ALREADY COMES DARKNESS

THE SONG OF THE ASH TREE - THIRD EDDA

ALREADY COMES DARKNESS

THE SONG OF THE ASH TREE - THIRD EDDA

T L GREYLOCK

GRASS
CROWN
PRESS

Grass Crown Press

ISBN 978-0-9965366-6-0

For A & R, who gave me books.

-Midgard-

Already comes darkness, | and ride must we
To Valhall to seek | the sacred hall.

Hyndluljoth, Poetic Edda

ONE

THE HOUNDS CAME with the sun.

The day had dawned in shadow, the skies cluttered with writhing clouds, but at last the sun broke through following close on the breath of a stiff winter wind. The horse swiveled its ears, nostrils wide, at the first notes of the chorus, and Raef, icy water spilling through his cupped fingers, sprang to his feet. Dead, dry leaves clinging to the branches of the aspens towering above him whispered as he sought to pinpoint the direction of the barking and baying. The strong, eager voices of the hunters rose and fell on the air, and though at first they seemed to call from every corner of the world, Raef closed his eyes and soon knew they were yet behind. They had not flanked him. But it was only a matter of time.

Raef looked to Vakre, who sat limp and listless in the saddle, his face pale and slick with sweat. His eyes were open, but the fevered gaze gave no sign that he heard the hounds. He would not survive a fight. Raef wrapped the reins in Vakre's hands as securely as he could, then slapped his palm to the horse's flank, sending the grey mare reeling through the trees and leaving Raef alone with only his thudding heart and the knowledge that he might have sent his friend away to die. Turning east, Raef began to run in a desperate attempt to lead the hunters away.

His path was perilous and steep, the snow masking jagged spurs of rock, slick ground giving way beneath his boots. He sprinted when he could and crawled when he had to, but always he went up, and when he gashed his hand on a splintered tree trunk, he let the blood drip freely to mark his trail. The hounds would follow, but their progress would slow and the men that trailed after would have to abandon their horses and continue on foot.

The voices of the pack rose and fell, and more than once they went silent for stretches of time that dragged on Raef's nerves. But always they returned and he drew strength from the knowledge that it was his trail they followed, not Vakre's. Raef forced himself to focus on his pace and each stride as he pushed onward while the bright winter sun slid across the sky. Sweat dripped from his nose and his lungs burned with each breath of cold air he drew in. The swords, his and Vakre's, banged against his legs, and his long cloak caught on the rough ground. He risked no glances behind, his mind bent only on moving forward.

The sun was sinking behind him, spilling his shadow across the snow, when he broke through the tree line and emerged onto the open ground of the high hills. Behind and below him, the fjord was a black snake, stark against the snow-covered slopes, stretching west to the hall he had lost and the sea beyond. Ahead and above, the darkening sky loomed. If he could reach the stones before losing the sun to the sea, the cloak of night would be his ally. Raef pushed on, ignoring his protesting legs, and climbed a rocky outcrop to gain his first look at his pursuers.

In the low light of dusk, there was little to see. All was grey and white and purple shadows, but Raef picked out movement here and there as he fought to slow his breathing and his skull thudded with rushing blood. Two, three, six men. Perhaps more. As many dogs, though the swift-legged hounds were harder to spot even as the trees thinned around them. He wondered if Isolf led them, or if his traitorous cousin had sent other men to hunt him. It made no difference; he could not fight them all. Taking a deep breath, Raef turned away and ran on, making his way toward a narrow spot between two peaks.

The statues were silent sentries under a deep blue sky by the time he arrived at the saddle between the peaks and stumbled upon the ring of stones. In daylight, Raef knew, the faces would stare down at him with bleak stone eyes carved by ancient, unknown hands. Now, in darkness, they were only black shapes blotting out the light of the first stars.

The snow had formed drifts around the base of each statue and Raef skirted the edge of the ring until he stood between the eastern most pair, a woman who faced away from the rest, her gaze turned to await the rising sun, and a stern man wielding an axe as tall as Raef. There Raef remained, letting the hunters come to him as the wind banished the last of the clouds, revealing the pale face of the moon.

The dogs came first, bounding through the deep snow as they finished the ascent. The men lagged behind, but the moonlight did nothing to hide Raef and a voice, heavy with ragged breaths, called the dogs off. The men slowed their pace as they approached, hungry eyes pinned on Raef. They were seven in number and sure of victory.

"Did you really think we would not catch you, Skallagrim? We would not hunt you down?" One man led the rest and Raef's heart burned with fury at the sight of him. "And this is how you have chosen to die. Here in the wild, a fugitive on the land your family ruled for more than five hundred years, without a friend to watch your back." Tulkis Greyshield spat in the snow. "At last the Greyshields will reclaim their rightful place. My sons will carry on my name while yours turns to dust and is wiped from memory."

"You are wrong, Tulkis." The arduous climb was but a distant memory, the exhaustion that had crept up on Raef for three sleepless nights was pushed away, forgotten. Raef put a hand on the hilt of his sword and felt the familiar anticipation of battle swell within him. This was blade-work, this was the steel song, and though the numbers called for his death, he knew he would not be the first to die.

Greyshield let out a barking laugh. "About what?"

"Everything. Your sons will die this night," Raef said, nodding at the young, freshly-bearded warriors who flanked Tulkis, "and I am not without friends."

Two of the warriors behind Tulkis glanced beyond the circle of statues, wary now of every shadow.

"Your friend? The one on the horse?" Greyshield's smile burrowed into the knot in Raef's stomach. "We have him, or will soon enough." Raef said nothing and Tulkis, grinning still, gestured to the axe-wielding statue at Raef's left. "Will he fight for you, Skallagrim? Will he strike us down with a single blow?"

"Even now, Isolf is sitting in my father's chair, Tulkis, tightening his grip on Vannheim. You will never have it."

"Vannheim or Garhold, it matters not."

Raef wanted to laugh. "If you think you will have Garhold, then you do not know Uhtred's daughter."

"The lady Aelinvor will do as she is told."

Now Raef did laugh, a bitter, scornful sound. "She craves power and helped murder her father to grasp it. She will not bend to you." Raef was glad to see a flicker of uncertainty in Greyshield's eyes, but words would do nothing to alter the situation.

"Kill him, father," one of the sons said. Raef could see fear in this one's eyes, fear masked by eager words.

"No, father, let me drain his life's blood." The other son was shorter and smaller than his brother, but his eyes were alive with the promise of bloodshed.

"Better yet, let me fight you both." Raef spread his arms wide, inviting them in. "I will gut you as Finnvold Skallagrim did Thannulf Greyshield. You are boys still clinging to your mother's skirts, so weak the Valkyries will never carry you to Valhalla."

The brothers moved together, snarling and cursing Raef and all his ancestors, swords drawn. They raced into the ring of statues and Raef let them come.

Three strides later, they were screaming and the snow was bright with slick blood as the sons of Tulkis Greyshield impaled themselves on sharp stakes buried beneath the snow. The false cover of skins and branches broke and vanished, revealing the pit that stretched to the feet of the silent, stone onlookers.

Tulkis was as still as the statues, his mouth gaping as he watched his sons die. One went quickly, for he had caught a stake in the throat, and his corpse sagged into the snow. The other, the second, younger son who had been so eager to kill, writhed still, legs jerking, blood coursing from his mouth and seeping out around the stake buried in his belly. His screams turned to shuddering moans of agony, but he lingered and the smell of urine reached Raef, who had eyes only for Tulkis.

The shock and horror frozen on Tulkis's face thawed into rage and his roar of anger drowned out the cries of his dying son. "I will cut off your cock and feed it to the crows, Skallagrim. I will flay you and make you eat your own skin. You will sob for death before I am done with you."

Raef kept his voice even. "You spoke true, Tulkis. Here in the wild we are and I am alone. But the wild is mine." Raef stepped behind the stony-faced woman who watched the eastern horizon and circled around to the north, every step taking him closer to Tulkis and his remaining companions. He had hoped the pit might claim three or even four warriors, for now he was left with five men to fight, but seeing Tulkis watch his sons be ripped from him was worth it. He drew his sword in his left hand and the axe in his right, reveling in the calm their sharp edges brought to his mind.

"Greet the corpse maidens for me, Greyshield. I will send you to Valhalla."

Tulkis charged and his first swing was full of power and wrath, meant to slash Raef open across the chest. He jumped back, the steel passing by harmlessly, and countered with a lunge of his own that Tulkis only just deflected away, heaving his sword back around in time to keep Raef's blade from burying itself in his gut, but the axe that followed was too quick and Tulkis could not prevent it from biting into his shoulder. Bellowing, Tulkis stumbled back, nearly falling into a snowdrift, and Raef pressed on. The swords clashed again, Tulkis keeping his sword arm raised despite the fresh wound, but the snow claimed Greyshield's balance and Raef's next swing cleaved into his ribs, splitting flesh and splintering bone with ease. Tulkis dropped to his knees, his eyes staring, mouth hanging open, and he did not move, did not try to defend himself as Raef's axe came to rest against his neck. Blood began to spill from his lips, streaking down his beard, but their eyes locked, hatred and fury blazing in Tulkis's face. With a short, brutal chop, Raef hacked the axe into Tulkis's neck and watched the eyes dull, the skin grow slack, and then Raef knew Greyshield was dead. Wrenching his weapons from the body, Raef let it fall backward so the dead eyes might stare at the stars. Only then did he face the four remaining warriors, his heart heaving with the battle-lust.

Two were faces he knew, men who had fought with him at the burning lake. He focused on them.

"So ends the line of Greyshield. Would you suffer the same fate, Olarr? Or you, Hakon? If you fight me now, I will kill you and hunt down your children and my blade will know the taste of their flesh. Is this what you want, to die a traitor, unremembered by the gods?"

Olarr looked down to the snow as though he might find an

answer or his courage buried there, but Hakon grimaced, his lips tugged sideways by an old scar, and Raef knew he would have to kill at least one more man that night.

"I broke an oath once, lord," Hakon said, "when I took mead from Greyshield's hand and drank for him. I will not break another, even if it means my death."

"You would stand by a dead traitor?"

Hakon shrugged. "It is all I have left, lord. What am I if I beg for my life now?"

"Then draw your sword."

There was grit and determination in Hakon's eyes, but also a measure of resignation. He was a strong man, and tall, but made for chopping trees and hauling loads, not battle. He had never been a skilled warrior, and Raef wondered what had tempted him to Greyshield's side, but found he did not wish to ask.

It was over quickly and Hakon fell not far from where the hounds crouched, whimpering now as the scent of the blood of men filled their nostrils. Olarr fell to his knees and begged Raef to spare him, or if not him, his wife and children. The other two warriors, unknown men from Silfravall, said nothing, though one fidgeted with his hands. He made a half-hearted attempt to draw his knife, but Raef, pivoting in the snow, hurled his axe and it sank deep into the man's chest. He fell heavy and hard and did not move again. The other warrior paled and Raef could see the fight fleeing from his eyes.

"Go," Raef said, weary now, but his voice still sharp with anger. "Run, run back to my cousin. Tell Isolf he will never be free of me."

Olarr and the other man turned their backs and fled, the hounds at their heels, and Raef watched them tread the snow-sea until they disappeared down the slope. He pulled his axe from the dead man's chest and wiped the blood from its edge. Only then did he allow himself to expel a deep breath, and he sank against the closest statue, resting his head between his knees, his cloak pulled tight against the wind.

The lone howl of a wolf jerked him awake. A quick glance at the moon told him he had not slept long, but it was not safe to linger. Rest could come when he was better sheltered. Raef hauled himself to his feet and walked to the edge of the pit that had claimed the sons of Greyshield. The bodies were stiff and cold and looked younger in death. With silent thanks to Odin, Allfather, Raef turned his back and began the descent, fixed now on finding Vakre, if the son of Loki lived.

TWO

THE TRACKS WERE not hard to find. Three sets of horse prints in the snow, all headed south from the place where Raef had separated from Vakre. Dawn was breaking in the east, golden light filtering through the valleys, as Raef picked and ate a handful of tart, frost-dusted berries and began to follow the tracks. His stomach raged for sustenance, as it had often since Raef had fled from the smoke and the death and the sound of Isolf's voice carrying through the darkness, but Raef had little to offer it. He had no bow with which to hunt the rabbits that crossed his path, or the deer whose tracks he had followed to water, and he hungered for meat. He did not have the time to linger over traps that might catch nothing. But it was Vakre he worried about. Vakre needed warmth and food and care that Raef could not provide.

For two days, Raef had led the horse through the trees, winding among the hills he knew so well, the hills that were no longer his. Their progress was halting, slowed by Vakre's wound, but Raef had found relief in the need to care for his friend, for it kept the other thoughts at bay, the thoughts that threatened to steal away with Raef's resolve to endure. Even so, he could not banish the sights and sounds from that night outside the walls of the Vestrhall, the battle, the treachery of Isolf, the loss of Siv, the deaths of Finnolf, valiant Finnolf, and steadfast Uhtred, the village burning, always burning. And Hauk of Ruderk, within his reach, and yet he had been unable to strike down his father's murderer. He saw it all again in the bitter, dark hours of the nights while Vakre slept a fever sleep. In the daylight hours, he buried his grief and trudged onward.

It was midday when Raef caught the scent of fire. The grey mare had continued south at first, but then her steps had taken her back toward the fjord, and where she went, the two other sets of tracks followed. Raef hurried on, passing a long-abandoned farm, and then coming to the shore of the fjord. He followed the water until he reached the jutting spit of land that marked the joining of the small, southern arm of the fjord to the main body. The burned air was sharp, biting at Raef's nostrils, and the bodies had already attracted a pair of crows.

The corpses were sprawled close to the shore, stretched out on the great, flat rocks that divided land from water. One would be carried away by the high tide. Both were black and charred, split open as a sausage would when held over a fire. Their faces were beyond recognition though one wore three arm rings, loose now over the shrunken flesh and white, exposed bone. When the tide carried him away, the silver rings would slip to the depths, prizes for the fish to fight over. The other had drawn his sword in the moment of death and the blade now gleamed in the bright sun as water lapped at its edge. A horse was there too, its grey coat unblemished by burns, but its fate made clear by the arrows that bristled from its neck and the dark stain that spread onto the snow. A single pair of footprints, a man's, led away from the carnage and back into the trees.

Two horses watched Raef from the safety of the trees and they seemed glad to see a living man when he approached them. Raef patted their noses and told them they were brave for not having fled from the fire. Then he mounted one and, the other in tow, went in search of Vakre.

He did not have to go far. The tracks took him up a gradual slope alongside a narrow fall of water that would spill into the fjord below. In spring it would be a rush of snow melt; now it was only a trickle and the rocks were crusted with ice. He found Vakre face down in the snow, as still as the ice, and Raef feared death had claimed him. Raef dismounted and knelt in search of a pulse, but he jerked his fingers back in surprise, for Vakre's flesh was hot. Not the heat of a man crippled by fever and wound-rot, but the heat of a rock long warmed by the sun. Raef rolled Vakre over and watched as his chest rose and fell in shallow but steady breaths. His face, though drawn with exhaustion, was free of pain. Raef expelled his relief in a long, shaky breath and felt his own fatigue weigh heavy on his shoulders. And yet he could not rest, not yet.

Vakre stirred only a little as Raef lifted him and carried him back down to the fjord. There he collected the swords of the dead men and one spear, for they were good steel, and draped Vakre over the back of one of the horses. The bow that had felled the grey mare was charred and splintered by Vakre's fire. It would break at any attempt to draw an arrow, so Raef left it with the corpses. Searching in the saddle packs, Raef found cheese and dried meat, and he ate a portion quickly, hardly chewing. Then, after washing it down with a splash of fjord water, Raef turned the horses away from the shore, leaving the bodies to the creeping tide.

ᚠ ᚠ ᚠ

The hidden fortress of Vannheim was as Raef remembered it, though he had last visited as a boy of twelve carrying his first bat-tle-ready sword and in awe of the great bowl cut out of the side of the mountain. It was not a fortress of walls and stone, but a natu-ral refuge invisible to prying eyes in the narrow valley below. The eagle's nest, his father had called it. The way up was steep and Raef was forced to carry Vakre rather than risk him falling from his precarious position on the horse, and the trees were thick, blocking the way with tangled branches and heavy underbrush weighed down by snow. But Raef climbed, given strength by the knowledge that he was close, so close. To his left, the end of the fjord sparkled in the moonlight and the sheer cliffs that flanked it on both sides reared up out of the water like guardians to watch over the hidden place. Below him, the river rushed through the valley, a constant murmur in conversation with the owls and the wolves and the other creatures that called this wild, bleak place home. This was not a place for men, or farms, or warm fires in stone hearths, but Raef, as he summited the slope and came over the rise into the bowl, felt a measure of peace fill him for the first time since he had lost everything he held dear, everything that warmed his blood.

The vertical walls of rock lining the bowl were set far back in the shadows and were punctured by a few caves, but Raef had not come so far to crawl into a hole and shiver in the dark. Leaving Vakre with the horses, Raef went back into the trees in search of dry kindling and branches that might burn despite the snow cover. The prevailing winds and the southern winter sun kept the eagle's nest largely free of snow, a fact Raef was glad of as he worked his flint with frozen fingers and coaxed a spark to life. He watched the newborn flames lick a handful of crispy leaves and dead pine needles, then spring up, eager for more fuel.

The warmth of the fire seemed to revive Vakre, and the son of Loki shifted, his eyelids fluttering, but it was some time before he opened his eyes. When he did, he stared at the cheerful fire for a long moment, and it was only when Raef pulled a whetstone from his belt and began to stroke it along his sword that Vakre stirred and looked around, first to the stars and then to Raef.

"I thought it a dream," Vakre said, his voice weak.

"It was no dream." Little else needed to be said. Raef put the whetstone aside.

"Where are we?" Vakre pushed away the fur Raef had taken from the pack belonging to the dead men and prodded at the makeshift bandage Raef had fashioned over the left side of his abdomen, where the knife had gone deep. Raef had changed the binding and cleaned it twice during the flight from the Vestrhall, but he knew it was not enough. It needed to be stitched. And yet Vakre's probing fingers did not seem to cause pain.

"A refuge in a storm. Somewhere Isolf will not know to look." Raef lifted his head from where it rested on his arms, his knees drawn up close to his chest, and looked over his shoulder at the walls of rock that shielded them from east, north, and west. "We are above the end of the small, southern arm of the fjord that runs to the Vestrhall and the sea. The secret of this place is known to only a few."

"And the fire? Will not the smoke be seen?"

Raef shook his head. "Only the wolves walk these hills. And maybe the gods."

Vakre frowned as though remembering something and glanced around. "Siv." He looked back to Raef, a question in his eyes.

"She was inside the walls." Raef found he did not want to look at Vakre. He focused on the bright fire. "Many lives were stolen by Isolf's treachery."

"She could yet be alive."

Raef closed his eyes but Vakre's words burned into his gut as the red flames did into his eyelids. "It was too much. Isolf's warriors, the men from Silfravall, the warriors lured by Tulkis Greyshield's words, and the advantage of surprise. Any resistance would have been put to death."

"Do not let go of hope, Raef," Vakre said.

Good words, strong words. And yet hope seemed a distant thing to Raef, a tiny boat far at sea, at the mercy of the volatile waves and storms. If Raef tried to swim the distance, he would be swept under and drowned.

In Raef's silence, Vakre turned back to his wound and peeled away the soiled cloth.

"It cannot be," he murmured.

Raef looked and was stunned by what he saw. The wound that had been so red and angry and filled with yellow puss was pink and clean and closed.

"Just yesterday, I thought the rot would kill you," Raef said. "You burned those men." He gestured at the thin cloak that had belonged to Loki. "Do you remember? By the fjord."

Vakre nodded. "Yes, though the effort nearly sent me to the gods. My father's gift must have cleansed and sealed the wound, but I am weak. I will be a burden to you. Find a farm, someone who will take me in."

Raef shook his head and felt his hands begin to tremble. "No."

"You have work yet to do," Vakre said, his voice stronger and insistent. "You are the lord of Vannheim, no matter what deceitful, cruel things Isolf has done."

"I will not leave you and you will not die." Raef clenched his hands into fists, his voice sharp with anger that was not meant for Vakre.

Vakre's eyes narrowed. "What happened in the trees, Raef, after we fled from the walls? What eats at you?"

Raef stared into the fire. "I chose your life."

"Over?"

Raef could see it in the flames. "You bled. Even in the dark, I could see the snow turn red with your blood. My hands were all that kept you alive." Raef looked at Vakre at last. "I let him go."

"Hauk." Understanding came to Vakre's face. "He was there, watching. You could have gone after him."

"I could have sent him to Valhalla," Raef said, a snarl bursting out of his throat. "I could have earned justice for my father at last."

Vakre was quiet for a moment. "Do you regret your choice?"

"No." It was the truth, but it did not make Hauk of Ruderk's escape any easier to accept. "You are my brother and I hold true to that. But now you see why you cannot die."

"I will do my best." Vakre lay down and pulled the fur across his chest once more. "Thank you for my life." Raef nodded and settled down opposite Vakre. The warmth of the fire began to dull his senses, the fatigue that had slowly gathered strength now overwhelmed. Raef let his eyes close and it was only moments before he drifted off. He dreamed of Siv.

THREE

THE FOG WAS thick, so thick that even Raef, perched high in his eagle's nest above the valley and the fjord, could see nothing beyond Vakre sleeping next to the cold ashes of the fire. Above him, the clouds were thinning and the day promised to be bright, but it would be some time before the sun burned through. Raef worked a piece of dried meat around his mouth to soften it, then chewed and swallowed. The cheese was nearly gone, but there was plenty of meat, so he left it all out where Vakre might see, for the son of Loki had not eaten the night before, then Raef collected the empty water skins and the spear he had taken from the dead men and descended down into the fog-filled valley.

The fog had gentled the winter morning and softened the air, and it hung in thick shrouds around Raef as he emerged from the trees at the bank of the swift, rock-strewn river. Raef stepped from stone to stone until he was in the middle of the rushing water, then dipped the water skins into the tumult and filled them until they bulged. Then, the skins reattached to his belt, Raef worked his way upriver, his feet sure on the slippery stones, until he reached a rock large enough to sit on. There he waited, spear at the ready, eyes searching for nimble silver fish in the pale blue, glacier-fed water.

He had never mastered spearfishing, preferring instead to work with hooks and line, and his first four throws were poor. The fifth found its mark, though, and Raef clambered over the rocks to retrieve the good-sized trout pierced on the spear's point. It wriggled still, caught only by its tail, and Raef slapped it against a stone to kill it, then returned to his boulder. Patience and persistence rewarded Raef with four more fish, all speckled brown trout, and he retraced his steps up to the bowl, emerging above the fog to find a brilliant blue sky, unblemished by clouds, spreading over the mountain peaks.

Raef deposited his catch on the ground and began to revive the fire, then used his slender, small knife to gut and clean the trout. Vakre, curled away from the fire, did not stir, but Raef, as he pulled the guts from inside the largest of his fish, felt eyes on him. Slowly, Raef got to his feet and turned, knife and hands slick with fish.

The raven was perched above him, clinging with sharp talons to a spire of rock on the side of the bowl. It was alone, its brother in some far corner of the world, no doubt. The black eyes bore into him, wreaking havoc in Raef's mind as surely as his knife had torn up the trout's small organs. Long had it been since he had seen a raven, and he knew not whether to be glad of it.

"I survive, still, Allfather," Raef said, his voice small against the great bowl around him and the fathomless sky above. "My fate has not yet caught up with me." The raven made a quiet sound deep in its throat. "Do you laugh at me? You see me now, bereft of everything, I who stood before you and refused a place in a distant, star-strewn hall, all for the hope of a home I have now lost. But I endure, Allfather, with or without your eye upon me, no matter the runes that have been carved next to my name in Yggdrasil's bark." The raven cocked its head and flapped its wings once. "You are listening? Then hear me now. I will reclaim Vannheim and I will bring the blood eagle to the oath-breaker, Isolf. This I will do, even when the stars have gone black, even when Jörmungand rises from the sea, and even while Surt's fires blaze across the nine realms. Even in your darkest hour, when the jaws of Fenrir slather before your face, I will split open my cousin's back and draw forth his ribs and then his lungs and loose his screams to the world."

For a moment, Raef's words hung in the air and the raven was still, then its massive wings spread wide and it took to the sky, riding the low clouds that yet covered the valley before disappearing to the east. Raef turned back to the fire and saw that Vakre was watching him now, and though his face was pale and thin and the shadows in his eyes were deep and dark, there was something of his old self there, too, and he grinned as Raef sat down to finish cleaning the last fish.

"Good words. The gods love a man who challenges fate," Vakre said. He helped Raef spit the fish on sticks and held two over the flames.

"Your father most of all?"

Vakre looked thoughtful. "No more than Odin, I think. Does not the Allfather defy fate with each rising sun? Loki may be cunning and full of hate, and he seeks to bring doom to the gods, but that fate will come, with or without Loki. It is Odin who works against what is known and what will be."

"Futile labor. It does not matter how many men he plucks from the battlefields of Midgard, or what knowledge he gains from Mimir's well, or how tall he builds the walls of Asgard, the fires will come and the world will break and Yggdrasil will burn."

"Odin fights because he must, and his spirit lives within us. We go on because we must."

And Raef nodded at this because those very words were in his own heart.

They waited until the fish were charred black, their skins crispy, before tearing into the white flesh with eager teeth. Raef ate with abandon, but Vakre's appetite did not last long, and he did not finish his first trout. Raef gave him a questioning glance but Vakre's only response was that he was tired. He turned away, wrapped tight in a fur, eyes closed to the vast sky, and seemed to sleep.

Leaving the warmth of the fire, Raef explored the bowl from end to end. There was little enough to see, a pile of cracked rocks where they had come to rest after tumbling down the cliff above, a shallow dip in the ground that had collected rain water now frozen to ice. The caves offered up only a pair of empty, rotting barrels, stashed there long ago, but Raef had not expected to find anything useful, for the nest had never been stocked with weapons or food stores or anything of value. Such preparations would require constant attention and a vigilant guard, which meant spilling the secret to more and more ears. And so the nest was sparse and Raef had known this and sought it still, for his father had told him once that the nest could not provide, but it could protect, and in the most desperate of times, that was enough.

His exploration complete, Raef settled down on the edge of the bowl, his legs dangling over the sharp drop, and slid a silver arm ring from its place on his wrist. His fingers ran across the familiar twists in the metal and along the beaks of the twin raven heads, but his eyes remained fixed on the clouds below as the valley and the fjord began to take shape. He would have given much for a bow to hunt with, and more for one hundred men to stand at his back with bright swords and strong shields, but he had none of these things. The nest might keep him safe, but it would not bring him Isolf's head.

By the time the clouds burned away, the sun was high and Raef's stomach was rumbling, the early morning fish long forgotten, but no sooner had Raef stood than the ship appeared, rounding the final bend in the fjord's long journey, slipping through the last of the fog.

Raef, rooted to the spot, his heartbeat quickening, could only stare. The ship was small, manned by only four or five men if necessary, and the beast on its prow had been removed, as was customary in friendly waters. And yet its presence in this isolated, uninhabited piece of water was unnerving, no matter how few warriors it could hold. Seldom, even in summer, did ships venture so far up the fjord.

Up in the nest, the air was still, but Raef could see by the patterns on the surface of the fjord that the winds were brisk, and the ship's grey sail was full. It would not be long before she made landing. Returning to the fire, Raef gathered every weapon he could carry and then hurried down into the valley, intent on reaching the shore before the ship.

He chose to wait and watch on a small point of land that arced out into the fjord. Should the ship aim for the shallow waters and safe beach at the mouth of the river, his position would give him a good look at the crew. Crouching between boulders, Raef watched a sea eagle cut across the sky and waited, the sharp wind numbing his cheeks.

The ship drew close, its prow pointed toward the river mouth, and Raef peered out at it, expecting to see men working the sail, to see the oars splashing into the water to guide her to land, to see a helmsman at the rudder, but he saw nothing. The sail rippled, the thick wool snapping in a gust of wind, but her deck was empty and the oars were stowed or missing. She was abandoned.

Raef, wondering if perhaps the crew had jumped ship, frightened or forced overboard, but suspecting that something more cunning was at work, stayed hidden. The sheer strake was unburdened by shields, but high enough to conceal a crouching man. The rudder might be fixed in place with ropes, the sail left in the care of the wind, all for the sake of stealth and surprise. Isolf had shown cunning in his capture of Vannheim; such an ambush would appeal to him. And so Raef waited.

The ship, with a groan and a shudder that made Raef wince,

slid up against the rocky beach. The sinking tide would leave her stranded before nightfall, her hull riding slick, kelp-covered rocks instead of salty waves. But no orders were shouted and no men leaped over the side, splashing to shore with spears in hand. All was silence and still Raef waited.

Clouds filtered in from the west, high ones this time, streaking the sky with orange and pink as the sun sought the horizon. The winds that had battered the fjord by day vanished, leaving calm waters to lap against the shore. The fish would be stirring, searching out insects that walked the water, and the birds would be watching for telltale signs of silver scales in the blue fjord.

As the light died, so did Raef's suspicions, and at last he allowed himself to rise and, rounding the curved shore to the beach, approach the strange ship, axe at the ready. No arrows were launched to pierce him, no spears were hurled to savage him, and Raef hauled himself over the sheer strake and landed with light feet on the smooth deck.

The ship was not deserted. A funeral pyre had been built at the stern. The wood was unburnt and freshly cut, rich with the scent of pine. A nest of kindling, ready to spark, sprouted from the sturdy logs. The body was richly dressed in a thick fabric of shimmering gold, the cloth threaded through with delicate strands of silver and copper, and for a moment Raef could not bring himself to look upon the woman's face, for in his mind he saw Siv's green eyes and red-gold hair.

But it was not Siv. She was a stranger to Raef and yet the sight of her caused Raef's heart to leap, for surely she was golden-haired Freyja herself. Raef took a deep breath and looked closer. She was adorned with gems. A thick rope of gold hung from her neck, the bright metal cradling stones of icy blue. Her hair was free and loose save for a single small braid that caressed her temple. There, entwined with her golden locks, was a strand of silver. She bore a pair of rings, one crusted with glittering black gems, the other small and plain and yet made from the finest copper. And yet despite all those riches, a strange thing caught his eye. A single golden arm ring encircled her upper arm, lost against the rich cloth, its serpent head chasing after the tail. A fitting prize for a warrior or shield-maiden, but this woman did not have the look of battle about her. Her shoulders were slender, her hands smooth, her skin unscarred. Raef bent closer, drawn in by the well-worked gold, for he had never seen finer craft, when he saw something that took the breath from him.

There, at her throat, a pulse.

ᚾ ᚾ ᚾ

She was alive. Raef touched the Thor hammer that hung around his neck and took a step back, his eyes fixed on the faint, drumming muscle beneath the pale skin of her neck. It flickered unevenly, a candle threatened by even the slightest hint of air, and Raef reached out a hand to rest on her shoulder.

She sucked in a gasp of air, her eyelids fluttering open violently, the cords of her neck straining as she raised her head. Raef released his hold on her shoulder but before he could retreat, she was clawing at his arm, her fingers latching to his sleeve, and then she was twisting and falling from the top of the pyre and Raef thrust his arms around her and caught her as together they went to their knees.

It was her eyes that Raef could not look away from. They were black and full of stars, and that dark gaze gripped Raef's heart. And then he blinked and her eyes were a calm sunlit sea, blue and vivid. She seemed unaware of the change, but as those blue eyes focused on his face, she pushed him away and staggered to her feet.

"You dare to touch me?" Her voice was rich and deep, but hoarse, and her beautiful features were distorted by a snarl Raef would have looked for on a wolf. "Bold. But fatal." The snarl remained, but there was something new there, some wild pleasure, and she reached to her hip as a warrior would for a sword, but her fingers grasped only air. As her hands came up empty, the snarl turned to horror. Raef could see her fight to take in a breath and her hands began to shake as she raised them to her face. Before Raef could reach her, she crumpled to the deck.

She did not sob, she did not scream. Her eyes were dry and she drew even breaths. And yet those blue eyes flashed with stars once more and Raef could see a tide of burning rage and crushing grief, so sharp he felt it in his own heart, and the sun and the waves and the birds all seemed to vanish.

The sky was deep blue by the time Raef ventured to speak. He did not stir from his place beside the sheer strake, but let his voice cross the vast distance that seemed to swell between them.

"Lady, who are you?"

"Many names have I had, Spear-Breaker, Axe-Wielder, Crushing-Wind. But now I am nothing. I am no one."

"Surely there are some who would rejoice to know you live?"

She frowned. "What do you speak of?"

Raef gestured to the ship around them. "You were set upon the pyre, but it was unburnt. Your ship drifted here. Was it an illness that made them think you dead?"

Her eyes took in the mast and sail, the smooth timbers beneath her, the funeral pyre. "I died, but am not dead," she said. "No one will be looking for me."

"Perhaps you have judged them harshly. A woman like you is not easily forgotten."

She laughed then, a bitter sound. "Why? Because I am beautiful? Because men will wish to have me spread my legs? Yes, my father has seen to that. It is all he has left me."

"Your father?"

For a moment, the stars returned to her eyes and her voice

grew stronger. "He who sits on Hlidskjalf, he who wields Gungnir, he who rides Sleipnir and sends his ravens forth into the nine realms." She fixed a piercing stare on Raef, daring him to question her, but she had said enough and Raef knew why her changing eyes sent shards of icy fear burrowing into him. She had nearly killed him with her sword of sunlight. Her voice had made bold warriors tremble and lose control of their bladders. She and her sisters had descended on the burning lake, carrying chaos on their shields.

"The Allfather has cast you out?"

The Valkyrie nodded.

"Why?"

"My sisters and I, we are loosed upon the field of battle, free to choose among the slain as we will. We bring the best to Valhalla, to line Odin's long tables and await the last battle. But the Allfather has his say and he is not to be denied. I dared to disobey, choosing a man marked for the cold embrace of Hel. And for that I am banished to the world of men, to live out numbered days, I, who rode fleet-footed death and lived among the stars." She fell silent but got to her feet and went to stand at the stern of the ship, her gaze searching for something in the dark fjord. "I can no longer see the shining hall, the shields that line the walls, the faces of those who were chosen." She turned and faced Raef and even in the darkness, he could see the anger flashing in her eyes. "I am not meant to live among men. I have drunk mead at Odin's table, I have tasted the wind that beats from Hraesvelg's wings at the end of the world, I have slain frost giants and smelled the breath of Fenrir. Am I to spend my days serving a man? Am I to die without a name that men will speak to the end of days?" The anger was not enough to mask her fear.

"I will speak your name." Raef crossed the deck and came to stand at her side. "A name of your choosing."

"Why?"

"You may not be a shieldmaiden of Asgard anymore, but I will not forget it. We have met before."

"Have we?"

"I have seen you in the thick of slaughter, I have heard you promise death, and I have looked into your eyes and seen my death there. I will shout your name to the world of men and they shall hear it and tremble." As he spoke, the eyes of starlight returned and the Valkyrie was as he remembered her at the burning lake, a storm of terrifying beauty, a wild, blazing thing, as though his words had somehow summoned the pieces of her she had lost. But then she was golden-haired and blue-eyed once more and Raef, though he could see pride and valor and strength yet in her face, knew in his heart the stars would not return, knew the last skin of the Valkyrie had been shed.

"Then you shall have the name my father gave me. I am Visna."

"Well, Visna. I have nothing to offer you but a fire, and fish, and a heart full of vengeance, but I will share it all with you."

"What would you have of me?" Visna's voice was tinged with suspicion.

Raef shrugged. "I would have you live. Live a bold and brilliant life, so that your sisters yet in Asgard will look down and know envy."

This seemed to please her. "I will need a sword."

"You shall have it."

"And clothing. My father has seen fit to send me into the world of men dressed as Freyja." She smiled then, and it was pure and true and a vestige of the light of those who dwelt in Asgard.

Raef laughed. "I am rich only in birch bark and pinecones."

He led the way through the now dark forest, past the rushing river, and up the steep slope to the eagle's nest. Visna followed easily, despite the long gown, but she drew up as they neared the edge of the bowl, her eyes on Vakre, who stood at the overlook, hand on the hilt of his sword.

"Raef?" Vakre called to them and Raef heard a sharp intake of breath from Visna beside him.

"Here, we are here," Raef answered. He stepped into the circle of firelight.

"You were gone a long time." Vakre was pale, but he seemed stronger. His gaze flickered between Raef and Visna, who stood still in the shadows.

"I know, forgive me."

"The ship?"

"Bore only her." Raef gestured and Visna stepped forward.

"You did not say you knew a half god," Visna said. Her voice was quiet but tense and Raef could see her shoulders were stiff.

"How could you know that?" Vakre's eyes were wary.

"I know the blood of Asgard when I see it."

And so Raef told Vakre of Visna and the punishment the All-father had given her. When he had finished, Visna stepped closer to Vakre.

"Tyr?" She frowned to herself. "No. And not Thor. Perhaps Njord, but you do not have the look of the sea."

Vakre looked over Visna's shoulder and met Raef's gaze. Raef could see the hesitation and struggle brim in Vakre's face, but his voice was calm and clear when he spoke. "My father is Loki."

Visna lunged, eyes blazing, hands grasping for Vakre's throat. Vakre leaned back, surprise turning to feral savagery, and then he was flame and smoke and a flashing sword and it was Visna's turn to recoil or face death.

"Enough!" Raef shouted, his voice ringing off the walls of the eagle's nest. He could not see Vakre's face, so thick was the fire, and it was a long moment before the son of Loki released the blaze. Even then, the air around him shimmered with heat.

Visna spat on the ground. "Tainted and accursed, you are. All men and gods know the children of Loki to be monstrous."

"If this is so, let us finish it, then," Vakre said. The flames that had sapped him of strength the day before now seemed to have brought him new vitality, and he stood, sword in hand, ready to strike.

"No," Raef said. "You will both have to kill me first."

"I am a daughter of Odin, a shieldmaiden of Asgard," Visna said. "Loki is our foulest enemy and I am charged with bringing death to what he has spawned into the nine realms."

"But you are not a shieldmaiden of Asgard," Raef said, his voice harsh. "You are a mortal, banished from Odin's hall, and though once you might have cleaved me in two without drawing breath, now we are more than a match, lady. Vakre is bound to me and I to him and you will not touch him."

For a moment Raef thought Visna might turn on him, but with visible effort the Valkyrie fought the urge to lash out and stalked away from the fire, disappearing into the dark confines of the bowl.

"What do you mean to do with her?"

Raef shook his head. "I do not know."

"She is proud." Vakre returned to the fire and offered Raef the last of the dried meat they had taken from Vakre's pursuers.

Raef followed and seated himself on a flat stone. "And she is afraid." He drained the water from one of the skins to wash down the chewy venison. Vakre tossed him the second skin but only a few drops remained.

"I will go." Vakre gathered the skins and descended into the dark valley, leaving Raef with the dying fire. He stood and went to the saddle packs, rummaging until he found the bag of grain the men had carried for the horses. As he gave each horse a portion, he could feel Visna's eyes upon him, though where she lurked in the darkness he could not say. He might seek her out, speak to her, perhaps plant a seed of trust between her and Vakre, but he was weary of such thoughts, of playing the peacemaker when his own heart was so filled with fury. And so he settled into his furs, drawing them tight to his chin, and watched the stars behind the shifting clouds.

He thought of the raven, of Odin, Allfather, watching him. He wondered at the arrival of Visna, Odin's own daughter, banished to a corner of Vannheim where only he might find her. He had questions, questions only the Allfather could answer, but it was thoughts of Siv that consumed him.

The horn sounded a moment after Raef let his eyelids close, but as he threw off the furs and jerked to his feet, so still was the night that for a moment Raef wondered if he had dreamt it. But then it sounded again, low and long, a single note, and Raef held his breath, waiting to hear the baying of hounds, the shouts of men, but nothing else interrupted the darkness. Keeping low to the ground, Raef crept to the edge of the bowl, scanning the slope below for torchlight and finding it.

The torches flickered in a faint line between the slope and the river. They were not many in number, but the horn was surely meant to signal others so that a host of men might climb to the eagle's nest together. Raef thought of Vakre and hoped he had eluded capture, but even so, he was most likely caught between the river and the torches, cut off from the slope and unable to rejoin Raef. Of Visna there was still no sign, though Raef did not doubt that the Valkyrie was watching. They did not lack for weapons and the edge of the nest was a strong position. Together he and Visna might turn the steep final ascent into a killing ground, but they could not hope to hold it for long.

Raef crouched there, his mind racing, when a sudden movement to his left caught his eye and he drew his axe in haste. But it was only Vakre scrambling up the slope. Raef helped him over the edge, but the son of Loki stopped short, his gaze staring over Raef's shoulder.

Visna stood there, a sword in each hand, and her eyes were hard in the last light of the fire. The glowing embers at her feet cast a dull red light across her golden gown, shading her skin an unnatural color, and for a moment she had the look of Asgard once more, but then she stepped away from the fire and the moment passed. She approached Vakre, who put a hand on the knife at his belt, and they stared hard at each other. Raef tensed, ready to intervene, but then Visna was handing a sword, hilt first, to Vakre, her attention turning to the torches that were growing closer.

"Do you mean to fight?" Visna asked Raef.

"We are but three. They will be many." It was possible to escape the nest by climbing the walls of the bowl and taking to the mountains, but the climb was perilous and would take time.

Visna nodded. "I will fight. And I will show Odin what he has lost." She hefted a shield that had hung from one of the saddles and stepped to the edge of the bowl.

Raef looked to Vakre, who, now armed with axe, knives, and sword, was assessing the second shield. It was well worn and notched in many places, and Vakre let it lie on the stones. "You know the way?" Vakre asked. Raef nodded. "Then go. We will give you what time we can."

"No." Raef felt a flush of shame spread through his chest. "I will not flee, not again. I will stand with you and we will die together."

Vakre shook his head, his eyes filled with sorrow. "You have much to live for Raef, much to do. We," he looked over his shoulder at Visna, who met his eyes, "we are outcasts. I do not speak for her, but gladly would I go to Valhalla so that you, my brother, might live."

Raef's legs seemed turned to stone and he could not tear his gaze from Vakre as his mind and heart warred with each other. To go meant a chance at survival and the hope of vengeance. But it also meant unending shame. Raef drew his sword and went to stand at Vakre's side.

"No more running," Raef said.

Vakre accepted this with a nod and then, as three, they turned to face whatever emerged from the trees.

FOUR

THE CLEAR VOICE of the horn rang out a third time as the torches paused at the tree line below the bowl. But the call was different, a pair of notes, one long and curving up into the second, higher one. In the silence that followed, Raef's heart pounded in his ears.

The line of torches moved forward again, passing out of the sanctuary of the snow-covered pines, and now Raef could see shapes of men, though he could not count them. The illuminated figures, night blind by their own flames, had not yet seen the three warriors waiting at the summit, and this lack of caution, this careless approach, sowed a seed of doubt in Raef's stomach. These did not seem to be men expecting a fight, though what the horn was for, he could not say.

Placing a hand on Vakre's shoulder, Raef stared hard at the son of Loki. "Do you trust me?"

"You know I do."

"Then do as I say." Raef directed Vakre to stand back from the edge of the bowl, deep in the shadows of a pile of boulders. Vakre frowned but obeyed, and Raef placed Visna opposite Vakre, so that they might flank the entrance to the bowl. When they were hidden from his sight, Raef raked dirt over the last embers of the fire and stepped back into the darkness to stand by the horses, hoping to keep them quiet. A soft nose bumped into his back and the other horse blew hot breath in his ear. Raef placed a hand on the horse's muzzle, his own breath released in the barest of whispers.

The figures hauled themselves over the edge of the summit and stepped into the nest, giving Raef his first good look at them. They were perhaps ten in number and their swords were yet at home in their sheaths. The torchlight danced over their bearded faces and one voice cursed quietly about a stone in his boot.

"He is not here," one man said. "I told you. He is crow food."

"I will believe that when I meet him in Valhalla." The man who spoke shifted his torch, sending a flash of light through his eyes, but still Raef could not see him well. "If he is not here now, he will come." Raef did not need to see the man's face, for the voice was one he had known since childhood.

"Ruf." Raef stepped from the shadows and the men whirled to face him, some sliding steel out to gleam in the firelight, but all went as still as the stones they stood on.

Rufnir Bjarneson dropped his torch and closed the distance between them in four long strides, his arms wrapping tight around Raef. Then he let out a great shout of laughter that echoed off the stone walls.

"I knew you lived yet, you skinny-arsed dog." Rufnir laughed again and slapped Raef on the shoulder.

"It is good to see you, Ruf." Raef gripped the young man's arm. "We were making ready to fight."

"We?" Rufnir's eyes lit up. "Then you are not alone?"

"There is no host of men at my back, if that is what you mean, but I am not alone." At Raef's words, Vakre slid from the shadows, earning more than a few muttered curses from the men who had followed Rufnir up to the eagle's nest, men who did not like to be surprised. The sight of Visna clad in her rich gown drew even more murmurs and Rufnir raised his thick eyebrows. But the coal-haired man soon returned his attention to Raef and sank down onto one knee.

"Lord," he began, "my sword is yours, and my shield." It was then that Raef saw that Rufnir's left arm ended in a stump at the wrist. He stooped to raise his friend, but Rufnir refused. "I know not what strength runs through my veins, but I swear to you, I will see you returned to the Vestrhall."

Raef nodded, then pulled Rufnir to his feet. "Your hand." He spoke quietly as the other warriors, having uncovered the remains of the fire, used their torches to rekindle the charred wood.

Rufnir shrugged. "I can still strap on a shield." There was defiance in his voice, as though he feared Raef might strip him of his weapons and cast him from the shield wall. "I can still gut a man."

"When did it happen?"

Rufnir looked down at the stump. "After the burning lake. The wound rot went deep." His gaze rose to meet Raef's. "But I was fortunate. The gods let me live and the healer who took my hand knew his work. Asbjork was not so lucky."

Raef bowed his head and closed his eyes. "It grieves me to know he is dead, and I am sorry that I have only now learned of it." The brothers had been inseparable since the day Rufnir could walk fast enough to keep up with Asbjork. Raef could not remember a time when they had been apart. As boys, the three of them had fought and laughed and grown, and together they had fallen in love with the sea, entranced by the ever-stretching ocean and the secrets that lay beyond the sunsets off Vannheim's shore.

"He sits at Odin's table," Rufnir said, his voice gruff. Then he forced a grin and laughed. "And the troll spawn is surely laughing to see me now, forsaking the arms of a pretty girl in exchange for the cold embrace of winter and this bloody lot," he said, gesturing to the men who now huddled around the fire, sharing skins of mead and breaking apart a loaf of bread. Then Rufnir grew serious once more. "They followed, but some more eagerly than others. They did not trust that you lived, or that I could find you. But I knew," he said, thumping his chest, "I knew you would come here."

Raef smiled. "Then I am glad I shared the secret of the eagle's nest with you all those years ago, though it earned me a lashing."

"We have some good supplies, but I did not dare bring more men, for fear of catching the eyes of that red bastard who sits in your chair in the Vestrhall. His men patrol the closest hills for any sign of you or those who might seek to fight for you. I watched him drown four men who were caught trying to sneak through the gate in the black of night." Rufnir's sorrow turned to glee. "But he could not find me, no, and I slit the throats of two of his men in turn when they strayed too far from their friends."

"The village?"

Rufnir hung his head. "Much was burned. I am sure the dead were many. In this, too, was I fortunate. I had planned to visit Engvorr, the shipwright, but fate delayed my journey from my father's farm and I arrived the day after the slaughter. The smell, the smoke," Rufnir shook his head. "I did not approach the gate and took refuge in a hunter's shelter until word spread of your cousin's great betrayal."

Raef asked the question that was nearest his heart, though he felt his lungs clench and the words nearly caught in his throat. "Tell me, Ruf, did you ever see a woman with a braid of red and gold? Isolf would have relished her death, would have made certain it was known."

Rufnir shook his head. "But for the warriors he sent into the hills and the men he took to the fjord to drown, the gates remained shut. I saw no women."

It was the answer Raef expected, but it knotted his stomach nonetheless. He forced himself to nod and push away thoughts of Siv, but Rufnir broke in.

"The hounds," he said. "The hounds left, too, with seven men at their heels. They slipped through the gate at dawn, so quick and quiet in the grey light, I almost missed them as they passed beneath my perch above the valley. I waited a day before leaving so that they might not catch my scent."

Raef nodded. "Greyshield. He is dead and his sons with him." Rufnir grinned. "I am glad to have you with me, Rufnir, son of Bjarne. We have much more to discuss, but the hour is late."

Raef greeted the warriors who had followed Rufnir. Four were poorly armed, farmers convinced by Rufnir to pull their dusty spears out of the thatch and trek into the wilderness in search of their lord. The other five were hardened warriors known to Raef, men he had fought beside in Solheim and Garhold. All were accustomed to hardship, though Raef knew, as he looked from face to face, the task before them would test their wills.

"Men of Vannheim, brothers of Vannheim," Raef said, speaking so they all might hear. They faced him, some with bold faces yearning for battle and glory, others with uncertainty and questions in their eyes. "You are first to answer the call, first to fulfill your oaths, and I shall not forget it. Others will come. Others will brandish their bright swords and boast of what they will do to the enemies of Vannheim. But you, you are the first. There is no certain path before our feet. There is no promise of victory that I can give that would not ring hollow in your ears. I see in your eyes the same fear that eats at my heart. But there is one promise I can make to each of you. All of Asgard will know your names, for we are wolves, unyielding and fierce, and we will scratch and claw and savage until the Allfather himself gazes down on us with his terrible eye."

It seemed a feeble attempt at binding them to him, a paltry means of bolstering the hearts of those who wavered, but the response was better than Raef could have hoped for. A roar went up from the men, shields were beaten, spears were hammered against the ground, and the eagle's nest filled with the sounds of blood-thirsty defiance.

That night, just before the dawn, stars streaked through the sky, more than a man might count. Silent bolts of lightning split the darkness, and Raef watched and knew the god of thunder was at war.

FIVE

THE CROWS WERE thick in the morning sky, a seething cloud of dark wings over the treetops in the valley, greeting brother and sister with harsh voices. Raef watched from the edge of the eagle's nest, an uneasy feeling in his stomach. The others rose and stretched and grumbled for food, but only Vakre seemed to share Raef's apprehension, for only Vakre had sat awake in the last hours of darkness and watched the ominous sky with Raef while the others slept. They had spoken only a little, for little needed to be said. Balder, bright son of Odin, beloved of the gods, was dead, and the doom that came for the gods and all the nine realms was at hand. That Thor had battled his eternal foes while the world of men slept, there was little doubt.

"Ever does the thunder god clash with the giants, Raef," Vakre had said, his face flashing white as lighting forked overhead. "It may signify nothing." There was little conviction behind his words.

"And yet stars fall from the sky before our very eyes. This is no skirmish. Even now the walls of Asgard may be besieged. Fenrir may be at the gates, lusting for a taste of the Allfather. Black Surt may be setting Valhalla ablaze with his flaming sword."

"The end is yet to come," Vakre had said, sure of himself then. When Raef had frowned and questioned this, Vakre sat quietly for a moment before answering. "There are times when I can feel him. Loki." Another pause. "He is angry." Vakre closed his eyes. "Betrayed." Vakre's eyes snapped open, a hint of fire retreating with his eyelids. He took a deep breath. "If this were the end, I would feel his joy."

Raef had accepted this, not questioning the Loki-blood in Vakre's veins, and the lightning storm had ceased not long after, but as the sun rose and the crows flocked, he knew whatever drew the corpse eaters to the valley was connected to Thor's anger.

Leaving a pair of men behind to watch the nest, Raef and his small band of warriors descended into the valley. The stench that rose to meet them was that of foul and rotten flesh, so putrid and choking that, as they drew closer to where the crows blackened the treetops, Raef pulled his cloak up to cover his nose and mouth in an attempt to blot out the smell. He could hear the moans of those who followed him, and more than one man spit up watery remains of the past night's mead.

They advanced in tight formation, though Raef did not expect to find a live foe beside the river's edge, and, after exchanging a look with Vakre, Raef signaled for the men to halt before continuing on with just Vakre at his side. Here the crow song was deafening, the voices mixed with the beating of wings as the birds swirled from tree to tree. Axe in hand, Raef carried on, pressing through the trees.

The giant's corpse was a swollen mass of flesh and bone, so savaged it was nearly beyond recognition. The chest was caved in with a mighty blow, the splintered rib bones protruding from pulpy flesh. Half the head was gone, revealing grey brain matter and broken bits of skull all tangled together with strands of bloody, once-blonde hair. A single eye stared upward, rich brown in color. The giant's legs were broken at the knees, the fingers torn from their sockets, dangling from limp skin.

"Mjölnir," Raef said, unable to take his eyes from the ruin that had been the giant's chest, the foul smell forgotten in the presence of such brutal death. Thor's hammer had done its work well.

The giant had been tall, not so tall as the brute Mogthrasir, Raef reckoned, but taller than his fair-faced kin Hrodvelgr, and his weight had toppled more than one tree while several others leaned at dangerous angles, their trunks threatening to snap where the giant's limbs rested.

Raef looked up to the sky, but it was Visna, dressed now in borrowed clothes pieced together from among the men who had arrived with Rufnir, moving silently to stand beside him, who spoke the words in his mind.

"This is wrong," she said. "A giant slain in Jötunheim should remain in Jötunheim."

"This is the fourth," came a new voice, young and high-pitched. Raef whirled, ready to fight, but the speaker was a boy draped in furs so thick and long that they dragged behind him and tripled the breadth of his shoulders. The boy stared straight ahead at the giant, his eyes bright but his expression blank. He paid Raef and his axe no mind as he walked close to the corpse and knelt beside the broken head. A slender hand reached out of the furs and closed the eyelid. When the eye popped open again and refused to stay shut, a small smile came to the boy's face.

"Who are you?" Visna said. The Valkyrie had not been idle, but had moved closer to the boy, and, though she spoke with a pleasant voice, Raef saw deadly intent in her face should the boy prove to be dangerous.

"Some call me He Who Burned, others say I am Fire-Born, my father gave me the name Barek in the hopes that I would be mighty in battle, but the name I have chosen for myself is Anuleif, for I shall be the ancestor to those who inherit the world." The boy fixed Raef with a calm gaze, those light blue eyes full of certainty, and Raef knew him for what he was.

"You are the son of Gudrik of Karahull, the boy lord who would not grant the Hammerling Karahull's spears and shields," Raef said. The boy was changed from when Raef had seen him in the smoky hall of Karahull. Then he had sat, nearly naked, in his father's massive chair, his shaven head glistening with sweat, the raging fires in the pits threatening to start the whole hall ablaze. Raef had thought him mad then and, though the boy had grown hair and layered himself with reindeer pelts, the madness was still there.

"Yes," the boy said, content to leave it at that, though Raef had expected him to lash out, for the Karahull warriors had made their own choice and followed the Hammerling to battle against his will. "But I am no longer the lord of Karahull. Let them fight this war as they see fit, let them choose one king or another. That is their right. I let them choose a lord from among the warriors and they are happier for it. And I have no need of a lord's seat or a lord's hall. I did not know it when I last saw you, Raef Skallagrim, but my fate moves beyond the circle of Karahull, beyond, even, the circle of this world."

"You said this was the fourth," Vakre broke in, returning all thoughts to the giant's corpse. The crows remained at bay, though why Raef could not have said.

"I found the first in the far south of Karahull. The second lay on the border between my father's lands and Silfravall. The third fell further west, half-submerged in a river. And the third led me here."

"Led you?" Vakre's voice was full of suspicion.

The boy who called himself Anuleif shrugged, though the thick pelts over his shoulders masked his movement. "I discovered the first by chance. Palest white and hairy that one was, the crudest example of their race." The boy's gaze flickered over to the crushed chest. "It smelled even more foul." Those bright eyes lingered on the ruined form of life before returning to Vakre's face. "The moment I

saw it, I knew there would be more and I knew I had to find them."
The boy looked at Raef. "I think I was meant to find you."

"Why?"

"The gods have not seen fit to tell me."

"You came all this way alone?" Raef asked.

"I am a good walker."

Visna stirred and scowled at the boy, her derision plain. "You
should walk home, boy. This is not your concern."

"A giant's corpse falls from the sky and you would brush it off
as you would a spider?" Anuleif's voice, though still high and childlike, rang out with new strength. "Balder is dead. Ragnarök is upon
us. It is very much my concern."

Raef saw the anger flush Visna's cheeks and he laid a hand on
her shoulder. "You know much, Anuleif, son of Gudrik. Tell me,
then, how is it that these giants have fallen like rain upon Midgard?
Has Thor sent them here?"

"They fall because the boundaries between the nine realms are
weakening. Races that have been kept apart since the dawn age will
soon collide. Yggdrasil is old and tired and cannot withstand the
war that is coming." The words were grave and spoken in earnest,
but Raef saw a gleam of something in Anuleif's face that told of
awe.

"Once you told me you must protect your people from the
frost giants. Now, you speak as though you look forward to seeing
their triumph."

"Triumph? The giants will succumb to the same fate that follows us all, that haunts the Allfather. They are the instrument, but
not the victor." Anuleif smiled. "But you speak true. When last we
met, Raef Skallagrim, I had much to learn."

"You are a boy. You have seen ten winters," Visna said, her eyes
narrowed by mistrust. "What could you know?"

Anuleif continued to smile and did not allow Visna to provoke him. His strange eyes looked up at Raef, unwavering. "I dreamed of you. And here I am standing before you, summoned by the blood of giants."

The other warriors had ventured among the broken trees. Many touched the hammers of Thor that hung from their necks. All stared at the mutilated corpse. Raef saw the fear in them and, though he knew not what to make of the boy from Karahull, of one thing he was certain. That fear would spark like tinder if they heard what the boy had to say.

"Come." Raef reached out and put a hand on Anuleif's shoulder. "Your journey has been long. You must be hungry. Let us go fishing, together. Just you and me."

The boy chewed on his lip for a moment. "What of him?" He indicated the giant's corpse.

Raef glanced at Vakre, who nodded in understanding, and asked Rufnir to lead the men back to the nest. Only when they were out of sight and Raef had begun to walk with Anuleif to the river, did Vakre, kneeling beside the giant's ruined head, send a tendril of flame out to latch onto the matted hair. The flame flared and grew and spread, and soon engulfed the giant from head to toe.

It was only after Raef had reached the river and begun to search the water for silver fish that he realized Vakre had not been wearing his father's cloak.

ᛉ ᛉ ᛉ

"You had a sister," Raef said as he watched Anuleif bound from one river-washed rock to the next, nimble and quick. Raef held a spear borrowed from Rufnir in one hand, poised to let fly should a fish dart near enough. "What became of her?"

Anuleif paused, balancing on a rock that knifed up from the river bottom like a mountain ridge and fixed his gaze on Raef. "She died." He smiled, then, and leapt to the next stone, this one nearly submerged. The boy watched the water rush around his feet and did not say more.

"Do the warriors of Karahull still follow the Hammerling?"

"Perhaps. They are no longer my concern." Anuleif reached down and stuck his fingers in the cold river, letting the water drag against them.

"You dreamed of me?"

At this the boy stood and stared hard at Raef, all traces of childishness gone. Then, with slow, deliberate movements, he stripped the reindeer skins from his shoulders, one by one, until he was barechested and the skins dangled in the river. His chest was puckered with scars, white and shiny. Not scars from battle, not scars made by a knife or sword or axe. These were a tumbling patchwork that swirled up from his navel and over each shoulder. Anuleif turned, showing Raef his back. The scars were thickest there.

A gust of wind blew across the river but the boy seemed not to notice.

"Do you know what it feels like to have flames lick across your back? To watch your skin burn away? To be consumed by fire? My people called me Fire-Born, for I lived when I should have died."

Raef lowered the spear, the fish forgotten. "I heard you say once that you would cure the weakness in your skin. That you would never burn again."

Anuleif smiled. It was not a happy thing. "I was foolish. I thought to become stronger than a man so that I might not perish as my father did. But I burned, and then I dreamed. Of you and many things. I did not understand them at first. When I gave up my father's hall, only then did I begin to see. I have not gone near a fire since. Fire is what will claim the world, Raef, and so I must distance myself from it."

ᚾ ᚾ ᚾ

The warriors gave Anuleif a wide berth in the nest that night, and the boy himself kept well clear of the campfire. He ate only a single fish and did not ask for more, though he eagerly drank from Rufnir's skin of mead when offered. Raef saw more than one guarded glance cast the boy's way

The mead skins were emptied, laughter was shared, and stories of battle and women and ruined crops were told. There was no talk of the giant's corpse, as though giving voice to its presence would give strength to its meaning. Raef found his thoughts punctured repeatedly by Anuleif's words burrowing into his mind, but, pushing the boy's madness away, Raef stood and went to Rufnir, who was lamenting the empty state of the last skin of mead.

"I am sending you to Axsellund, Ruf. Tomorrow. Choose two of these men to go with you."

Rufnir frowned. "What for?"

"Torleif of Axsellund made a promise, one that I kept secret from most, though Isolf may have learned of it. You must go to him and determine the strength of that promise."

Rufnir shook his head. "My place is at your side."

Raef put a hand on Rufnir's shoulder. "Who among these men can I trust to go in your stead? They have cheered my name and they sit around my fire, but when our hopes fade around us, when our enemies close in, when blood is spilled, will they stand firm? I need you. You can speak with my voice for you know me better than most. And I know you will honor your oath to me until your last breath."

Reluctance remained on Rufnir's face, but he gave a slow nod. "I will go, if that is what you require of me."

"It is. When you see Torleif, give him a sprig of cedar. He will understand."

Rufnir nodded again. "I will take Fjolnir with me. He is quick with a blade." Fair-haired and sharp-eyed Fjolnir was the youngest of the men who had followed Rufnir to the eagle's nest.

"And the other?"

Rufnir's gaze roamed over the warriors gathered around the fire. "Gullveig." He was one of the farmers, a burly man with thick arms who spoke little.

"You must leave at first light and travel with all speed."

Rufnir was quiet for a moment, his gaze fixed on an empty spot in the darkness over Raef's shoulder. "Do you think we will ever take the sea road, Raef?" His voice was full of longing and Raef knew he thought of his brother, for Asbjork would never ride the waves again.

He was looking for hope and Raef chose to shatter it. "No, Ruf. Balder is dead. The last battle will be upon us soon. We have time only for blood and vengeance. I will win back Vannheim before the floods and the fires come, but the sea road," Raef paused, his heart heavy, "the sea road is beyond us, a dream we will take to our deaths."

Rufnir's face filled with grim understanding, and there was new determination there. "Blood and vengeance, then." He seemed to warm to the task Raef had given him. "I will return with the strength of Axsellund at my back, and we will descend upon the Vestrhall with swords and spears and your treacherous cousin will die screaming."

"And a son of Bjarne will bring me victory." Raef grinned and planted a kiss on Rufnir's forehead. "I mean to send out others into the valleys of Vannheim. We must gather more men to us. And I will wait for your return."

Rufnir, Fjolnir, and Gullveig descended from the nest in the grey light before dawn. The men who remained watched with solemn faces, their breath forming clouds of vapor that hung in the still air, until the three figures disappeared into the trees below. One by one, they turned away until only Raef and Anuleif lingered at the overlook.

"Will the lord of Axsellund fulfill his promise?" Anuleif's voice was small in the cold, grey morning, but the words rang in Raef's ears as though the boy had shouted.

Raef chose not to answer.

"You are without a hall and you are hiding in your own wilderness. He may choose to turn his back." Anuleif cocked his head. "But that would mean risking the wrath of Odin, for to turn his back on you would be to turn his back on his named king."

Raef flinched and turned to stare at the boy. "Why do you call me a named king?"

"Because that is what you are."

"Not once have I been called king in your presence. How could you know this?"

"I have told you. I have dreamed."

The rising sun saw more men depart the eagle's nest, six sent out to delve into the deep valleys and high hills in search of warriors to bolster Raef's strength.

"Keep clear of the Vestrhall," Raef told the men, "and speak only to those known to you. I will not have strangers brought back to the nest." He looked each in the eyes, searching for signs of betrayal. If any deceit festered in those irises of brown and blue and green, it was well concealed. The six men left the nest as one. They would fill their skins with river water and then separate, carrying Raef's hopes to the east, north, south, and west.

The man left behind, called Tuli, planted himself on the overlook, spear in hand, as though he meant to keep watch, and he did not stray from the edge until the sun was past its highest point, and even then he only stepped away to relieve his bladder. Vakre muttered something about Tuli's watchfulness putting him on edge and left the nest. Raef did not try to stop him. Visna separated herself from the others, climbing a short distance up the sides of the bowl to a ledge, her dislike of Anuleif apparent in her scowl and narrowed eyes.

When the sun began to sink out of the sky, Raef went to Tuli and placed a hand on the warrior's shoulder. "You watch as well as Heimdall, Tuli. Come sit by the fire and warm yourself." Tuli grinned at the praise, his wide face spreading to show uneven teeth, and did as Raef said. As he stoked the fire, Anuleif, who had spent much of the daylight carving bits of wood with a small knife, retreated to the back of the bowl, ducking into the mouth of one of the small caves. In the growing shadows, Raef soon lost sight of him.

With the boy gone, Visna descended from her perch.

"The boy is mad. Let me slit his throat so that we might be rid of him."

"No," Raef said. He had been waiting for this. "He has done us no harm."

"Do you not see it in his eyes?" Visna stepped close to Raef.

"I see it." Raef refused to say more.

Visna frowned, marring her blue eyes with anger. "Then send him away," she said. "He will bring only misfortune and suffering."

"You show little sympathy for one who has much in common with Anuleif." Raef let his voice grow sharp and was glad to see Visna felt the sting. She drew back and spit on the ground between them.

"We share nothing."

"He is alone in this world, as you are. Do not be so quick to denounce him for that."

Visna's eyes flared in recognition of this unwanted truth. "His delusions and dreams will poison the minds of others and you will regret not emptying his life blood into these stones." She turned away and brushed past Vakre, who had returned with silent footfalls and heard all. Raef watched the Valkyrie stalk away, then turned to Vakre with a heavy sigh.

"She will be at his throat soon enough," Raef said. "I have gathered a pair of wolves into my nest. I must find a way to build a truce between them."

Vakre dropped an armful of wood by the fire. "You cannot tame her, Raef. She was born and bred for a single purpose, to kill that which she has condemned. If they both stay here, they will not survive each other."

"I will not choose between them. They are both drowning, though they do not know it."

"The choice may not be yours to make. But tell me, do you pity the boy, or do you hear some truth in his words?"

Raef looked at Vakre but found he was unwilling to answer. Vakre did not seem surprised at the silence.

"I hear what you hear, Raef. Though why Anuleif has come to us and what his purpose might be, I do not know." Vakre held out a slender object wrapped in brown linen. "Here."

"What is it?" Raef asked.

"I will let you see for yourself. I discovered it on Visna's ship."

Raef unwrapped the cloth with careful hands and felt leather beneath. When the linen fell away, he was holding a scabbard of simple leather, unembellished and dark with age. The sword's hilt was black and glossy, smooth as ice, and it felt warm to Raef's touch as he wrapped the fingers of his left hand around it. He had revealed no more than a finger's width of the blade when Visna was there, her hand grasping tight over the naked steel. When Raef looked up, her eyes were hard and fierce.

"That is mine."

"And yet you left it, forgotten, abandoned," Vakre said. Raef did not release his grip on the sword.

Visna flinched at Vakre's accusation. "It is mine by right." She stared hard at the sword. "And mine to part with."

Raef pried the sword from her grip and eased the blade out of the scabbard. The steel was dark and rippled with shadows. "I saw you wield a sword of sunlight, bright and blazing and hard to look upon. There is not a spark of light here."

Visna was pale now and her voice scarcely more than a whisper. "No. Nor will there be until it is claimed by the right hand." Her hand shook as she reached out for the sword. Raef let her take it. The steel remained dull and Raef saw a glimmer of hope fade in Visna's eyes. When she spoke again, her voice was flat. "This is the sword of a Valkyrie. Once it was mine and once I looked upon the faces of men and chose who would die by its edge. I can no longer remember their faces." She sheathed the sword. "My father has given me a final task." Visna looked from Raef to Vakre and back again. "There must be nine. Nine Valkyries riding the storm clouds, nine streaking to the battlefield, nine at the Allfather's side."

Visna let out a sharp laugh and cast her gaze to the sky. "Is this your final punishment, Father? That I must seek out and discover she who will replace me? That I must hand over the weapon that exists as a part of me, a limb, an eye, a piece of my heart? That I alone must sever the last link to the life I have known?" Tears spilled onto Visna's cheeks and she did not attempt to hide them. "I would curse you if I knew how, Father, but I do not have the words for there is only love in my heart for you. And that is the hardest thing of all. I want to hate you, but I cannot." Visna stared at the stars for a moment longer and then let the sword fall to the ground. She looked at Raef through tear-laden eyes, her face more open and honest than he had ever seen it, then turned and left the fire's light. When she returned at dawn, she was cold and hard and would not speak of the sword

For five days and five nights, Raef kept his vigil in the eagle's nest, each day wearing longer than the last as his uneasy, guarded companions circled around him in a tangle of unspoken threats. On the sixth day, they were no longer alone.

SIX

THERE WAS NO banner, no horns, and few enough men, Raef could see, even from his high vantage point. They had come not long after the sunlight had cascaded into the valley, spilling over the snow-covered trees with a golden glow that reminded Raef of summer. The icy air that nipped at his ears and reddened his cheeks banished those warm thoughts as Raef caught sight of the men that came from the east, following in the footsteps of the sun. They might have passed under the nest and reached the edge of the fjord unnoticed were it not for a bare patch of open land just east of the nest that grazed the shore of the river. It was there that Raef spotted them by chance, catching the glint of sunlight on something that was not water, tree, rock, or snow.

A quick word to Tuli and their fire, hissing and spitting in protest, was smothered, sending a spiral of smoke skyward that was soon lost in the blue. Vakre stepped to Raef's side as the men reached the end of the bare land and disappeared once more into the trees.

"Yours?" Vakre asked, his eyes not leaving the valley, searching always for the next sighting.

"Perhaps."

They waited in strained silence, hearing nothing but the river rushing over rocks and the faint calls between birds. At last Raef could stand it no longer.

"If they were mine, they would be here, not skulking among the trees." Raef retreated from the overlook and retrieved his scabbard, then slid his axe into his belt on his left hip next to the long knife that already lay there. Vakre armed himself as well and Visna began to do the same, but Raef stopped the Valkyrie before she reached her borrowed sword.

"Stay. Keep watch for others." Visna began to protest but Raef was in no mood to hear it. He turned and climbed over the side of the nest, leaving the Valkyrie to sulk.

"Will she listen?" Vakre asked as he followed Raef down the slope.

"Unlikely."

They reached the tree line and slowed their descent as they headed for the river. The woods around them were quiet and still, the snow marked only by the prints of small animals and a few deer, and they, after passing by the melted snow and scorched ground where Vakre had burned the giant's corpse, reached the river without sight or sound of the party of men. Raef turned east, following the riverbank, and now they walked with great care, keeping close to the thickest bushes and branches to avoid unwanted eyes.

"Do you hear that?" Vakre asked, frozen in his tracks. Raef stopped and strained to listen. There, the sound of voices, one first, dim and distant, then others joining in. Raef crouched and crept onward.

The men were gathered at the river's edge, clustered among slender birch trees and sturdy oaks. Some held the reins of horses and were heavily armed, others carried only spears and shields, once painted, now worn to dull reds and yellows and chipped black.

Raef nodded to Vakre and the son of Loki slipped through the trees to circle around the clearing and get a full count of the warriors. Raef, his view barred by snow-laden pine branches, ducked low and crawled closer, eager to glimpse the faces of those who trespassed so close to the eagle's nest.

One man still sat in his saddle, his horse hemmed in by the others, and he was speaking, though the river water carried away the sound of his voice. With a tug of the reins, he turned the horse and dismounted and Raef sucked in breath at the sight of his face. Fengar, lord of Solheim and the would-be king, had come to Vannheim.

Vakre reappeared at Raef's side and whispered that he counted forty-three men but some were there against their will, bound at the wrist by ropes. The crowd parted as one of these captives was pushed forward by a man of ancient face and hunched back. A black crow's feather was tied in the old man's white hair and a pair of pale medallions that hung from his neck rattled against each other as he prodded the prisoner toward Fengar. The old man delivered a sharp rap to the prisoner's shoulder with a stout shaft, sending him to his knees.

"This one, lord," the old man said.

War had changed Fengar. When first Raef had seen the would-be king, Fengar's face had been open, almost friendly, the face of a man surprised to be named king. Later, he had gained a measure of confidence and poise, as if he were beginning to believe in the fate that had swelled up around him. Now his cheekbones were more pronounced, his eyes less bright, his whole posture closed off and wary. He eyed the man at his feet with obvious distaste, but he was no warmer toward the old man and Raef sensed Fengar would be rid of both if he could.

Fengar said something too quiet for Raef to hear, but the old man's reaction spoke loud enough for both.

"The gods do not bestow victory upon cowards. You have lost their favor, Fengar. We must win it back."

"With this man's blood?" Fengar's voice rose but held no conviction. "What is this man to Odin Allfather, or to Thor?"

"Does the Hammerling shrink from such duties? Does he fear the necessary sacrifices? A skinny winter rabbit is no longer enough." Though bent and brittle, the old man spoke with utter belief.

Fengar scowled and Raef could see his nostrils flare, but whether it was from anger at the old man or at the mention of his rival, the Hammerling, Raef could not say. Perhaps both. "Do it." The words were uttered through clenched teeth and Fengar turned away and pushed through the men until he reached the riverbank.

The old man took no joy in Fengar's decision, but grabbed the prisoner's cloak with a bony hand and pulled, forcing the man to scramble after him on hands and knees. The gathered men spread out, giving the old man a clear path to the closest tree, their eyes watching every move with nervous anticipation. Two other bound men and one woman cowered as the old man passed them by, but they might have been worms in the dirt for all the attention he gave them. He gave a sharp whistle, summoning a beardless boy, and together they stripped the captive to the waist and lashed him to the tree, arms stretched wide to echo the shape of the oak's branches. Without a word, the old man pulled a small knife and skewered the man's left hand to the bark. The shriek pierced the uneasy silence and the old man stepped back as though to admire his work. The boy produced another knife, this one long and lean and set in a bone handle. The old man took it and, with a few muttered words that Raef could not make out, stepped close to the shivering, sobbing prisoner and began to carve into his pale belly. The sobs turned to moans and screams and then the air was filled with the smell of piss and shit.

In a moment, the prisoner's head sank to his chest, though Raef could see his eyelids fluttered still, and the old man went on with his work with precision. The warriors watched with horror and fascination etched on their faces. Fengar kept his back to the bloody sacrifice.

When the old man had finished, the captive was dead, his entrails strung up around him, the ravaged belly a mass of mutilated, bloody flesh. With a last flick of his knife, the old man cut a lock of hair from the dead man, held it to his nose, then tied it next to one of the medallions that hung from his neck. Raef saw then that the fresh strand of hair was not alone and the medallions were smooth, worn bone.

Only then did Fengar turn and survey what had been done and Raef saw him lick his lips and swallow at the display before him. "What now, Griva? Will Odin himself descend from Asgard and fight alongside me?" There was mockery in Fengar's voice and face, but a sharp look from Griva sent it fleeing, leaving only weariness behind. "Let us be gone from this place," Fengar said, his gaze roaming back to the river and the trees on the far shore. "I do not like it here."

"No," Griva said, and though Fengar had returned to his horse, it was the old man whose voice commanded the warriors. Not a single one stirred and all watched Griva, who was assessing his sacrifice. He traced a finger along the dead man's chest until he reached the savaged belly, then he touched the lock of hair he had taken, his mouth forming silent words. "This is a good place. We must stay."

Fengar looked as though he wanted to argue, but something made him hold his tongue. "Very well." The king summoned a warrior to his side. "Send out riders so the others might find us. We will await them here." Now the warriors surged to life, and soon they separated, two returning to the east on fleet-footed horses, the rest surging further along the river in search of decent ground to make camp. Raef and Vakre drew back into the trees and underbrush and waited until they had passed from sight, then followed at a distance.

A spot was chosen close to where the river spilled into the fjord and it was not long before the smell of charred wood brought curious men to the place where the giant had fallen from Jötunheim. One by one they filtered through the trees until Fengar's entire host stood in the clearing. Raef and Vakre watched from higher ground. The clearing was free from snow and scorched where Vakre had set his blaze. Nothing remained of the corpse and the only sign of violence was the trees splintered by the giant's limbs. Fengar's men muttered to each other and a few reached out to touch the Thor hammers that hung from their necks, eying those around them to see if they did so alone.

"A lightning strike." Griva seemed sure of himself and the men agreed, some with quick laughs and crude jokes to shake off the nerves that had sent them reaching for their amulets.

Fengar ordered the men back to the river to set up shelters, but they had gone only a few steps when shouts rang out and swords were drawn. In the confusion, Raef could not see what had caused the commotion, but then, with a sharp word from Fengar, the warriors went still, giving Raef a better view. Beside him, Vakre swore under his breath.

Visna stood at the edge of the clearing, her arm wrapped tight around Griva's chest, her sword pressed against his long, thin neck. The old man did not struggle and his face was calm.

"Your skald dies if any of you move," Visna shouted. "And then I will kill the rest of you."

For a moment Fengar seemed content to let her kill Griva, but Raef could see the agitation on the faces of the warriors and knew the king would lose the loyalty of each and every man if he let the old man die. Fengar knew it, too. He held out his hands to show he did not threaten. "He is no skald."

Visna frowned. "What other purpose does an old man have?"

"He is," Fengar paused, "skilled in many things." Raef had thought the old man a priest of Odin and was surprised to not hear him named so.

"Then if you value his skills you will do as I say."

With a cry, a warrior charged from Visna's right. Moving with deadly speed, she shoved Griva to the ground, whirled, sliced, and killed with a single motion. Griva was collared and the steel, dripping now with a dead man's blood, returned to his throat before he had a chance to move.

Fengar grimaced. "Name your price."

Visna's gaze shot across the clearing, behind Fengar, to where the three captives stood. "I want her."

The woman turned and ran.

For a moment, no one moved, then Fengar shouted for someone to chase after her. Three men sprinted into the trees, but Raef had moved first. There was little time to think, but he did not intend to leave Visna alone. No matter how deadly she had proved herself to be, she was no longer a Valkyrie and he did not trust her to remember this.

The woman was headed toward him and Raef only needed to step out from the trees to bring her down. They landed with a thud and the woman began to scream, but Raef was deaf to her pleas as he led her back to the clearing, Vakre at his side. The three warriors slid to a halt as he approached, hands going to sword hilts, but a burst of flame from Vakre sent them reeling, their faces ashen, eyes staring. Raef entered the clearing unimpeded.

"Skallagrim." Fengar's voice was hushed, but then he rounded on Griva, who was still in Visna's bloody grasp. "You said he was dead."

"The gods love chaos," Griva said, grimacing as his throat moved against Visna's blade.

Fengar looked once more at Raef and gestured to the woman in his grip. "This woman means something to you?"

"No."

Fengar frowned. "Then why interfere?"

"Because these are my lands."

"And I am king."

"Not my king."

Fengar's gaze flickered and he did not look Raef in the eye. "Well, woman," he said, facing Visna now. "There is your prize. Let him go."

Visna shoved Griva to the ground, her gaze fixed now on the woman who clutched at Raef in fear. But she had taken no more than two steps when Griva hissed a curse at her and Visna turned, eyes flashing, steel carving a path through the air toward the old man's chest.

Raef saw the blonde women too late. Like wolves, they sprang at Visna, and her death blow turned into a desperate, swinging defense as they attacked her from both sides. Raef leaped forward, his movements hampered by the woman at his side, and the butt end of a spear plowed into his chest, sending him backward. Before he could move again, the spear point was at his throat and a grizzled warrior, face hidden by a thick black beard, barred his way. Behind the warrior, Visna was on her knees, panting, blood running down her face, her sword out of reach, and the blonde women, two of the so-called Daughters of Thor, stood over her in triumph.

Raef felt the rush of heat and thrust his arm back, palm out, to where Vakre smoldered just behind him. "No, Vakre." The heat faded but did not disappear. Raef looked at Fengar, who had not moved, had not given an order. "Call them off. We are not here to fight."

Fengar hesitated, uncertainty clouding his eyes. Griva sidled up beside the king and whispered into Fengar's ear. Fengar flinched away from the old man's touch, but the doubt fled from his face. "Bind them."

They fought, Visna screaming in fury, Raef beating back the bear-like warrior, Vakre lunging for one of the blonde sisters, but the opponents were too many. An arrow pierced Raef's shoulder and dizziness swarmed over his vision in an instant. Raef, sluggish, stared down at the white fletching and then at his empty hands. His sword was gone, though he did not know he had dropped it, and then he was on the ground. The beating was merciless and Raef fought to stay conscious, sucking in air when he could, striking out with his feet in vain. By the time he felt the ropes cut into the skin of his wrists, his vision was reduced to a blur of light slashed through with shadows, and then all was darkness.

SEVEN

"HE IS NO use to me dead."

The voice was both grating to Raef's ears and hard to hear, the words a jumble in his mind until sense was made of them.

"The poison will wear off, lord. It is my own blend." The second voice was faint, light, a drop of water beyond reach. Raef fought to open his eyes and for a moment thought he had failed to do so. Then the stars came into focus. He could see little else and nothing of the voices in the dark. The ground was cold beneath him but free of snow and he began to understand the shape of a crude half-shelter fashioned together of wood and branches and skins.

"For your sake, I hope you are telling the truth." The third voice was deeper than the first two, harsh and unfriendly.

"I do not make a habit of lying to lords." Female. Yes. The second voice belonged to a woman. "He will wake. The wound itself is minimal and has been cleaned and stitched. It was my poison that brought him down so quickly." Raef traced a finger along his shoulder, feeling the puckered skin and gut stitches beneath his woolen layers.

"And the others?" The first voice returned and Raef, certain it belonged to Fengar, could now tell the three speakers were to his left.

"Brought down by more uncivilized means." There was no doubting the disdain in the woman's voice. It had to be Vakre and Visna she spoke of and Raef's heartbeat spiked. "But they, too, will return to the light." Alive, then.

The deep voice said, "Cast off the spares, lord. They are of no use."

There was a moment of silence. "Perhaps. But better to wait and see."

Raef heard a shuffling of feet and a sigh that suggested impatience. "As you wish," the deep voice replied.

"The moment any of them wakes, bring them to me," Fengar said.

"Yes, lord," the woman said. Boots crunched on snow and then all was silent. Raef, his head clearer now, twisted to his left side. A single figure stood not far from him. The woman. She turned and walked out of Raef's sightline, leaving him to lie in the dark, trying to summon the will to overcome the poison in his limbs. He struggled into a sitting position, his movement hampered by the ropes around his wrists and ankles. Discerning a shape slumped against a thick spray of pine branch, Raef scooted over the ground until he could make out a face by starlight.

A bruise covered Vakre's left cheekbone, but there were no other visible injuries. The son of Loki's breathing was steady and Raef prodded him with a toe, then his elbow, until Vakre stirred. Blinking, Vakre raised his head.

"Raef?"

"Yes."

"What were you thinking?" Vakre grinned and then winced and touched the bruise on his cheek. "Had to get involved. Reckless."

Raef tried to smile, but it quickly slipped from his face. "I could not leave a daughter of Odin alone among them."

"No," Vakre said, solemn now, "though I would like to know what inspired her foolish action." Vakre leaned back and closed his eyes. "Are you hurt?"

"I took a poisoned arrow. Bruised ribs. Little else."

Approaching footsteps silenced them and Raef looked over his shoulder to see the woman returning.

"Awake, I see." She stood over them, her face obscured by darkness and a hood. Raef said nothing. "Then it is time you were brought before the king."

The king was ensconced in a circle of warmth, shielded from the night air by thick skins. He was half-dressed, and the woman who Visna had risked all for was tugging her dress down over her shoulders, her face hidden by strands of dull brown hair. She did not react to the arrival of Raef and Vakre, but kept her head down.

"The prisoners, lord," the female archer said. A sharp finger in Raef's shoulder, near the wound she had given him, prompted him to take a knee.

"Now? I am busy." Fengar plucked at his belt, loosening the buckle, his voice impatient, but little enthusiasm showing.

"You said the moment either wakes, lord."

Fengar looked about to argue, to impose his will as king, but Raef could see his heart was not in it. "Very well. She smells of sheep." The woman was ushered out, and Fengar gestured for the female archer to go as well, leaving Raef and Vakre to bear the full brunt of Fengar's scrutiny.

"So. Skallagrim. Once more you are at my mercy." Fengar resettled his cloak on his shoulders and clasped it. He did not look Raef in the eye. "Stefnir wanted me to kill you last time. He would say so again if he were here."

"What do you say, lord? You are king, are you not?"

At last Fengar met Raef's gaze. "I am." There was nothing fierce in his voice and Raef wondered how much conviction lingered in the lord of Solheim. "I let you live once. I am not inclined to do so again."

"Yet?" For Raef was certain there was more.

"Yet you are likely to possess knowledge that would be valuable to me." Fengar's gaze slid to Vakre, who had remained silent. "And yet this one," Fengar cocked his head, "this one I think is more trouble than he is worth. I have heard what you are, Vakre Flame-cloak, heard about the battle at the burning lake. Your uncle has told me all." Vakre stared hard at Fengar and the king looked away first. "As for that woman, the wild one, perhaps she will be more appealing than the sheep woman. Perhaps I will take her into my bed. What did she want with my prisoner?"

"Griva does not have the answer for that? Your men hang upon his every word, Fengar. I do not think they would know how to find their own cocks if he did not tell them. I had thought to see him here."

Fengar scowled. "Griva has his uses but he does not command me." He stepped close to Raef, his breath heavy with the scent of ale. "I ask again, what did the woman want with my prisoner?"

"I do not know. You would have to ask her."

"You are free with your words, Skallagrim. A wiser man might make an effort to be humble. Your father was such a man."

Raef let the barb slide over him. "And yet I am wise enough to see you for what you are, a lost king, fleeing through the wilderness from a stronger foe, clinging to your last few warriors in hopes that their shields will stay strong."

With a roar, Fengar buried his fist in Raef's ribs. Gritting his teeth against the pain, Raef hunched but did not bow his head. Fengar's shout drew the blonde sisters into the shelter, and they waited only for Fengar's command, teeth barred and ready to strike.

A hand raised by Fengar kept their weapons sheathed, though they strained like foxes trapped in a snare.

"Get them out of my sight," Fengar growled. The sisters gripped Raef and Vakre by the arms and pulled them from the shelter back into the biting embrace of the winter night.

"You were three once," Vakre said, eyeing the sister who led him. Her long braid hung down to the small of her back and she did not respond. "Daughters of Thor, they call you." Vakre let the words whisper into the night. "Invincible," he taunted. "Where has your sister gone, I wonder?" The sisters walked on, undeterred, but Vakre persisted. "Strange that only two should stand guard over Fengar now."

They had returned to the makeshift shelter and in silence the sisters bound them to each other. As one, the blonde women rose from their task and turned their backs on Raef and Vakre. Neither looked back as Vakre called out one last time.

"I know her fate." The slightest hitch in one's stride brought a grin to Vakre's face and he looked to Raef. "That one will be back before morning."

"You have your father's sly tongue," Raef said. Vakre's grin grew wide and wolfish.

⋈ ⋈ ⋈

The daughter of Thor did not return before dawn as Vakre had predicted, but Visna was brought to share the same open-faced shelter, and bowls of hot broth came not long after. Raef and Vakre emptied their bowls quickly, but Visna's remained untouched, the steam rising furiously at first, then in feeble bursts until the heat was gone. The Valkyrie sat unmoving, her face, once bright, now dull. A gash at her hairline was crusted with blood. Her lower lip was split and bruised. Her golden hair was matted and her blue eyes were grey. If not for the tiny pulse at her throat, she hardly seemed to live.

Raef encouraged her to eat, to speak, but if she heard him she did not respond. She stared at the ground, hands clenched in her lap, and at last Raef left her to her silence.

"Tuli will wonder at our absence," Raef said. Though he knew the eagle's nest was out of sight, masked by the tall trees, he yearned to look up, to seek out the steep slope leading to the bowl, the dark shadows hiding horses, a man, and one small boy. But he dared not risk even the briefest glance.

Vakre nodded. "Let us hope he is not overcome with sudden bravery."

"Fengar has not asked why we have crossed paths in such a remote place."

Vakre scoffed. "Fengar is not clever enough to wonder about such things."

"He has asked me nothing about Vannheim, Vannheim's warriors, about the Hammerling."

"He is lost, as you said. Without Stefnir of Gornhald to guide him, to pull a string of wit from his skull, he is nothing. He is riddled with uncertainty."

"Or he intends to ask us nothing at all." Raef met Vakre's eyes and saw his own thoughts mirrored there, despite the son of Loki's words. "If he gives us to Griva's knife, he will please his warriors."

Vakre's eyes flashed with anger. "The sun will sink and the seas will rise before I let that old man gut me."

"Then let us hope the nest soon becomes home to a hundred warriors."

The day passed in slow agony, measured by the lengthening shadows. Those of Fengar's men who ventured close enough eyed them with furtive glances, but most kept their distance and none spoke a word. Griva came to stand at the river's edge once, lingering there while the sun started to slip behind the trees, and he carried the sword that Visna had threatened him with, not as a warrior would, but as a man studying something unknown. He let it rest across his palms, the dark steel stark against his pale skin, and examined the edge, holding it out over the rushing river, and once Raef caught him staring at Visna, but even he did not open his mouth to the prisoners.

It was dark when a face in the moonlight stirred Raef out of his thoughts. Anuleif, his thick array of pelts pulled high over his ears so that only his narrow nose and blue eyes showed, was suddenly at the side of their shelter.

"They will catch you," Vakre muttered. Alert now, he and Raef had crawled forward to speak. Raef peered over Vakre's bent head, gaze fixed on the closest group of warriors. The three men with tall spears stood over a small, flickering fire and their eyes were turned inward. For now.

"Yes," Anuleif said. There was no concern in his voice. "They are many and I am but one. But they are tired and their minds wander to the homes they have left behind and the ale skin they emptied two days ago. I have time to say what I have come to say."

Raef's heartbeat quickened as Anuleif's gaze shifted to him and he felt the stare of those uncanny eyes as surely as he felt the sun on a warm day. It beat into his bones, into his core, and for a moment, there was nothing but Anuleif's face, no Vakre, no Visna, no ropes binding his arms.

"Son of Skallagrim, I know now why I dreamed of you. You know what lies ahead, what hurtles toward us, unyielding. You know our fate. Balder is dead and even now the wolf has gained his freedom. Jötunheim is seething with fury and Jörmungand stirs in the watery depths he calls home. Alfheim is all darkness and despair. Midgard is breaking at the seams. It will not be long now before the cocks begin to crow." Anuleif paused and a strange smile came to his mouth. There was color in his lips and cheeks where none had been before and Raef felt sure that if the boy were to strip naked, the scars that circled his skin would smolder and crack, revealing fire beneath the surface.

"This is the end we have all come to know, to wait for. This is the end Odin fights against, knowing he fights in vain. But oblivion is not all that lies ahead, Raef. There is hope."

Raef's heart was pounding, his blood hammering in his ears as he tried to take in Anuleif's words. "What do you speak of?"

"I am the ancestor. There can be life after the darkness, after the fires burn and the seas swallow. I am meant to survive."

"Impossible. You do not know what you are saying."

The blue eyes flared and for a moment no longer than it takes lightning to streak across the sky, Raef saw something other than a child in Anuleif's face. "I do know what I am saying. The world can go on. Not without great sacrifice and trials beyond reckoning, but it can. You must believe this."

The shout of alarm broke the bond that had formed between Raef and Anuleif. The boy did not move, did not take his eyes from Raef, as a warrior rushed toward him, did not flinch as a spear point came to rest against his spine. And then others were there and a dozen voices were ringing in the darkness. Anuleif was pulled to his feet.

"It can be done, Raef," the boy said. "The swift knows the way." A warrior's strong arms dragged him backward through the snow and cast him at Fengar's feet. Griva loomed behind the king, his lined face alive with the promise of blood.

"A brave boy," Fengar said. Anuleif trembled on his knees, the fear he had eluded now gripping him tight. "But foolish to attempt such a rescue. How old are you?" Anuleif's teeth chattered as he opened his mouth to reply and nothing came out. The warriors roared with laughter. Fengar bent over and reached out a hand to brush snow from the boy's hair. "Do with him as you will, Griva."

"No," Raef shouted as Fengar straightened. The king's shoulders rose and fell and Raef could hear the heavy breath escape from his lungs before Fengar turned to face Raef.

"You are in no position to argue, Skallagrim."

"He is a child, Fengar."

"Boys grow into men who wield spears and shields."

"No, not him."

The king's gaze narrowed and Raef halved the distance between them, the lie forming on his tongue. "He does not know where he is. His own name comes and goes from his mind like the rain in spring. He is no threat to you and never will be." Raef spoke quietly and came within an arm's length of Fengar. "The gods would find no pleasure in this child's death." Raef did not dare break eye contact for fear that Griva would slip into the gap he left behind. Fengar glanced down at the top of Anuleif's head once more and when his gaze rose to Raef again, there was burning hatred there.

"Then let him live his pitiful life," Fengar said. He turned away into the darkness, leaving Anuleif surrounded by men who were looking for blood. Griva was but a step away and Raef wondered how quick the old man would be.

Raef stared hard at Anuleif, who was getting to his feet. "Run." The boy frowned and Raef could see the fear still gnawed at him, still clouded his mind. "Run." The boy's gaze darted left and right, and then he was gone, feet churning through the snow. One man reached out to snag him, but Anuleif was alert now and he slipped out of reach and into the trees. He would not get far if those loyal to Griva wished to hunt him down, but it was with satisfaction that Raef saw their blood-hungry eyes focus on him instead.

Three came on him at once, fists flying. Raef ducked one and upended the second with his shoulder, but the third struck hard in his ribs and then a boot buckled his knee, sending Raef, unbalanced and unable to use his arms, face-first into the snow. He caught himself on his shoulder, rolled, but his knee, the same that had suffered damage in Jötunheim, would not take his weight and he could not get to his feet. The blows came hard and fast, raining down, and Raef took them gladly, for each one put more distance between Anuleif and Fengar's warriors.

When the frenzy of pain passed and Raef knew something other than the taste of blood in his mouth, he was on his back, the shelter blocking the light of the stars, and Vakre's face hovered over him.

"The boy is away," Vakre said. "They have not gone after him."

Raef accepted this information by closing his eyes and trying to breath without pain lancing through his chest. When he opened his eyes again, Vakre was still there, and Raef saw that the son of Loki was not untouched. His nose leaked blood and the bruise that spanned his cheekbone was now accompanied by a fresh one and a laceration along his jaw.

"You too?" Even that sent spasms along Raef's ribs and he winced.

"Two have my boot print in their backs," Vakre said. "They did not care for that."

"Visna?"

Vakre's face grew solemn. "I do not think she is here. Not really. She has not moved."

"She must eat. She must stay warm."

"You cannot make her want to live, Raef. But you must. Are your ribs broken?"

Raef took as deep a breath as he dared and to his relief his ribcage felt better than he had expected. "I do not think so." He prodded at the arrow wound on his shoulder. The stitches held. His hands sought the knee that had failed to hold his weight. It ached with dull fury.

"How is it?"

"Weakened as it was when I returned from Jötunheim. It will need time."

"The boy spoke strange words," Vakre said.

Raef met Vakre's eyes, but he was hesitant to speak, to give voice to Anuleif's beliefs.

They fell into silence and Raef felt the weariness return. He slipped into a sleep spotted with dreams, fragments of images only. Siv, her red-gold hair tied in a neat braid, laughing. His father, speaking to Raef despite the gaping hole in his belly. Griva, the crow feather glistening in his white hair, holding back a tide of water with nothing but his bare hands. A raven, pecking at Raef's skin. Raef wanted to chase it away, to wave his arms and see it burst into the air, but his arms would not move and the raven's beak began to draw blood. A voice called, the words muffled, and then Raef was awake and the voice was Visna's and the raven's sharp beak was her hand, light and tentative on his shoulder.

"Help me," the Valkyrie whispered.

Raef struggled up onto one elbow, though it pained him. "Are you well?"

"In body, yes, but in spirit, no."

Raef looked over his shoulder; Vakre slept curled on his side, hunched as though burdened even in sleep. "What troubles you?"

Visna closed her eyes and for a moment Raef thought she might not speak. "I begin to forget who I am. More and more with every rising sun. One day, I will wake and be a woman, bound to the earth, to a husband, to death, knowing only the smell of the dirt I work with my hands, knowing only the feel of the wind when rain follows behind, knowing only that my life is fading. Visna, who flew to the stars, who watched the Norns work their carvings into the great ash tree, who knew the Allfather's embrace, will be lost, forgotten, forever." Visna opened her eyes and sought Raef's. "Do not let me forget."

Never before had Raef heard such a desperate plea and it dug into his bones, heralded by the knowledge that he could not save her from this fate. "I will help you remember," he said, though he knew not how.

Visna shook her head. "My father has been cruel, but sometimes I think even he does not understand what he has done to me, what terrible future he has given me."

"To know the wind and the rain and the sun and the earth, is this so terrible?"

Visna's sorrow turned to pity. "Knowing those things is simple. Common. I am like a blind woman who remembers what it was like to see a sunrise."

The Valkyrie's pride aggravated Raef. "I am a lord of men, descended from lords. I rule the lives of others. I can claim their sons for battle, I can condemn those who have committed grievous offenses, I can allow or forbid marriages as I see fit, and I can give land to those who please me and take it from those who do not. Power is mine and I wield it. And yet I take a thousand times and a thousand times again more pleasure in the warmth of the sun on my face, the smell of the salt breeze, the feel of good, green earth between my fingers."

"Because you are a man, content with these things. You do not rise above."

"Rise above to what? To a cold and callous thing who looks only to the stars and the gods? The stars are beautiful and I take joy in them, but they are far away and the earth and the growing things and the cool mountain water, they are near." Raef watched Visna's face in the moonlight as the Valkyrie struggled to make sense of his words. "You have already lost what you were," he went on, and he could see the pain his words caused her even though he spoke gently. "Remember it, cherish it, be proud of it, but do not be disdainful of what you have now. It is all you have."

Visna was quiet for a long time, but the troubled emotions that had clouded her face seemed to have faded.

"I have seen men who wish to rise above," Raef said, letting his thoughts slip away to a burning lake where men had died with ice and fire. "One such was the Palesword and he was willing to tear apart this world to achieve his desire for fame in the eyes of the All-father, to impose his will on the realm of men. He woke a terrible host that sowed death and destruction in its wake. Men should seek battle-fame, men should seek wisdom and a place at the long table in Valhalla, but men must not forget what it is to plant a seed and watch it grow."

Their eyes met and for the span of two deep breaths that seared Raef's chest, he thought he saw a glimmer of understanding there, but then he let himself lie flat on the ground once more.

"That woman, what did you want with her?" Raef asked.

Visna was quiet for a long time. "I must find the one who will take my place in Asgard, who will ride with my sisters." Another pause, this one filled with a heavy sigh. "When I saw her, I was sure it was her. I wanted to rip her heart out and I wanted to see the sword burn with light once more when she held it. I am not sure what I would have done had I had her within my grasp."

"And now?"

"She is not the one. I do not know whether to be glad or grieved that I must continue to carry this burden."

Raef closed his eyes but Visna's voice came to him again out of the darkness.

"What will you do?"

"Survive."

Raef slept and the dreams that had plucked at the strings of his mind returned, this time with the weight of a heavy, suffocating snow. He was outside the walls of the Vestrhall, the smell of ashes sharp in his nostrils. There was blood everywhere, and on Raef most of all. Crows settled on the corpses, pecking half-frozen flesh. He tried to scare them off, but they stared at him with bottomless black eyes. And then he saw her. Siv, sprawled under the dark sky, eyes staring at nothing, her hair caked with the drying, sticky blood of other men. He reached for her but the crows drove him back, sharp talons and outstretched wings beating him away. He tore the head off of one and the rest, screaming, took to the sky, disappearing on black wings. The other bodies were gone now, only Siv remained. So pale. So empty of the life that had coursed through her. He felt a cold wind on his neck and turned, then staggered back as he saw the labyrinth of Jötunheim open up before him, twisted and cruel, forever bleak. And then he knew he was meant to choose between the punishment of staying beside Siv, so close to her and yet to never see her smile again, or reentering the labyrinth, never to return. He would not leave her again. He stretched out his hand to her cheek, but then he felt the labyrinth pull him in, sucking, reaching, devouring. And then it was gone.

Anuleif appeared, and the boy's words of the future seemed to fall from the sky like bolts of lightning. Fear made Raef cower, but in time the lightning seemed less monstrous, less deadly, and Raef stepped from his hiding place and let the bolts strike the ground at his feet. And then he knew hope.

When he awoke, it was to shouting and the sun on the horizon. A pair of warriors dragged him to his feet and through the snow, and for a moment Raef was sure he was about to meet Griva's knife, but then all was quiet and he was let go at the edge of the river. Vakre was given the same treatment. A man waited for them there, but it was not Fengar. He was unknown to Raef and he picked at dirt beneath his fingernails. He wore his hair long and his beard short and from his left ear hung a bead of glass. In the bright morning, it caught the sun. Raef was sure he had never seen him before, but there was something familiar about him, something that only grew more certain when he spoke.

"Lost your taste for battle, Skallagrim? I thought you to be at the Hammerling's side."

"I was. As Fengar promised to be."

The man scowled. "Do not speak of promises. Speak instead the truth, and you might earn an easy death. Why do you skulk about in this corner of Vannheim? What does the Hammerling want with you?

Raef thought quickly, glad to learn that his separation from Brandulf Hammerling was unknown. So too, then, would be his naming as king. "We were sent to treat with Torleif of Axsellund."

"What then?"

"That was to depend upon the manner of our reception."

The long-haired man nodded as though Raef had imparted a piece of wisdom, the glass bead dancing with his movement. "Go on."

"If Torleif agreed to give the Hammerling his oath, we were to remain and gather the Axsellund warriors. If not," Raef took a stab in the dark, "we were ordered to do the same in Bergoss."

Again, the man nodded. "Strange that you would make such a journey alone," he said.

"The Hammerling hoped we might travel undetected."

"Then he sent no gifts, no treasures to sway the lords he hoped to win?"

"Those were to come later," Raef said, aware that his lie might unravel at any moment. "We rode swift and light. Speed was our aim."

"And where were you to meet the Hammerling with your new-found spears?"

Names and places flashed through Raef's mind, but he abandoned them all and held his tongue lest he betray himself.

"Lost your tongue?" The man cocked his head at Raef and grinned. He was missing a tooth just right of center. "I wager you will sing to us soon enough. But let me ask you one more question,

Skallagrim, one question that is not the king's." He leaned in close and Raef could smell his foul breath. "Did my cursed brother still draw breath when you left the Hammerling?"

"To answer this, I would need your name," Raef said.

The man grinned again and the glass bead twinkled. "He calls himself the lord of Kolhaugen, but I am the true lord."

"Then you are Alvar, twin of Eirik," Raef said, at last recognizing the hint of Eirik's voice in the other brother.

Alvar of Kolhaugen spat. "I am Alvar, son of the last king."

"He lives," Raef said.

Alvar scowled. "By Odin's will, not for long."

"Even in Valhalla, all the pretty women will smile at him and avoid you." Vakre's voice was sharp and teasing, a sudden spark that reddened Alvar's face. The lord of Kolhaugen lashed out, striking Vakre across the cheek. Vakre managed a grin, though Raef could see blood on his tongue. "You must hate him, always the fortunate favorite, beloved by your father, admired by every village girl at the long tables." Again Alvar's fist cracked across Vakre's jaw, but the lord of Kolhaugen did not strike a third time.

Alvar fought to control his anger. "Best not mar that pretty face before Griva gets his hands on you. He likes a clean surface to work on." Alvar forced a laugh and turned, leaving them alone with their guards.

Vakre spit and ran his tongue over his teeth. "I heard a rumor once that the twins of Kolhaugen were ever at each other's throats, that Alvar had always loathed his brother and writhed in a stew of jealousy." Vakre wiped his mouth with his sleeve. Raef could see a smear of blood on the cloth. "Seems the rumor was true."

"We are not winning any friends, Vakre," Raef said. "Would you stab a weakened spear at an angry bear?"

Vakre stared at Raef for a moment. Raef saw something distant and wild there. "If I want the bear dead, I would." Vakre blinked and seemed more himself. "If they are going to kill me, I want them to earn it."

A chorus of voices reached them and they turned to look east, down the valley. At first, Raef could see nothing, but then he heard horses and more shouting, and soon the river camp was crowded over with new faces. Men had come with the first rays of the sun, traveling through the night to swell Fengar's numbers. Chief among them was a man the sight of whom made Vakre's face darken with hatred, for his uncle, Romarr, lord of Finnmark, had come to Vannheim.

EIGHT

"YOU. I THOUGHT you dead."

Romarr, lord of Finnmark, had been deep in conversation with a captain when he stopped in his tracks and drew back at sight of Vakre. In the confusion of the arrival of the new warriors, the prisoners had gone unnoticed at first and Raef was sure he saw a burst of fear, quickly masked, in the lord of Finnmark's face.

"And wished it, I know," Vakre said, chin held high, contempt in every line of his face.

"I should bleed you now, right where you stand." Romarr's hand twitched to his scabbard, but his feet stayed rooted to the stones. "I should have known I would find you hiding in a useless corner of the world such as this, choosing to save your own skin rather than stand your place in the shield wall." Only then did Romarr take in Raef's presence. He barked out a laugh. "And the lost lord of Vannheim with you, nephew. How fitting. I will see to your deaths myself. It is time you joined your mother in Hel."

Vakre was moving before Raef could react. He did not touch his uncle, but the flames that sprouted from his hand licked at Romarr's face, causing him to jerk backward, nearly losing his footing. Then Vakre, his hands left unbound from when he had relieved his bladder, grabbed the fur collar of his uncle's cloak and hauled him in close, singeing Romarr's thick, dark beard with his flaming hand.

"Would you like to burn, uncle?" Vakre's voice was soft, soothing, almost wistful. Romarr had eyes only for the tendrils of fire and could not find his words. "I thought not," Vakre said. Raef was the only one to react, the only one who did not stand in mute shock, and he laid a hand on Vakre's arm. But a quick glance at Vakre's face told him the son of Loki was in control. An ocean of anger swelled within, but the surface was calm and unthreatening. It was an unnerving sight.

"You cast her out, ashamed and afraid of your own sister, when all she did was bear a child, a child of your own blood."

"The gods will curse you, Vakre Lokison," Romarr shouted, finding his voice at last, spit flying from his mouth.

With a flick of his wrist, Vakre released his uncle, who lurched back, and the flames vanished. Vakre flashed a feral smile and said to any who might listen, "Take care with this one. There is no honest, true bone in his body."

His voice broke the stillness and the captain Romarr had been speaking with lashed out. A long knife flashed from his belt and another, this one short and brutal, appeared from behind his back. He advanced on Vakre, twirling the short knife, his rugged face cracked open by a cruel smile, but a shout brought him to a halt. It was not Romarr who stopped him, but Fengar, approaching and flanked by the two daughters of Thor.

"The time for their deaths will come, but it is not now," Fengar said. The captain grunted and, smiling still, lowered his blades. He did not take his eyes from Vakre and Raef felt a twisting in his gut at sight of the eager glint in the knifeman's expression. Fengar would not look at his prisoners. "Come," the king said to Romarr, whose fear had turned to rage and reddened his face. "Valdemar, the only eyes I have left to me, will be here soon and we must talk."

It was some time before Vakre opened his mouth to speak after they were shoved back into their shelter. Visna greeted them with only silence. Raef, his hands newly bound, worked on the fire as best he could, sending a shower of sparks into the air as he stirred it with his boot. He maneuvered a fresh log onto the embers, then sat down to wait. The log was black on one side before the son of Loki unknotted his tongue.

"My uncle never ceases to remind me that my birth made my mother's life difficult, that she lost everything. I only sought to remind him that he is as much to blame. He treated her like filth. I should have killed him long ago."

"What stayed your hand?"

"Killing him is what my father would have done. It would have confirmed everything my uncle believed about me. My mother made me understand this. To seek justice for what he did to her, while I still feel in my heart is right, would brand me forever as Loki's murderous son. I must not be that."

"The knifeman," Raef said, "who is he? I do not like him."

"Nor should you. He is Ulthor Ten-blade, or so he calls himself. He is cruel beyond measure. I was a boy of eight when I learned this. I watched him feed a dog a sausage, then, when the mutt rolled on its back, begging for a belly scratch, Ulthor slid his knife in again and again. More than once I have asked my uncle to rid himself of such a beast, for he knows only malice. My uncle likes to think him a loyal hound, well leashed. He will break the leash, and when he does, Finnmark will suffer for it."

"He means to kill you," Raef said.

"He may try." Vakre snarled his response and Raef felt heat gushing from his friend's skin. He tensed, thinking the flames might burst out and consume him, but the warmth faded, leaving Raef with a question on his tongue, a question he had delayed asking.

"How long has it been, Vakre, since you no longer needed your father's cloak?"

Vakre's gaze darted to Raef's face and there was surprise hidden there. "You saw? When?" He would not look at Visna, who was watching them carefully, her eyes no longer empty.

"You were not wearing it when you burned the giant."

Vakre opened his mouth to speak, but he hesitated and Raef heard uncertainty in the silence. "I did not intend for anyone to know. Even you." Raef waited until Vakre continued. "It was the day the fog blanketed the valley, our first morning in the nest. You went to catch fish and I," Vakre paused, "I discovered that my skin had become cloak enough." Vakre looked at Raef. "The flames no longer weaken me as they once did."

Visna, who had listened in silence, broke in. "Surely a cause to be glad. Many would give much to have such a gift."

Vakre did not share her enthusiasm. "I feel only dread."

The early morning sunshine soon vanished behind a thick wall of clouds and the storm was upon them before midday. The valley waited under a boiling, writhing sky, and then the snow fell in sharp, windy bursts that stung Raef's eyes. He, Vakre, and Visna huddled in their shelter and watched as the world grew white around them.

When the storm broke, shafts of light split through the clouds and Raef crawled from the shelter. The world was even more brilliant than he had imagined. Beyond the close pines, the valley stretched out, awash in glittering snow, and a stiff breeze blew the last, lagging clouds westward, freeing this small patch of the world from the storm's grasp. Raef drew deep breaths of crisp, cold air, his eyes closed as he listened to the chatter of birds in the high branches. The horses, massed together nearby, stomped their feet and shook their manes, glad to be under the sun once more.

Raef, shutting out the sounds and smells of men, let himself find a moment of joy in the harsh beauty of the world, let himself imagine that Siv stood at his side, her hand in his, a smile on her face, her heart beating in time with the earth.

Raef rubbed his bound wrists against his chest, massaging the cold away as best he could, then went to empty his bladder. Before he had finished, a figure brushed into the corner of his vision and then leaned in close and blew a hot breath into Raef's ear.

"Should I fetch the girl? She could help you with that." Ulthor Ten-blade's breath stank of garlic and rotten teeth but Raef resisted the urge to draw back while fastening his belt as best he could without full use of his hands. "Or perhaps you would prefer to have your friend, Lokison, lend a hand?"

Raef did not rise to the bait. "Be gone." He turned away but Ulthor grabbed him and Raef spun around, coming face to face with Ten-blade.

"You think to tell me what to do? I am Ulthor Ten-blade."

"I know who you are."

"Ah, has the cursed half god told you? Did he mention my fondness for eyes? Yours are very fine. Perhaps I will take them from you." The knife was out, twirling in Ulthor's hand. Raef could see it though he kept his gaze fixed on Ten-blade's face. At that close distance, the knifeman's gaze was unsettling, for his eyes were mismatched, one blue, one brown.

Ten-blade laughed, but there was no mirth in it, and then the knife was gone as quickly as it had come and Raef was alone by the river once more.

The storm had delayed the anticipated arrival of Valdemar, and the king's anxiety at this spread through the camp. Raef heard mutterings about ill luck, about the gods laughing at them, and he saw Griva and Fengar arguing, though the distance was too great to make out their words. They parted with angry gestures that did not go unnoticed by many, but then a long, low note of a horn sounded, racing to them on the swift river, and followed by five riders. As Fengar's men began to gather, one man slumped and fell from his horse. Three others dismounted and clustered around their companion, but the fifth remained tall and straight in his saddle. He was dark of hair and eye, and his gaze bore down on Fengar. A scar, puckered and pink, ran down the side of his neck, curved around to the front of his chest, and disappeared beneath his cloak. This was Valdemar, the broken man. Raef had heard his name, had wondered why he was called such. Now he wondered how far the scar descended.

"What news?" Fengar looked as though he would rather not hear the answer.

Valdemar dismounted, his face grim, and stood close to Fengar to speak in the king's ear. The wounded man was carried away, and the crowd thinned until Raef had a good view of the king and his captain.

"Perhaps the Hammerling has sniffed out Fengar's trail," Vakre said.

"Or perhaps Valdemar brings word of Vannheim, of my naming as king, of the men I sent to gather a host here."

Fengar was speaking and Raef watched as Valdemar's frown grew deeper. The broken man glanced at Raef, then he was striding toward them, Fengar not far behind. Raef stood his ground as Valdemar seized him by the shoulder and pressed a knife to his throat.

"What brought you here, Skallagrim? Speak!"

"I am unarmed. My hands are bound. You need not threaten me."

Valdemar snarled and pressed the blade harder against Raef's skin. "Answer me."

Visna looked to Fengar. "Lord, we are your prisoners. Skallagrim has done you no harm."

Fengar looked uncertain and it was a different voice that snaked into Raef's ears. "Soft words from a soft woman." Ulthor Ten-blade stepped between Visna and Fengar, just on the edge of Raef's vision. He took a strand of Visna's hair between his fingers and raised it to his nose, inhaling deeply. Visna stiffened and recoiled. "Taken a liking to the lord of Vannheim, lady? Do you wish to save his pretty skin?" Ten-blade twisted the hair around his fingers. "If you want a good fucking, you need only ask."

Fengar came to life. "Enough." Ten-blade grinned and released Visna's hair, then came to stand by Valdemar. Raef could feel his hot breath, could feel those mismatched eyes bore into him, but he kept his focus on the broken man.

"The knife stays until you speak," Valdemar said, paying no mind to Ten-blade. "The truth now, son of Einarr."

"What is truth, when it is balanced on a sharp blade?" Raef said.

Fengar stepped forward. "You told Alvar you were to visit Bergoss on behalf of the Hammerling."

"Yes."

"It seems your tongue is twisted with lies, Skallagrim. You see, my good eye was in Bergoss not five days ago." Fengar stepped close to Raef, a hint of a challenge in eyes that had been dull and defeated only a moment before. "And he heard a strange tale, of an envoy sent from the Hammerling and led by none other than Hauk of Ruderk. Twenty men with gilded tongues and a banner from Finngale. And the lord of Ruderk spoke with Sverren, drank mead with Sverren, laughed and hunted with Sverren. They talked of war and bright blades, of battle, of shield walls and the men to fill them. Tell me, why would the Hammerling send two men to speak with Sverren Red-tail and Torleif of Axsellund? Why would he send you with only this cursed bastard for a companion, only to send out Hauk of Ruderk with a party of warriors at his command? Answer now with the truth."

Raef took a deep breath and prepared to line his tongue with another lie. The movement was so quick, he almost missed it. Ten-blade's hand flicked to his belt and then up again, slicing a piece of Raef's hair off before he even saw the blade in the fading light. The knife came up again, the point grazing Raef's temple and then curling through his hair. "You are too patient, Valdemar," Ten-blade said. "Or do you not mean to make him bleed?"

With a roar, Valdemar turned on Ten-blade, a long-fingered hand wrapping around his neck, the other hand releasing his knife to twist Ten-blade's wrist and force him to empty his hand. Throwing Ten-blade to the ground, Valdemar retrieved his knife and advanced, while Ten-blade, cursing, scrambled for his own blade.

"I will skin you, maggot-mouth," Ten-blade said, coming to his feet and drawing a second knife from his belt. "And then I will scatter your bones so you will never reach Valhalla."

They came together in a tussle of limbs, Valdemar perhaps the stronger of the two, but it took only a moment to know that Ten-blade was more skilled with his blades. Ten-blade was all quickness, darting, striking, his movements easy. Raef backed away as a streak of blood splattered across the snow as Ten-blade slashed at the broken man's arm, leaving a deep gash that soaked the cloth of Valdemar's sleeve in an instant.

Fengar did nothing. His hands were clenched at his sides, white knuckles showing, and behind him Romarr, Vakre's uncle, watched with a gleam in his eyes. The fight ended quickly. Valdemar, his clothing shredded, his wounds many, lay spread out on the snow, the hilt of a knife protruding from his belly. He writhed for a moment, each scrape of his boots against the fresh snow a plea that went unanswered by all save the river, and then lay still. Ten-blade, unscathed but for the red marks where Valdemar had grabbed his neck, spit onto the broken man's blank, dead face.

"Your dog needs a leash, uncle." Vakre's voice penetrated the silence and Ten-blade turned on him. Raef stepped between them, though he could not hope to defend himself, much less Vakre as well. The blow fell hard and fast on his temple and then Ten-blade was on Vakre, doubling him over with a savage punch to the gut that had Vakre gasping before Raef's knees hit the ground. Lunging, Raef flung himself on Ten-blade's legs, his movements clumsy as his skull throbbed, but his weight and force was enough to bring them both down. Without the use of his hands, Raef's struggles were in vain and it was only a moment before Ten-blade was straddled over his chest, his arms a blur as he hit Raef again and again.

Time seemed to slow and the pain swelled in his chest and head. Blood trickled into his eye and he tasted it on his lips. In the corners of his reeling vision, he caught glimpses of feet, but all seemed still. If anyone moved to stop Ten-blade, Raef was blind to it. Before the darkness came, Raef focused on Fengar's face. The king's gaze was on the crimson spotted snow, a twitch in his cheek, his mouth clamped shut like a bear trap, his eyes those of a panicked animal facing fate.

↑ ↑ ↑

He saw Odin, one-eyed and terrible, his mighty spear splintered. He saw Isolf in the Vestrhall, seated in his father's chair. He saw Hauk of Ruderk, cloaked in shadows, sharpening a sword. And he heard the voice of a flute, high and wavering at first, then growing in strength. It was a song Gudrik had played and when Raef stirred into wakefulness, the poet's song pulsed on in his heart.

The night was dark, the moon shadowed by clouds that slid across the pale face. Raef's face was raw and scrapped, one eye puffy and swollen.

Something cold was pressed against his temple, and Raef flinched away, only to realize it was snow, and it was soothing, and he wanted it desperately. The snow pack sent rivulets of melted water running down his cheek. A dribble caught in the corner of his mouth and Raef let it wet his lips.

"Can you hear me?"

It was Vakre's voice and Raef turned his head to locate him. The son of Loki was bruised and beaten, but, as Raef stirred, a pulse of flame bloomed in the palm of his hand, then spread until Vakre's fingers were shrouded with fire. The warmth was as welcome as the icy water and Raef closed his eyes and savored the heat.

"Our death comes at dawn," Vakre said. "Fengar means to give us to Griva's knife."

Raef struggled to sit and Vakre helped him lean against the shelter. His flaming hand continued to burn and Raef was glad of it for reasons he could not say. Visna was peering out of the shelter, but she ducked back in, shaking her head.

"Even if we subdued the two who watch over us, there are too many," the Valkyrie said. "Perhaps if I were armed, I could cut down enough to get you into the trees."

"I will burn them," Vakre said and Raef could see the resolution in his eyes. "Or enough of them to let you get away."

"And leave you to have your guts strung up in a tree? No."

"Do not argue with me, Raef. If I do not, none of us will survive. If I do, there is a chance, a small one, but a chance, that one of us will make it." The fire dimmed in Vakre's hand and then went out. "It is a better death than most." Vakre got to his feet and offered Raef a hand. "Can you stand?"

Dizziness swept over Raef as Vakre pulled him up, but it passed quickly and he began to protest again.

"I am going out there and I mean to bring upon them such a blaze that the gods themselves will feel its heat. If you hesitate, I will die in vain." Vakre's gaze hardened. "Do not hesitate."

Vakre ducked out of the shelter and Raef hurried after, his hand reaching to pull Vakre back, but both were brought up short before taking another step by the approach of a tall blonde woman, her hair silver in the moonlight.

"I will watch them." The daughter of Thor pushed past the two warriors assigned to stay with Raef, Vakre, and Visna. "Go." The men were eager to comply, no doubt thinking of the skins of ale that awaited them. The woman raised her voice to address the remaining warriors who clustered around two small fires or stood on watch at the edge of the clearing. "All of you, the king would speak with you. I will stay with the prisoners." The woman watched them go and then moved to confront Raef and Vakre. She looked long and hard at them before speaking. "My sister is dead?" The daughter of Thor was as tall as Raef and well-muscled. She gazed at Raef over a once-broken nose.

"Yes. What was her name?" Raef said.

"She was Tora."

"And yours?"

The blonde woman scowled at Raef but answered. "Inge."

"I am sorry for your sister's death, Inge. I am sure Tora sits at the Allfather's table."

The scowl deepened. "I hope she does not. I hope she is freezing in the darkness of Hel." Inge spit in the snow. "Was it you who took her life?"

Raef was about to answer with the truth, that he had only stumbled upon Tora's frozen corpse in the deep snows of Hullbern, but Vakre spoke first.

"I did."

Raef's heartbeat quickened and he held his tongue, letting the son of Loki spin the lie.

Inge nodded at Vakre. "Then I thank you." Her hand went to the knife at her belt and Raef tensed. "What would you have in return?"

Vakre held out his bound wrists. "Release us."

Inge stepped forward and sawed through Vakre's ropes with ease, then turned and began to work on Raef's.

"Fengar will kill you when he discovers what you have done."

"If he discovers it, yes, he will. Or he will have that dried up cock do it. But he will be right to do so, for I am dishonoring and disobeying him."

"Then why do it?"

Inge's pale grey eyes bore into Raef's. "Because I will go to my death knowing I have outlived one sister, perhaps even two if the king sends Gudra after me, and that is worth the price." Raef's ropes fell away and Inge, jaw clamped shut now, freed Visna, then led them to the edge of the river camp, far from the largest fire where the men gathered.

"Wait here. I will bring your weapons."

She disappeared, leaving them to wait in tense silence. Raef had nearly decided to abandon their weapons and slink back to the eagle's nest unarmed when Inge returned. Raef and Vakre armed themselves quickly while Visna stared at her sword for a moment before taking it in her hands.

With nothing more than a nod exchanged between them, they left Inge and slipped away, Raef hunched over from the pain of his injuries. They took precautions, weaving a course that led away from the eagle's nest before doubling back and beginning the steep climb, but Raef did not think Inge would follow and they met only a pair of startled foxes as they returned to the nest.

Raef crested the summit and his heart swelled with gladness, for no longer was the nest shelter to Tuli alone. For a moment, he went unnoticed, and then the bowl came alive as his presence was first challenged and then welcomed with eager voices as more than twenty warriors of Vannheim recognized and greeted him. But one face caused Raef's gut to clench and the voices grew quiet as the men saw what drew their lord's gaze.

⚡ ⚡ ⚡

Dvalarr the Crow has shorn his beard. The hulking warrior stood before Raef, bereft of the great symbol of his long life and success in battle. Where once his head and been shaven only on the left, now his entire skull was hairless, the left dark with the ink of three crows, the right pale and free from scars. But there was no mistaking the Crow's heavy brow and deep, dark eyes that bore into Raef.

"Crow," Raef said, trying to mask the apprehension that fluttered in his chest. For Dvalarr the Crow had been the voice that had proclaimed Raef king, a voice urged to speak by Isolf, Raef was sure.

"King," Dvalarr said, his voice strong and solemn.

"Am I?"

The Crow faltered, searching for words. "I know what you must think."

"And what is that?"

"That I am a snake, a spy. That I ate from your cousin's hand like a worthless dog, that I saw my own rise in your defeat." With every word, the Crow seemed to grow more certain. "That I made an oath and broke it, that I spoke words your cousin whispered in my ear, that I named you king and sought your death."

"Are you guilty of these things?"

Dvalarr was quiet for a moment. "My father once told me that the naming of a king is a thing most sacred, that the gods would strike down a man who spoke those words with a false heart. He told me of Olfin of the seal sons and Aedric Stonefoot and I listened with wide eyes. It is a story for children and I am a man long grown, a warrior who has sent many to Valhalla. But I never forgot my father's words. You are my king, and may Odin deny me Valhalla if he thinks me a traitor."

Raef let the Crow have his say and was quiet for a long moment. "Why have you shorn your hair and beard, Crow?"

"To show you that I come to you with nothing." Dvalarr tossed something small and gleaming into the air. Raef caught it and held open his palm to the light of the fire. The thick ring of gold was plain and battered in more than one place.

"You wore this to tie your beard," Raef said. Dvalarr nodded. "Why give this to me?"

"To show you that I come to you with nothing," the Crow repeated. He stepped closer to Raef. "All men knew the Crow, he who scorned the wearing of arm rings, he who did not need a ring-giver, a lord, to make a name that the gods might hear. He was a proud man."

"Are you not still a proud man, Dvalarr?"

The Crow knelt. "I could be, if I might serve you."

Raef scanned the gathered warriors and found one clutching a skin. Raef nodded at the man and held out a hand. The warrior threw it to Raef, who uncapped it. The mead smelled rich and strong and made saliva fill Raef's mouth. The weakness in his legs swelled and blood pounded in his temples, but he went to stand before Dvalarr and placed a hand on the Crow's shoulder.

"Then be a proud man and share a drink with me, Crow." Raef took a swig from the skin as he pulled Dvalarr to his feet, then handed the mead to the larger man. The warriors cheered as Dvalarr brought the skin to his lips, but quieted at a gesture from Raef.

"We are not alone here. Fengar of Solheim is in the valley below," Raef said. The men began to talk all at once and then went silent when Raef raised his hand. "I have been his prisoner these past three nights. I do not believe he will find us here, but we must take precautions. I will allow a fire in the largest cave," Raef said, gesturing to the back of the bowl, "but we must come and go with care. We will use the goat paths to climb into the mountains to find game and slip down to the fjord at night to fish. And we will wait for more men to gather here and then we will descend upon Fengar as the white owl does a mouse in the night, with deadly silence and ready talons, for I will tolerate no foe on Vannheim soil."

The men were glad, their hearts full of promise and ale, but Raef's vision swam and it was difficult to conceal his exhaustion and the extent of his injuries as he, gathering warm thick reindeer skins, limped to the cave where a pair of men were already at work building a fire. Raef sank to the ground and leaned back against the stones, but the sight of the growing flames reminded him of Anuleif, He Who Burned. The boy was nowhere to be seen. Raef called for Tuli, who had remained in the nest when Raef ventured into the valley.

"The boy, Anuleif. What happened to him?"

Tuli's cheerful face turned sour and grim. "He went in search of you. I tried to stop him, lord, but he was quick."

"Do not burden yourself with him, Tuli. The boy found me and I sent him off again. I meant for him to return here."

"He did. But only to say that he could no longer remain. He was gone before morning."

Raef nodded, keeping his face calm, though his mind was a sea of turmoil. Like a fisherman on the wide waves, the boy had cast a line into the depths of Raef's heart and hooked something there, something that would not be tugged free. But now the fisherman had returned to shore, leaving the fish to wriggle, unaided, on the hook.

Tuli turned to go but Raef called him back. "What were the boy's exact words?"

Tuli frowned and Raef could see him pulling the words from memory as though each were a fragment of glass. "He said he could no longer remain in the land of the rising sun."

"The rising sun? Vannheim stretches to the west, not the east," Raef said. Tuli shrugged and left the cave, leaving Raef alone to fall into a heavy, dreamless sleep.

NINE

FOR NINETEEN DAYS, Raef bought back his strength with hot stews of venison and rabbit, with charred, briny fish, with rest and careful ministrations to the arrow wound and the bruises lacing across his torso, and in those nineteen days, the number of men in the eagle's nest swelled. The warriors trickled in, sometimes in pairs, sometimes alone, and once half a shield wall of eighteen men came at sunset, and each brought axe or spear or sharp sword.

Of the men in the valley, Raef saw little. Fengar seemed content to linger there, fishing in the river and foraging in the forest. No more men joined him there, Raef's scouts said, but whether Fengar waited for more warriors or simply was too uncertain to venture beyond the valley, the men could not say. There was no sign of pursuit from the Hammerling, or reinforcement from Stefnir of Gornhald, and Raef yearned for news of both men.

On the twentieth day, a wedge of shields descended from the hills just east of the nest. They came in the fading light, the last rays of sunlight glinting off the tips of their spears, their painted shields burnished over with golden orange, and they did not come quietly. Drawn to the edge of the bowl, Raef frowned, trying to make out if the warriors were friend or foe, and he knew those in the valley would see them, too. Gathering his weapons, Raef took Vakre and a few men from the nest and approached the horde, which had lumbered to a halt near the tree line. Keeping in the shadows of shrubs and boulders, Raef stayed out of sight until he drew near enough to see one man separate from the pack and move west along the slope, toward where Raef hid and toward the eagle's nest. His stride was purposeful, as though he knew what lay ahead, and Raef tensed and readied his grip on his axe.

As the warrior came closer, his curly, coal-black hair grew distinct, as did the stump where his left arm ended. Raef grinned to himself and stepped out from his hiding place.

"Ruf."

Rufnir's face broke into a wide smile and he loped the last few strides until he reached Raef. They clasped arms.

"Have you brought me Torleif?"

"With forty warriors at his back," Rufnir said, the smile growing wider. "More will follow."

Raef clapped his friend on the shoulder, but then let the pleasure drop from his face. He gestured to the valley, which was already in shadow.

"So has Fengar."

Rufnir grimaced.

"The lord of Finnmark is with him, as is Alvar of Kolhaugen. They are perhaps seventy in number and they will have seen you just as I did." Rufnir began to apologize but Raef brushed it away. "Bring me to Torleif."

The lord of Axsellund was young, younger than Raef, and he had an open, honest face shadowed with a trim blonde beard. He did not look like a man who had been lord of Axsellund since the age of thirteen when his father had died of a fever. He did not look like a man who could command warriors in battle. But his warriors were a hard, grim-faced lot, whose backs were stiff with pride, and that pride was for their young lord as much as for themselves, Raef saw as he approached. The eyes of the Axsellund warriors were not hostile toward Raef, but neither were they friendly.

"Torleif, you are welcome to Vannheim."

Torleif gave a slight nod. "Skallagrim."

Raef did not have time for further pleasantries. His mind was on the eyes that watched from the valley floor.

"Are you prepared to honor the promise you made to me?"

Torleif's gaze showed a hint of irritation before smoothing over. "I would not be here if that were not my intent."

"Then we have work to do." Raef pointed down into the valley. "Fengar is down there. I mean to slaughter him and all who follow him, but first we must buy ourselves some time. Your arrival will not have gone unnoticed and I cannot take you further and risk discovery. Are you prepared to do as I ask?"

"I will not send my men down into a death trap, lord, if that is what you mean to ask."

"I am not wasteful," Raef said, staring hard into Torleif's eyes and ignoring the bristling warriors around him. "We do not have the time to spar. You sent your chosen king a sprig of cedar, Torleif. Did that mean nothing?"

"It meant everything." Torleif's voice was low but sharp and at last Raef saw the backbone, the strength, which had allowed him to rule from such a young age. "I do not make promises lightly." They locked eyes for a moment longer.

"Then let us be friends. But first we must trim the wolf's claws. Fengar will be wary at the sight of your men. We must put him at ease. Do as I ask, and your men will share the shield wall with mine when I win back Vannheim."

The idea had been forming in Raef's head from the moment he spotted Rufnir, but even then it was a shadowy, unfinished thought and the risk was high. If they failed, Raef would lose the Axsellund warriors, who would be outnumbered by Fengar's, and chance discovery of the nest. Everything he had built to challenge Isolf could be destroyed before the sun rose again.

But there was no time to question the directions he gave Torleif and it was only moments before he was watching the lord of Axsellund lead his host down into the valley, carrying his hopes on their shields. Raef waited the span of forty heart-shuddering breaths, then followed with Vakre and Rufnir at his back.

The shield walls at the river's edge were still compact and bristling with spears, but by the time Raef crept close enough on the boulder-strewn river to hear, the initial flare of hostilities had been subdued and Fengar and Torleif were speaking to each other. Vakre crouched next to Raef, a silent, watchful shadow, while Rufnir waited out of sight behind them.

"How is it that you have found me here, Torleif?" Fengar stood several paces from the lord of Axsellund and it seemed to Raef that he leaned away from the confrontation, as though he expected the younger man to pounce.

"It was Valdemar, lord," Torleif said and Raef felt his tongue go dry in his mouth as Torleif spoke the first lie. "He came to me, calling your name, urging me to join your cause. It was my duty, he said, to the king who was named."

Raef had insisted on that last part, for Valdemar would not have extolled Fengar's virtues or strength, or even promised vast rewards. That was not the broken man's way.

"He told me where I might find you, where I might make my oath," Torleif went on. He gestured to the men who stood with overlapping shields behind him. "These are but a taste of the warriors I can bring you, Fengar." The young lord's face was bright in the torchlight and Raef searched it for a sign of hesitation, but Torleif did not falter and he looked the king in the eye without blinking. "Axsellund is home to many more brothers and sons eager to stand in the shield wall and prove their valor."

"So you will join the fight against the Hammerling and bring peace back to these lands?" Fengar's back was to Raef, but the king's eagerness could be heard in his voice.

"What will you give me in return?"

Romarr, to Fengar's right, broke in. "That depends upon you. He will reward those who serve him well." Romarr twisted a ring on his left hand. Even in the faint light and from a distance Raef could see how large the jewel was. He wondered what corpse it had come from.

"Serve?" Torleif cocked his head to stare at Romarr and Raef held his breath. "Am I a common beast to do his bidding?"

"We are all beasts when it comes to war."

"Tell me, that ring there, was that one such reward?" Torleif asked.

Romarr seemed unsure of the younger man's intent. "The king has been generous to me. This is but a taste of what he has given me."

"Arm rings? Torcs? A jeweled necklace for my wife, perhaps?"

Romarr's hesitation was slight, but he answered. "All these and more."

"Ah, but you see it is the more that I want, not a ring, or a pretty gem to put in my wife's hair." Torleif's voice had lost its curious, youthful lilt. "Would he give me land that I might spread to the sea and ships to sail upon the glistening waves? Would he make me a lord superior to all others? Would I be master of the western lands?"

Raef's heart pounded in his chest as Torleif made his demands, wondering if the young lord pushed too far. The wrong words, the wrong look, would start a battle. He would have given much to see Fengar's face in that moment.

Romarr threw back his head and laughed. "Is your brain addled? Have the vaettir run away with your senses, boy? What you ask is impossible."

"Then Axsellund will not stand with you or your king."

"That is all?" Romarr was all blistering anger now. "You think the war will pass you by? That Axsellund will remain unscathed simply because you wish it to be so? To deny the true king is to guarantee your destruction."

Torleif smiled a little. "Is that so? Have the Norns whispered in your ear? Have you seen the carvings on Yggdrasil?"

Romarr flushed in the firelight. "You will regret your choice, boy. I will cut your wife's throat myself, but not before I have her."

"Enough." Fengar spoke at last and laid a hand on Romarr's arm. "Young Torleif has come to us with good will. We should not banish him simply for his brash words." The king turned to Torleif. "You ask much, Torleif, son of Audvin, and it would be within my right to claim your life. But I am not so rash as to throw away a chance at alliance because you have insulted me." Fengar's right hand jerked as though he were about to offer it in friendship and then thought better of it. Instead he indicated the shelter behind him. "Come, we have much to discuss."

Raef watched Torleif disappear with Fengar behind the skins and swallowed hard to loosen the clenched muscles of his chest. Romarr followed, as did Alvar of Kolhaugen, leaving the shield walls to face each other in silence. Fengar's men began to disperse, peeling away from the wall one by one until only twenty or so men remained to watch the newcomers, but Torleif's kept a good formation that Raef was glad to see. It would not do to have the Axsellund warriors drop their guard.

Raef signaled to Vakre and they slipped back along the river, meeting up with Rufnir, and then into the forest.

"It is done." Raef breathed the words out in a puff of white vapor, both relieved that the first part of the scheme was done and knotted with tension over what was to come.

"We should have stayed. Kept watch." Vakre seemed restless and Raef could guess why.

"Torleif's ruse will stand or fall with or without us hanging on their every word. He is on his own. Yes," Raef continued as Vakre began to protest, "your uncle will push back. He will not be eager to let Fengar accept Axsellund, not after the demands Torleif has made. But Fengar is desperate. We must hope that desperation bolsters his will."

"Unless Torleif has asked for too much." Rufnir was quiet, unsure, and Raef could not read his face in the darkness.

"It was necessary, Ruf. Axsellund has kept out of this war. Torleif must show he had reason for this, must show a great deal of foresight, and above all, must show that he burns with ambition. Asking for lands stretching to the western sea is reckless, but bold, and Fengar needs bold if he is to defeat the Hammerling. He needs to believe that Torleif will bring him victory, or Romarr will convince him not to let Torleif leave that shelter alive."

Despite Raef's assurances to Rufnir, it was with a restless mind that he returned to the nest with them. The men were quiet but in good cheer, carving portions off a pair of deer brought down just before Torleif's arrival in the valley. But Raef found he did not have the stomach to eat, and instead kept a constant vigil at the nest's overlook, staring into the dark valley and the faint light of torches that seemed to hum in the heart of it.

It was not until just before dawn that the warrior came. The valley was thick with mist and Raef, drifting somewhere on the edge of sleep, was slow to rouse himself, for the figure that took shape before him out of the swirling mist seemed no more solid than a dream. It was the man's voice that broke through Raef's weariness as the warrior leaned over Raef and shook his shoulder.

"Lord."

Raef blinked and, with a groan of discomfort, pushed himself away from the wall of rock that he had slumped against in the night. "What is it?" he managed, his tongue thick in his mouth. He focused on the warrior's face, so pale in the mist but for the dark ink that crept up his neck in the guise of a serpent. Raef recognized him now. He and Torleif had spoken in private before descending into the valley, though Raef did not know whether the man counseled for or against the plan.

"It is done. A bargain has been struck."

Raef felt the relief rush through him like the spring flood that would come to Vannheim's rivers. "Good. Good. Then we will begin our preparations at once." Raef got to his feet but something in the warrior's face halted him there on the edge between rock and air. "What is it?"

"The terms. They are not what they should be."

"What do you mean?"

"Torleif must prove himself, must show he is worthy of the demands he has made. Only then will Fengar accept his oath."

"Then Torleif cannot be called an oathbreaker when he turns on the would-be king." Raef knew his words sounded hollow, knew the warrior had more to say.

"Fengar means to have the Vestrhall. And Torleif must win it."

Raef swore. "This was Romarr of Finnmark's notion."

"It was the agreed upon task. Torleif was left with no choice. Fengar needs a place of safety; the Vestrhall is near. And he has seen you away from your hall, in the wilderness with only a few men, a strange thing in a time of war. He does not know what has gone on here in Vannheim, does not know of your cousin's treachery, but he believes the Vestrhall is ripe for the taking." The warrior of Axsellund stepped close to Raef and gripped his forearm. "The valley will be emptied today."

Raef's gaze roamed over the men stirring in the nest. There were not enough to be sure of victory, even with the surprise of Torleif's deceit. He turned back to look at the serpent warrior. "Then Fengar dies today."

TEN

THE MIST WAS a friend at Raef's back, a silent companion as he watched the riverside camp empty. The warriors snaked into the trees in a column three shields wide, led and trailed by men on horseback. From Raef's vantage point, there was little enough to see, but the warrior from Axsellund at his side was quick to point out that Torleif and his men were scattered throughout the host. There would be no easy way to alert and organize them when the fighting began. Fengar rode at the front, flanked by Romarr of Finnmark and Griva, the two blonde sisters just ahead of the king. The old man looked frail and birdlike, perched atop a large, heavy-hoofed horse meant for field work, but this did nothing to lessen the sharpness of his knives, Raef knew. Torleif was given a place of honor just behind the king, but the presence of Ulthor Ten-blade at his shoulder told Raef the honor was tinged with suspicion and the promise of a quick stab to the ribs should Torleif show any signs of falsehood.

"He will be killed the moment we attack." The warrior's snake tattoo seemed to writhe with anger as he crouched next to Raef.

"Do you have so little faith in your lord?" It was a cold answer but Raef could not afford to be swayed by emotion.

"Are you so eager to see your newly-won ally slaughtered?"

"Torleif knew the danger," Raef said, his teeth clenched against the frustration building into a knot in his throat. "He knew this battle would come."

"In days, yes, perhaps even weeks. You do not have the men to win this fight."

Raef rounded on the warrior. "I have men who are willing to do what must be done, who are willing to go to the gods. That is what I have. What I do not have is time. Should I hand the Vestrhall to Fengar? Should I let a king take up residence in my hall and watch him fortify it with an army?"

"Is that no less than your cousin has done?"

Raef seized the warrior's shoulder. "And what if your lord should have a change of heart? What if I, secure in our alliance, let Fengar take the Vestrhall, and then throw my men against the walls expecting our friends inside to unbar the gates, to find only foes on the other side?"

"Torleif is not a faithless dog," the warrior growled.

"We fight Fengar today. Here." Raef kept his voice quiet though he longed to unleash his anger. "You are free to keep your sword clean if that is your wish. I care not." Raef turned away, knowing the warrior of Axsellund would do no such thing. His devotion to Torleif ran too deep. Scrambling across the rocks, Raef returned to the eagle's nest, where his company of warriors waited in grim silence, their freshly sharpened spears and swords piercing the mist. Raef glanced up to the top of the bowl where a lone figure stood, stark against the sky. Vakre. The son of Loki raised a hand in greeting and Raef turned to the men. He put a wide smile on his face that he did not feel in his heart.

"It is time. Show me how well you climb. An arm ring for the first man to reach the top."

With eager grins, the warriors hurried to the walls of rock that formed the back of the bowl. Some worked their way up the narrow paths riddled with empty air, others sought unconquered ground, finding finger holds and ledges as well as any goat. They took to it with a quiet determination that made Raef glad, but one man Raef pulled aside just before he began to climb.

"Not you, Ruf." Raef patted Rufnir on the shoulder.

"I can make the climb." Rufnir's jaw was set but there was fear in his eyes. "I can."

"I do not doubt you," Raef said. Rufnir would try without complaint, he knew, but Raef would not risk his friend's life to save his pride. A one-handed man had no place climbing a wall of rock. Even the paths would be treacherous. Raef grinned to set his old friend at ease. "I have another task for you. You will be coming with me."

The first warriors had reached the top by the time Raef and Rufnir dropped out of the bowl and crept close to Fengar's column, which was leaving the valley by the same route Torleif had come. Visna was already there, her sharp blue eyes unblinking as she traced the warriors through the trees, and Dvalarr watched her back. The way would take them into a high valley, thick with grasses and flowers in high summer, wide and white with snow in barren winter. And above, as high as the eagles that nested there, the Vannheim warriors would watch and track them as the wolf does the wounded deer, and ready themselves for battle. Following behind, Raef would stalk Fengar and wait for the right moment and the place where the terrain might give them the greatest advantage.

That place was a narrow gorge where the valley thinned, penned in by sheer walls of rock on both sides. Raef had described it to Vakre, sure it was their best hope, for there they could trap Fengar's force, closing in from behind and blocking the way forward with a wall of shields.

The thick snow made for slow progress and Raef and his companions trudged along up to their knees, keeping enough distance between them and Fengar's rear guard to avoid being seen.

"We will be the first to close the trap from behind, Ruf," Raef explained between breaths as he pushed through a high drift of snow. "It is vital that none escape." It was the truth. The Vannheim men who descended to close off the front of the gorge would have an easier path. Those who were sent to join Raef and seal off the rear had a more treacherous descent, and if the attack was not perfectly timed, Raef and those with him would have to stand alone until reinforcements came. But he also said it to bolster Rufnir's spirits, and Raef was rewarded by a grin that brightened his friend's face.

"I will sing the steel song for them all," Rufnir said, tugging at the Thor hammer that dangled from his neck, his shield strapped tight against his stump.

"Try to leave a few for me."

As the gorge came into sight ahead of them, Raef did his best to narrow the gap between them and the last of Fengar's warriors, though the lack of cover kept them from getting as close as he would like. He saw nothing of the warriors that lay in wait, nothing of Vakre, and for a moment Raef felt alone in that windswept valley, but then he glimpsed a soaring shape high in the sky, an eagle, its wings spread wide to catch the air, and he thought of Siv and the nerves vanished, supplanted by the first tremors of keen anticipation. With a nod exchanged between them, Visna broke away from Raef, Rufnir, and Dvalarr, heading to the eastern side of the valley, an arrow already knocked on the string of the borrowed bow. She would make her way to the top of the gorge opposite Vakre to make visual contact with him and signal the start of the attack, then rain down arrows until she had none left.

Dvalarr watched her go, openly admiring her long, sure strides and the wave of her golden hair where it vanished into her hood.

"Where did you find such a woman?"

There would be a time to tell Visna's story, to reveal her to the world so her name might ring across the skies as Raef had promised, but it was not now. "Only the gods know." It was true enough. Raef grinned at Dvalarr. "Come, Crow. Do your axes hunger for the taste of blood?"

Dvalarr loosed the pair of axes from his belt and kissed the cold steel heads in turn. "Their thirst is great, lord." There was no grin on Dvalarr's face, only a promise of death.

Fengar's host had almost reached the gorge and Raef glanced up to see that Visna was nearly in position. Throwing caution away, Raef hurried forward, Dvalarr and Rufnir at his heels, every pounding step taking him closer to battle.

As the last of Fengar's warriors filed into the narrow path between the walls of rock, Raef looked to the sky. An arrow streaked across the gorge and dark figures began to emerge from between the jagged slopes and boulders that framed the cliffs. One by one, the warriors of Vannheim trickled down to reach Raef, each man sliding into place, shield overlapping shield until they were twelve across and two deep. Ahead of them, the gorge rang with the voices of men, but not with alarm, and then at last the shout came, echoing back along the cliffs, reaching Raef as only a ragged cry. The warriors in Fengar's column came to life. The retreat came quickly, pressed on by the sudden appearance of a shield wall blocking the forward exit, Raef knew, and he braced for impact.

The charge was hard and fast, a great press of men and sweat, but uneven and without order, and Raef's line held with ease. Then a voice came to Raef, sharp in the cold air, shouting commands, and Raef, tucked behind his shield, knew the next push would come with greater precision and less fear. He risked a glance and saw Alvar of Kolhaugen on horseback, sword in hand, spit flying from between his teeth as he barked orders. If there were men from Axsellund among those about to charge, Raef could not say. Raef ducked as the opposing shield wall came forward, this time with even, measured steps mixed with angry insults and roars of defiance. As the walls clashed a second time, sending shudders through Raef's bones, the hacking and the bloodletting and the dying began.

It was the Crow who broke through, his great strength beating back the man opposite him, and then, his shield forgotten, he began to unleash his axes in a fury. One, longer hafted than its sister, stroked through the chests of two men, while the shorter one hacked through the leg muscles of another. Raef, at Dvalarr's side, pushed into the space the Crow was cleaving open in Alvar's shield wall, battering one warrior down with his shield and finishing him with a swift chop through the skull that sent shards of bone flying. Behind Raef, his men poured into the hole they had created, driving Alvar's men apart until they could no longer help defend each other, and Fengar's rear guard began to crumble.

Given a moment of respite behind Dvalarr's bulk, Raef wiped blood from his face with his shield arm. Only when he nearly gouged out his own eye with a splinter did he realize how battered his shield was. It would offer little in the way of protection, so Raef let it fall to the gore-slick snow and drew his sword. Ahead, he could see Torleif rallying the warriors of Axsellund to him and Raef felt a hope of victory swell in his chest. Calling on Dvalarr and Rufnir to follow him, Raef pushed onward, ready to meet Fengar in the thick of it.

The scream was piercing, fierce, and demanded death. Raef, having slashed through a warrior's neck, looked up to see Griva, all bones and knife blades and wild eyes, throw himself from his saddle and onto Torleif, landing like a deadly cloak on the young lord's shoulders. Torleif turned and twisted, trying to shake the old man off, but Griva sunk in his hold as a wolf does his teeth when he has latched onto prey. A knife flashed, someone shouted, and then blood was gushing from Torleif's neck. Again and again Griva

"Because these are my lands."

"And I am king."

"Not my king."

Fengar's gaze flickered and he did not look Raef in the eye. "Well, woman," he said, facing Visna now. "There is your prize. Let him go."

Visna shoved Griva to the ground, her gaze fixed now on the woman who clutched at Raef in fear. But she had taken no more than two steps when Griva hissed a curse at her and Visna turned, eyes flashing, steel carving a path through the air toward the old man's chest.

Raef saw the blonde women too late. Like wolves, they sprang at Visna, and her death blow turned into a desperate, swinging defense as they attacked her from both sides. Raef leaped forward, his movements hampered by the woman at his side, and the butt end of a spear plowed into his chest, sending him backward. Before he could move again, the spear point was at his throat and a grizzled warrior, face hidden by a thick black beard, barred his way. Behind the warrior, Visna was on her knees, panting, blood running down her face, her sword out of reach, and the blonde women, two of the so-called Daughters of Thor, stood over her in triumph.

Raef felt the rush of heat and thrust his arm back, palm out, to where Vakre smoldered just behind him. "No, Vakre." The heat faded but did not disappear. Raef looked at Fengar, who had not moved, had not given an order. "Call them off. We are not here to fight."

Fengar hesitated, uncertainty clouding his eyes. Griva sidled up beside the king and whispered into Fengar's ear. Fengar flinched away from the old man's touch, but the doubt fled from his face. "Bind them."

They fought, Visna screaming in fury, Raef beating back the bear-like warrior, Vakre lunging for one of the blonde sisters, but plunged the blade into Torleif until at last the young lord's legs gave way and they both went down in a heap of blood and limbs.

Raef plunged forward, desperate to reach Torleif, but he was not the only one. The warrior with the serpent tattooed on his neck got there first and he flung himself on the bodies, separating Torleif from Griva, flinging the old man's skinny frame aside with vicious force. Raef reached for Griva, his axe ready to split ribs, but he never got the chance.

The thunder came without warning, cracking across the narrow sky between the two cliffs, and the earth shook beneath Raef with such violence that he was sure Thor himself had come. The ground lurched underfoot, the snow tossing and heaving like Jörmungand in the sea, sending Raef to his knees, and there he locked eyes with Torleif and saw the fear there that only a dying man knows.

In the next instant, Raef was hurled in the air and beneath him he saw man and horse and rock and snow all collide as though in the grip of a giant, flesh mashing against stone, snow burying faces and hearts and lungs that clawed for air. And then Raef landed, his arms caught beneath him, and watched as a tide of snow peppered with rocks chased him down. His world went white as the avalanche caught him up in its icy folds. He tumbled, he knew not how far, and then all was still and dark, the only sound his heart pounding in the cocoon that would soon be his tomb.

ELEVEN

HE WAS LUCKY. The avalanche had deposited him with the crook of his elbow and his forearm up around his head, creating a pocket of air. Raef mustered his saliva and let a drop of spit leave his lips. It dripped down his chin, not into his nose. He was upright. And he was still alive and conscious.

Raef took a deep breath to still his frantic heart and quiet his mind. His axe and sword were gone, flung far afield in the tumult, but a knife lingered in his belt. He could feel it press against his hip, a presence that would have been reassuring if he could have snaked his arm around and drawn the blade. It seemed a small, useless tool against the heavy press of snow that covered Raef, but it was all he had. Except that he did not have it. His left arm had created the air bubble and his right was trapped against his side. He had a small amount of wiggle room around his chest, but his limbs might as well have been severed from his body for all the good they would do him.

Raef swallowed and tried to take small, shallow breaths to conserve what air was left to him, but the panic swelled in his chest like waves battering a rocky coastline. Raef shouted, called for Vakre, Visna, anyone who might hear, but the snow only threw his pleas back at him and Raef soon fell silent.

"Forgive me, father. I have failed you in every way." The voice hardly seemed to be his, so hushed, so broken. But it was a voice that spoke the truth and Raef closed his eyes and hoped the cold would take him quickly.

The sound came to him from a different world, a world of wind and waves, of canvas collaring the air, of sleek longships riding the ocean. It was the sound of well-worn wood rubbing against itself, a familiar, tender sound. But then the wood became brittle sheets of snow pierced with shards of ice, and something was scraping, scraping, soft at first, and then the sound roared in Raef's ears and he was sucked through the snow so suddenly he could not catch his breath. Raef felt air, empty air, and then he was caught, cradled in a sharp but gentle embrace, and at last he opened his eyes to see the ground give way beneath him as he rose up, up into the blue, driven skyward by a pair of smoke-colored wings.

〈 〈 〈

The kin refused to leave his side. She curled around him, her wings enfolding him with a leathery warmth, but it seemed to Raef as he stroked her neck that she stayed close to him out of fear as much as for concern for him.

They were perched above the gorge, out of sight of the battle that was now buried under the snow, for she had flown high and fast to the summits above. Below, Raef could just see small, dark figures, survivors, though how many and who he could not know from that distance.

The kin blinked her sunset eyes and shivered. She seemed skinny to Raef, her bones more obvious beneath the stretched leather, her talons sharper, and he rubbed the spot between her eyes while whispering to her.

"How is it that you are here?" He rubbed harder as she leaned into him. "I would give much to understand your thoughts, to know what brought you here, to know how things stand in Alfheim." Raef thought of Anuleif's words. The boy had said Alfheim was in darkness and ruin. And he thought of the corpse of the giant, fallen from the sky. The boundaries between realms were weakening. "Do not be afraid. You have saved my life more than once. Let me look after you now."

Raef got to his feet and the kin did the same, coiling around him as she rose up to tower over him.

"You have grown." He smiled at her. "Now we must put some meat on those bones, give you strength to match your speed." Raef looked down into the valley, trepidation at what he would find there rubbing away at him as surely as the winter wind. "And I must go back."

As if she understood, the kin crouched and Raef swung himself onto her back, the exhilaration at what was to come rushing over him as she unfurled her wings. They were away before he had time to take a breath, diving down the face of the mountain as straight as an arrow and far more deadly.

The human figures below grew and grew and Raef saw arms point skyward, saw astonished faces take in the sight of him on the kin's back. They landed on the northern end of the gorge, where the survivors were fewest in number and where the western cliff face had crumbled. But as he walked the length of the gorge, the smoke-colored kin a shadow behind him, he saw the faces of both friend and foe alike. Some were digging, calling to comrades, searching for friends, dead or alive, others sat against the broken, shattered rocks, their faces white with shock. Most stared at Raef with a mixture of fear and awe, but one gave him no notice at all.

The snake tattooed warrior knelt in the snow, a corpse cradled across his knees. In death Torleif looked at peace, the fear Raef had seen staring back at him in that final moment now closed behind eyelids that would not open.

Raef stopped and went to one knee, the kin nudging her nose against his back to let him know she was there.

"Do not pretend to mourn him, Skallagrim." The warrior's voice was full of bitter anger. He looked up and Raef saw a face streaked with tears, though the brown depths of his eyes seemed dry now. "You do not deserve to mourn him."

Raef fingered the hammer that hung at Torleif's neck. It was finely wrought, delicate silver stamped with intricate patterns. "You are right." He met the warrior's gaze. "I do not."

Commotion at the southern end of the gorge drew Raef's attention and he left the warrior to his grief, continuing on to see what fate awaited him there.

The shouts were angry ones, but tinged with dread, and men had clustered together, almost close enough to form a shield wall. Raef watched the grey kin fly up to perch above the crowd, then pushed through and found Vakre on the other side, head held high, defiance in his eyes.

A Vannheim warrior clutched at Raef's elbow. "He did it, lord, he started it all." The man's eyes stared down at Vakre's feet, and it was only then that Raef saw that snow was melting where the son of Loki stood.

"Fengar was fleeing. I did what I had to." Vakre's jaw seemed to grind together as he spoke, ice against stone, and Raef saw in him the same ruthless, wild, single-minded hunter that Raef had first met in the forest of Balmoran.

"Is Fengar here? Does Fengar lie beneath the snow?" One man, bolder than the rest, stepped forward. "No, Fengar is out of our reach."

Raef's heart sank in his chest and he looked over his shoulder to the mountain passes that lay to the north. The would-be king would have had many paths to choose from.

"What happened?" Raef's question was for all, but it was Vakre he stared at. The son of Loki's gaze was frozen as thick as a waterfall in winter and Raef knew he would have no more answers there.

"I will show you." It was Visna who found the words to answer him. Raef had not seen her, had not heard her approach. She took his hand and led him back through the gorge

"We have all seen fire burn. Today I have seen fire do things I did not think possible. The flames blazed through rock and snow, shattering the cliff face." The rocks were streaked black with smoke, Raef saw, licked by fire. "He stood just there," Visna said, gesturing, "and the ground broke beneath his feet."

"Why?"

"Fengar and the one with the knives got loose, carried past the shield wall by their horses. The lord of Finnmark followed. Vakre was not willing to watch them get away." Visna pushed hair from her eyes and looked hard at Raef. "He is your friend, I see that. But he is dangerous. A wise man would not be friends with the son of Loki, or of any god."

The words were so like the one's Raef's father had spoken so long before that Raef heard his father's voice once more. "And you? Are you not the child of a god?"

"I was. There is nothing of Asgard left in me." Visna took Raef's hand once more. "I fear what Vakre may become."

"I cannot believe he intended," Raef flung an arm out to encompass the destruction around them, "this."

"Does he deny it? Do you see regret and remorse in those eyes?"

Raef had seen nothing but cold fury in Vakre's eyes, but he was not about to admit that to Visna. He looked north once more.

"So Fengar is gone, and Ten-blade and Romarr with him. Let the winter take them." Raef turned his attention back to the gorge. "How many survive?"

"Tell me how it is that you ride a skeiflyng of Alfheim and I will answer that."

"Skeiflyng. So that is their true name." Raef could not help but feel that knowing the true name of the dragon-kin was a betrayal to Finnoul. He wondered if she lived yet, if devastation had come to Alfheim as Anuleif said, befouled by the wolf Fenrir, broken by giants once more. "She is an old friend." He did not have the will to say more.

Visna held his gaze for a long time and then nodded. "If we are lucky, we may dig up a few more before they perish beneath the snow, but I count no more than thirty-eight survivors. Fengar's men are all but wiped out." She pointed to a small group that huddled near a pair of nervous horses. "What will you do with them?"

Raef looked over the eight warriors. They avoided his gaze and their faces were those of men who wait for death. "If they will fight for me, I will not turn them away." A dark shape in the snow caught Raef's eye and he knelt to pluck up a black crow's feather. It was bent and tattered, no longer the shiny piece of plumage that Griva had worn in his hair, but Raef flung it away in disgust. "What of Griva? Is the old snake buried with the rest?"

"I have not seen him."

"Lord." Dvalarr the Crow approached, his tattoo savaged by a blooming, bleeding gash across his head. A purple bruise was already spreading down to his cheek and up over the top of his scalp. The Crow's hands were unsteady as he handed Raef something wrapped in a dead man's cloak.

Raef let the wool fall away to reveal his sword and axe. The axe blade was crusted with dried blood but the sword shone bright and clean. Raef wiped the axe on the cloak and then secured both to his belt, more comforted by their presence there than he could say, and rested a hand on Dvalarr's shoulder.

"I thought these would lie under the snow until spring. Thank you."

The Crow nodded and Raef tightened his grip on Dvalarr's shoulder as he felt the large man sway.

"Look to your wound, Crow."

"It is nothing. It was only a rock."

"I insist. The lady Visna will help you." Visna stiffened beside Raef and he turned to her as Dvalarr sank down into the snow. "You are the sunrise and the sunset and the sweetest cup of mead to him. Be kind." Visna rolled her eyes with good-natured tolerance and knelt to clean the blood from Dvalarr's pale skull.

When Raef returned to the southern end of the gorge, he found Vakre unchanged. He stood apart, stiff and unrepentant, and met Raef's questioning look with indifference. The crowd of men around him had dispersed as the warriors gathered what they could from the snow. Corpses were discovered, men out of breath and out of time, men who died without knowing that the surface, the sunlight, was less than an arm's length away. Others would be buried deeper, left to freeze into the ice, their terror preserved for the spring thaw. Raef swallowed, feeling the snow close in around him once more, and wondered how deep he had been.

One was found alive. Alvar of Kolhaugen's red glass earring had been ripped from his earlobe. It dangled now from his hair, caught up in the long tangles that had nearly strangled Alvar. He was blue in the face and his lips were a deep purple as though stained with the juice of blackberries. His horse was found nearby, lanced with a spear through the belly, but somehow alive. Raef leaned close and slid his knife across the horse's throat with a swift jerk, glad to spare the animal some pain, and he was about to grant Alvar the same peace when a shout rang out over the broken stones.

The snake warrior had Griva by the neck and the old man was as limp as a meadow flower wilted under the hot summer sun. And yet when the warrior reached for his sword, a flash of white struck first, slicing through the warrior's arm. In pain, the warrior bellowed and dropped Griva, who squirmed away like a wounded rabbit. The warrior clutched at his arm, blood dripping between his fingers, and Raef, closing the distance between them, saw now that Griva held a sharp wedge of bone, a crude weapon, but deadly.

"Stay where you are, Skallagrim," the warrior said, his voice the growl of an angry bear. "The wretch is mine."

"Shed my blood and you will lose the favor of the gods," Griva shrieked.

"I lost that with his death." The warrior charged and Griva hopped back, but the blade still carved into his torso, cleaving through flesh and bone to split the old man from shoulder to ribs. Griva collapsed, the bone knife slipping from his fingers, but the snake warrior was not content with that. Howling with rage, he threw himself to the snow and shoved the white blade back into Griva's outstretched hand.

"Keep it, maggot, that I might kill you a thousand times again in Odin's hall." But Griva was still, his lifeblood coursing from the wound to congeal on the snow, and only the snake warrior could know if the death rattle of Griva's last breath had come too soon.

The shadow of the kin's wings passed over the bloody scene in the snow as she came to land by Raef, a deep hiss in her throat warning off any threat, but all else was silence.

Raef looked up and down the length of the gorge, taking in the worn, frayed, disoriented faces, and raised his voice so all might hear. "Any man who wants to live, let him follow me. The wolves will be here by nightfall."

It was a wretched procession that left the gorge behind and filtered down the alpine valley. Rufnir, acting on Raef's orders, led the way. Visna and Dvalarr steered the horses that had survived. One carried Alvar of Kolhaugen, who still drew breath through his blue lips. Around them flowed men of Vannheim, of Axsellund, of far-flung places who had followed a king and found death. Raef watched them go from the back of the smoke-colored kin, but the sight of two men in the snow, still hemmed in by the high walls of the gorge, kept him from urging her to fly onward. Instead, they circled to the ground and Raef saw the faces of the two men who had chosen to stay behind. Both filled him with sorrow.

He went to the warrior of Axsellund first, who had not moved since avenging Torleif's death. Raef's presence received no reaction, not until Raef knelt and untied the knot that held Torleif's silver Thor hammer around his neck. Raef offered it to the warrior.

"Would he want you to have it?"

"What difference does it make? I will join him soon enough." The man's voice was dull, but it was his eyes that told Raef of the depth of his grief.

"What is your name?"

"Eyvind."

"You loved him?" The question hung between them and Eyvind looked up but did not answer. "Then live for him." Raef lowered himself to sit in the snow, tucking his knees to his chest. He kept his eyes trained on Torleif's face as he spoke. "It is no easy thing. To know you will live the length of your days without a glance at his face, without the sound of his laughter or the sight of his smile. It is enough to draw the life from you, slowly, painfully, leaving you wracked with loneliness." Raef was quiet for a moment, then leaned forward and pressed the silver hammer into Eyvind's empty hand. "I see her in the stars, in the rushing river, in all the things she loved in the world. It is not enough. But it is something to live on."

Raef let out a heavy breath that clouded the air in front of him. The sky was darkening and the choice was not his to make. He stood and walked away from Eyvind, the snow crunching underfoot the only sound between them.

Vakre stood at the base of the gorge, his gaze drifting far afield, though whether he watched the horizon or was fixed on something only he could see, Raef could not say.

"Leave me." Vakre's voice was raspy from disuse.

"Why?" Raef had wanted to be calm, had meant to speak without anger, but all the frustration of the day welled up into his voice. "Why should I? Because you will burn me, too? Because your selfish action sent good men to Valhalla, or worse to a death unremembered, to a cold place far from Odin's hall? I was there under the snow, Vakre." Raef was shouting now. "I felt the weight of it, I could see my last breaths before me. Is this what you wanted? To break my only alliance before the mold was hardened? To show the world that the son of Loki is as cruel and thoughtless as his father?" He was ranting, he knew, his scrambled thoughts spilling from his mouth without sense, and it took effort to swallow them back. Chest heaving, Raef held his tongue until he could see straight once more. "Perhaps it is my own fault, my own single-mindedness that has brought us here. You have made me many promises, Vakre, and perhaps it is time I made you one." Raef looked hard at his friend's face, willing Vakre to show him something other than stony silence. "Ruin will come to your uncle, if that is your wish. He will face what he has done to you, and he will beg for death. This I swear to you. You do not stand alone."

The slivered moon hung low, riding the mountain crests in the eastern sky. A wolf's howl raised the hair on the back of Raef's neck.

"Leave me," Vakre repeated. "Please. I have broken the trust of the men who follow you. If I stay, I will only do more damage."

"They will forget it if I tell them to."

Only then did Vakre turn his head and meet Raef's gaze, and it was as if that single action brought forth a flood of emotion. In Vakre's eyes, Raef saw fear and sorrow and, most frightening of all, self-loathing. "I heard him laughing. My father." Vakre blinked and the words rushed out. "The flames, they came before I knew I wanted them. I wanted only to catch Fengar and my uncle, but they blazed so bright that all else was lost to me, all was beyond my control. And then I heard him. And he was proud." Vakre closed his eyes and Raef felt the wall begin to rise up again between them. "I do not trust myself, Raef. You must let me be, let me go to whatever fate my father has made for me."

"No. Your father is not your fate. I will not believe it." Raef stepped forward and gripped Vakre's sleeve, pulling the son of Loki close enough to see the flecks of gold in his eyes, even in the growing dark. "I will not."

To Raef's surprise, Vakre smiled. It was small and sad, but there was a kernel of brightness in it, like the scales of a silver fish flashing through the deep blue of a sleeping fjord. "You cannot save us all, Raef, no matter how hard you try. Some people are not meant to be saved."

"I will not turn my back on you."

"You are a true friend. The singers will spin tales of your glorious victory at the burning lake, of your journey to Jötunheim and back again, of your pursuit of vengeance, of triumph over treachery. But if I could tell them to sing of one thing and one thing only, it would be of this." Vakre reached out and placed his hand on Raef's chest. "This heart that beats for others, for the stars in the sky and the green trees in the wind. Even for all the nine realms. It is a great heart."

"Come back with me, Vakre. The gods are not through with us."

R R R

The fire was tall and blazing by the time Raef returned to the eagle's nest with Eyvind, who had shouldered Torleif's corpse, and Vakre at his heels, and its light did nothing to conceal the looks of discontent and apprehension at the arrival of the son of Loki. Raef ignored the glances and pushed through the crowd to warm himself by the fire, watching as Eyvind melted into the group of survivors from Axsellund and the kin settled onto a large flat rock that gave her a vantage point over the entire bowl. Vakre came to stand beside Raef and the warriors closest to them shifted, opening up more space for him, but one, a short, thickset man Raef recognized as being one of Fengar's stood his ground, his mouth curled in a sneer, and muttered something about Vakre setting his own fire rather than taking the place of a wounded man who needed the warmth.

Vakre grimaced. "I will go," he said, and made to move off into the shadows.

"No," Raef said, gripping Vakre's arm. "You will stay."

"Yes, stay and roast us over the fire, Lokison," the short warrior said, growing bold in the face of Vakre's mild reply.

"He is ill luck, Skallagrim," a voice called out. Raef swiveled but could not determine the source.

"Let him answer for the destruction he has brought." A few cheers followed this one, and suddenly the warriors gathered around the fire, enemies under the light of the sun, banded together in the light of the moon. Men began to press forward, calling for justice for their lost shield brothers, their voices finding strength in numbers.

"Silence," Raef shouted, earning a brief respite, but then the voices swelled and Raef felt the heat of the fire sear his skin as he was pushed closer to the flames. His sword slid from its scabbard in silence, but the blade, bright in the firelight, spoke for him. A ripple of movement beside Raef made him spin, ready to defend Vakre with his own life, but he held back at the sight of Dvalarr, axe in hand.

"Any man who wants to see the Flamecloak dead will have to get through me," the Crow said and the crowd grew quiet, though the faces were no less angry.

"He is the spawn of Loki," came a shout. "He will bring darkness upon us."

"His death will please the Allfather!"

Vakre's gaze flickered here and there, Raef saw, but he did not draw a weapon.

The rush came with surprising speed, a single body leaping at Vakre with a yell, but Dvalarr thrust out at the man's head with the butt end of his axe handle, knocking the assailant to the ground. He groaned and lay still, blood pumping from a growing welt on his temple.

"The next man to move will die," the Crow said. All was still and Raef sought words that might muster a peace, even an uneasy one, but Dvalarr spoke first. "You who followed Fengar," Dvalarr spread his arms to encompass the warriors, "that spineless wretch who called himself king, be glad you draw breath and thank Skallagrim for it, for you would be lying in the snow, your frozen eyes staring at the crows that come to peck them out, if not for this man who let you walk away from death." The Crow took a deep breath and went on, his voice ringing over the stones. "And you, men of Vannheim, you should be ashamed, you who swore oaths to the Skallagrim, our king. Do your words mean so little? You have sworn to lay down your lives in service to him, to uphold his will and word, but now, in his hour of need, you dishonor him and in doing so, you tarnish the names of your fathers who came before and your sons who will hope to follow. Are we oathbreakers? Are we cowards, fit only to die old and frail by the hearth, beyond all dreams of glory? No, we are wolves of war and we are sworn brothers. Conquer your fear and hold your tongues or I will tear them from you!" The Crow was red in the face now, and shaking with anger. "Will none of you stand with me? Will none of you hold true to the oaths you swore?"

"I will stand with you, Crow." Rufnir stepped forward and planted himself beside Dvalarr.

"And I."

"I will."

Three, five, then ten men came to the edge of the fire and formed a wall between Vakre and his accusers. A log cracked, sending a shower of sparks into the air, and so silent was the eagle's nest that Raef was sure he could hear each and every spark hiss against the cold stone ground.

Raef nodded at Dvalarr and then pushed through the barrier. He looked from face to face, trying to discern the minds behind the shadowed eyes.

"I speak to those who came to this valley with Fengar and to those who came with Torleif. I do not ask for your oaths or your loyalty or your lives. I will not keep malcontents here simply to fill my shield wall. I will not let disgruntled minds sow dissention and doubt among the rest. If your heart longs for a far off place, a home left behind, then go. I have no quarrel with you." Raef let that hang in the air for a moment. "Unless," he went on, sharpening his voice, "unless you threaten that which I hold dear. You have until the sun rises to make your decisions." Raef paused again and let his desperation, his fury well up to fill his lungs. "And to the rest, to you who were born and bred in Vannheim, whose fathers and fathers before have called these hills and waters home, to you I say this. Are we not brothers of Ymir? Are we not raised on that mighty giant's blood? Is his heart not our heart, beating still? It is not in my nature to succumb. Let the gods do as they will." Raef's voice dropped. "Will you lend me your shields? Your hearts? Your lives?"

For a long moment, the crowd of warriors stayed rigid, and then they scattered like raindrops in a pond. Some went with quick, furtive steps, others with careful, deliberate strides. A few spoke, their voices coming to Raef like the sound of water falling in the distance, but it was the Axsellund warriors who moved as one, collecting their belongings and then huddling together away from the light of the fire.

"Is it wise to let them go?" Rufnir asked.

"Perhaps not. But I meant what I said. Resentment is like a rotten wound. It spreads." Raef reached up the sleeve of his left arm and unhooked one of the silver rings from his forearm. He held it up so the others might see. It bore the head of a bear and its eyes were tiny blue gems. "Crow," Raef said, "I want you to have this."

Dvalarr took the ring in one large hand, a hand still crusted with the blood of dead men, a hand that cradled it as though it were a gift from Odin himself.

"And I am proud to bear it, lord." The Crow curved the bear around his wrist and pushed the ring up his arm as far as it would go. "But what will you do with him?"

Alvar of Kolhaugen had been propped up near the fire, so close that the blanket wrapped around his legs was beginning to smoke. Visna shoved his legs to the side and stamped out the sparks that were smoldering at the edge, but her movement caused Alvar to slump sideways to the ground. Dvalarr grabbed Alvar's shoulder and hauled him upright again, but Alvar was as limp as an eel and he flopped to the other side the moment Dvalarr released him.

Raef squatted down to peer in Alvar's face. His lower lip hung open, revealing brown teeth, and his glassy eyes stared at the flames without seeing. Without his red glass bead, Alvar was nothing more than a common warrior, and Raef wondered what the farmers and fishermen of Kolhaugen would think if they saw him now. They would surely not see him as a lord, a ring-giver, a fame-bringer.

"Will he last the night?" Raef spread the lids of Alvar's right eye but even this got no response.

"I do not think it is the cold that will kill him," Vakre said.

"If he has not changed by morning, I will bring him a good

end, lord," Dvalarr said. Raef nodded, thinking of Alvar's brother Eirik, who fought for the Hammerling. Visna and Dvalarr drifted away from the fire, leaving Vakre alone at Raef's side.

"How many families will be torn apart by this war? How many brothers will fight brother? How many sisters will smile at the deaths of their kin? Inge drew her last breath under the snow today," Raef said, referring to the blonde sister who had freed them from Fengar. "Do you think she wept for the hatred she bore in her heart? Or do you think she spent her final moment wondering if her sister died first?" Raef stood and faced Vakre. "Would Eirik be glad to see his brother like this? Or would he think back to when they were boys, when they played and fought together, and wish they had walked a different path as men?"

"Freyja herself could not grow a tree in barren soil, Raef. The bonds of blood do not run deep in some." Vakre's voice was bitter and Raef knew his mind was on his uncle and his mother, cast out and forsaken.

"Hate is a strange thing. So often born out of so little. Erlaug, son of Hymar, do you remember him?"

Vakre grimaced, his teeth glistening in the firelight. "I would not soon forget the lord of Grudenhavn and his son."

For a moment Raef stood once more in the forest of Balmoran, staring at a face full of enmity. Erlaug of Grudenhavn might have taken his life that moonlit night if not for Vakre.

"Once we promised eternal friendship. We swore that nothing would come between us. We were eight and we were foolish. I remember being caught up in the moment of meeting him, knowing that one day we two would be lords. I had dreams of brave alliances and hard won battles. Four years later, he summered in my father's hall, and we loathed each other from the moment he arrived all because I had not grown so tall as he and he was quick to be sure I knew it. I disarmed him and threw him flat on his back and that was the end of our dreams." Raef was not sure why he spoke of Erlaug in that moment, but then the question came to him, the one he had never asked. "What did you do to him?"

Vakre was quiet for a long moment before answering. "There is a plant that grows in the deepest forests in Finnmark, in the ravines that hardly see sunlight. My mother showed me these places when I was very young. A single seed is deadly." Vakre looked at Raef. "I smeared the arrows with a paste made from one hundred such seeds."

"A foul way to die."

"For a foul man." Vakre nudged a smoldering piece of wood back into the flames. "He needed to know agony." The son of Loki frowned. "Be glad that you never knew your mother, Raef, for you never had to see her suffer."

"And yet I never saw her smile," Raef said, his gaze fixed on the smoldering embers of the fire. Vakre accepted this with a nod and Raef turned to his friend. "What now?"

"Now you wait and see what the sunrise shows you."

TWELVE

RAEF RUBBED HIS hands together and blew hot breath on his palms. The morning was frigid and frosted over and though the sun spilled into the valley below, it was a cold light made even colder by the ripping gusts of wind that battered against the walls of the nest. The day would be cold, perhaps the coldest yet that winter, but somehow it made Raef glad, for it suited his mood, and his own clear mind was a reflection of the clear, pristine sky above.

The fire burned still, but it seemed to be a fire without heat so quickly was the warmth swept away by the wind. Men clustered around it all the same, furs pulled tight over their ears. Others huddled at the entrance to the largest cave, waiting, though whether they waited for him or for death, Raef could not say. Their faces were grave, the faces of men who did not know if they had chosen well.

Seventeen men had made the choice to stay. The last of those who departed the nest were still in sight, their descent made tricky by slick frost on stone, but some had slipped away in the night, as though the sun might shame them into staying. Each and every man of Vannheim had answered Raef's challenge, and each had come to him in the night with words of fervent loyalty on their lips.

Of Fengar's men, none remained and Raef was sure they had been the first to vanish in the night. But one face he was surprised to see. Eyvind, the warrior from Axsellund with the snake tattoo, had chosen to stay.

Alvar of Kolhaugen was dying. It was a peaceful death, his blood draining away from the slice Dvalarr had made into his neck. They had set him up by the edge of the nest, as though giving him a last view of the world might either wake him from his stupor or send him gladly into death, though Raef was sure he was conscious of nothing around him, not even the cold. His eating knife, for that was all that remained on his belt, was pressed into his hand in the hopes that the gods might see him and take him to Valhalla, and Vakre had hooked the red glass bead into his ear once more. It glistened now and Raef stepped forward to close Alvar's eyes.

"Little of Alvar remained in this husk of a body," Raef said, "but we will build him a pyre nonetheless and let the gods see if him if they can." Raef looked to Eyvind. "They will see Torleif, I know."

Raef took to the task with vigor, leading a few men into the valley to select and fell a pair of young trees. Their axes chopped into the trunks, sending chips of bark and wood flying, and the forest came alive with the rhythmic sounds of steel meeting wood and labored breathing. They dragged the trees back to the nest and soon the pyre was stacked high. Dvalarr and Rufnir lifted Alvar's stiff corpse onto the wood, and Eyvind did the same for Torleif, but for Raef this was no longer a pyre for the man who wanted to be lord of Kolhaugen or for the ally who had gone to Valhalla too soon. It was a pyre for those he had not been able to burn, who had not had the light of a fire to lead them to Valhalla. In his mind's eye, he placed their bodies on the pyre. Asbjork, Rufnir's brother, was among them, but last of all was Siv.

With a nod from Raef, Dvalarr held a burning log to the base of the pyre. For a moment there was silence and then the kindling and pine needles began to smoke and spit and a fire was born.

Without oil to help the flames spread and burn hot, the pyre would burn slowly and linger through the daylight hours and well into the night, and yet Eyvind took up his vigil as Raef had known he would. When Raef came to stand at his side, the warrior of Axsellund did not begrudge him a place.

"Do you stand vigil for all your foes?" Eyvind asked. "Alvar of Kolhaugen would not have done the same for you."

"I do not stand here for him."

Eyvind nodded, his eyes clear with understanding.

"I did not think you would stay," Raef said.

"There is little enough to return to," Eyvind said. "And I want no part of what will follow?"

"And what is that?"

"Torleif's widow, she carries his child. She will fight for that child's inheritance."

"And you do not wish to see a child of Torleif claim what its father left behind?"

Eyvind looked away, his brow furrowed. "I do not know what I wish for a child of Torleif."

"What did Torleif want for Axsellund?"

When Eyvind looked back at Raef, his eyes were clouded with suspicion. "You mean the demands he made to Fengar."

"Were they just a ruse? Or did Torleif hold this dream in his heart? Did he wish to rise above his ancestors and be marked the greatest of them all?"

When Eyvind answered, there was a smile on his lips. "No. It was never about his name, his family. All he did, he did for Axsellund. But the sea did not speak to Torleif. He never craved ships or the influence they can grant."

"I would have given it, all he asked for," Raef said. "If he truly wanted it and he brought me victory, I would have carved a path from Axsellund to the sea for him."

Eyvind seemed surprised. "And the Hammerling? Axsellund and Finngale have not quarreled in many generations. Nor, I think, have Finngale and Vannheim."

Raef took a deep breath. "The Hammerling will come for me in time. There is no chance of reconciliation now." Even if the Hammerling remained ignorant of Raef's naming as king, even if he might yet harbor good will for Raef, he had a serpent whispering in his ear, for Raef was certain Hauk of Ruderk would slander the name of Skallagrim. Raef waved away a gust of smoke. "I see you are not the only man of Axsellund to remain behind. Will they fight for me and uphold Torleif's oath? Will you?"

Eyvind was quiet but his face betrayed little emotion. "Your friend. Is he truly the son of the silver-tongued god?"

Raef nodded. "He is."

"Fire is a dangerous plaything." There was no judgment in Eyvind's voice, but Raef felt a twinge of ire creep into his chest.

"Those flames have saved my life more than once."

"And if he should choose to end it? What then? Will he set a fire in your flesh? How many deaths will he be responsible for? How many bodies will he leave in his wake?" This last was hissed in Raef's ear, the vehemence bursting into Eyvind's voice with sudden strength, and then Eyvind turned and retreated from his vigil, striding as far from the pyre as the bowl would allow.

Raef closed his eyes and when he opened them, Vakre had come to stand by him.

"He blames you," Raef said.

"He is not wrong."

"We do not know that Torleif would have survived that battle."

"And still, he is not wrong."

"He fears you," Raef said, then corrected himself. "No, not fear.

He does not understand you. I think he only feared one thing and that has come to pass."

"Let me speak to him."

Raef searched Vakre's face, though he knew not what he was looking for. He nodded. "Go."

He watched from a distance and through a veil of smoke as the two men, perched at the edge of the nest, conversed. There were no wild gestures, no raised voices, only cloaks lifted by the wind and silence. The sun had ridden far across the sky by the time they finished. Vakre returned alone.

"He will stand with you. As will the rest of Torleif's warriors who remained."

Raef felt his stomach unclench. "What did you say?"

"I think perhaps that should stay between us."

Raef frowned. "Did you threaten him?"

Vakre shook his head. "No."

"Then I will ask no further questions."

The stars burned bright when Raef finally released himself from his vigil. The bodies of Alvar and Torleif were nothing but bones and ash, and Raef's throat was dry, his eyes burning with smoke. He stepped away and filled his lungs with cold night air, clearing his senses, and when he had breathed his fill, it seemed to him that the walls of the nest were closing in around him, that the only thing holding them back was the icy air that swelled within him. Raef scanned the walls of the bowl and found her, her sunset eyes dancing with firelight as she watched his every move from on high. He did not need to call, did not even move, for the kin was already sweeping down to land at his side.

Around them, warriors drew back, uneasy so near to the strange beast, but Raef was blind to them. He felt the life that had been drawn out of him by the funeral pyre return with new force as he climbed onto her back.

She took to the dark sky, rising higher and higher until the nest was the size of Raef's fist and the moon and stars were spread before him, so close it seemed he might stretch out to touch them. If Hati, the wolf who chased the moon was near, Raef could not feel his vile presence.

They soared high above the mountains, then dropped with terrifying speed back to earth, skimming the surface of the fjord. For a moment, Raef's thoughts turned west and he longed to fly her to the Vestrhall and descend upon Isolf, but the thought faded in a heartbeat for the kin was tiring, he could see. She pushed onward, her joy in the flight boundless, but Raef tapped the side of her neck to steer her back over land. They climbed once more, this time up above the slopes on the southern side of the valley and landed on a ridge between two summits. Across the way and beneath them, the bowl was aglow with the light of the funeral pyre, but Raef turned away from it and let the darkness of the mountains fill him.

Raef put a hand on the kin's rib cage and felt her heart beating there. The pulse was strong and sure but the lack of meat on her bones and her faltering flight knit Raef's chest with concern.

"You are not well. Tomorrow we will find you a good meal." Raef patted her shoulder and sat down on the narrow crest of the ridge. Below him on both sides the ground dropped away in steep cascades of stone spotted with snow. The kin folded her limbs close and settled next to him. "I know you do not care for moss. Perhaps birch bark would suit you better?" She blinked her bright eyes and Raef laughed. "No, no, you need meat. A nice, fat pig would do." Raef leaned against her and she rested her nose on his knee. "You may have to settle for some leggy hares and a barrel of fish."

A pair of wolves struck up a distant song, their voices carrying in the empty, windless night. Raef closed his eyes and listened until they grew quiet.

"I do not have enough men. Twenty-one swords will not win

the walls of Vannheim." Raef leaned back and looked at the stars, seeing the shapes of the bear and the bow and the longship, trying to imagine the night sky empty of stars. "But time is against me. If I wait, gather more men, strengthen my shield wall, the Einherjar and the giants may go to war before I am ready. Ragnarök may come while I sharpen my sword in this lonely valley, and my cousin will sit in my father's chair while the world of men falls."

The stars listened to Raef in cold silence and the kin closed her eyes, leaving Raef to hope that the light of a new day might give him answers.

ᚠ ᚠ ᚠ

The newly risen sun showed Raef one thing. The kin was dying.

Her eyes were dull, the sunset colors muted and listless. She seemed unwilling to rise, to stretch her wings, and the heartbeat that had seemed so strong under the moon was now slow and hesitant.

"Tell me what to do, skeiflyng," Raef said, whispering her true name. His toes were numb with the cold, his hands longed for the warmth of a fire, but all was forgotten when he understood the extent of the kin's weakness. "It is not fair, that you have saved my life so many times, but have come to me too late so that I cannot save yours."

She responded to the sound of his voice by lifting her head off the rock, but only for a moment.

Raef felt tears sting his eyes, tears of frustration mixed with grief. "Must I lose you, too? Am I to be stripped away until I have nothing left?" Raef pulled her head onto his lap and bent over it. "I do not know how much more I can bear."

Raef stayed with her, unmoving, until the end. She lingered through the day and endured the bitter watches of the night, and she saw the rising and passing of the sun one last time. Only when the mountains grew purple and drew tight their mantles of deep shadows in the fading twilight of the second day did she breathe her last.

Raef, his hand on her chest, felt her heart go still, felt her shudder into quiet death. He kissed her between the eyes. "Sleep now, beautiful one, and dream of your home in the sky."

As if heralding the smoke-colored kin's death, a coil of clouds wrapped themselves around Raef's ridge and snow began to fall in thick, heavy flakes that soon coated Raef's shoulders and hair. He might have lingered, might have watched the snow cover her body, might have waited until the storm passed and descended to the valley with the morning light, but there was nothing to keep him.

"Enough. Enough," Raef said to the snow and the grey eyelids that covered the sunset eyes. "I have been gone long enough." And so he trudged down from the ridge, through the tree-covered slopes, across the rushing, snow-capped river, and up to the eagle's nest, arriving dressed in frost and snow to face the bewildered faces of those he had left behind. The men watched as he went to stand by the fire, he who had flown away on a creature of legend and returned on foot two nights and two days later.

It was Vakre who came to him, a question in his eyes, as Raef felt the heat of the fire sink into his chilled skin.

"I am well," Raef said in answer to what Vakre did not ask. "I have not eaten nor slept since last you saw me, but I am well enough." The words, though, seemed to sap him of what strength remained in his muscles, and he was glad to feel Vakre's strong arm take hold of his. "She may have been the last of her kind and now she is dead. She came here for me and I think it killed her." He had left his grief on the mountain, locked it away so that he might only look forward, ever forward, and not back where despair waited for him.

Raef looked into Vakre's eyes. "But I know how to win the Vestrhall."

The thought had come to him on the ridge. He could not have said when, but by the time the kin had breathed her last, it was firmly planted in his mind, an ember, a delicate thing that he must protect and cherish, something secret that would slip away if he did not take care.

"Rest," Vakre said. "Eat. And then tell me."

THIRTEEN

T HE SHIP HAD been left to the whims of the tide, rising and falling on the slick green rocks, sharing a berth with pieces of driftwood that bumped ceaselessly up against the shore. The hull bore a few scrapes and scars, visible now that she was in low water, but from Raef's distance she appeared to be seaworthy. High tide would tell.

Vakre was already climbing over the sheer strake, and Raef stepped from rock to rock until he, too, could pull himself over the side and onto the wide, smooth planks of the deck. The funeral pyre meant for Visna was still standing, a forlorn thing dusted with snow, and Vakre set to work disassembling it in order to clear the deck. Raef walked to the stern to examine the rudder and was glad to find it in working order. Together, they lowered the grey sail and bundled it up to carry back to the nest to be greased with animal fats as protection against the wind and snow.

"No oars," Vakre said. "But we have plenty of pines to work with."

"The Allfather has given us good ropes," Raef said, fingering the fine cords made of seal skin. He knelt by the mast and opened the ballast hold. It was filled with a few large, flat stones and one fine iron anchor.

"She is small," Vakre said.

"She is enough." Raef caught Vakre's glance. "She has to be enough."

"And what of her?" Vakre gestured over Raef's shoulder.

Visna stood yet on land, reluctant to venture closer to the ship that had carried her from Asgard. Her arms were hugged tight across her chest and even from a distance Raef could see her brow was furrowed by a frown. She had followed Raef from the nest willingly enough when he told her he meant to claim the ship from the tides, but the sight of it had stilled her curiosity.

"Everything hinges on her," Raef said.

ᚾ ᚾ ᚾ

The hot fat glistened on Raef's palms as he worked his hands across the weathered woolen sail. Down in the valley, men were at work felling the six young spruces he had chosen to fashion oars from, and still others were maneuvering the small ship off the rocks now that the tide was up. Theirs was a cold, bone-chilling task, and they would return soaked and grumbling, but the fire waited and Vakre had promised each man who braved the icy fjord the best cuts of meat from the pair of deer they had taken that morning. As for Raef, he would have preferred to work with bear grease, but the deer fat would do, and he was glad of the labor.

Rufnir worked from the opposite end of the sail, his one hand useless for anchoring ships or cutting trees, but sure and practiced at the job at hand. They coated the sail in silence, each caught up in the rhythm of a task they had first learned as children, and by the time Dvalarr returned to report that the trees were down, there was only a small section left ungreased. Leaving Rufnir to finish, Raef wiped the fat from his hands and descended into the valley to show them how to make oars.

They had few woodworking tools between them, but Dvalarr

had produced a file from a pouch at his belt, and another man a chisel, and Raef had converted a borrowed knife into a makeshift draw knife that he could use to shape the wood. The trunks were split into pieces Raef could work with and the bark was removed, and then Raef settled down on a stump with a long piece of smooth spruce and began the slow task of drawing forth an oar from the wood.

For two days Raef worked the wood, leaving the valley only to sleep a few hours each night, returning with the sun. He ate when Vakre brought him meals, drank from the river when he was thirsty, and inhaled the scent of spruce with each and every breath. In the end, he had six crude oars, rough things made from rough tools that he might have scorned once. But they would take him the length of the fjord if the wind failed to fill the sail and for that they were most dear.

With Dvalarr's help, the oars were carried to the nest and set before the fire, alongside the sail, thick now with cold fat.

"She will hold ten oars," Dvalarr said, brushing the wood dust from his hands. "Should we not make more?"

"Four more oars would go to waste, as would the time spent to make them."

Dvalarr nodded, accepting this, but there was confusion on his face for Raef had shared his plan only with Vakre. The Crow moved away, his shaven head bristling with new hair, and Raef looked across the nest, through the mire of smoke and sparks, and found Visna.

The Valkyrie was watching him, arms wrapped around her knees, the sword that was no longer hers set by her feet. The blade was unsheathed, and though the day was bright, the metal was dull and dim, as though a darkness was buried deep within it.

Raef approached Visna and held out his hand, but did not offer any words until she, with hesitation in her eyes, took it and came to her feet.

"Will you come with me?"

"Where?"

"To my home by the sea under the setting sun."

Visna frowned and Raef led her to the edge of the nest.

"She floats." Raef pointed down at the fjord. The small ship was anchored just off shore, motionless on the smooth surface of the water

"You cannot think to make her into a warship. She will not hold even this many men."

"I do not intend to make war with her. And she need carry only six."

Visna's frown deepened, her blue eyes dark and her brows drawn close. "You mean to sail to your home, to your cousin, and then what? Throw yourself on his mercy?"

"I mean to make an offering."

"Of peace?"

Raef felt the corners of his mouth turn up in a smile. "I will explain, but you must promise to listen to all I have to say before giving me your answer." Visna nodded, though her face was now shadowed with suspicion, and so Raef unraveled the knot of his plan to her.

She listened in silence as he had asked, but her face grew tempestuous with each word, and when he had finished speaking, she was rigid with fury.

"No." Visna spat out the word with contempt. "I will not." She turned on her heel, but Raef reached out and pulled her back. She lashed out as though to strike him, but Raef caught her wrist and forced her arm down. Visna snarled but went still. "You would dishonor me and complete my father's punishment. I should never have trusted you." She twisted away and this time Raef let her go, but not without calling after her.

"Dishonor, no. I would give you fame. I promised you the world of men would know your name, that the skalds would sing of you. Take this chance and live forever, or cower and die unremembered." Raef's words went unanswered. She did not turn, did not slow her step, but Raef had not expected her pride to give way in that moment. That would come later, if it came at all, and only after she went to war with herself.

And so Raef waited. Outwardly, he was patient. He ate a meal with the men. He helped fill water skins from the river. He sharpened his sword. But on the inside Raef was a knot of tension and he could think of nothing but Visna and whether the words he had chosen might sway her.

She came to him at last with the rising of the moon. A low, sad song rose up from one of the voices around the fire, a song that spoke of a lonely death far from home. The voice was joined by two more and the song swirled with the smoke as Visna approached. Raef was seated at the edge of the firelight and she was nothing more than a whisper of boots on stone. Raef stood to face her, questions threatening to flood from his mouth, but he held his tongue and waited.

"You will need to carry these for me." Visna held out the sword of dark steel, waited until Raef grasped the hilt, and then plucked a knife from her belt and rested that in Raef's other palm. Then she was gone as quickly and quietly as she had come.

FOURTEEN

RAEF CLOSED HIS eyes and listened to the beating of his heart in the dark. The five men were silent except for their breathing and the cramped space had grown warm with the heat of their bodies and the smell of their sweat. Raef shifted his shoulder, trying to maneuver away from Vakre's knee, which dug into his ribs, but doing so pressed his face up against Dvalarr's boot, so Raef shifted back again and focused on the sound of the water around him.

As a child, more than once that sound had lulled him to sleep after a long day on the waves and under the sun, but there would be no sleeping now.

Above Raef, a foot tapped once, twice, and then the faint glow of firelight trickled down to cast the faces around Raef in shadow in place of darkness. Though he could see none of it, Raef knew well enough what the scene above looked like.

The torch at the prow had been lit, sending light jumping over the small waves of the dark fjord. Ahead of them, the shore would be growing closer, though it would be hard to see where the water ended and the land began. But someone, somewhere on that land, would be watching and be first to witness something astonishing.

The eyes on land would see a small boat gliding across the deep waters, they would see the torch, a fearless beacon calling to the shore, blazing at the prow, but most of all, they would see a figure standing by the mast.

She would be small at first, but golden, and then, as the ship drew ever closer, the firelight would pale and grow dim in the shadow of her radiance, for Visna the Valkyrie had come to the Vestrhall.

Grim-faced and hard-eyed, Visna had donned the golden gown in a cove out of sight of the walls of the Vestrhall just as the sun slipped below the horizon. She had shivered a little, bereft of furs and cloak, but she had refused the woolen blanket that Raef had offered her, instead throwing back her shoulders and raising her chin in rebellion against the cold. She had raked her fingers through her hair, then swiftly plaited a few tresses and pulled them back from her face. Last of all, she slipped the rings on her fingers and settled the heavy necklace over her slender collarbones. The arm ring she had worn since her arrival aboard the funeral ship now came off over her wrist and she had handed it to Raef with reluctance. He had not asked her to remove it and he could see the sorrow it caused her, but she had insisted.

A close inspection would reveal dirt at the hem of the dress and a slight tear in one of the sleeves, but in darkness and lit by fire, Visna would be a vision to slacken jaws.

"I do not need to tell you what you look like," Raef had said.

"Must I smile shyly and look down at my feet?" The scorn had been plain in Visna's voice.

"No," Raef had said. "You must be extraordinary and irresistible and unlike anything he has ever seen. Be fierce and proud and they will believe you have been sent from the gods."

Doubt crept into Visna's face. "Will your cousin believe?"

"He will want to believe it, and he will want you, and in the end that is all that matters. Consume him with desire so that he does not think twice about a small boat left behind in the dark."

And so they drifted to the shore, their small ship bringing an offering, a bride sent from Asgard for Isolf Valbrand.

The first voice rang out across the water to challenge the boat's sudden and strange appearance, and Raef, tucked into the corner of the ballast hold along with Vakre, Dvalarr, Rufnir, and Eyvind, felt that challenge in his bones. There was no turning back now.

"Name yourself, stranger."

Above them, all was silent on deck for a moment and Raef held his breath as he listened for Visna's answer.

"Where is Isolf Valbrand?" Her voice was clear and strong and Raef could hear the defiance in it. "Where is he who shall have my heart?"

The silence that followed this was even longer and Raef could imagine the confusion among Isolf's men.

When an answer did come, it was a new voice, deep and commanding, but not without hesitation.

"Again we say, name yourself."

"I am Light-Bringer, I am Sun-Singer, I am Storm-Rider. I have seen Valhalla and the heart of Yggdrasil, and I come from Odin, Allfather."

By this time, Raef could hear commotion on the pair of docks that jutted out into the fjord between the walls of the water entrance.

"Do you come in peace, lady?" The deep voice was perplexed now.

"I come leashed to fate and with purpose that shall not be denied. Bring me Isolf Valbrand."

"Will you not come ashore, lady?" The warrior's voice was full of genuine doubt and deference.

"I will wait and you will not touch me." Visna let a snarl taint the edge of her smooth voice and Raef could imagine the men on the docks with readied ropes to capture the ship. A moment later, her foot tapped once more against the deck, a signal Raef took to mean that Isolf was being fetched from the top of the hill.

In his mind's eye, Raef took the path up the hill with the messenger, passing the blacksmith's forge, the small market hung with drying skins and the ever present smell of smoked fish, up and up to the stone steps that led to the door of his father's hall. His hall. It seemed an interminable wait before at last he heard the voice he had been waiting for, the voice that had taunted him in the darkness as his village burned and his men died, and then taunted him in his dreams ever since.

"Lady, will you not come in from the cold?" Raef could hear the smile in Isolf's voice. His cousin was pleased with what he saw.

"Are you Isolf Valbrand, the great war leader?"

"I am." The smile was growing wider.

"Then I bring you greetings from the Allfather."

"And what does the Allfather say?"

"He says the lord of Vannheim has earned more than a wooden chair and the company of savage warriors. He says the lord of Vannheim must rise above the rest and have a woman worthy of him."

"The Allfather is generous. Let me welcome you to Vannheim."

The boat shifted slightly and Raef heard Visna walk to the sheer strake. Then came the sounds of rope securing the small ship in place. He heard her climb over and land gently on the dock.

"Will you not give me your name?" No doubt Isolf had taken Visna's hand in his.

"I am Visna and I am your fate."

The dock thrummed with footsteps and the voices of those who had gathered at the shore began to fade away. The light that filtered down between the boards of the deck jumped, then grew faint as the torch was removed from the prow, leaving the five men in darkness once more. But not alone. A gentle tread of feet told Raef that at least one guard remained to watch the water. He was pacing, no doubt trying to ward off the night's chill, which meant there was no fire lit on the shore to warm hands and feet. When it came time to creep from their hiding place, whoever was out there would not be night blind.

Raef waited, trying to measure time, but his mind would not release the image of Isolf slaughtering Finnolf Horsebreaker and Uthred of Garhold, of fire and smoke rising above the walls of the Vestrhall as Raef's people died and he did nothing to save them, and so all sense of how long they had been waiting was lost. He raised his head from where it was nestled among the limbs of the others and straightened his shoulders and neck as best he could, though he had to hunch to avoid smacking his skull on the boards above. Raef closed his eyes and listened. The guard had slowed his walk. His movements to the end of the dock had become less frequent, but the tread of boots now came to Raef and he nudged Vakre, then fumbled in the dark for the edge of the board that marked the hatch to the ballast chamber. The boots paused at the end of the dock while Raef waited in agonizing silence for the man to turn his back once more.

Vakre, crouched now next to Raef, tapped him on the shoulder to signal he was ready, and when the telltale shuffle began, Raef raised the hatch and climbed from the hold with deft, quiet movements. Not looking to see if Vakre was following, Raef sprang forward and launched himself off the prow just as Vakre's knife whirled past him. The blade imbedded itself in the warrior's back at the same moment that Raef landed and caught hold of the man's shoulders. The warrior tried to suck in air, staggered, and Raef lowered him to the dock without a sound. Crouching next to the dead man, Raef's gaze darted around and only when he was sure that the docks and shore were deserted did he get to his feet and signal for the others to follow. Vakre, perched on the sheer strake, a second knife in hand, grinned, his teeth catching the moonlight, and Raef felt a shiver of anticipation race across his skin, as though the wolf inked on his shoulder was stirring and preparing for battle.

Dark and fluid like a swarm of creatures from the deep, Dvalarr, Eyvind, and Rufnir crawled out of the ballast chamber and over the side of the boat. Vakre fetched his knife from the dead man's back, and together they paced the length of the dock until their feet crunched on the pebbly shore.

The village lay before them in darkness. Some homes were charred and empty, remnants of the night of Isolf's betrayal. Others were whole and smoke drifted from their roofs, but Raef heard nothing, no music, no laughter, and he wondered if his people shuttered themselves against Isolf and his men out of fear or spite.

The Vestrhall was out of sight, up the hill and around the bend, but Raef could not resist staring up at where it lay for a moment, then with a nod at his companions, he headed west along the curving wooden wall.

The small western gate was no more than a door carved out of the timbers that formed the wall. Beyond it, the hills rose in earnest, dwarfing the mound the Vestrhall held dominion over. The gate was little used, being too narrow to allow passage of goods and animals and, since it led only to the hills and the sea beyond, it was impractical for those who wished to travel to the rest of Vannheim.

But for Raef it was a gateway for a boy eager to explore, to test his aim and his new bow, to roam in search of hidden places only he might know. The hills between the Vestrhall and the sea had been Raef's first retreat. And so it had been simple to sketch a crude map of the area for the rest of the men, to show those who had not come by boat the easiest path that would skirt around the walls and take them to the thick pines that waited thirty paces from the small gate.

Raef slowed his steps as he approached the gate and signaled for the others to halt, then he crept forward until he could see the door and the horizontal timber that barred it. Two men stood there, illuminated by a single torch in a bracket by the door. One, lean and sharp-nosed, picked at his teeth with a splinter of wood. The other was large, his neck nearly as thick as Raef's thigh, but less alert than his companion. He leaned against the wall, arms crossed over his belly, his chin resting on his chest. Each man was armed with an axe and Raef guessed more than one sharp knife he could not see. Neither was known to Raef, but he had not expected his cousin to trust Vannheim warriors to guard the gates, if any even lived yet behind the walls. The men on watch would no doubt be those who had followed Isolf to Vannheim or the men from Silfravall who had made false promises of friendship to Raef.

Raef retreated to the others and held up two fingers, then gestured to Vakre, who understood and hefted a knife once more from his belt. Creeping forward, he let the blade fly at the lean warrior, but the man shifted his stance and the knife lodged in the wall a finger's breadth from his throat. Startled, the warrior lurched sideways, fumbling for his axe, a shout stuck on his lips, as Raef and the others attacked at full speed.

The big man was slow to move, but his eyes widened at the sight of Dvalarr bearing down on him and he managed to get the haft of his axe free in time to take the worst of Dvalarr's swinging blow. But his evasion knocked him squarely into the smaller warrior, who was retreating from Raef's sword. The lean man buckled against the unexpected jolt, his neck snapping back with violent force. He pitched over into the snow and tried to crawl away from death, but Eyvind's swinging axe caught him in the neck and he jerked once, then lay still.

The brute was fully awake now, and grunting as he swung at Dvalarr. From behind, Vakre hacked into the man's upper arm, nearly severing it, just as Raef slashed into his ribs, and the axe fell from the warrior's hand. His momentum carried him forward, a growl of rage etched on his face, but he collapsed at Dvalarr's feet. His muscle and fat kept him alive, though, and he writhed on the ground until Dvalarr swung the larger of his two axes and took off his head.

Raef was already at the gate and lifting the timber from the iron cradle it rested in. Throwing the log away, he pulled the door open until it stuck in the drift of snow that had blown up against the wall. Raef whistled sharply and the pines came alive as the men waiting there brushed through the branches. The greeting was silent and grim as they clustered inside the wall in the light of the single torch. Eyvind and Vakre hauled the dead men out of sight into the forest and Raef looked from face to face of the warriors gathered around him.

"Any men yet loyal to me within these walls will not stand against you. Strike down any who wield a blade and resist. Except my cousin. The man with the red hair is mine."

They moved up the hill as quickly as they dared, keeping clear of the main gate. It irked Raef to leave Isolf's men at the gate alive, for they might present a threat from behind once the fight at the top of the hill broke out. But he dared not waste the lives around him in a drawn out, bloody skirmish at the gate, a skirmish that would draw men down the hill and leave Isolf out of reach. They had to concentrate their strength on the hall.

The first person they encountered was a drunken warrior pounding on the door of a small house. He turned at the sound of so many feet, but his bleary, bloodshot eyes did not seem to comprehend what he saw, for he began to ask if anyone had a skin of ale, a question cut short by a blade drawn across his throat. Leaving the body where it fell, they moved on.

They had reached the midway point of the climb when Raef

stopped in his tracks and ducked behind a skin stretched out to dry. Lights bobbed ahead of him, revealing ten figures striding down the hill. Others around Raef followed his lead and sought hiding places, but Raef knew it was futile, for they were too many and the dark shadows too few. No doubt the warriors were headed to the gate to change the watch and there was little chance they would not stumble upon Raef's men.

A hand on Raef's shoulder nearly earned a blade in the ribs, but it was only Rufnir.

"Go," Rufnir said, indicating the path ahead. "We will keep them dancing long enough for you to get up there." Before Raef had a chance to reply, Rufnir slid away, five men trailing close behind him, and moved to the east toward the wide wagon path where the warriors were sure to see them.

Raef moved on, sprinting now and followed by his pack of remaining warriors, his ears straining to pick out the first sounds of battle below them while his eyes looked only ahead. The shouts came quickly, surprise, questions, then an indistinguishable clamor as the steel song began.

The steps to the hall were watched by a single man, but his eyes were focused solely on the woman straddling his lap and his hands were engaged far from his axe as Vakre rushed forward and silenced him. Blood gushed from his throat and the woman screamed and twisted away in desperation, but Vakre caught her up and held her fast with a hand over her mouth. Raef stared hard at the woman, who was a stranger to him, and put a finger to his own lips. She nodded vigorously beneath Vakre's grasp and Raef signaled her release. She fled into the darkness and disappeared down the hill.

Raef turned his attention to the door. Behind it, the hall was bursting with music and drunken laughter and Raef would have given an eye, like the Allfather himself, to see what went on behind the walls, to see if Visna was safe, if Isolf was enamored.

"Will she get him out?" Dvalarr asked in Raef's ear.

"We do not have the time to wait anymore, Raef," Vakre said.

Raef hesitated, his heart pounding madly, threatening to leap out of his chest as he saw his chance at taking Isolf grow smaller. Visna was meant to draw Isolf out, to lead him away from the crowd and into Raef's waiting arms. But the commotion down the hill was growing louder and Raef did not doubt that Rufnir was surrounded on all sides, for men from the main gate would surely have joined the fight. The six warriors would not last long.

"Then we will go in and fetch him."

There was no telling how many men Isolf had with him in the hall. A good number might be too drunk to fight, but Raef had only fifteen men left at his back.

"Follow me."

Raef led the men around the side of the hall, seeking a different entrance that would mask their arrival.

The kitchen yard was empty. The well and the chicken coop and the winter garden were as Raef remembered, but the moment he stepped from the shadows, the kitchen door opened and a short, round woman stepped out, dusting flour from her hands as she went. Raef was caught out in the open and she squinted to make him out.

"No scraps to be had here. Best try the front door." She sounded tired and one hand went to her hip, as though it pained her. Raef didn't move. "You hear me? Be off with you."

Raef smiled to himself, for she had said those words to him as a boy often enough. "Perhaps you could spare something."

She went still and Raef could see her frown. "Who are you?"

Raef meant to answer, meant to give his name, but he found he could only step forward and let the lights of the kitchen wash over his face.

Darri's hands went to her mouth and Raef could see her sway.

He stepped forward and caught her beneath the arm. She stared up at him, her pale blue eyes wracked with shock and tears.

"You died."

"Is that what he says?"

Darri wrapped her arms around Raef's waist in a sudden embrace, the top of her head tucked under his chin. Raef smiled and kissed her hair.

"It is good to see you, Darri." Raef took her hands and drew back so he could look down into her joyful face. "But I must not linger. There is work to be done here."

Darri's joy vanished, replaced with malice. "You mean to kill him."

"Yes."

The old woman wiped the tears from her cheeks and nodded, as firm and resolute as a warrior. "Half of them are so drunk you could dunk them in the fjord and they would hardly notice."

"How many are warriors?"

Darri thought for a moment. "No fewer than thirty."

"Armed, all?"

Darri snorted. "If they can tell their swords from their spoons, yes."

An urgent gesture from Vakre reminded Raef they were running out of time. He smiled once more at the old cook and then hurried into the kitchen, the men at his heels.

The passageway between the kitchen and the hall was narrow and stuffy and smelled of bread. Raef opened the door to the hall a crack, shedding a beam of light onto the faces behind him, and peered out.

Isolf sat at the high table, a horn of mead in one hand and a handful of Visna's golden hair in the other. She was perched on his lap, her back to Raef, and Isolf was laughing, head thrown back, that mane of red hair shaking with his delight.

The source of his mirth was in front of the high table. There, two men were stripped to the waist and smeared in remnants of food. The fats and oils from the pig carcass hanging on a spit over a low fire now gleamed on their skin and they were locked in a half-hearted, drunken hold, each trying to force the other to the ground. One turned and vomited over his shoulder, causing Isolf to laugh once more, and then the man slumped against his opponent's chest. Together they went down in a heap and the men at the tables banged their fists and hollered for a new bout.

To Isolf's right, a dark-haired woman sat stiff and straight in her high-backed chair, eyes staring out into the hall, but from the hard line of her jaw and the taut muscles in her neck, Raef was sure that Aelinvor, daughter of Uhtred of Garhold and conspirator in her father's murder, was blind to the antics of the men, all her attention focused on ignoring Isolf and Visna beside her.

Raef removed Visna's sword from his belt and handed it to Dvalarr.

"See that this gets into the lady Visna's hands."

The Crow gave a solemn nod and then Raef turned his attention to the rest of the men huddled in the passageway. They were all sweating, their faces gripped with the knowledge that the real fight was just ahead. Raef knew each name, each place called home. Even the men of Axsellund who had chosen to remain were no longer strangers and their faces were etched into Raef's skull.

"Some of us will go to Valhalla this night. Know that whatever the outcome, you have earned your place there. The gods will rejoice to see you," Raef said, his voice nearly drowned out by the deafening noise in the hall. "May Thor bring strength to your arms and bite to your blades."

Without another word, Raef turned and strode into the hall. For a moment, his presence went unnoticed. But in that moment, the slaughter began.

Isolf was the first to react as Raef plunged his sword into an unsuspecting warrior, but Visna was faster. The Valkyrie twisted and jabbed her elbow up into Isolf's throat. Isolf roared, reaching blindly for her, and the chair toppled over backward. Visna landed on top but Isolf's strength was great and they grappled for a moment before Isolf broke free and scrabbled away from Visna. Finding his feet, Isolf, his face red with rage and drink, drew his sword and screamed for men to gather close. Visna snarled and might have gone after him, but Raef, separated from Isolf by more than one table, shouted at her to fall back. Dvalarr reached her side and extended the dark sword to her, hilt first. The Valkyrie grasped it, spit in Isolf's direction, and then dropped back to join Raef's line of warriors as they began to wreak havoc in the hall while men scrambled for weapons and cover. Aelinvor, unarmed and not practiced in the ways of a shieldmaiden, withdrew to the closest wall and looked for protection from Isolf, who made no move to reach her side.

The first man's death had been met with angry roars, but Raef's sword carved into unprotected flesh twice more before any resistance came his way. A pair of warriors lurched at him, one barehanded, the other thrusting with a knife. Raef ducked the first and sliced upwards into the second. His blade stuck and was ripped from his grasp as the man fell to the floor. Raef let the sword go and drew his axe as he spun to face the first, empty-handed man again. A quick chop and a kick to the chest sent the man reeling, blood spurting from a gash in his wool shirt.

A new opponent launched himself at Raef with a knife. Raef braced and then was swept sideways as Eyvind and a warrior plowed into him. Losing his balance, Raef went to his knees. The knife slashed down. He caught the blade on his leather forearm guard, then hacked his axe up into the man's groin. The axe wedged into flesh and bone while the man screamed, then ripped out through his belly. A spray of guts and blood spattered across Raef's face. He blinked and moved on as the screaming warrior fell to the floor.

The hall was awash in blood by the time Raef reached the far wall. Behind him was a trail of savaged corpses. Isolf had retreated into a corner near the high table, surrounded by a cluster of warriors, but the rest of his men were dead, dying, or too drunk to have noticed the fight.

"Isolf!" Raef's voice thundered across the hall as he leapt upon the closest table. He held out his arms, both streaked with the blood of other men, his axe haft slippery with gore. "I am the wolf song." He began to walk the length of the table, his gaze fixed on his cousin's red hair and fearful, enraged face. Behind him, Vakre followed off his left shoulder, Dvalarr the right. "I am the serpent breath." Each word rang off the timbers of the vaulted ceiling. When he reached the end of the table, he paused. "I am your death."

Isolf pushed past the warriors that huddled around him. His sword was clean, the steel still bright, but he did not return it to its scabbard. He looked up at Raef from under his thick eyebrows.

"If your men stand down now, they will live," Raef said.

Isolf hesitated, then gestured to his sword, unstained by blood. "And me? If I draw no blood this night, what of me, cousin?" There was something still of his old charisma, his easy nature that had tamed Raef's suspicions.

"Nothing you say or do can change your fate now."

Isolf's face hardened with resignation and he nodded over his shoulder. One by one, the warriors sheathed their weapons and, on Raef's orders, disarmed themselves. Vakre watched with sharp eyes while two of Raef's men collected armfuls of swords and axes.

"There, cousin," Isolf said. "You have won the hall." He smiled, a tight, anxious thing that showed the frayed edges of his composure. "Shall we go to the yard and I will place my head upon a block for you?"

"No, cousin, there will be no swing of an axe. Not for you." Raef hopped off the table and strode close to Isolf. He circled around him once, then came to stand in front of him, so close their noses almost touched. "The eagle is coming for you, Isolf."

Now the fear ran rampant over Isolf's face and he shuddered visibly. His jaw moved up and down as he gaped at Raef. "Please," he whispered at last.

But Raef turned away, heedless of the plea. He called out for Isolf's men to be ushered from the hall and Isolf was bound hand and foot and roped to one of the tree-shaped pillars.

"Crow." Raef beckoned for Dvalarr. "Take those who are not wounded. Secure the gate. Find Rufnir. If he lives."

Only when the Crow left the hall did Raef exhale a long, trembling breath, and only then did the battle-lust seep away from his bones and his heart. In Dvalarr's wake, a flurry of movement caught Raef's eye as Aelinvor stirred and reached for a knife on the high table. Vakre snatched her wrist just as her hand closed around the antler handle. She strained against his hold for a moment, her heartbeat visible in her neck, her nostrils flared wide as she debated her course of action, and then she released the knife. Vakre led her around the high table and sat her down on the bench closest to Raef. She held her head high still, but her gaze was cast down and her knuckles were white from the force of her own grip as she clutched one hand to the other. Raef could not help but think of how young she was and he wondered if she would have rather stayed in Garhold.

But it was Aelinvor who spoke first, her eyes rising to meet his. "What will be my punishment, lord?"

"Is that what you want? For me to strike off your head? Leave you as carrion for crows?"

She rose in a stiff, jerky motion, anger brightening her face. "What I wanted was power. For you. For me."

"Your ambition killed your father."

"His death freed me."

"Freed you for what? To sit beside my cousin and watch men drink until they cannot see straight? To see Isolf lust after another woman after making promises to you? To know that your ambition had cost you much and earned you nothing?"

Aelinvor was shaking now and Raef could see he had struck upon the truth. "You are to blame, Raef Skallagrim. And when you kill me, my death will sit heavy upon you."

"Perhaps I will let you live, and then we will see who is burdened with guilt." Fear crept into Aelinvor's face for the first time and Raef had her taken to a sleeping chamber where she might be kept under watch until he decided what to do with her.

In her absence the hall was quiet and Raef closed his eyes for the briefest of moments, but he could not savor his victory, not yet.

Three of his men were badly wounded. One clutched at a hole in his side, but his pale, sweaty face told Raef he would not last. Another had taken a blow to the face that had loped off half his jaw. He was conscious, though just, and seemed oblivious of all, even the pain. He kept attempting to get to his feet, and did not understand why others were trying to keep him still. The third might live, Raef thought, though he would never heft a weapon again. His right arm was slashed to ribbons and the wounds went deep, severing tendons and ligaments. Eyvind was already at work wrapping the arm with cloth, but it would need stitching.

Raef looked to Vakre, who bore no sign of injury, but the son of Loki's face was full of concern.

"Are you hurt?"

Raef looked down at himself and saw that he was coated in blood. He wiped a hand over his face but only succeeded in smearing more sticky wetness across his forehead.

"I do not think any of it is mine. Come, we must see to the village," Raef said. Leaving Eyvind and Visna to watch over Isolf and the wounded, Raef and Vakre stepped out into the night once more.

The village was quiet but for the frantic barking of a single dog. Raef hurried down the stone steps and began to wind down the wagon path. As he went, he noticed that a few doors were cracked open and he thought he caught glimpses of faces staring back at him.

He found the Crow kneeling in the middle of the wagon path halfway down the hill. Several bodies lay in the snow and dirt around him. Dvalarr straightened at the sight of Raef.

"Some were taking for the hills," the Crow said, gesturing down to the main gate, whose torches flickered in the distance. "Gullveig is keeping them under guard. The rest are dead." A fresh cut ran down Dvalarr's face but the Crow seemed not to notice. He glanced down to the body at his feet and Raef followed his gaze.

Rufnir was still alive. His breaths were shallow and forced, his eyes unfocused, though they settled on Raef as he knelt on the ground beside him. A wound gaped high on Rufnir's inner thigh, the flesh matted and tangled with cloth. A dark stain had already spread down to his knee and the snow beneath him was crimson. His right hand clutched the handle of his sword and the left stump reached for Raef as he choked on thick blood that spilled down his chin.

Raef took Rufnir's stump and held it close to his chest, his eyes stinging with tears as he watched his old friend die.

"The Vestrhall is ours, Ruf," Raef whispered, his voice hoarse. "You have fulfilled your promise."

Something that was either a smile or a grimace of pain twitched on Rufnir's blood-streaked face and Raef could only hope his words had been heard and understood.

"Go in peace and sail the seas of Asgard. The gods await you. As does your brother." Raef leaned over and placed his lips on Rufnir's forehead. When he drew back, Rufnir had gone still and his blue eyes stared at nothing. Raef closed the eyelids and detached the hunting horn that hung from Rufnir's belt. He got to his feet and handed it to Dvalarr.

"Sound the horn, Crow. The people must learn what has happened. They must know it is safe."

Raef retreated to the stone steps, flanked by the surviving warriors. Dvalarr raised the horn to his lips and let loose a single note that drove into the darkness. The Crow let the sound die away before repeating it and the second note was still echoing in the hills when the first, curious, wary faces drew near.

Fathers kept close grips on their children. Mothers looked over their shoulders with nervous eyes. But as more and more of them caught sight of Dvalarr, his bald head shining in the torchlight, of Vannheim warriors they knew by name and face, and, last of all, Raef standing tall at the top of the steps, the crowd began to murmur and the worry on their faces turned to wonder.

Raef opened his mouth to speak, but a voice in the crowd shouted first.

"Hail, Skallagrim!"

Others echoed the call, their voices rising in the dark until Raef raised a hand, asking for silence.

"There is a Skallagrim in Vannheim once more." This was met by a loud cheer. "The traitor and oathbreaker Isolf Valbrand will be put to death. And then we will mourn our dead and rebuild what we have lost. I ask only one thing. That you might forgive me. I was blind and Vannheim suffered for it."

"We are the heart of Ymir," Dvalarr roared.

"The heart of Ymir!"

"Blood of the giant!"

After the crowd quieted, Raef descended the steps and greeted his people by name. Hoyvik the blacksmith was there, though he walked only with the aid of a wooden crutch. Old Grandmother, who had inked the wolf onto Raef's shoulder, smiled, her pale, delicate hands steady and cool against his blood-stained cheeks. Then came a young woman, Hanna, the sister of Finnolf Horsebreaker, and, but for the length of her brown hair and the slenderness of her arms, she could have been mistaken for the young captain who had been slain outside the walls on the night of Isolf's treachery. There was no sign of her young sister, Tolla, and Hanna's eyes were full of grief. Ulli the steward was as trim and tidy as ever, though it seemed to Raef the neat little man had lost the sprightliness in his step.

Many faces were missing. Engvorr the ship builder and his sons. Yorkell the silent captain who could not grow a beard. And still others who had made their homes inside the shelter of the Vestrhall's walls.

A cask of mead was brought to the steps and cups were passed until each man, woman, and child shared a drop in remembrance of the fallen, and then the crowd faded back into the night.

FIFTEEN

THE EARLY DAWN light found Raef at the shore of the fjord. It slipped across the water in streaks of silver and gold and danced along the shoreline, nipping at Raef's toes before racing onward. A pair of gulls wheeled overhead, searching the waters for fish beguiled to the surface by the sun.

Raef sat on a boulder, flat and smooth across the top and marbled through with bolts of deep red stone. For him, it was a different morning, one that seemed far away and long ago, a morning like this one. Siv had perched on the same rock and waited for the ice bear to come to the fjord to drink. He could see her smile, see the way the sunlight brightened her hair, see the peace and joy she felt in that simple moment.

Sleep had eluded Raef in the few hours before the dawn. His chamber was as he had left it, for Isolf had claimed the lord's chamber, but Raef had not lingered there, choosing instead to begin the work of cleaning the hall. One by one, he dragged the bodies through the carved doors, heaping them high at the base of the stone steps. He collected the refuse from Isolf's final feast and threw it in the rubbish pit to be burned. And then he sluiced bucket after bucket of water over the bloodstained floors.

When sounds of life came from the passages and chambers

adjoining the hall, Raef knew the servants were stirring and so he slipped away in search of further solitude.

It was only later, with the rising sun and the memory of Siv warming him, that Raef at last began to feel relief. It was done. Once a funeral pyre was built and burnt to send Rufnir and the others to Valhalla, all that remained was bringing death to Isolf.

ᛗ ᛗ ᛗ

Isolf had been stripped to the waist and he shivered now in sight of gods and men. The bare, rocky hilltop faced the sea and the winter wind bore down on the gathering without mercy. Waves crashed against rock below them, filling the air with the sharp smell of salt spray, and beyond the shore, the grey sea was spotted with shafts of sunlight that pierced the dull clouds.

Raef stepped close to Isolf, whose skin was prickled with the cold. "Tell me, Isolf, of Siv's fate."

"Will you grant me an easier death if I do?" Isolf bore a tattoo on his chest of a bear, a reminder of his ancestry. The blue ink stood out against his pale skin.

"No. But you can go to your death with a clear heart if you speak."

Isolf's face twisted in a grimace and he spat at the ground at Raef's feet. "So weak. So sentimental. You were never fit to rule here." Dvalarr jerked the ropes that bound Isolf's hands and growled a warning, but Isolf went on. "I earned this hall. You do not know what it is to be born in isolation, hidden away from the world and forced to scratch out a reputation, a name for myself, when it ought to have been my birthright as the only worthy descendent of Tyrlaug."

"No, Isolf. You earned this death."

"Please, cousin," Isolf said as he was forced to his knees, his defiance turning to panic. A rope around each of his wrists ended in a loop and, though Isolf struggled, Dvalarr's strong grip forced him to extend his arms and the loops were hooked on a pair of sturdy, forked branches that had been driven into the frozen ground and wedged there with piles of small rocks.

His pleas were lost on Raef, and so Isolf began to thrash against the bonds that held him, his face twisting with fear and snarling hatred.

"You will defile yourself if you shed the blood we share," Isolf shouted, his voice whipped across the hilltop by the wind. "The gods will curse you."

Raef removed his heavy fur cloak and the thick woolen tunic until he stood before Isolf in breeches and a thin woven shirt. He began to roll up his sleeves, never taking his eyes from Isolf.

Isolf strained against the ropes. "You will answer for this when you reach Valhalla. I will kill you with every rising sun." The watching crowd drew back from Isolf's fury, but Raef stepped close and leaned in so that he might whisper in Isolf's ear.

"This is all that shall pass between us, cousin. It is not my fate to see you in Valhalla. You will never have a chance at eternal retribution."

Isolf pulled away and looked at Raef with new dread. Raef stood straight once more and drew his chosen knife, a long-bladed thing.

"The Valkyries will shun you, Isolf. The Allfather will not have you when I am through. I mean to make you scream. All men know that he who screams while facing the blood eagle will never sit at Odin's table."

Isolf barred his teeth and clamped his mouth shut and Raef could see him shudder with the force of it.

Raef stepped behind Isolf and gripped the other man's chin, forcing him to look out at the cold, indifferent sea.

"Look your last upon the world."

The knife sank into Isolf's back, near the base of his spine.

His right hand still holding tight to Isolf's neck, Raef ripped up through flesh, dragging the blade with tender slowness up and up until he had carved open the length of Isolf's back, exposing white bone. Under his grasp, Isolf writhed and twitched, but his mouth remained closed.

Raef, his hand slick with blood, traded his knife for an axe, then shifted his right hand to Isolf's shoulder and brought the axe down with a swift, short hack, severing the first rib from Isolf's spine. Isolf lurched against the ropes, his weight sagging more and more as Raef worked up the spine, the ribs cracking with ease under the sharp steel. When he reached Isolf's shoulders, he reversed direction and did the same on the other side. When he had finished, Raef flung the axe to the ground, reached into the wound with his bare hands, and began to bend the bones backward out of Isolf's back, opening up the cavity of Isolf's chest. Some broke off clean in his hands, snapping with horrific noises that had more than one witness shuddering at the sight. Others splintered and held, the jagged shards of bone jutting out of the skin at terrible angles.

The scream came when Raef shoved his hands inside the ruin of Isolf's core and found the lungs nestled there. Isolf's head snapped up, the cords of his neck bulged, and his voice ripped unbidden out from between his teeth, and Raef could feel the agony throbbing through him.

Raef drew forth one lung with both his hands, felt it move in his palms, felt Isolf's life beat against his skin as the man trembled beneath him. Raef placed the lung gently on Isolf's shoulder blade and then returned for the second one and set it opposite the first. There they pulsed and then went still and Isolf died.

Raef stared at the bloody work his hands had done and at the crimson gore that had dripped to his elbows. He closed his eyes and took a deep breath and knew satisfaction. Not triumph. But satisfaction ran through his veins unlike any he had ever known and with the exhalation of that breath, he released all the anxiety that had gnawed at him, all the anger that had burned within, all the grief over the loss of so many.

Raef dipped his forearms into a waiting bucket of water and scrubbed off the congealing blood. Dvalarr waited with his cloak and tunic, but Raef knelt first before Isolf, whose weight now hung fully from the wooden supports. His face had slackened at the moment of death, but the terror and pain were still there, and Raef was sure he saw something like shame, for in the moment that he screamed, Isolf would have known his fate. When he stood, Raef looked to Dvalarr and Vakre.

"Leave him for whatever scavengers will claim him."

Raef lingered on the hilltop as those who had gathered to watch the execution began the descent through the forested hills and returned to the Vestrhall. The wind had grown faint, as though the savage gusts had been sated by the blood spilled there, and he watched the ever-changing sea, the shifting colors and shadows, as he waited for the last footsteps and subdued voices to fade away.

When at last there was silence, Raef turned away from the view and saw that Vakre was still there, as he had known he would be.

Raef gestured to Isolf's corpse. "Is Vannheim avenged?"

"Only you can decide if Isolf's life was payment enough for what he did."

Raef thought for a moment. "For the lord of Vannheim, it is enough."

"And for Raef Skallagrim?"

"It will never be enough," Raef said, thinking of Siv, of Finnolf, Rufnir, and Uhtred of Garhold, and all the others who had died because of Isolf's treachery.

"Death does not bring life, Raef," Vakre said. His voice was gentle, his eyes shadowed with his own private sorrow.

Raef sighed. "I know."

To the west, the sunlight shattered the cloak of clouds, spilling over the surface of the grey sea, but there on the rocky hill, snow began to fall.

"Come," Vakre said. "They will be waiting for you."

Raef nodded, but they had not gone far when a rustle of wings drew Raef's gaze up to the bare branches of an ash tree. Two black ravens had just come in to land. They snapped their beaks at each other as they shuffled their wings and feet, but then they grew still save for their black eyes.

Raef exchanged a glance with Vakre, wondering why the Allfather's ravens followed him so persistently. One raven croaked then took to the air, the other waited, staring at Raef, then followed its brother. But the second flapped once, twice, and then plummeted to the earth.

It was dead before it landed, Raef knew, and still he watched it for some sign of life, not daring to believe that one of Odin's ravens was dead. The creature was even more massive when spread out on the snow, one black wing stretched wide, the other tucked close to the body. The eyes stared up at Raef still, but they were unseeing now and held only darkness in their glassy depths.

Raef looked to Vakre, whose face mirrored the muddle of emotions that churned in Raef's belly. Then Vakre knelt and stroked the glossy feathers of the bird's head.

"Your watch is done, friend," Vakre murmured. The fire that spread from Vakre's fingers took hold of the raven's tail feathers first, and for a moment Raef could imagine the bird soaring once more, tail blazing, but then the flames smothered the raven's body, burning hot and fast and reducing it to ash in a moment.

"How long do you think we have?" Raef asked as the smoke curled up and away on the air.

"Not long. The death of Odin's ravens heralds the coming battle." Vakre shivered, but not from cold, and Raef could see a fleeting shadow of loathing pass across his face. "My father is pleased."

↑ ↑ ↑

They feasted that night in remembrance of the dead. The villagers and those who served in the Vestrhall filled only half of the hall's long tables, but when they followed Raef's lead and raised their glasses and their voices and hailed the dead, there was strength and gladness in them, the sharp edges of sorrow softened by solidarity and mead.

Word of Raef's return had spread outside the walls and by the time the second cask of mead was opened, men who made their homes in the first ring of hills around the Vestrhall had joined them, bringing bright faces and good cheer and freshly butchered venison. A few had brought their older children as well and in time the hall swelled with laughter. Raef drank and ate and laughed with them and felt a measure of peace.

He honored those who had made the journey from the eagle's nest with words and riches, bestowing arm rings and jeweled belts and fine cloth from the Vestrhall's stores. He praised Eyvind and the others from Axsellund, spoke of Torleif's loyalty, of Visna's courage. The Valkyrie was much admired. She had replaced the gown of gold and sunsets, ruined in the fight in the hall, with simpler, borrowed clothes, but she was still a vision, radiating strength and poise, and the crowd gasped and murmured in awe as Raef told her story.

"I am a poor skald," Raef told Visna after.

Visna laughed. "A dog would have howled better, but it will do."

"And I have kept my word. They know your name and will not soon forget it."

Visna had smiled at that, her pale skin flushing with pleasure, but Raef was glad to see that she also took pleasure in Dvalarr's humble courtesies toward her and in the laughter of the children as they chased the dogs here and there.

Eyvind came to him late in the night, when the mead had soaked into the skin of many and more than a few pairs of eyes were fighting off the shroud of sleep. The hall was filled now with the noise of quiet contentment as the warrior from Axsellund came to sit at Raef's side in the place vacated by Dvalarr.

"Lochauld wishes to make his oath to you," Eyvind said. He spoke of the youngest of the surviving Axsellund warriors, a blonde bearded youth who was quick with a spear.

Raef was quiet for a moment, then nodded. "I would be glad to have him."

"Svor and Engred wish to return to Axsellund. They have families there." Eyvind seemed about to say more but he shifted in his chair and held his tongue.

"They shall have whatever they require to make the journey," Raef said, eyes on Eyvind, who gazed across the hall. He waited but still Eyvind hesitated. "And you? What is your wish?"

At last Eyvind looked at Raef. "I, too, will return." Raef said nothing, sensing that Eyvind had more to say. "Whatever comes of Torleif's death, whether the lady Oddrun has a boy child, the bravest boy since Ketill Kringa himself, or a girl, as strong and wise as Frigg in Asgard, whether this child can cling to Torleif's legacy or a warrior rises up to claim what is ripe for the taking, I owe it to Torleif to be there. It is my home."

"Then you will not make a claim for yourself."

Eyvind shook his head, confirming Raef's assumption. "Ruling is not in my nature. But more than that, I do not think I could bear to sit where he sat."

"Then I wish you well, Eyvind. Know that you are always welcome in Vannheim, that you will always have a friend here."

Eyvind nodded his thanks and pushed the chair back from the

table. He signaled for the other three Axsellund warriors to come forward. Svor and Engred gave thanks, which Raef gave them in return, and Lochauld took a knee, eager to bind himself to his new lord. Raef was about to raise him up, to say that could wait for another time, but the great doors at the far end of the hall creaked open and a gust of cold air that made the closest fire cower brought Raef to his feet instead, a warning beating in his heart.

The figure in the doorway was tall and narrow, all sharp angles and gaunt bones even under the weight and bulk of a heavy furred cloak, but so steeped in the shadows of night still that Raef could not make out a face. The hall had gone quiet and it seemed to Raef that he could hear the smoke swirling off the flames of the torches and the fires.

"Hold, stranger," Raef called out, breaking the silence. "Give me your name or you may come no further."

"Ever do you greet me with harsh words, Raef Skallagrim. Are we not friends yet?" The voice thrummed into Raef's bones, smooth and strong and tinged with amusement. It was a voice not soon forgotten.

The Far-Traveled reached up and pulled back his hood, then stepped into the light of the hall. The distance between them seemed to dissolve into nothing, for Finndar Urdson's blue eyes were piercing and forceful and not to be ignored.

"I have learned to be wary of those who claim to be my friend," Raef said. He nodded at Dvalarr. His boots thumping across the floor, the Crow strode to the Far-Traveled's side and searched him with rough hands. The Far-Traveled endured this without complaint, indeed, without removing his gaze from Raef.

When Dvalarr finished, his hands coming up empty, Finndar spread his hands before him, palms up, a beseeching, questioning gesture from most men that looked far more like a demand when expressed by the half god.

"You are welcome to the Vestrhall, Finndar Urdson."

The Far-Traveled smiled and began to pace the length of the hall, coming to a halt when he reached the high table.

"It seems I have interrupted a joyous occasion, forgive me."

"What little joy you see has been cruelly bought with blood and sacrifice."

The Far-Traveled's face betrayed nothing. "Then what I have to say can wait." His words and his eyes were at odds, the one meant to put the villagers at ease, the other, fixed on Raef, flashed with warning.

Raef walked around the table, seizing an empty cup and filling it with mead from a jug as he went. At this gesture, conversation returned to the hall as men and women whispered among themselves and Raef was glad to feel the weight of fewer eyes upon him.

Raef handed the cup to the Far-Traveled. "A drink, to revive your limbs after long travel."

Finndar took a long swallow and handed it back to Raef. "A drink, for the king named in Vannheim."

This caused a stir as Raef, too, took a drink, draining the cup. He wiped his mouth with the back of his hand, then called for Ferrolf, a man skilled with the flute, to play music and take minds away from the Far-Traveled's presence.

Three songs later, Raef could bear it no longer and he slipped from the hall, taking a passage lined with heavy tapestries and little light. After rounding a corner, Raef halted and waited until the footsteps of Finndar Urdson caught up to him. In the dim light, the Far-Traveled's blue eyes grew grey, as a sea in a storm.

"What brings you to my home?"

The Far-Traveled studied Raef for a long moment. Behind them, the hall was a blur of noise, the distinct sounds of Ferrolf's flute melting with voices and laughter.

"Is it true you have seen Jötunheim?"

Raef felt his nerves sharpen and push to the surface. "What have the runes told you? Surely you, above all, would know the words I will speak before I have even formed them."

If Raef's irritability ruffled Finndar, the half god did not show it. "Have I offended you?"

"I risked the lives of my friends to keep you free from the Palesword's clutches. You gave me nothing in exchange." Raef felt his cheeks flush with anger.

Now the Far-Traveled's face darkened and the blue eyes narrowed. "I gave you a means to free your friends. You were satisfied at the time."

The flush turned to shame but Raef was not prepared to give in yet. "You might have offered a warning," Raef shouted, his voice caught in the tightly knit threads of the tapestries.

Finndar looked away, his gaze burrowing down the length of the passage. Whatever he saw there brought a heavy sigh up from deep within his chest. He looked at Raef once more. "I told you once that I speak what I am given. Sometimes, it is as though my own hand is carving the runes on Yggdrasil. They are branded into my mind, as sure and certain as the beating of my heart. This makes me glad, even if the words are grave, for there can be no doubt, no questioning. But more often I am given smaller, slighter things. A glimpse of a dawn-shrouded forest cloaked in mist, the call of a proud eagle as he rides the setting sun, the scent of honey carried on a summer wind. Tell me, Raef Skallagrim, what would you make of such things?"

"But you suspected." The anger had fled from Raef.

"There is much I can suspect. I saw pain and sorrow in your future, Raef, but is not this so for all men and women? I would have done you no service by giving you such a feeble warning as that. But it is true, then, that you have walked the land of the giants."

The Far-Traveled's words summoned the vast darkness of

Mogthrasir's hall, the deafening roars of Hrodvelgr's arena, the mind-numbing, heart-eating oblivion of the labyrinth. Reflexively, Raef stretched his hand against the solid stone wall at his back, as though somehow the cold, rough rock might anchor him. He swallowed and tried to work saliva into a mouth that had gone dry. Then Finndar Urdson blinked and Raef felt the weight of the words lift.

Raef gestured to the narrow passage around them. "Come, I can offer you better than this."

They retreated to a grove of bare apple trees awash in moonlight and guarded by the eyes of four stone wolves. The night was still and far milder than the recent days. The brutal winds had subsided and it seemed to Raef that the stars shone with new warmth.

Raef stroked the nose of one of the prowling wolves, a habit formed in boyhood. "It was Alfheim I visited first," he said. The wolf stared back at him with blank eyes. Raef turned to the Far-Traveled and the story of his strange journey tumbled forth, halting in places, as fast and fluid as a racing river in others. Through it all, Finndar listened with little expression and when Raef finished the account, he was quiet for a long time.

"But that is not all," Finndar said at last. "I can see it in your eyes."

It was more difficult to speak of Isolf's betrayal, for that anger was fresh, and that grief and pain far more devastating than any injury he had suffered while away from Midgard. But the tale came out under Finndar's watchful eye until there was nothing left to tell.

Clouds had drifted in so that the stone terrace and the sentinel wolves gleamed less brightly, but the snarling teeth and raised hackles were all the more fierce for their newfound shadows.

"What now, then, son of Urda?" Raef asked. "I ask again, what brings your feet to my door?"

For the first time since crossing the threshold of the Vestrhall,

Finndar looked uncertain. To Raef's eyes, he sank deeper into the shadows, or perhaps the shadows came to him.

When he spoke, though, the uncertainty vanished. "The Hammerling is coming for you." Finndar looked to the stars, as though the Hammerling's horde of warriors and their spears might be found marching across the sky. "He grows weary of chasing Fengar through the wild and looks for different prey."

The news did not surprise Raef. The bonds between them had been brittle to begin with and were now severed beyond repair. "Has he stopped to think why Fengar eludes him still?"

At this, the Far-Traveled's mouth turned up at the corners but he kept his thoughts to himself.

"So the war will come to Vannheim and the west at last. Once before you came to the Vestrhall and brought tidings of war. The lord of Vannheim did not live long after."

It was not a slight or an insult or meant as a condemnation against the Far-Traveled, who was only a bearer of news. But Finndar's face drained of all color and he clutched at the snout of one of the stone wolves with both hands. His breaths came short and fast and Raef saw beads of sweat form at his hairline. Only with effort did Finndar regain his composure, and even then he retained his grip on the wolf.

"Are you well?" The son of Urda seemed not to hear Raef, who took a step toward the other man and tried again. "Forgive me."

At last Finndar stirred and the look that he gave Raef was full of fear. "The fault is not yours, nor mine. It was not your words, son of Einarr, but something else, something I have felt before and know that I will feel again. It reaches out, from darkness, through darkness, its grip both trembling and terrible, and leaves me stripped bare, bereft of all that I am, have been, and will be. And then it passes, vanishing like a moth in the night when the last flame is blown out."

"What does it mean?"

"I have walked these lands for years beyond count. My memories are packed away in here," Finndar tapped a finger against his skull, "all the fates of men, the knowledge, the things I have seen, all kept tidy and neat and under lock and key, as a steward might. Endless vigilance is required to maintain this tidiness, to maintain my mind. If I let it, my brain and what it holds would grow restless and wild." Here Finndar looked at Raef. "You know that the twilight of the gods is at hand, you have not said it, but I can see it in your eyes. You know that Black Surt will soon rise and stride forth and swaddle the golden halls of Asgard in fire and blood." Finndar turned again to the stone wolf. "Before Odin succumbs to the jaws of Fenrir, before Thor and Jörmungand destroy each other, before Yggdrasil crumbles, before, even, Hati and Skoll catch the moon and sun, and before the cock crows to summon the Einherjar to battle, my mind will break. Those tidy bundles of memories will burst free, savage and cruel, and, unfettered, unchecked, they will rampage through my mind and heart and destroy me with both the speed of a swift, violent death in battle and the agonizing creep of a slow, debilitating illness. This is my fate, Raef Skallagrim, and it will come soon enough." Finndar was pale when he finished speaking, but calm.

"I cannot imagine," Raef began, but Finndar cut him off.

"No. No, you cannot imagine." The sharpness of his voice was countered by the hint of a weary, gentle smile. "Nor would I want you to." The Far-Traveled heaved a sigh.

"Let me show you to a chamber where you might rest," Raef said.

"Is there not more you would say, son of Einarr?" Finndar's voice betrayed genuine surprise. "Are there not questions you would ask of me?"

"The Hammerling comes. If Odin wills it, Hauk of Ruderk, my father's murderer, will be with him. That is all I need to know."

SIXTEEN

BRANDULF HAMMERLING WAS coming, but it was not that impending clash that occupied Raef's mind, to his surprise, as he finished clearing the last remnants of Isolf's presence from the Vestrhall and began the work of rebuilding the homes that had burned. His dreams were not of Hauk of Ruderk, that false friend, nor of the Hammerling and his righteous anger, but instead his sleep was filled with stranger things, things unlooked for and only half-remembered when he opened his eyes, things that turned to ash and dust and smoke when he tried to stretch his mind out to meet them. Always, he felt as though something was just beyond his reach, and his mind and body grew restless.

When he wasn't hauling timber or laying turf on newly raised roofs, Raef slipped into the forest outside the walls. He carried no weapon but his axe, for he was in no mood to hunt, and he found himself walking the hills, from the high, bare saddles to the deep, hidden valleys. Some days he traveled far afield, striding over snow-covered ground without rest. Other days he lingered, once by a frozen pool that would surge with snow melt in the spring, once at the shore where he tasted the salt sea in the air, and many times he did nothing but sit within a ring of old, weather-beaten stones whose carvings were too worn to make out, but always he returned with the cover of darkness and always Vakre watched for him from the stone steps of the Vestrhall as Raef made his way up the slope. The son of Loki asked no questions and Raef offered no answers, but it was the Far-Traveled's eyes that Raef felt on him as the mead and meal were shared each night.

The Far-Traveled stayed for three days and three nights. At first the people of the Vestrhall were wary of him and whispered to each other when he passed by, but by the third night he was telling tales by firelight to an enthralled audience. When the hour grew late and the hall had emptied save for a few men debating the merits of seal skin rope, Finndar returned to the high table.

"It is time I left Vannheim," Finndar said. He refilled his cup with golden mead and sat in the empty chair to Raef's left.

Raef nodded, for the Far-Traveled's restlessness was not unexpected. "The men from Axsellund are prepared to make their journey home. They leave in the morning and I am sure would welcome your company."

"The dawn is too far off," Finndar said. "Though I would be glad of friends upon the road, I must be satisfied with only the stars." And yet the son of Urda hesitated and stared into his cup of mead.

"You were right," Raef said. "There is a question I would ask you."

Finndar's smile was that of a young man, quick and easy, and he gestured for Raef to ask.

"We spoke of what lies ahead. This grim knowledge has settled in my heart, but sometimes I wonder if I should keep it there." Raef waved out at the hall. "My people, they live as they always have. They hunt, they fish, they farm, they build. And they see many tomorrows yet ahead of them. Do I owe them the truth, or is it right to keep silent?"

It was not the question the Far-Traveled had expected, Raef

could see. The laughing eyes had grown subdued as Raef spoke and Finndar Urdson no longer looked young.

"It would change their lives to know the truth, Raef. Are you prepared for that burden?"

"What I am prepared for makes no difference. I would do what is right."

Finndar drained the last of his mead. "I think you know already what I will say. You must decide for yourself. This question is not one I possess an answer to." The Far-Traveled got to his feet, cast a glance at Vakre, who relaxed with his feet up on the table next to Raef. He nodded once to the son of Loki and Raef wondered what might have passed between them while they were beneath the same roof. But then Finndar's gaze came back to fix on Raef and he felt the blue eyes pull him in. "Farewell, Skallagrim. You and I will not meet again."

And then he was gone from the hall.

ᛋ ᛋ ᛋ

Four days of confinement had muted some of Aelinvor's defiance, though Uhtred's daughter bore no visible burden of guilt on her slender shoulders, or if she did, she hid it away under a careful face when Raef came to visit her at last on the morning after the Far-Traveled's departure. Her keepers said she had eaten and drunk what was given and had suffered her isolation without complaint, indeed, without many words at all. But he would not have called her meek, no, and she greeted him with poise.

Silence followed their initial words. Aelinvor seemed content to wait for Raef to continue, but he found he still did not know what to say.

"The strength of your ambition was always clear to me, Aelinvor. You were not shy about conveying your desires to me. But what I do not understand is when it all became worth your father's life."

Raef had meant to sit, as she was, next to the fire, but instead he paced between the pair of windows that overlooked a grove of trees. "He was proud of you. Your happiness and future were important to him."

"Have you ever set about a task and found that, through no fault of your own, the desired end result was out of reach and impossible to attain?"

Raef frowned. "If I believed that, I would still be starving in the wilderness, not standing once more in my hall."

Aelinvor smiled a little. "These are the words of a man. A man who has been bred and trained and taught to be as he is. Imagine instead that you were raised without all this," she said, gesturing to the walls around them. "That your place in the world was much smaller and that no one had any expectation of you but that you would exist as you have always existed. Imagine that you wished to rise above your small place, but that you do not have the tools to do so."

"Then I would make persistence my friend."

"As I have done." Aelinvor's voice sharpened and she stared hard at Raef. "It is no easy thing for a woman to make her mark upon the world. I have done little but weave cloth and ride horses and comb my hair for most of my life, and no one, least of all my father, has expected me to do more than this. I have chafed, Raef," she said, desperation creeping in, "chafed against this since I was five years old."

"I have known many women who are not content with weaving."

"Not all of us, even men, take to the blade and the warrior's way with ease. I did not have the skill or the talent or the teaching to become a shieldmaiden. And I have always meant to rule, Raef, not fight."

"Why? Why do you wish to rule?"

Aelinvor frowned. "Because I am suited to it. More so than many men."

"Torrulf Palesword was suited to be king. You know his fate. But let us not speak of that," Raef said, as Aelinvor began to argue. "Let us speak instead of your father. You were his only surviving child. Would Uhtred have cast you aside and named someone else to rule Garhold after his death? I think not. Many women have ruled after their fathers and have done so without murdering them. Bryndis rules well in Narvik, despite her youth, and long has Kollumheim prospered under Leska, lady of the sapphires. They have earned places of respect on their own merits. You sought to bind yourself to me, or even Isolf, in an effort to raise yourself above others. You are driven by greed."

Aelinvor had gone still and stiff, and her voice was cold when she spoke again. "You will not cause me to regret my actions. I would have wielded the knife that killed my father myself, if need be."

Raef looked at her, so young, so beautiful, and felt the strength of her resolve as though it had struck him. "I will grant you a quick, clean death, for your father's sake." He pushed off the window ledge he had been leaning against and left the room.

But in the end Aelinvor denied Raef. She was found at dusk, a ragged cut carved into her wrist by a dull piece of iron meant to stir the logs in the fire, her blood emptied across the fine cloth of her gown, her determination and persistence carrying her into death, for it would have been no easy thing to end her life in that manner.

A funeral pyre was built in haste, small and not fitting for the daughter of a lord, but Raef did not feel he owed her anything else. He watched the first flames lick against the oil-slick logs and then turned away as the heat flared and left Aelinvor to burn alone as the stars unveiled in the darkness.

By dawn, all that was left of the daughter of Uhtred was a hint of smoke in the air, and it was under this shadow that Raef said farewell to Visna.

The Valkyrie had been restless, Raef could see even in his distracted state, since the victory over Isolf, and so he was not surprised when Visna came to him in the early light of the morning dressed for travel. She said nothing at first, and went to look out his window, but her mind was clear to him and so he said it for her.

"You mean to leave."

She turned from the glass and nodded, her hand going to her belt and the sword that was sheathed there. "I must not fail my father. There must be nine Valkyries. Too long has he been without me."

"You know you do not need my permission," he said, glad to see his teasing bring a smile to her face.

"No, but I find that I would not wish to part without knowing that I have your friendship."

"You have it."

"And I would thank you." Visna paused, her uncertainty forming furrows in her brows. "You have shown me something of this world that I did not understand and because of you my heart is not so darkened with fear as it was." She stepped close and placed a light kiss on his cheek, then brushed past him and out of his chamber. Raef listened to her footsteps fade and then, from the wide ledge outside his window, watched her descend the hill. A tall, broad figure approached her, the bald head gleaming in the sunrise, a horse in tow, and Raef watched with a smile as Dvalarr offered the mount, which Visna quickly refused only to be won over by Dvalarr's humble doggedness. She took the reins and the Crow watched until long after she was out of sight.

SEVENTEEN

THE HAMMERLING'S BANNER fluttered outside the gates of the Vestrhall on the sixth day after the Far-Traveled's departure. A single rider carried it in the afternoon breeze and braved the spear-lined path to reach Raef. Warriors had come from across Vannheim, boys no more than fourteen, men with grey beards and gnarled hands, women with long plaits in their hair, each answering the summons to defend their home, and now the walls were flanked with their makeshift shelters and the smoke of many fires.

The rider was not a stranger to Raef and he was sure the choice of Eirik of Kolhaugen was no accident, for the Hammerling was no doubt aware that they had struck up a friendship while fighting together in the east. But Eirik's strong face displayed no warmth or eagerness at seeing Raef.

"Greetings, Eirik, son of Brynvald."

Eirik did not return the greeting. "Raef Skallagrim, I name you oathbreaker." The lord of Kolhaugen's voice rang out and gripped the ears of the watching warriors. "I charge you with treachery and deceit and summon you to answer for these crimes. All this do I do in the name of Brandulf Hammerling, lord of Finngale and king above all."

"How does the Hammerling wish me to answer?"

"As you must, as dictated by the laws of gods and men. You swore your life belonged to the Hammerling and now he will take it as punishment for the breaking of your oath."

"Be gone, cur," Dvalarr shouted from beside Raef. The Crow took a step forward as though he might leap at Eirik and Raef put a hand on his shoulder to restrain him.

"To demand my life, the Hammerling himself must come for it. This is the way of both gods and men, as he well knows," Raef said.

"I speak with his voice and authority. I am the mouth of his justice and in this way I am the Hammerling."

Raef moved past Dvalarr and Vakre and went to Eirik's horse, placing a hand on the brown mare's bridle. "Then I have no choice but to give Brandulf a name in exchange for the one he has given me. I call him coward, for that is what he is if he will not speak to me in person, if he will not demand payment in the flesh."

For the first time Eirik's stony countenance shifted, betraying a hint of sorrow. But his voice remained as sharp as a blade. "With these words you have sealed the death of those around you. All of Vannheim will pay for your arrogance and betrayal."

Raef lowered his voice and spoke now only for Eirik's ears. "Do you condemn me so easily, Eirik?"

"What has passed between us will not sway me."

"I would never ask you to be disloyal, but I will not let my friend depart without offering him meat and mead. Will you refuse?"

Eirik's eyes lost their edge and at last Raef could see that he bore the Hammerling's task with an uneasy heart. "No," he said quietly, "I will not refuse."

Dvalarr was loath to leave Raef with Eirik, but Raef was firm and Vakre soon led the big man away, leaving Raef and Eirik alone in the hall.

Raef prodded at the lone fire with a half-charred branch, sending up a shower of sparks, then added a pair of fresh logs. After he was sure they would catch, he turned to the jug of mead that had been set out on one of the long tables and poured two cups full to the brim. Eirik hesitated when offered one, but then took it and drank as Raef did the same.

A long silence followed the draining and refilling of their cups, and then both men sat on benches facing the fire. Raef spoke at last.

"Your brother is dead."

Eirik glanced up from the fire. "I come to you as your enemy, Skallagrim, and now you tell me this."

"I did not kill him." Raef spoke of the battle in the gorge and the avalanche, of Fengar's flight and Alvar's death. "Your brother's mind was gone, his body not far behind. We sent him to the gods as best we could." Raef watched Eirik's face but could read little there. "Is that what you would have wanted?"

"He was my brother."

"That is no answer. The enmity between you was known to all."

Eirik sighed and ran a hand through his wild, pale hair. "Yes. I hated him with all my heart and he felt the same for me. I often wonder which of us is to blame for that. Some part of me wishes I might have been there to see his end, perhaps even to bring death to him myself, but then I see him as the boy he was and I grieve for the both of us, for the brothers we might have been." Eirik paused and then changed the subject. "The Hammerling outnumbers you," he began.

"Let us not speak of the Hammerling," Raef said.

"For the news of my brother," Eirik said, trying again.

"You owe me nothing. For my part I am sorry that I do not know you better, and that it comes to this between us."

"Yes," was all that Eirik said.

They drank another cup of mead, the golden liquid warming

Raef's belly, and whether it was the drink or the heavy silence that prompted him, he could not have said.

"I do not know if I speak now as a friend or an enemy, if these are words that you would want to hear, or if you will dread the knowing of them, if I am warning you or filling you with fear, but I find that I must speak." Raef took a swallow of mead and studied Eirik as the other man frowned. "The twilight of the gods is at hand." Eirik met Raef's gaze and did not look away. "Believe me or not, as you see fit. Tell the Hammerling if you wish, or keep this to yourself, it matters not to me."

"The time of the wolf," Eirik whispered.

"Yes."

"Then why fight? Why bring suffering to your people when instead you might fill their last days with peace? He will spare them if you give yourself up."

"Will he also hand me a sword so that I might take Hauk of Ruderk's life? I have made a vow I hold above all others, and that is to my father and to the gods. Hauk Orleson will answer for my father's murder before the end comes."

They did not speak again of the Hammerling, or Hauk of Ruderk, or the fate of the nine realms. A small meal was brought and shared and they parted after nightfall as friends who will face each other in battle.

"I will ask Thor to strengthen your sword arm," Eirik said in the torchlight at the gate.

"And I will ask the Allfather to shield you."

Eirik turned his horse into the darkness and was soon gone from Raef's sight.

⟨ ⟨ ⟨

"The captains know their places. The warriors know who to follow." Raef looked across the snow-covered ground that would see battle the next day, at the fires that smoked there and the warriors sharing bread and meat. Vakre and Dvalarr stood beside him. The Crow was now inked all over his bald head, the three crows joined by fresh patterns weaving together to form a winged creature that resembled the smoke-colored kin. Vakre was as quiet as ever, but his eyes rested on Raef, rather than the spread of warriors before them.

"I expect the Hammerling just after dawn," Raef said. They had word that the Hammerling's men were just beyond the first ring of hills and the Vestrhall's walls had been crammed to bursting with farmers and fishermen seeking shelter. "If he times it well, the sun will aid him and blind us." Raef turned to Dvalarr. "See that the extra spears are shared among the captains."

Dvalarr nodded and walked off, leaving Raef to confront Vakre.

"Your words blaze unspoken behind your eyes, Vakre. What would you say?"

Vakre walked to the fjord, leaving Raef no choice but to follow. There, the son of Loki spoke. "You do not mean for there to be a battle, do you."

Raef sighed and let his gaze drift to the grey, shifting waters of the fjord. "I should not have tried to keep it from you. I will leave under cover of darkness and make my way to the Hammerling's camp."

"What did Eirik of Kolhaugen say that could convince you of this?"

"He spoke the truth." Raef looked at Vakre. "I broke my oath. I cannot deny that. But more than this, I have sought this fight for a single reason, and I can no longer let that reason outweigh the lives of my people." Raef shook his head, angry with himself. "The vengeance I seek for my father must not cause suffering among the people of Vannheim, and I am ashamed to have let it come so close."

"Would not many gladly lay down their lives to know that you have brought justice to your father's murderer?"

"Yes. But they will lay down their lives soon enough for the gods."

"Giving yourself up to the Hammerling will shame them."

Raef was quiet for a moment. "In the heat of battle, amid the chaos and the screaming steel song, am I certain to come face to face with Hauk Orleson? Will we meet at last and clash swords as we should have done long ago? I do not know the answer to this, Vakre, and this uncertainty is a ruthless companion. If I go to the Hammerling, I will see him there and, if Odin wills it, I will kill him."

"Then let me come with you."

Raef was ready for this. "Eirik says Brandulf will spare my people if I submit to him. But if he does not intend to fulfill this promise, my people will have to fight and they will have need of good men to lead them. Dvalarr is strong, Dvalarr is fierce, and Dvalarr will die for Vannheim, but he is not enough. I will not command you, Vakre, but I ask that you do this for me."

Vakre was quiet and together they watched the gentle waves lap against the shore. "Vannheim will stand," he said at last.

The southern shore of the fjord had sunk into purple shadows and the deep waters were dark and fathomless without the sun to light them. Raef pulled his fur-lined hood over his head.

"It is time."

Vakre nodded and they returned to the camp and the walls. In the growing dark, it was simple enough for Raef to lead a horse unnoticed from the firelight. Around him, voices carried from fire to fire, the voices of warriors who look for a dawn red with blood. Vakre accompanied him across the strip of open ground to the trees, but neither man said anything and Raef did not look back. When he could no longer hear the murmurs of the camp, Raef mounted and rode into the hills.

The Hammerling was farther west than Raef anticipated, but no attempt had been made to mask the presence of his warriors. Once Raef caught the scent of smoke, his first glimpse of fire between the dark, sentinel trees was not far behind. The Hammerling's camp overflowed a narrow glen split down the middle by a frozen stream and Raef approached from a steep descent on the northern side of the camp after leaving his horse among the trees above. He had chosen his path well, for the rocks and heavy underbrush were free from patrolling scouts, and Raef was able to reach the light of one of the outer fires before he was spotted.

He made no effort to stop the four men who wrestled him to the ground and his silence might have earned him a quick knife to the gut had one not recognized him and drawn back in trepidation. A quick argument was won by the one who insisted Raef must go before the Hammerling, though the other three did not hide their disappointment at being deprived of their prize, and he was hauled further into the camp.

Brandulf Hammerling did not at first notice the growing com-motion as Raef was led close. He was bent over a boulder, brush-ing snow from a map drawn on a delicate skin. At his side, a boy pointed at the map and Brandulf answered his questions in a quiet tone. The boy had grown since Raef had seen him last; his shoulders were broader, his chest thicker, but he still had a boy's lankiness and a boy's face, and Raef wondered when Asmund, Brandulf's elder son, had joined his father at war.

"Lord," one of Raef's captors began, but the Hammerling waved him off without raising his head. It was another voice that finally caused him to stir.

"Skallagrim." Eirik of Kolhaugen burst from the growing crowd of men, his face torn between sorrow and relief, his hair tamed for battle and drawn back from his face into a knot at the crown of his head. He pulled up short between Raef and the Hammerling.

The Hammerling straightened, the map dropped and forgotten,

left to curl up in the snow. Even in the dim light Raef could see that the Hammerling was still hale and strong, undiminished by the rigors of battle and the long roads he had traveled. This was a man in his prime.

If the warriors encircling them spoke, Raef was deaf to it. He could hear only the beating of his own heart as the Hammerling came to stand in front of him. The lord of Finngale had grown his beard and taken to splitting it into three braids. He wore a massive black-furred cloak across his shoulders, held in place by a thick gold chain, and he walked without any trace of the injury that had nearly claimed his life after the battle in Solheim.

When he was three paces from Raef, the Hammerling halted and it was then that Raef could at last see his eyes, see the triumph mixed there with something that Raef could only name disappointment.

"You surprise me, Skallagrim."

"Will my people live?"

The Hammerling shrugged, a great rolling of his shoulders. "That depends. Have you left instruction for them to accept me as king?"

"They do not know I am here."

"Then likely many will die." Brandulf beckoned Asmund forward and the boy came to stand at his father's side. The Hammerling rested a heavy arm across Asmund's shoulders. "This war has gone on long enough, Skallagrim. I mean to see it ended. Vannheim must kneel."

Raef swallowed back the bitterness in his mouth. "I ask only that you offer them the choice before the slaughter begins. Many lives might be spared."

"And I should listen to the request of an oathbreaker?" The Hammerling, his voice suddenly full of ire, released Asmund and took a single, menacing stride toward Raef.

Raef did not flinch or break the stare between them. "The oath was mine, as was the breaking of it. Your justice ends with me."

"We shall see." The Hammerling turned away and gestured at Eirik. "Secure him." And it was in that moment, as Eirik of Kolhaugen bound Raef's wrists with rope and his weapons were stripped from him, that Raef saw the face he had come for, the face that filled him with raw fury and bile. Hauk of Ruderk stood to the side, watching, arms folded across his chest.

"There is a traitor in your midst," Raef shouted at the Hammerling's back. Brandulf stopped and turned to face Raef once more.

"Yes, here you are." The Hammerling grinned and the warriors laughed.

Raef, undeterred, went on. "Have you ever wondered why Fengar continues to elude you? How many times has he been within your grasp only to slip away and vanish?"

"If this is some means to plead for your life, you are wasting your breath." But there was a flicker of hesitation in Brandulf's eyes.

Raef, his mind racing across possibilities, continued, his thoughts tumbling only a step before his tongue. "Ever has the lord of Solheim been two steps ahead of you. But deception is not in his blood. And neither does the faithful Stefnir of Gornhald have it in him to weave a tangle of lies. Someone is feeding you false information sprinkled with enough morsels of truth that you are kept in ignorance, just as someone warns Fengar when he ventures too close to the bear's jaws."

"These are dangerous words, Skallagrim."

"You know there is truth in them. I can see it in your eyes."

The Hammerling flushed underneath his beard and snorted. "Then name this foul traitor if you know so much."

A wild thought bloomed in Raef's mind, a spark that seemed to lead him, blindly, into the darkness. Taking a deep breath, Raef took the plunge. "Once, Fengar was your captive. Who set him free?" The Hammerling frowned and Raef went on. "Who fostered the peace between you, who saw the prudence in fighting your common enemy, the Palesword, together?"

Out of the corner of his eye, Raef saw Hauk uncross his arms, his face marred like the sea before a storm. The Hammerling's gaze shifted, sliding across the faces around him until it came to rest on the lord of Ruderk.

"Fear for his life births lies on his tongue, lord." Hauk had smoothed his face over. "Was I not among the first to name you king? Have I not ever been at your side, in victory and defeat? We need a strong king to unite us. Fengar will only divide us further and this I will not bear."

"No," Raef said, his mind seizing upon a thought not yet fully formed. "No, Fengar will do as he is told." Raef swung around to face the Hammerling, one arm still held by Eirik of Kolhaugen. "Imagine that this war is over, the last battle fought. Imagine that you rule from Finngale with a firm grip and with wisdom. You heed the opinions of good men, men you trust, but always every choice is yours. No man will sway you when your mind has been made up. I know you well enough to know this. Tell me, then, what place is there for those who seek to influence the king, who would move in the shadows to see their will done?"

The Hammerling was still. "None."

"And he knows it," Raef said, pointing at Hauk without breaking eye contact with Brandulf. "Fengar does not have your strength of will, does not command the respect you do. He was only meant to appear to rule while others did so in truth."

Hauk broke in, laughing. "You have spun a fine tale, Skallagrim. But your story would have me control the elements, not just a man. The fire at the gathering nearly killed Fengar of Solheim."

"And yet by lucky chance it did not. It was heralded as a sign from Odin. What better way to be sure that a dozen voices would pledge themselves?"

Hauk scowled, his derision at Raef's words plain for all to see. "You cannot," he said to the Hammerling, "believe him. My men have died in your name."

Brandulf looked from Raef to Hauk, then focused on Eirik of Kolhaugen. "Take them both."

Hauk howled in protest but soon he and Raef were both shuffled away and placed under watch beside a small campfire. They sat in mutual hatred and enforced silence until the Hammerling came to them. A hooded figure behind him slipped into the firelight and Raef felt a knot of apprehension grow in his gut as the hood was swept off to reveal Eira. The shieldmaiden gave no sign of recognition and her grey eyes were sheltered from his sight by her downcast lids.

"Eira tells me you have a grievance against Hauk of Ruderk, Skallagrim. A personal one." The Hammerling stood over them, the black fur wrapped close, shielding the glinting gold from the hungry firelight. His voice was carefully measured and betrayed nothing. "Once before you accused someone of murdering your father. You were wrong then."

"He admitted it to me," Raef said.

"Another lie," Hauk said.

Raef lunged at Hauk but was brought up short by strong hands at his collar and his face was shoved into the snow. Raef fought to breathe and only at the Hammerling's command was he let up, though his lips still brushed the snow.

"You do nothing to help yourself, Skallagrim," the Hammerling said. Though Raef could not move his head to see the other man, he could hear weariness in his voice. "You have brought yourself within striking distance of the man you believe was responsible for the plot to kill your father. How am I, knowing this, to believe anything you have said? How am I to know that your warriors are not creeping through the trees at this very moment? How do I know an arrow is not trained on my neck as we speak?"

"I came alone," Raef said, spitting snow as he spoke. "I came to spare my people if I could and to kill him. There is no threat to you."

"What do you call the rumors spreading among my men? What do you call the distrust you have sown? Your death will not wash that away."

"Once you said you would rather have me as an ally than kill me."

The Hammerling was quiet for a long moment and Raef wished he could see his face. "The time for that is long past, Raef, son of Einarr."

"Perhaps, but I am still that man, and you found it in yourself to trust that man's word once, despite the differences between us. I ask only that you trust it again now."

Silence again. Raef waited, straining against the hands of the men who held him down, but the only sound that came was that of footsteps going through the snow. When Raef was allowed to sit up, the Hammerling was gone.

Eira remained. Her dark hair spilled out from within her hood as she leaned over to poke at the fire.

Raef knew he should keep his mouth shut, knew he should not try to delve into the shieldmaiden's mind, for he had swum there once before and had found the dark depths foreboding. But the words were out as though spoken by someone else.

"Why, Eira? What did I do to deserve your betrayal, your hatred?"

"I do not hate you." She looked surprised. "I only saw that you did not have the strength of will to do what needed to be done."

Raef saw Isolf's spine before him, saw the shattered ribs, the pulsing lungs laid out across his shoulder blades. "You might be surprised to learn what I have the will to do."

Eira shrugged as though she did not care. "I have said this before. You are like a dog. A good dog. But only a dog. It is wolves that shape the world."

"And the extent of your treachery?"

She met his eyes briefly, then pulled a long knife from her belt and began to sharpen it. "Do you remember when we rode west from the burning lake? We passed my shieldmaidens and later I told you they had chosen a new leader."

"I remember."

"That was a lie." Her words were as simple as the movements of her hand. "They are as loyal to me as ever and were on their way to pledge themselves to the Hammerling."

"You mean to Hauk."

She ignored this and went on with her task as though there was nothing else to say.

"It was you who set me adrift on that boat. Your shieldmaidens."

She nodded. "You were not supposed to survive."

"Then why not kill me?"

Eira looked up. "Bodies have a way of inspiring revenge. Better that your fate be uncertain."

"And you came back when you heard I lived. All the while communicating with Hauk."

Eira's lips remained pressed together and Raef sensed he would get little else from her.

"I cared for you." The words were foolish and Raef regretted them immediately.

Eira shrugged again. "Would you have me say the same?"

The shame vanished, replaced by a heated anger. "No." Raef hunched his shoulders and drew his knees up to his chest for warmth, his mind on the small knife wrapped against his inner thigh. In their haste and surprise, the Hammerling's men had not searched him with care. He wondered how far he would get before Eira slashed his throat.

The arrow lodged in Eira's neck with such speed and silence that Raef was not roused from his thoughts until the shieldmaiden began to choke on her own blood. A second arrow found one of the Hammerling's guards, then a third, and by then Eira was dead. Raef reached for her long knife and launched himself at Hauk, but he was thrown to the ground mid-stride by the falling weight of the last of the Hammerling's men. By the time he scrambled out from under the dead man, his fingers searching for the knife in the snow, Hauk was out of sight and Raef was seized by hooded figures and dragged into the trees.

Behind them, voices rose in alarm but Raef could only stumble along within the iron grip of his new captors, his hood slipping over his eyes, as they rushed over rough ground. The hill rose before them and up they went, the only sounds those of their feet churning through the snow and their harsh breathing.

When at last they came to a stop, Raef stumbled into one of his captors and dropped to his knees, then righted himself and flung his hood away from his eyes. A pair of shadowed faces stared back at him, both unfamiliar.

"Who are you?" Raef asked, his chest still heaving from the effort of climbing.

"You misplaced your sword."

That voice. Gone, gone to Valhalla. Raef's heart slammed in his chest, the sound of that voice thrummed in his ears, and all else was numb. The faces of the two men before him seemed to fade from sight and Hauk of Ruderk vanished from Raef's mind.

"Lost your tongue as well?" He could hear the smile now, see the laughter in her eyes. His skin prickled and his heart pounded relentlessly, but the rest of him was rooted as deep as Yggdrasil. "It is a fine sword. Perhaps I will keep it for myself."

She stepped from behind a gnarled pine, sending showers of snow to the ground as she brushed through the branches. She was dressed in black from toe to hood, a bow in hand, and the grin faded, but the eyes sparkled still, green, so green, even in the cold light of the moon.

And then she was in his arms, her heart beating against his own, her face buried into his neck, his hands tearing away her hood to reveal the face that had filled his dreams.

"Siv."

She smelled of pine and woodsmoke. Her nose was cold against his skin, her hands wrapped tight around him in a furious embrace. At last Raef released her and took her face in his hands.

"How?"

Siv smiled. "There will be time for that later." She stood tall to kiss him, a quick, light touch, her lips cold on his. "Come, we must go." Taking his hand, she pulled him through the trees, her feet swift and sure in the snow. Branches slapped against Raef, sending shivers of snow across his face. Some landed on the back of his neck and melted, soaking in icy rivulets under his cloak. Brushing the dusting of snow from his eyes, Raef plunged after her, heedless to everything but the feel of her hand in his.

Horses were waiting just over the crest of the hill. Behind them, Raef could hear a swell of voices rising from the narrow glen, but Siv and the two men conferred in low voices and they seemed content to wait. Moments later, a third man burst through the trees from the east, leading the horse Raef had left behind. Strapped to the horse's saddle were all of the weapons Raef had been stripped of in the Hammerling's camp. Laughing, Raef wrapped his arms around Siv once more and, spinning, lifted her from the snow. A moment later, all five were mounted and picking a careful trail through the trees with as much speed as they dared, but rather than head directly west back to the Vestrhall, Siv led them north, following a ridge toward a pair of bright stars that hovered just above the horizon. When the ridge veered sharply right and began a steep climb, Siv turned left and they descended to a small mountain lake, the snow-covered ice a smooth empty surface gleaming bright in contrast to the black of night.

There were no fires and little enough sound or movement, but as they neared the lake's shore, Raef caught sight of warriors and their horses clustered there. The man riding closest to Raef puckered his lips and let out a sharp, three-note whistle, mimicking the call of a mountain sparrow. A moment later, an answering call sounded from below. Not a word was spoken until Siv came to a halt and dismounted, and then it was only whispers between her and a single man whose face was obscured by a deep hood.

Then, without any command uttered or signal given that Raef could see, the warriors mounted and, as though riding a single horse, began to flow along the lake. Caught up in the pack, Raef was swept along and he soon lost sight of Siv. Their path carried them up and down through a series of rough steps in the land, each dotted with another lake in the chain that ran the length of these high plains.

They came to a halt along the last lake, this one the smallest yet. Across the water, steep walls of rock rose out of the snow, the shoulders of one of the tallest mountains in Vannheim. A pair of small buildings, dwarfed by the mountain, were nestled on the lake's shore and it was there that the party of warriors dismounted. The summer farm consisted of two turf-roofed buildings built from stout timbers and meant to house young boys and girls charged with watching the sheep or goats as they grazed the rich grass in the high meadows. Now firmly entrenched in winter's domain, it was clear the only people to trespass here in recent days were the warriors.

Only ten or so men might fit in each building, but they did not cram into either in search of warmth. Instead, each man remained by his horse and each seemed to keep a silent vigil over the tiny lake. Siv appeared at Raef's side and placed a hand on his arm, then nodded toward one of the huts. Inside, three men waited for them. One was the man Siv had exchanged words with, though his hood was now removed to show a wide, solemn face and a head of streaky grey hair. He was not a large man, though he commanded the small room without question, and the gaze that focused on Raef as he crossed the threshold was full of intent.

The interior of the hut was bare but for a single low bench. There was no pit for a fire, no smoke hole, for the farm was warm enough during the long days of summer, but a small lantern set on the bench provided a bit of light that danced across the faces of all those present.

"You are Skallagrim." The grey-haired man's voice was deep and filled up the dirt-floored hut with ease, and yet, for all that, was still soft.

"I am. Will you give me your name so that I might offer my thanks?"

The man considered this for a moment. "You have her to thank," he said at last, nodding his head toward Siv. Then he swung around to the pair of men behind him and continued the conversation they had been having. To Raef's surprise, Siv grinned and, taking Raef's hand, led him back into the open air.

"Now you have met Ailmaer Wind-footed," Siv said. They walked toward the lake, weaving between the unmoving, silent warriors, her hand still tucked in his. "And now you can say you know him as well as most."

"He is," Raef paused, "grim."

"Yes.

"And them?" Raef gestured to the warriors. "Are they under oaths of silence? Does he command their very breath?"

"They understand where their meat and mead come from. They understand what keeps them alive. Earn a place among them and you will not want for anything. These men do not come to him as the most skilled, strongest warriors. But they learn discipline and control and, right now, they are at work."

They had reached the lake and Raef looked back, taking in the warriors, perhaps fifty in number, under the expanse of the star-filled sky. "Was it so with you? You told me Ailmaer took you in."

"I was treated as any new warrior would be." Siv grinned. "I learned how to stand still until I was commanded otherwise, even if my nose itched."

Raef laughed and pulled her close. "I am glad you did not lose your cheerful heart to them." He drew her long, red-gold braid over her shoulder and ran a finger down the plaits. "Now, tell me, how is it that you live?" His heart caught in his chest as he spoke the words, so sharp was the joy of holding her, of seeing her breath mingle with his in the cold air.

Siv was quiet for a moment and Raef could see her memories of that night flare to life in her eyes. "I watched you. I saw the betrayal on Isolf's face. The gate was barred and guarded on the inside. When the fires began, the safest place for me was the walls, so I stayed for as long as I dared. But when one of Isolf's men spotted me, I fled, taking refuge in the forge, for I could find none of your warriors and no way to resist on my own. When everything grew quiet, I emerged. It was not yet dawn. I crept amid the still-burning buildings. There were bodies strewn here and there. Warriors, women, children. From atop the wall, I could see death, and standing there hand in hand with death was Isolf and Tulkis Greyshield and the men of Silfravall, and I knew the Vestrhall had fallen." She reached up and touched Raef's cheekbone. "I knew my best chance at escape was through the small gate. Isolf had posted two men there. They died with my arrows in their throats."

Raef planted a kiss on her forehead. "As did Eira."

"Was that her? I could not be sure."

"How did you find Ailmaer Wind-footed and his company?"

"By the will of the gods, I think." Siv drew back and they began to walk once more. "I believed you dead and I had only my vow to find my sister driving me onward, so I began my search once more. I reached the border between Vannheim and Finngale when a familiar sound caught my ear."

"The mountain sparrow?"

Siv smiled. "I was glad enough to see a friendly face, and Ailmaer did not ask questions I did not wish to answer."

"What was Ailmaer Wind-footed doing at the border between Vannheim and Finngale?"

Siv shrugged. "He does not say. We raided no one. I think he was looking for something." Siv turned her head to look at Raef. "Word came that you lived, that Uhtred of Garhold had won back the Vestrhall for you, that you were dead but your spirit called forth a storm of eagles to destroy Isolf. I persuaded Ailmaer to go south, though I think he was of the same mind. We stumbled across the Hammerling two days ago. It was only by chance that we were watching his camp when you rode out of the darkness."

"And your sister?"

Siv shook her head. "As elusive as ever." She squeezed his hand. "And now you owe me your tale."

And so Raef told her of the eagle's nest, of Visna, of the strange boy Anuleif, of giants falling from the sky, of Rufnir and the first loyal few, of Torleif and the doomed alliance. He spoke of the battle in the gorge, of the avalanche and Vakre's increasing burden, of the smoke-colored kin's death, of the return to the Vestrhall, and, last of all, of the eagle he had spread across Isolf's back.

Siv was quiet for a long time and they walked in silence to the far side of the small lake.

"Did you mean to die at the Hammerling's hand?"

"I meant to kill Hauk of Ruderk if I could, and then, yes, die if the Hammerling required it. My people have suffered enough. I had thought to spare them battle with the Hammerling."

Siv's face was sorrowful. "There is little hope of that now. And given a second chance I would have shot Hauk instead of Eira, though she drew my arrow because she was armed and he was not. But I am not sorry for taking you from the Hammerling's clutches." She wrapped her arms around Raef. "I am not sorry that I am standing here with you."

Raef leaned in. "Nor am I," he said, his voice as quiet as the gentle wind that blew across the open ground. They stayed still for a long moment, the stars turning slowly overhead, and though Raef's cheeks grew numb from the cold and his toes were frozen, he did not wish to move.

"Uhtred is dead," he said at last. "And Finnolf. Yorkell. Little Tolla. Many others."

Sorrow filled Siv's eyes. "And what of Uhtred's daughter? Did Isolf spare her?"

With a heavy heart, Raef told Siv of Aelinvor's part in her father's death and the end she had made for herself. When he finished, they returned to the shadow of the mountain and the two huts. A handful of Ailmaer's warriors remained on their feet, as vigilant as the stars above, though the rest had been released to seek sleep. Raef and Siv took to the chilled, dirt floor of one of the huts with a pair of thick reindeer furs and slept curled against each other for the last hours before dawn.

EIGHTEEN

"WILL YOU FIGHT?"

The Vestrhall was in sight, the walls stark against the snow, the hall golden in the bright morning. The shelters of Vannheim's warriors had been cleared away, leaving only a few smoking remnants of night fires, and the walls were lined with men wielding shields and spears. All eyes were looking west in expectation of the Hammerling's arrival and Raef and the party of warriors on the hill to the north had not been spotted.

Ailmaer Wind-footed surveyed the Vestrhall and Raef could see the experienced warrior calculating the lay of the land, the strength of the walls, the number of spears and blades that might be brought to battle.

"It seems to me you and yours will be outnumbered." The mercenary cast his heavy gaze on Raef, who knew better than to look away.

"Yes. But your fifty swords would change things."

"The Hammerling would still have the advantage."

"Is your reputation falsely earned? I have always heard that the Wind-footed warrior has won every battle." Raef goaded the man with good humor.

"Not every battle." Ailmaer did not share Raef's mood, but neither did he take offense. "Do you know that the first time I was called that it was in jest, an insult, after I had fled from the field of battle?"

Raef frowned. "Then why take the name as your own?"

"A wiser man than I had a sense of such things. He said a man needs a name, something to fling to the wolves in lean times, something wild that lives on air alone, something like a mountain stream that rushes downhill and becomes the wide, coursing river. He said it sounded good," Ailmaer said with the slightest hint of a grin, "and I heeded his counsel."

"What would this wise man counsel now?"

Ailmaer's jaw and mouth hardened, his lips tightening as he looked once more at the Vestrhall.

"He would say I would be better served by turning east and siding with the Hammerling. Or, even better, taking my men far from here."

It still was not an answer and Raef pressed him. "I can offer you gold, riches. Vannheim is wealthy."

Ailmaer's stare turned to Raef again. "What if I did not ask for riches?"

"What price, then?"

"Land."

"I cannot make you lord of Finngale even if the Hammerling is defeated."

Now Ailmaer laughed, a coarse sound as solid and unflinching as the man. "Lord? I have names enough, Skallagrim. I care not to rule over a hall. Nor do I seek a vast tract of land to farm and breed horses and sons on. No, I speak only of a single hill that looks out over the sea."

"Any hill?"

"I am partial to one that sits on your northern coast."

"Why?"

Ailmaer's face remained blank. "The view is pleasing to me."

"I think there is much you do not say."

"Do you want the fifty swords I can give you?"

Raef grimaced, his mind turning as he tried to grasp Ailmaer's motives. "Yes."

"Then we are agreed."

Raef's hesitation was no more than a heartbeat. "We are."

As one the warriors moved down the hill, navigating the descent with ease, and they thundered across the open ground to the Vestrhall's gate, Raef at the head, his horse eagerly matching strides with Ailmaer's larger mount.

Shouts from the watchtower heralded their arrival and the gate swung open to admit them. There to greet them was Vakre, rushing down the wooden ladder that led to the tower, and Dvalarr the Crow. The Crow's face showed only delight at seeing additional shields to fill their wall; Vakre's was awash with relief. But neither Raef nor Vakre could speak of what had passed in the night, for others were too close, too eager to speak to their lord and hail him for bringing reinforcements. But Vakre grasped Raef's forearm, his grip firm and glad, and then wrapped Siv in a joyful embrace and Raef was pleased to see the son of Loki smile and forget his burdens, even for just that moment.

"The Hammerling has not come with the sun," Dvalarr said, looking to Raef for guidance.

Raef glanced at Siv. "Perhaps Brandulf has not had a restful night." Siv bit back a grin and Raef forced himself to give Dvalarr his full attention. "He will come, Crow, and we must be ready."

"Everything is prepared, as you commanded, lord," the Crow said.

Raef nodded. "Then the rest is in the hands of the gods."

Dvalarr and several other warriors touched the Thor hammers they wore around their necks and then the Crow was barking orders and they rushed off to do as he said. Dvalarr and Ailmaer Wind-footed put their heads together and Raef watched the two hardened warriors walk off, discussing the role Ailmaer's shields would play.

Raef was famished. Taking Siv's hand, he led her to the Vestrhall's kitchens. The serving men and women and most of the villagers who would not fight were already sequestered in the hall, a place of safety should the Hammerling break through the gates, so Raef and Siv helped themselves to bread baked at dawn, soft, smooth cheese, eggs boiled until the yolks were still creamy and then put out to chill in the snow, a warm, brown broth that had been left to bubble over the hearth, and thick slices of reindeer meat, dried and salted.

When they had eaten their fill, Raef and Siv joined Vakre at the walls, their gazes fixed on the eastern hills and the day grew from youth to middle age as the sun slid across the sky, and still the Hammerling did not show his face. The narrow stretch of land that separated the Vestrhall from the eastern hills remained empty, but if Raef closed his eyes he caught a glimpse of its fate, corpse-strewn, the pure white snow soiled with blood and urine, the crows descending to feast on the dead. Behind him, the village was still, the market empty. The warriors who waited atop and behind the walls spoke in hushed voices if they spoke at all. It seemed to Raef that they all stood upon a precipice, waiting, waiting for a fall that was inevitable with only the outcome yet to be discovered.

Only when the shadows had lengthened and twilight threatened to spill forth and cloak them all did the Hammerling's spears and shields darken the edge of the trees opposite Raef. And then the strip of open land vanished beneath the marching feet of the Hammerling's warriors. On and on they came, in greater number than Raef had feared.

His own men flocked to the walls, bows at the ready, arrows nocked. Some men touched the hammers at their throats, others placed steady, worn hands on the solid oak barrels that stood next to them on the wall walk, their lids cast aside to reveal a glossy, dark liquid that trembled at the slightest touch, sending shivers of rippled light playing across the surface. Some men knelt on the wall walk, oblivious to the army a bow shot away, though Raef was sure they yearned to peek over the walls. Instead, they were resolute, shoulders hunched, hands cupped to shield tiny flames, their sole purpose to keep the fires alive when the chaos started.

The Hammerling rode at the front, head held high, flanked by his son Asmund and Eirik of Kolhaugen. He raised his fist and the horde of men behind him ceased to swarm onward. Wind curled inland from the fjord, bringing the smell of fish and seaweed to Raef's nostrils. It swept across the walls, tugging at the pair of green and gold banners that rose above the gate. The thick fabric snapped in the wind, a harsh sound carried to Raef on swift currents. The taut bowstrings to Raef's left and right seemed to cry out for release while the timbers of the stout walls creaked, the ancient wood protesting the silence, the waiting. Dvalarr looked to Raef with a question in his eyes, but Raef shook his head.

"Skallagrim." The Hammerling's voice rang out and Raef was sure he felt the heartbeats of those on the wall quicken. "Has it come to this, then? Will your people name me king or will they die?"

Next to Raef, Dvalarr sucked in a great breath of air and Raef knew what the Crow would shout, knew it would seal the fates of many, knew he might stop it and yet he did nothing.

"Vannheim has a king, one of our choosing." The Crow's voice was thick with pride and defiance. "We will not kneel to another."

A pause, one the swirling wind consumed. "At last I see the depth of your treachery, Skallagrim," the Hammerling called. "At last I see why you fled from the burning lake. You sought to quench your own burning ambition."

No, Raef might have said. He might have said that his only

ambition was to see justice brought to his father's killers. He might have said that the only seat he wanted was his father's wooden chair in the Vestrhall, or even a rowing bench on a ship sailing west. He might have said much. Whether by the will of Odin or the will of something that dwelt within himself, Raef swallowed all the words that lingered in his throat. He could feel his blood coursing through his veins, feel each breath he took surge into his lungs, feel his heart beat with the anticipation of battle. His sword and axe sang to him, whispering of death and bloodshed, and it seemed to him their voices were joined by those of his ancestors, those who had not knelt to any king.

"I will ask once more. Do we fight or do we bury the axe between us?" the Hammerling called.

"We fight."

The roar that rose up from the warriors atop the wall was echoed by the voices of the Hammerling's horde below. Spears clashed against shields, naked steel slid from scabbards, and the snow writhed with the long, unnatural shadows of the warriors spread before the walls. Raef looked to Dvalarr and gave him a nod. The Crow bellowed an order that was carried down the wall by other voices, and in response the archers bent down to hold their pitch-smeared arrows to the sheltered flames.

The flaming arrows streaked through the darkening sky and for a moment there was silence as all eyes tracked them. As they fell, the Hammerling's men formed hasty shield walls and many arrows thudded uselessly into the snow, their flames snuffed out in an instant. But others pierced flesh, their steel heads burying into the unprotected chests and legs of those warriors who had been too slow to seek cover. And here and there small fires bloomed amid the clusters of men as the arrows sprouted on the painted shields. The archers on the walls fired at will, their keen eyes seeking those who scrambled yet for safety, or gaps between carelessly positioned shields, but it was only a moment before the Hammerling's army was safely ensconced behind their shields and every arrow that flew was an arrow wasted.

"Hold," Dvalarr called. He turned to Raef. "To the gate?"

"Yes." Raef had hoped to maintain their position of strength and safety behind the walls for as long as possible while whittling away at the Hammerling's men, but the Crow was right. Better to meet them now than wait until the Hammerling had a ram at the gates and they were penned in with few options. The inevitable clash of shield on shield was at hand.

Leaving a handful of archers on the wall to pick off strays, Raef descended to the gate where the bulk of his warriors waited. They filled the small market and the narrow passages between houses, their spears held in tight grasps, gazes flickering from face to face as each warrior fought off nervous fear.

Raef looked at them, trying to gauge the strength of their minds and the steadfastness of their hearts, and was pleased to see the fear in their eyes tempered by resolve.

"Once before we lost the Vestrhall to invaders," Raef said, his voice ringing out as the first stars unveiled themselves in the sky. "Never again." A shout of defiance swelled among the warriors and the ground trembled with the thundering rhythm of spears battered against the earth. "Fight for the man who stands at your side and let the bastards outside these gates feel the fire of Vannheim's wrath. He who falls this night will go to the gods." The screams were deafening, a sound born from the union of fear and bloodlust. Raef turned to the gate, feeling the press of men behind him, the shouts of the captains filling his ears. And then the heavy timbers were lifted and the gates swung open and the screaming warriors rushed past Raef, swarming through the gate.

A hand on Raef's arm pulled him up and then Siv's arms were around his neck, her mouth pressed hard against his in a fierce kiss that sent shivers flooding across Raef's skin. When he opened his eyes, her green ones were staring at him, their depths pulling him in so far that for a moment he forgot about the warriors preparing to die, forgot about the Hammerling, forgot, even, about Hauk of Ruderk, who still lived.

Without a word between them, they joined the crush of warriors and passed through the gate, filling their place at the center of the growing shield wall. Raef pushed to the front until he stood shoulder to shoulder with Vakre and Dvalarr, their shields overlapping, and Siv tucked herself behind him, spear and shield in hand, sword at her belt.

The shield wall stretched south to the shore of the fjord and north to the trees and the steep hillside that rose out of the land next to the Vestrhall's walls. Three shields deep it went and Raef looked down the line, then out across the empty ground to the Hammerling's force. With the threat of arrows reduced, the Hammerling's men had formed a single wall, the same length as Raef's, or near enough. No doubt the Hammerling had five or six rows of warriors waiting behind the first. For every man who went down, another would step over their fallen sword-brother and take his place. For a moment, Raef swept his gaze the length of the line. Searching for Hauk of Ruderk was as natural to him as breathing, but Raef could not afford to lose himself to his vengeance, not yet. With a deep breath, Raef focused on the Hammerling instead. He watched Brandulf's mouth open, watched him shout a command, watched as the warriors began to churn through the snow. Raef's heartbeat slowed with each step they took. Around him, voices called for the line to brace, and then at last the thunder of clashing shields filled the twilight.

Raef dug in, his feet slipping on the snow-slick ground, Siv's shield pressing against his back, but the force of the collision pushed him back and his own shield slammed into the side of his head.

Beside him, Vakre and Dvalarr had also lost ground, but as three they surged forward, regaining a step. A spear thrust beneath Raef's shield, just missing the flesh above his knee, and an axe came over the top, hooking onto the iron-edged wood and threatening to tear it from Raef's grip. Shifting to his right, Raef found an opening and thrust up with his short sword. He felt the blade strike bone, heard a scream, and the axe hung limply from Raef's shield. Already he was hacking at another exposed limb.

A bellow of pain from Raef's left told him Dvalarr had taken a wound, but the Crow did not stagger, did not falter, and the press of body against body was endless. Raef's world was reduced to his shield arm, straining to give him room enough to work the short sword, and the trampled snow beneath his feet. A sword sliced through the shields and glanced off Raef's forearm, but Raef jabbed forward with his shield, trapping the warrior's sword and hand in the gap. From behind Raef, Siv hammered down on the man's knuckles with the hilt of her sword while Raef stabbed under his shield into the man's groin. The warrior dropped to his knees, the sword falling to the snow, and Raef shoved the dying man aside with his boot, earning himself a brief reprieve from the constant crush. But another warrior surged forward to fill the gap.

They were losing ground. Bit by bit the Hammerling's wall was pushing them back, back, and soon they would be pressed up against the timber walls with no room to swing a sword. They would be hacked to bits.

"We must move forward," Raef shouted, his voice caught in the roar of battle, and for a moment he was sure Vakre had not heard, but the son of Loki finished off an opponent with a grimace and caught Raef's eye. Dvalarr gathered his voice in a yell worthy of the giants and fresh energy swelled from the rows of warriors behind Raef. One step, then two, finally a third, but the shields began to loosen, the warriors no longer in step as they battled for ground.

Raef, tucked tight between Dvalarr and Vakre still, could feel it, could feel the line weaken, and knew soon it would break, leaving every warrior to fight alone.

Vakre stumbled against Raef, caught with the haft of an axe, the head narrowly avoided, and went to one knee. When he rose, the gap between them had grown, and suddenly the wall was gone. Raef slashed into his opponent's shoulder, severing into the collarbone, the battle-joy contained in his gut flowing forth to fill his chest, his limbs, as he savored the freedom to move as he was meant to move. Raef dragged the short sword through flesh and bone until he had carved out a gaping hole in the warrior's neck, then yanked the small blade free. The warrior fell to the ground and Raef dropped the short sword, transferred his shield to his right arm, and drew the sword that sung a song of death in his ear.

The steel song hummed around him and warriors and shield-maidens died, some in empty silence, some with dreadful noises, but Raef knew only the feel of the blade in his hand, heard only his own heart beat with calm certainty, and dealt death to all who came within reach. And yet he knew it was not enough, knew that his men were too few, knew it was only a matter of moments before the enemy closed around him.

The thunder of hooves came to him like a wave rolling in from the sea in the same moment the hairs on the back of his neck stood up against a searing heat. He whirled and saw the flames envelop Vakre, flushing out from his torso to consume him from head to toe, banishing the warriors who had pressed close to him, and then the horsemen rushed out of the darkness, their spears impaling the enemy from behind, for Ailmaer Wind-footed had joined the battle at last, sweeping through the dark to fall upon the Hammerling's rear.

A shout turned Raef in time to raise his shield and catch an axe arcing toward his head. The bearer of the axe tried to rip the head free, but the steel was caught fast and Raef was too quick. He slammed his shield into the warrior's face and brought his sword down to plunge into his chest. As the warrior dropped to the ground and Raef wrenched his sword free, his gaze caught on a face, lit with Vakre's fire, and he felt fury rage in his heart.

Hauk of Ruderk was unscathed, his blade smeared with the blood of dead men, and he was close, so close. Raef raced forward, his boots sliding on snow and blood, but a shadowy figure, untouched by Vakre's light, hurled itself out of the darkness and planted itself between Raef and Hauk. A pair of eyes blazed out from beneath the hood, eyes set in a pale face, and Raef faltered, for there were stars in those eyes, and cold hatred.

"Visna?"

At last Vakre's flames shed light on the shadows and Raef felt horror slide down the length of his throat and settle deep in his belly.

"Eira."

Her throat was a ruin, crusted in dried blood. Her body trembled as if coursing with the strength of a sea at storm and those star-filled eyes bore into Raef so sharply that he already felt her sword pierce him. And yet she did not strike, did not lash out. Her head turned from him to Hauk, and she seemed a wild animal caught in a trap, unsure which way to run. Only when a Vannheim warrior launched himself at Hauk did she move, her sword, a dark thing that repulsed the firelight as she herself seemed to, darting out and opening the warrior's chest from groin to neck. Then Eira grabbed Hauk and they were gone, vanishing into nothing.

Raef stared at the blackness they had left behind but a surge of heat called him back to the battle and he turned to help Vakre. But the son of Loki was far from harm.

Vakre hung in the air above the battle, floating higher than the top of the wall, wreathed in flames so hot and white they brought day to the battlefield and Raef was forced to shield his eyes as he stared up at his friend. Beneath him, warriors of both armies cowered in fear. Smoke curled from more than one cloak and Raef could see one man clutching at his arm, the skin raw and bleeding. Raef took a step forward, but the heat was too intense and he dared not go closer.

The battle ground to a halt as all eyes turned to the fire in the sky and it was not until Siv appeared at Raef's side, her fingers brushing his elbow, that Raef stirred from the depths of his astonishment. He turned to her, scanning her for injury and finding little more than a slash on her upper arm. He wiped a smatter of blood from her cheek, and then Ailmaer Wind-footed was beside them. He dismounted and his horse, skittish under the flames, pranced away. Ailmaer held tight to the reins and lowered his eyes from Vakre.

"We have the Hammerling." The older man was streaked with sweat, the Thor's hammer at his neck gleaming in the light of Vakre's fire. Raef saw one hand twitch as though he might reach up to clasp the metal for reassurance, but the hand stayed at his side and Ailmaer kept his gaze on Raef.

Raef nodded, then turned his own gaze skyward once more, squinting to ward out the light, one hand raised, fingers splayed in vain.

"Vakre." His voice caught in his throat, a feeble, uncertain thing that he was sure the half god would not hear, much less heed. Raef tried again. "Vakre. Come back to us." The blaze did not dim, the heat did not weaken. "Come back to me."

At length the flames darkened, growing orange and yellow once more, and then Vakre drifted to the ground. Beneath him, warriors scrambled to keep their distance and at last he settled on the snow once more and the flames vanished on the night breeze. Raef blinked, struggling to see in the sudden dark. At last Vakre's face came to him, a face lit only by starlight and moonlight and free of the tangle of flames.

Raef rushed forward, ready to catch Vakre should he fall, ready to defend himself should the son of Loki not know him, but he pulled up when he saw the calm in Vakre's face. Their eyes met and Raef could still feel the heat pouring forth, but he closed the distance between them.

"Are you well?"

To his relief, Vakre nodded. "Yes." He looked over Raef's shoulder and inclined his head once more. "This is not over."

Raef turned and saw the Hammerling caught between two of Ailmaer's men. Brandulf fought to keep his head high, to keep from crumpling, but his face was etched with pain and Raef could see the wound in his side even from a distance.

Around them, the Hammerling's men were laying down their weapons, some with quick, nervous hands, others with reluctant faces, but all succumbing to the spears aimed at their chests by Ailmaer's mounted warriors. A few tried to flee, seeking freedom in the darkness, but these were quickly run down and herded together with the rest.

Raef approached the Hammerling, who had dropped to one knee, his head sunk against his chest. Raef nodded at the pair of warriors, who backed away, and he lowered himself so that he might look in the eyes of the man who had been his king, his ally, his enemy. Raef placed a hand on Brandulf's shoulder and the other man struggled to raise his head. Death ate at the edges of his eyes and the hand clamped to his wound, a deep slash that had ripped apart the thick leather, was dripping with blood.

"Say your piece, Skallagrim, and be done with me." A last torrent of defiance burst out from between Brandulf's clenched teeth and then the other leg gave way and the Hammerling pitched forward. Raef caught him by the shoulders and steadied him.

"How is it that I have had to watch two good men die, two men who might have made great kings, and the third survives still?"

The Hammerling coughed. "Your father would have been a better king than I. Or the Palesword." He clutched at Raef's shoulder with a trembling hand. "Is he dead?"

Raef frowned. "Fengar?"

"Hauk."

Raef thought of Eira and the blackness woven around her, of her starry eyes, of her disappearance with Hauk. "He lives."

"Find him. Finish him."

"Where is your son?"

"I sent him away. Home." The Hammerling's fingers tightened on Raef's shoulder. "Will you kill him?"

Raef shook his head. "No." He hesitated. "I never meant to make you my enemy."

"And yet you broke your oath."

"What would you have done for your father?"

Brandulf's courage fled from his face and he sank against Raef, who lowered him to the ground. "Perhaps you will yet become a king we might be proud of, Skallagrim." His voice was low now, rough and broken. "My sword, my sword." Raef glanced around them but the Hammerling's blade was not in sight. Raef drew his own and pressed the hilt into Brandulf's outstretched hand. The fingers curled tight, a warrior's grip still, and something like contentment came into the Hammerling's face. "I am ready. I will greet your father in Valhalla."

Raef felt his throat close up. "Tell him," he paused, unsure. "Tell him," he tried again, but then he saw that Brandulf Hammerling was already gone.

NINETEEN

THE FIRE THAT burned the Hammerling lasted to morning. Raef had stood vigil over it until the smoke drove him away, and then, after leaving instructions for the Hammerling's warriors to be released, he retreated to his chamber in the Vestrhall and did not emerge until a bright sun was high in the sky and the Hammerling's ashes were being swept into the fjord by a gentle wind.

He sought out Siv first, who waited alone in the hall, knees tucked to her chest as she perched on a bench. Raef slid onto the bench beside her.

"I am sorry."

She reached out and tucked a strand of his hair that had worked loose behind his ear. "For what?"

"For shutting myself away."

"I know what it is to seek solitude." She smiled and held out her hand, palm facing him. Raef placed his palm against hers and wrapped his fingers between hers, his heart full to bursting with joy over Siv's understanding. He stood and pulled her to her feet and settled a deep kiss on her lips.

"Come," Raef said when he pulled away. "It is time I spoke to Vakre."

They found Vakre by the fjord at the end of one of the docks. He stood with his arms crossed over his chest, his face turned toward the sun. He wore no cloak, nothing to keep winter at bay, and when Raef came close enough to touch him, he could feel the heat emanating from Vakre's skin. It was a tender heat, an easy warmth free of malice or anger.

Vakre smiled at Siv, but then his eyes sought Raef. "Did I kill anyone?"

"No." Raef watched the water shimmer in the sunlight and a deep longing for spring came over him. He swallowed that down. "I have to ask, Vakre, what did you do? How did you rise into the air?"

The son of Loki shook his head. "I do not know. I could feel my father, as I always do when wreathed in his gift. The power, the fury, the fear, they burned through me, and for a moment I could feel the lives of everyone below me as though they were beating hearts in the palm of my hand. Hearts I was meant to crush." Vakre's gaze met Raef's and the pain there was laced with sadness and guilt. "I could have killed you all."

"But you did not."

"Not this time."

There was nothing Raef could offer Vakre, no words of reassurance to counter the truth Vakre spoke.

"You told the Hammerling that Hauk still lived," Siv said, breaking the silence.

Raef's mind swam with visions of Eira as she had appeared on the field of battle under the stars. It seemed difficult to find the words to express what he had seen.

"Eira came for him."

Siv frowned and Raef rushed on.

"Her throat was ripped open, torn to shreds by your arrow. But the blood was dried, and she was angry, so angry, but," Raef paused, "uncertain, lost, somehow. She knew me and yet did not know me.

Her eyes," Raef hesitated again, then brushed past that image and continued. "She carried a sword, dark of blade and finely wrought." Raef looked at Vakre. "It is a sword we know well."

Understanding dawned in Vakre's eyes, but he said nothing, leaving Raef to speak the words to Siv.

"She is a Valkyrie."

The words hung over them, a shadow between them and the sun.

"Visna left to carry out her final task, one she dreaded and yet could avoid no longer. She had to find another to take her place, to carry her sword. There must be nine."

"Would that she had chosen any other," Vakre said. "And yet when you faced Visna at the burning lake, her sword was as a shard of sunlight. You said the steel was dark in Eira's hand."

Raef nodded. "Perhaps the sun will fill it in time. I do not know."

"She will hunt you," Siv said, her face darkened by a frown.

"I am not so sure. If she can remember, yes, if her hatred for me burns as bright now that she is of Asgard, if she still does Hauk's will. But she may lose something of herself, just as Visna began to forget pieces of herself and her past life when she came to the world of men." Siv did not seem convinced but she kept her doubts to herself. Raef put two fingers under her chin and drew her head up, his eyes searching hers. "Nothing good will come of thoughts like those. If Eira means to come for me, then she will come and I cannot stop her. But I will not live in fear of that moment. Not when there is so little time left to us."

"And Hauk?" Vakre's voice was soft but insistent. "If you find him, you may find her."

"Then I will ask Odin to guide my hand, to put strength in my legs, to fill my lungs with breath enough to do what I must, what I owe my father."

"Skallagrim." Ailmaer Wind-footed stood with one foot planted on the dock, his arms crossed, a fox-fur hood pulled over his grey-ing hair. "Our terms?"

Raef shifted his stance so that he faced Wind-footed head on. "Will be fulfilled. But I mean to see this view that pleases you so greatly."

ᚱ ᚱ ᚱ

The hill stood over a wind-swept stretch of beach and under a swirl-ing grey sky spitting snow. In summer, Raef knew, blue waters would lap at the sand and deposit new treasures dredged up by the sea's waves, but winter held dominion here and the waves rolled up to the shore with increasing vigor, battering the cover of snow molded so carefully by the relentless wind.

They had ridden north for three days under snow-laden skies, ferrying across fingers of grey water, passing within half a day's ride of the valley where Raef had left Rudrak Red-beard to be sniffed out by hungry wolves. He wondered if any of Rudrak's bones lingered yet under the spreading limbs of the oak Raef had tied him to, or if the wolves had long since removed any trace of the traitor. More than once on the ride north Raef had felt eyes watching them, but no threat revealed itself and he saw nothing.

"Old Troll, my father called it," Raef said, looking up at the crest of the hill, a misshapen, rocky thing. As a boy he had laughed with delight to discover, with his father's aid, the troll's bulbous nose, craggy chin, and narrow eyes. At the summit, tall waving grasses had served as the troll's unkempt hair. Now he saw only stones and Ailmaer Wind-footed's unspoken words.

Little had passed between Raef and Ailmaer during the journey, for the mercenary was not inclined to answer Raef's questions and Raef had forced himself to bite back words that might have sparked irritation.

"The earth is full of sand here," Raef said, his voice carried to

Ailmaer on the wind. "And the wind would eat away at a house." He did not think Ailmaer intended to build a home and farm the land, but he hoped his words might open a leak in the other man's stubborn tongue.

Ailmaer looked at Raef, said nothing, and put his heels into his horse, urging the beast to climb the hill. Raef grimaced and did the same, his cloak dragging behind him as the wind grew fiercer.

"A fine view, no?" Ailmaer's voice was laced with humor and the mercenary took in a deep breath of salt air as he gestured at their surroundings. From above, the site was even bleaker, the thick grey clouds pressing in, the sea a roiling mass of steel-colored water.

"What do you mean to find here, Ailmaer?"

To Raef's relief, Ailmaer did not ignore the question. The humor left his face and he confronted Raef with hard eyes. "I swore an oath to hold my tongue."

"An oath? Who holds your leash? Do you mean to hand over this piece of Vannheim to another lord?"

"Not that kind of oath. I will bring no harm to Vannheim, Skallagrim. But I will not say." Ailmaer must have caught Raef's glance to the beach below where the rest of the warriors waited, Ailmaer's and Raef's. "Nor will they," he added, not unkindly.

"I could make them talk."

"They will not say because they do not know. But I will not listen to you threaten them."

Raef sighed. "What would you do in my place? Would you ask no questions when a man you have known for a matter of days lays claim to a piece of land that has belonged to your family for generations?"

"No." Ailmaer turned his horse and began to descend from Old Troll's head and Raef was forced to follow. "I would do as you are doing, Skallagrim. And you would do as I do," Ailmaer called back, his words catching on the gusts of air that churned up the slope.

It was then, halfway between Old Troll's wrinkled temple and cracked ear, that Raef caught sight of a lean grey shape crouched alongside a downed tree a spear's throw from the base of the hill. He pulled up his horse, which had caught an unwelcome scent and stepped nervously under Raef's firm hold, but the moment Raef's feet touched the ground, the grey shape raced away, no more than a blur amid the drifts of snow, and Raef blinked, shaking his head at what was surely his imagination.

They shared one fire that night, finding a measure of shelter behind a crumbling shelf of rock, but there was little camaraderie to be had. Ailmaer's men were as Raef had first met them, vigilant and little given to talk, while those of Vannheim were uneasy around the strangers. They would part ways in the morning, Raef leading his men south again, Ailmaer remaining to seek whatever had drawn him to this remote piece of Vannheim. It did not sit well with Raef, but he had given his word and Ailmaer's mounted warriors had been invaluable in the defense of the Vestrhall.

It was Siv who spotted the glimmering eyes in the dark. They reflected the firelight, but they were far too low to the ground and far too wide and round to be those of a man. Raef took a branch from the fire and brandished the burning end before him as he ventured into the dark, his hand on the haft of his axe where it hung from his belt. Siv stalked forward as well, a knife in hand, but the eyes remained fixed on Raef as they drew closer.

A low growl caused Raef to halt and then something was hurtling out of the darkness toward him. The creature was around his legs in an instant, quick feet dancing between his, tufted ears rubbing against his shins. Raef dropped his burning branch and began to laugh.

He knelt down and stroked the lynx's sleek fur. "A brave little girl, you are, and a survivor." The lynx cub had grown since Raef had watched Vakre lead her away into the hills that stood watch over the Vestrhall's walls, enticed into the trees by the carcass of a freshly slaughtered deer. Raef looked around, searching for any sign of the female cub's younger brother. She butted her head against his knee. "All alone, then?"

Raef's laughter had drawn the attention of the closest men, who watched him now with curious faces and murmured to each other. Ailmaer pushed his way through from the other side of the fire, his brow furrowed with concern until he saw the lynx, content under Raef's hands, and then his eyes went wide and he froze where he stood.

"Do you toy with me Skallagrim?" Ailmaer's voice was sharp and full of apprehension.

Raef stood, his joy at seeing the lynx alive and well overshadowed by Ailmaer's sudden show of emotion. "I do not know what you speak of."

With effort, Ailmaer steadied himself and his face grew smooth and stern once more. "You encourage a wild animal to come near."

"She is an old friend," Raef said.

"Take care that she does not grow too fond of your scent." Ailmaer retreated through the crowd of warriors, but Raef was not blind to the two men who followed hard on his heels, the same two who had conversed with Ailmaer at the summer farm, and how they huddled close and conferred with each other in urgent whispers.

At length the warriors ceased to stare at Raef and the lynx, and many sought sleep in the warmth of woolen blankets and thick furs. Not Ailmaer. He sat across the fire, hunched over, hood drawn so far forward that Raef could not see his face, but he was sure the mercenary was watching.

It was dawn, though, before Ailmaer approached Raef, who had slept fitfully with the lynx draped over his chest. Ailmaer's boots scuffed against the pebbles strewn across the beach, drawing Raef out of a dream. Wind-footed stood over Raef, his face impassive.

The lynx stirred and drew back her lips at the intruder, but Raef lifted her from his torso and set her to the side.

"Come with me," Ailmaer said, his voice masked by the steady murmur of the sea.

Raef turned to Siv, who slept still, and lifted the edge of her fur to cover her exposed neck, then got to his feet and followed Ailmaer as he skirted the edge of the campsite and headed toward the base of Old Troll. The lynx padded after on silent feet, her nose twitching with the smells of the ocean.

Ailmaer followed the curve of the hill, his eyes tracing the uneven surface as though searching for something. More than once, Raef saw his gaze flicker back at the lynx, who would stop mid-stride every time Ailmaer looked at her. Only when they had gone the length of the base of Old Troll did Ailmaer come to a stop, halting where the hill's shoulder joined with the rest of the ridge overlooking the sea.

"How did you come to know her?" Ailmaer said, gesturing to the lynx.

"I killed her mother." Raef tried to hide his impatience, not understanding what Ailmaer wanted.

Wind-footed frowned. "And then?"

Raef sighed. "She followed me to the Vestrhall. Until last night, I had not seen her since."

"And yet she came all this way, drawn by your scent."

Raef threw up his hands. "What do you want?"

Ailmaer ignored him and his gaze swept over the lynx. "She is small for this time of year. A late cub. And yet she survives. Freyja has been kind to her."

"And the goddess has led her here, is that what you mean?"

"Her presence here is no accident." Still Ailmaer had eyes only for the lynx.

"Or she hungered after the deer your men took down in sight of the Vestrhall and followed us in search of a meal. I would have you speak plainly, Ailmaer. Enough of these secrets."

The calm face that had betrayed so little to Raef in the first days of their meeting was now awash with desperation and hesitation as Ailmaer warred within himself. He turned from Raef, clenched fist raised as though he would strike the bare rock, but he pulled up and instead let out a great shout of frustration that ricocheted out to sea where it was swallowed. Raef waited.

"Did your mother ever tell you the story of the quarrel between Freyja and Idunn?" Ailmaer's voice was soft and commanding once more.

"My mother died giving birth to me."

Ailmaer seized upon this with eager eyes. "Is there nothing you would not do to change her fate?"

"My mother is no concern of yours. Tell me of Freyja and Idunn."

Ailmaer took a deep breath. "Idunn keeps the golden apples and grants the gods eternal youth, as you know. Freyja, for all her beauty and power, has always been jealous of Idunn. She schemed for a means of depriving Idunn of her apples. She begged Odin, she threatened Bragi, Idunn's husband, and at last she donned her eagle skin and flew to Idunn's garden. There she dove from the sky and came to battle against the flock of thrushes that guards the apple tree. Despite her size and greater strength, the thrushes tore at Freyja's feathers and threatened to peck out her eyes, and Freyja was forced to flee. But not before she broke a twig from the tree and stowed it in her tail feathers." Ailmaer stepped close and grasped Raef's shoulder. "And on that twig was a tiny apple." Ailmaer released Raef and began to pace. "When she discovered the broken branch, Idunn suspected it was Freyja who had committed this act of deceit and treachery, but she had no proof, for an eagle is just an eagle in the eyes of the faithful thrush. Freyja, for her part, could not keep her prize in Asgard for fear of discovery and Odin's wrath, so she carried the tiny apple far from her hall to a place only she might know. There she plucked a seed from the apple's core and planted it, nurtured it, watched it grow until it was a strong sapling, until it, too, sprouted golden apples."

"And you think she chose this place?" Raef thought of the times he had visited the Old Troll as a boy, had clambered over these very rocks. The notion that Freyja harbored a secret apple tree there seemed beyond belief. "You have been deceived."

"Doubt me if you like, Skallagrim. You do not know the lengths I have gone to in search of this place."

"And all to quench your own greed? To defy death and place yourself among the gods?" Raef backed away from Wind-footed, his gut clenched with revulsion.

"No," Ailmaer said, shaking his head, tears filling his eyes, "not for me. Never for me." The proud mercenary dropped to his knees and buried his face in his hands.

Raef hesitated, uncertain, then stepped forward and knelt in front of Ailmaer. He put a hand to Ailmaer's arm and slowly drew the other man's hands away from his face. Only when Ailmaer lifted his eyes did Raef speak.

"Tell me."

Ailmaer swallowed hard and fought to control his tears. "To save a life other than my own, this is why I seek Freyja's tree." Ailmaer sank back on his heels and then sat in the snow. "The Norns are cruel, Skallagrim. Always they take that which we can least bear to part with." He ran a weathered hand down the length of his face, his fingers pulling at the skin around his eyes, the lines around his mouth. "The man who encouraged me to take the name Wind-footed, he is called Adalherr and I owe him everything. He was father when I had none, friend when I needed one, teacher always." Ailmaer cast Raef a bitter glance. "I have survived this long because of him, and yet for four years I have watched him waste away, watched the illness spread from limb to limb. First, he could not grip a sword, now he cannot drink from a cup without spilling. He can hardly feed himself, he loses control of his bladder more often than not. At times he grows angry, afraid, but then a moment later he will laugh and things will seem to be as they were before." The tears welled once more. "But things will never be as they were and my heart breaks to see what has become of him." Ailmaer blinked and his face grew hard. "Idunn's apples will forever be out of my reach, but now you must see, Skallagrim, why I must find Freyja's."

"An old man's time will come, illness or no," Raef said.

"Is forty and one so old? Should I relinquish myself to death in three years time when I am that age?"

"I am sorry," Raef said, realizing Ailmaer was younger than the grey streaks of hair suggested. "I will help you if I can, though I do not know how." Raef felt a tremor of apprehension in his chest as he spoke the words, for to help Ailmaer succeed would mean unleashing eternal youth into the realm of men. Gladly would men go to war over such a gift. And yet even eternal youth would not spare Midgard from the final battle.

"Freyja holds the lynx dear to her heart and no doubt she has smiled on this one, who lives when she should have died. Perhaps she is the key." Ailmaer got to his feet with new vigor.

"Do you expect her to sniff it out as a dog would?"

"She may see with the goddess's eyes."

It was a strange thought, and yet Raef did not doubt that Freyja was capable of such a skill, and so he walked to the top of Old Troll once more, the lynx trotting behind, and together they traversed the hill from side to side, in search of something unknowable. But not once did she show interest in the snow or the dead grasses that poked through in places. She wandered after Raef readily enough, but the only thing of note she did was urinate against a boulder.

Even so, Raef examined it, tried to shove it away from where it was lodged in the earth, hoping to find some hidden passage, some sign of Freyja's presence, but all to no avail.

Through all this, Ailmaer watched from a distance, his arms crossed, his eyes hungry. When at last Raef returned to him, Siv had joined the mercenary, her former leader, and Raef had seen them exchange enough words to know that Siv was aware of their purpose. The three of them turned their attention to the base of the hill and again the lynx followed Raef here and there, sniffing, but it was not long before she found a patch of sunshine warming a rock and curled up there to sleep. Ailmaer despaired and left Raef and Siv, stalking across the beach until the waves lapped at his boots.

"Do you know this Adalherr?" Raef asked.

Siv nodded. "Only a little. But enough to know that Ailmaer would do anything for him."

"And if we find what he seeks? How many will die for a taste of these golden apples meant for the gods?" Raef took Siv's hand between his and kissed her palm. Neither had an answer to his question.

The sky grew dark as the day waned and Raef watched as the sea frothed and clouds rolled in from the west. If they headed inland now, they might escape the storm and return to the Vestrhall with speed, but, though he felt the pull of the Vestrhall, Raef was reluctant to leave Ailmaer. And so he waited, all the while wondering if he would regret the delay.

When the storm hit, Ailmaer was nowhere to be found. The men clustered in the rocky shelter, cloaks and furs pulled tight. The fire fought valiantly against the wind that whipped around the barriers, but it was a brief battle and soon it was nothing but smoke swept up in the blowing snow. Raef wished for Vakre and the flames he could give them, then peered out from the shelter in search of

Ailmaer, but he could see only a few hulking boulders here and there. Beside him, Siv's face was creased with worry.

"He will kill himself out there."

The lynx, her fur dusted with snow, stood between them.

"I must find him." Siv stepped forward and Raef made to stop her, then thought better of it. Instead Raef pulled his hood down and together they plunged into the storm, the lynx darting ahead.

They shouted Ailmaer's name, their voices ripped away by the wind, and walked the length of the beach, finding nothing. Out at sea, lighting flashed, knifing from black clouds to the swelling waves below, and the lynx burst ahead of Raef and out of sight, vanishing into the thick snow.

Raef gripped Siv's gloved hand tighter and pointed up in the direction of Old Troll's summit. Siv nodded and together they fought the wind back to the base of the hill, then began the climb.

At the summit, Raef caught sight of a dark shape and began to make his way toward Ailmaer. But he had gone only a few paces when a blinding flash threw him back, sending him sprawling in the snow as thunder cracked above them. Blinking, Raef got to his knees, his legs unsteady, but another bolt of lightning plunged to earth, striking the ground just in front of him. In the wake of the flash, Raef fell backward, but not before he saw a black and white bird rise from the charred ground. The bird flapped its wings and passed so close to Raef that he felt feathers brush his face, and then the lynx was leaping after it, claws outstretched, teeth barred in a silent snarl. The bird twisted out of reach and was gone.

His heart thundering in his chest, Raef got to his feet as Siv rushed to his side. He clutched at her, his vision streaked with violent white light, and sank to the ground once more.

"Are you hurt?" Siv brushed hair from Raef's face as she cradled him on her lap. Raef fought to draw breath, his heart moving too fast for his lungs to catch up, and struggled to speak. He closed his eyes as Siv's hands searched him for injury and his breathing slowed, though he could not have said how much time passed before he felt himself again.

When he did sit up, Raef saw the black scar in the earth where the lightning had struck, saw that a hole had opened up, saw Ailmaer on hands and knees peering into its depths. Around them, the sky had cleared, the dark clouds vanishing, the snow faltering so that only a few flakes fell. Out at sea, shafts of sunlight pierced the cloud cover and illuminated the grey waters below. Raef found his feet, reassuring Siv that he was unhurt, though he did not let go of her hand as he walked to where Ailmaer knelt.

Between them, a tunnel had opened in the rock, burrowing deep into Old Troll's skull, a nearly vertical descent. Already Ailmaer was removing his fur cloak to prepare for the plunge but Siv convinced him to wait until rope might be found and he could enter the tunnel more securely. Ailmaer paced across the hilltop while rope was fetched.

"This is wrong," Raef said to Siv as he watched Ailmaer fasten the rope around him and hand the loose end to three of his warriors, who would control his descent. "Not for Freyja are the dark places deep beneath the earth." Siv squeezed his hand and said nothing, her unease written plainly on her face. They watched as Ailmaer disappeared into the shaft and then there was nothing to do but wait.

"Where did the bird come from?" Raef asked, more to himself or whatever gods might be listening than to Siv. He walked a circled around the hole in the ground, giving a wide berth to the three men holding the rope. "No nest, nothing," he said, speaking aloud what was already known. "What bird lives underground?"

"Cliff swallows, burrowing owls."

Raef thought of the black and white bird, its angular wings and short tail. "This was neither."

"A message from Asgard? Why?"

It was a question Raef could not begin to answer.

When Ailmaer tugged on the rope, he was hoisted up to the daylight once more. He blinked against the light, raising hands smeared with dark earth to shield his eyes, and as the shadow passed over his face Raef could see the sorrow in his eyes.

"What did you find?"

"See for yourself." Ailmaer looked away and said nothing else.

The walls of the shaft were narrow and grew narrower as Raef was lowered deeper and deeper into the earth. A man of Dvalarr's build would not have fit. Using his hands and feet, Raef controlled his descent, not caring to risk everything to the hands that held the rope above him. At last his feet touched bottom and Raef stood in silence for a moment as his eyes adjusted to the darkness.

A cavern took shape around him, its low ceiling within reach if Raef raised his arm, its earthen floor broken by sharp ridges of half-buried rocks scattered as though dropped from a great height. There was no tree, no sapling, root, or twig. The golden apples that would save Adalherr were nothing more than a dream.

But the cavern was not empty. The more Raef looked, the more he saw, for the walls were covered in carvings that seemed to glimmer at the edge of his vision as though they were fluid, living things reacting to the hint of sunlight that had followed Raef into the depths. Raef pressed his fingertips against the grooves that outlined a raven in flight, wings spread wide, beak open in a call only the stones could hear, as his eyes took in the shape of a mighty tree. This was no slender fruit tree. The roots spanned the circle of the cavern, twining over the rock in a tangle, the trunk rose straight and strong to the ceiling, the branches arched over all, the limbs filled with delicate leaves. Yggdrasil hewn into the earth.

How long Raef stared at the stone tree, his gaze running over every knot in the trunk, every whorl in the roots, he could not have said, but Siv's faint voice pulled at him until he remembered where he was. He tugged on the rope to show he was ready to rise to the surface, but his eyes lingered on Yggdrasil's likeness until it was out of sight.

When he reached the surface, Raef found a second rope and asked the warriors to lower Siv down, then waited until she had reached the bottom before following.

Raef took Siv's hand and led her to the nearest wall, his fingers already reaching to feel Yggdrasil once more, but the rocks were empty under his touch, their surfaces free of carvings. Raef spun, searching, but the cavern had swallowed up the tree and the walls were just walls.

"I saw it. I felt it." Raef walked around the cavern, his uncertainty growing with every step.

"Saw what?" Siv asked.

"Yggdrasil." Raef tried to describe what he had seen, the breadth of the world tree's limbs, the twisted roots, the way the carvings had seemed to move when he looked away, but his words sounded hollow in his ears and he broke off. "Do you believe me?"

"Yes."

"It was beautiful."

"Ailmaer made no mention of it."

Raef frowned. "Why would I alone see it?"

Siv was silent for a moment, her face thoughtful. "When I was a girl, before my sister and I went to live with my uncle, I wandered into a cave at the outskirts of our farm. I dug in the dirt and found a piece of wood shaped into a swan and it was the most beautiful thing I had ever seen. I hurried out of the cave, intent on carrying it home to show my family, but the moment I stepped into the sun and the wind, a strange thing happened. It crumbled to dust in my palms. My father told me he had heard of such things, of ancient artifacts destroyed once removed from their hiding places, places that had kept them safe for countless years. The air, the warmth of the sun, these things are deadly."

Raef closed his eyes and pictured the carvings once more. "The discovery of this cavern was its destruction?"

"I think you are fortunate to have seen it at all." Siv came to stand by Raef. "Its fate was not unlike that which will befall the true Yggdrasil." Raef put his arms around her and held her close, closing his eyes once more and feeling the beat of her heart against his chest.

"What will we do?" Her voice was no more than a murmur.

"What we can." Raef put her face in his hands. "We will go on. We will laugh and fight and live until life is taken from us. And I will love you."

TWENTY

THE LOSS OF the golden apples weighed heavily on Ailmaer and Raef could see from the stoop of the other man's shoulders and the emptiness in his eyes that the mercenary had lost his conviction, his determination.

"I was so sure." Ailmaer had not abandoned the hilltop, choosing to stay near the shaft's entrance even as the sun passed into the sea. Raef and Siv brought him a portion of dried meat and hard cheese and a skin of ale, but Wind-footed showed little interest in eating. "I will keep looking."

"What would Adalherr have you do?" Siv rested a hand on Ailmaer's forearm as she spoke.

"I cannot lose him."

Siv put her palm to Ailmaer's cheek. "Do not let your grief blind you. Does Adalherr wish for eternal youth? Do you search for golden apples for him or to put an end to the sorrow and rage in your heart?"

The pain that flowed over Ailmaer's face made Raef look away.

"He would have me let him die, let the disease run its course." The words were choked out. "He is tired of living."

"Then you know what you must do." Siv cradled Ailmaer's face now and the tears flowed freely from his eyes.

"I cannot go on without him. He made me what I am, gave me everything."

"And in your greed you would deprive him of peace." Siv's voice was gentle but firm. "Let him go, Ailmaer. Let the gods look after him."

Ailmaer closed his eyes, his head sinking to his chest. After a long silence, he got to his feet and walked away. Siv made to follow but Raef stopped her.

"He sees the wisdom in your words," Raef said. "Let him wrap his heart around it."

ᚨ ᚨ ᚨ

"The hill is yours, Skallagrim. I relinquish my claim on it." Ailmaer Wind-footed mounted his horse on the beach, the wind tugging at his long hair. Behind him, his warriors were ready to travel.

"Where will you go?" Raef asked.

"Home. Such as it is. And there I will say goodbye."

Raef nodded. "Go with the good will of Vannheim."

Ailmaer returned the nod and then urged his horse forward as Raef stepped out of his path. The company of warriors thundered after him, the horses' hooves spewing snow and sand as they raced by and leaving Raef and the Vannheim warriors alone with the gulls. Within moments, Raef led his men from the beach, taking a southerly course toward the Vestrhall.

"I dreamed of the tree. I see it still when I close my eyes." Raef rode at the head of the column as they passed into a notch between a pair of hills. The sea was far behind them, the sound of its waves long forgotten, but Raef could not keep the cavern from his mind. He looked at Siv, who rode beside him. "I cannot help but feel that it," he paused, struggling to find the right word, "that it matters. The lightning, the bird, all of it." He glanced down at the lynx keeping pace at his side. She wandered from the pack of riders when she wished, always finding her way back to them.

Siv listened, but she was quiet, her thoughts tucked inside her own mind. She had said little since they had left the beach.

"What is it?"

"I am wondering if I should heed my own advice." Siv shifted in the saddle to look at him. "I told Ailmaer to let Adalherr go, that holding onto him would only make the parting worse, the sorrow cut more deeply. And yet for years I have chased the shadow of my sister. Am I doing it for the sake of the vow I made or for her sake?"

"Both, I think. We are children of Odin. It is in our nature to make vows."

Siv was quiet and they passed out of the steep-walled notch into a wider meadow. "I have shaped my life upon the events of that day. If I let it go, if I let her go, have I wasted myself?"

Raef swung his horse in front of Siv's forcing her mount to halt. The Vannheim warriors flowed around them. "Do not speak such things. Doubt sows only grief." The words were worthless, he knew, a poor balm, and yet he was compelled to say them, to wipe the uncertainty from Siv's face, to ease the burden she brought on herself. Siv gave him a small smile and Raef could see he had accomplished nothing.

They rode on in silence until the stars came out and the night sky spread over the world. As Raef drifted into sleep, he saw shadows pass in front of the moon, shadows in the form of wolves. He dreamed of the wolf brothers Hati and Skoll, of the Einherjar preparing to battle the giants, of a black and white bird, and of Yggdrasil drenched in Black Surt's fires.

ᚾ ᚾ ᚾ

The Vestrhall lay a day to the south when a pair of riders came upon Raef's company. The horses were lathered in sweat and blowing hard, their heads drooping with exhaustion, their legs trembling as they came to a halt on the opposite bank of the river Raef's party was following.

"Hold your fire," Raef shouted, signaling to the three warriors who had nocked arrows to their bows. Vakre was already urging his horse across the water toward Raef, heedless of the threat aimed at him. Raef recognized Lochauld behind the son of Loki, the young warrior from Axsellund who had pledged his life to Vannheim. Raef's horse danced sideways as Vakre urged his up the bank. "What, what is it?"

"Fengar has been found."

"Where? Is the Vestrhall safe?"

Vakre nodded. "Untouched. Word came from the southern stretch of Vannheim of fighting in Narvik and Silfravall. The reports were contradictory save for one thing. All agreed that Fengar has been discovered." Vakre drew a tiny roll of parchment from a pouch at his belt. "This came yesterday. From Bryndis of Narvik."

Raef took the parchment from Vakre's fingers and broke open the blot of honey-colored wax that sealed it. The paper unfurled quickly and Raef read with eager eyes.

"She requests Vannheim's aid. Fengar has reunited with Stefnir of Gornhald and the greater part of his dwindling force."

"Her intent?" Vakre asked.

"To bring an end to the falsely chosen king. To call a new gathering." Raef signaled for the riders to move on and they splashed across the river. He tucked Bryndis's message into his sleeve and urged his horse forward. "Would that I knew the extent of Fengar's strength, how many men still follow his banner, how many lords still cling to him. She does not say."

"How will you answer her?"

"I do not know. Must more Vannheim blood be spilled? Have we not done our part in vanquishing the Hammerling?" Raef looked at Vakre. "And yet she speaks of a gathering, a chance to set right the wrongs done in the Great-Belly's hall." Vakre said nothing and Raef thought he knew the son of Loki's mind. "You mean to go."

Vakre's voice was calm and betrayed nothing. "My uncle will be there."

Raef hesitated. "I thought you did not wish to be Loki's murderous son."

"But I am Loki's son, Raef. It is time I accepted that. If I have learned one thing from my father's gift, it is that I cannot escape him." Vakre raised a hand and placed it on Raef's shoulder. "I am a danger to you. To Siv. Let me be a danger to my uncle instead."

Raef swallowed the words that were forming on his tongue, words to counter Vakre's, and instead said only, "Then I will not hold you back."

"And you?"

Raef thought for a moment. "I will speak to the captains. Put the question to them." They rode in silence for a long stretch and then Raef related the discovery of the cavern inside Old Troll, of the likeness of Yggdrasil and its strange disappearance, of Ailmaer's grief. "Tell me, Vakre, what do you think has happened to Visna?" She had been on Raef's mind much of late. "Eira has the sword and soon her transformation will be complete, if it is not already. What happens to a woman after she creates a Valkyrie?" It was a question neither could answer but Raef could see his dark thoughts mirrored in Vakre's eyes.

ᛉ ᛉ ᛉ

Vakre did not delay in his departure for Narvik. After their return to the Vestrhall, he slept for a few short hours before saddling a fresh horse and preparing for his journey. Raef walked with him to the gate, and then beyond into the open air. Siv lingered just behind, her goodbye already said. Raef could see that Vakre was eager to be away, but he did not pull himself into the saddle.

"I will send word when I know more," Vakre said, the horse's reins limp in his hand. Raef nodded but still Vakre hesitated. "If we do not meet again, I am glad to have known you, Raef Skallagrim."

Raef's chest constricted at the thought of never seeing Vakre again. "Save your words." He tried to smile, but there was no truth behind it and no jest in Vakre's eyes. The son of Loki swung up into the saddle, his gaze still on Raef as his horse tossed its head and stepped backward. Vakre turned the horse's head and dug his heels in, releasing his gaze from Raef in that moment, and they were off, smooth strides carrying them over the snow. Raef watched, trying to swallow down the sorrow that swelled within him, wondering if he had sent away his last friend, and did not move long after Vakre had vanished from sight.

"Your paths have diverged before." Siv had come to stand at his side. Her cheeks were pink with cold and she blew on her hands to warm them.

"So many have ridden away not to return. So many have died."

"Such is the nature of war."

"When will it be enough? When the seas rise and all of Midgard perishes at the end of all things?" He turned to Siv, consumed with the need to hold her, to feel her in his arms, and pulled her close. "Never leave," he said, breathing into her hair.

↑ ↑ ↑

The eight captains of Vannheim gathered in the hall at dusk. Raef greeted each in turn with a cup of ale. Only two faces remained of those who had served his father. The rest had gone to Valhalla, Thorald, entrusted with much by Raef's father, Finnolf, skilled beyond his years and a natural leader of men, Yorkell, reserved and independent but tireless and clever. The new faces were young, less experienced, chosen by Raef from the shield wall to fill the positions their dead comrades had vacated. Dvalarr, as Raef's right hand in battle, was there as well, as was Siv, but the absence of Vakre seemed a gaping chasm to Raef.

They ate well, feasting on pheasant smothered in garlic, fish baked in a crust of salt, mushrooms dripping with butter, dried apples dipped in honey, and steaming bread. Raef let the conversation wander where it wished, let the men laugh and boast. He spoke little, eager to let the good humor, the simple pleasures of food and drink and good company endure for as long as he could.

But at last the platters were removed, the cups filled once more with ale, the conversation dying away as more and more eyes came to rest on Raef. He took a swig of ale and stood to address them.

"We have a choice before us, and I urge you all to speak your minds, to speak what lies in your hearts." Raef looked from face to face. "We have a chance to end this war. Bryndis of Narvik sends word that Fengar has been discovered and that she is in pursuit. She means to bring him to battle, a last battle, and she asks for our aid." Raef let the words settle over each man before continuing. "I do not know Fengar's strength, I do not know who will fight at his side, or who will ride to aid Bryndis. But I do know that Vannheim has bled much of late, that our warriors have been left on far flung battlefields, that our people have suffered the loss of home and kin. In this matter, I am not the king you have chosen, I am simply a warrior among warriors. And so I put the decision to you, to all of you. What is Vannheim to do?"

It was Olund who spoke first and the others looked to him with respect, for Olund had served Einarr before Raef.

"It seems to me, lord, that Vannheim has done enough. Let someone else deal with Fengar."

"And if the lady Bryndis is defeated? Fengar must be overcome, his followers brought to heel." A younger captain, Skuli, got to his feet, his face bright, his challenge to Olund direct.

"Fengar will be destroyed with or without Vannheim's help. His numbers weaken, his conviction whittles away to nothing. We need only wait." This from Melkolf.

"Wait and be named cowards." Skuli's glare turned to Melkolf now. "Would you have it be said that Vannheim sat out the last battle? That Vannheim was too afraid to see it through?"

"I agree with Skuli," Njall said. "We have named Skallagrim our king. If he defeats Fengar, none will question his right to rule."

Raef held up a hand. "The lady Bryndis has stated her intent to call another gathering. Either she does not know of my naming, or she does not care. And I am inclined to agree with her. Regardless, do not make this decision with any thought of that. Rather think only on what is best for Vannheim, for your sisters and brothers, mothers and fathers, for the children you will one day have." Raef tried not to think of another battle, one that would be upon them all too soon, one that would wipe out any thought of the future and see the destruction of the gods. Better to give these men something to live for.

The voices around him went silent and he could see the confusion in the eyes of some, some who no doubt could not understand why he would support another gathering, when, with Fengar's death, he would be the sole surviving named king.

The silence lingered and Raef could see the split between the captains. Raef shared a glance with Siv before turning to look at Dvalarr. "Crow," Raef said, "you are quiet."

Dvalarr shifted on the bench, arms crossed over his thick chest. His discomfort was plain. "I would not have it said that Vannheim is weak, lord, or her warriors gutless." It was answer enough.

"Think on this," Raef said. "I expect to see each of you in the morning with your decision."

The hall emptied as the captains took their leave. Dvalarr lingered until Raef nodded for him to go, leaving only Siv. Raef sank into a chair and rested his head in his hands.

"There will be no consensus," he muttered. "Olund is too stubborn, Skuli too eager to prove himself. The others will flock to one or the other." He lifted his head. "Was it too much to ask? Should I have forced my decision upon them?"

"Do you know your own mind?" Siv asked.

Raef groaned. "No." He drained the last of his ale. "I would not drag reluctant warriors into a battle they do not crave. But nor would I leave Bryndis unaided. The Hammerling was right, Siv. It is time this war was ended." Raef took Siv's hand and pulled her into his lap. "But Fengar is not all that is on my mind." He kissed her earlobe and wrapped his arms around her, his gaze transfixed by her green eyes. "Siv. The darkness is coming for all of us. I would swear myself to you before it comes, in sight of all the gods. Will you have me?"

Siv traced two fingers along his jaw. "Yes."

TWENTY-ONE

THERE WAS NO priest to conduct the ceremony. Of Josurr, the young priest of Odin, there had been no sign since Raef had reclaimed the Vestrhall from Isolf. The sacred cave was abandoned, though whether Josurr had fled in fear of Isolf or seen an opportunity to lift the yoke of obedience Raef had shouldered him with, Raef could not be sure. He had given little thought to the priest's absence, but now it chafed at him, so impatient was he to bind his life to Siv's. Without the priest, they would have to wait, and so Raef was in a sour mood when he roused himself with the sun to hear each captain's decision. But before he could hear the captains, Raef had a visit to make.

Eirik of Kolhaugen had sustained a leg wound in the battle outside the Vestrhall's walls. The lord of Kolhaugen had intended to leave with the remainder of the Hammerling's men, whose lives Raef had spared, but Raef would not let him limp away into the wild with the surviving warriors of Kolhaugen. The wound was healing well, though it was still wrapped in heavy bandages and caused Eirik pain when he moved in haste.

"I will grow fat on this fish your kitchen woman keeps feeding me," Eirik said after Raef found him seated across from the warm kitchen hearth and under a string of dried herbs. The scent of baking bread filled Raef's nose.

Raef grinned. "She does make good fish." He gestured to the knife in Eirik's hand and the basket of trout at his feet. A small pile of silver scales gleamed on the dark wood of the long table. "Found a way to make yourself useful?"

Eirik shrugged. "A fish is only a fish. But a fish cleaned to perfection, now that is something to behold."

"I bet young Gurin could clean ten in the time it takes you to do one."

Eirik waved the little knife at Raef. "But does young Gurin know how to peel back the skin without damaging the flesh?"

"He learned from the best," Raef said, grinning.

Eirik laughed, a good strong laugh that Raef was glad to hear. A comfortable silence fell over them and Raef went to the hearth, where a broth simmered, waiting, no doubt, for the fish and the root vegetables Darri was peeling just outside the kitchen door.

"How is your leg?"

"Mending. I will be fit to travel by the time the moon is full."

"And then?"

Silence for a moment. "And then home for me, Skallagrim." Another pause and Raef turned away from the hearth. Eirik sighed. "I have been away a long time."

"And you return alone."

"Yes." Eirik's gaze went to the knife. He flicked a scale from its edge and then plucked a fish from the basket. "Yes." He ran the knife across the striped body once, twice. "It will be a strange thing to set foot in Kolhaugen knowing that my brother is dead."

"Strange, but better for your people, no?"

"Better for them, yes." Still Eirik did not look up from the trout in his hand. Raef waited. The knife came to a halt and Eirik laid it with precision on the table, then looked at Raef. "Sometimes I wonder what it would be like to go back. Back to the way things were, I mean."

"Before Alvar was dead?"

"Not just that. Before the Palesword raised an army of warriors that could not be killed. Before this war ravaged over the lands of so many. Before Fengar was named king. Before your father died. Things might be different."

"Perhaps," Raef said. "But Fenrir has the Allfather's scent and the drops of poison that will bring Thor to his knees hang already from Jörmungand's teeth. Things might be different, but all that would be very much the same."

Eirik was quiet. "You are right," he said at last. He smiled to himself, then the grin grew. "And so I shall go home to Kolhaugen and clean fish and drink mead until the twilight of the gods comes." He grew serious once more. "And then I shall stand with the Einherjar until the end."

Raef nodded.

"I will look for you there, Skallagrim."

Raef nodded again, but he could not bring himself to speak the lie, to say that he would stand beside Eirik. There was no place for him in the last great host of warriors, in the army of the slain that would succumb with the gods to Surt's flaming sword. He let the shadow of Eirik's words diffuse with the scent of hot bread.

"I will not be here when you are well enough to travel," Raef said.

"Fengar?"

"Is within reach. If only we have the strength to grasp him."

"I would aid you if I could."

Raef shook his head. "Go home. And may the gods give you peace before the end."

ϟ ϟ ϟ

The captains came to him one by one, Olund first and unwavering, Skuli last and bold. In the end, four wished to spare Vannheim from further bloodshed and four sought victory over Fengar. But no longer was Raef's own mind mired in doubt and so the split voices of his captains troubled him less than he had expected. Raef followed Skuli from the hall into the early morning light, where the rest waited.

"My mind is clear," Raef told the captains. "I will not leave Bryndis to face Fengar alone. But neither will I condemn he who wishes to keep his blade sheathed." The captains cast sideways glances at each other. "I ride to Narvik. Any warrior or shield-maiden who wishes to follow is welcome. Those who would stay will not face judgment."

"Except from the gods." Skuli's accusation bit into the chill of the morning air and Olund flushed red with anger. The older man lunged for Skuli, teeth bared, restrained only by Melkolf's strong arm.

"Would you threaten me?" Olund bellowed. "Say that again when my axe rests between your balls."

Raef descended from the stone steps and stood between snarling Olund and Skuli, whose lips curled up with disdain.

"Brothers, enough. Ill words between us will only sow discontent, and that I will not have. The warriors who remain in the village must be given the choice. Riders must be sent to inform others. See to it." Raef waited until the captains walked away, Olund striding stiff-legged with Melkolf at his shoulder, young Njall casting quick glances at Raef and Skuli, who was last to step away. Raef reached out and grabbed the edge of Skuli's cloak, yanking to turn the captain around.

"Insult them again and I will strip you of all that I have given you." Raef's gaze strayed to the pair of arm rings decorating Skuli's forearm to make his meaning clear. "My father's captains knew when to speak and when to keep silent. Think on this and save your nerve and your slurs for Fengar." Raef held Skuli's stare and only released him when the other man forced out a stiff nod. Raef watched him go and wished again that Finnolf and Thorald and Yorkell lived yet to stand beside him.

"The best of us have died and gone to the gods," Raef said to Dvalarr, who had watched all in silence from the highest step. "We are left to face the end without their courage, their wisdom."

"The end?" The Crow's face was creased in confusion and Raef cursed his clumsy tongue for saying too much.

"The end of this war," Raef said, "and whatever it brings."

TWENTY-TWO

DEATH AND DESTRUCTION had come to Narvik. Fifty-two warriors had chosen to follow Raef south and their course took them first through the western edge of Silfravall and then on into Narvik, a place of narrow valleys and small farms, a land surrounded on two sides by harsh, barren peaks. And yet the soil was rich, nurtured by glacial water, and much coveted was the wool shorn from Narvik's sheep.

The northern-most valley smelled still of smoke and fire, though the ashes were long since cooled. Four farms had perched on the hillsides, their pastures stretching from the valley floor and the stream that meandered there, to the high hills, home to eagles. But all four farms were burned, their buildings hollow shells or crumbled ruins. The carcasses of sheep and horses and cattle had been picked clean by scavengers, their bones littering the snow. The next valley was much the same, only Raef was not so sure all the bones belonged to animals. Once he thought he saw the grey, lithe form of the lynx slinking through the burned wreckage of a farm, for she had followed the warrior column as it wound away from the Vestrhall, but it turned out to be nothing more than an ash-smeared piece of cloth billowing in the breeze. He had not caught sight of the lynx since evening of the second day. She had come to Raef's fire that night, sniffed his hand, curled once around each leg, and then she had trotted off into the darkness without a backward glance. In his heart, Raef knew she had claimed her independence, knew he would not see her again.

Raef spotted the watcher at dawn on their second day in Narvik lands. A lone rider stood on the ridge above them, silhouetted against the eastern sky, a tall spear piercing the roof of the world. The horse trotted out of sight not long after the camp began to stir, but three times that day Raef caught sight of the lone warrior as they continued south, pushing deeper into Narvik.

The rains came that night, cruel shards and pellets spit from the sky, coating cloaks and boots with a slick shell of ice. Beards froze, stiff and matted, and hoods drawn tight still did not keep the sting from cheeks and eyelids. Raef called an early halt and they spent a miserable night hunkered down under thick pine branches without fire and only small bites of dried venison to sustain them. But with the dawn came blinding sunshine and every twig, stone, and dangling, brown leaf blazed in the new light, for the world was made of ice and nothing else.

Raef broke through the pine branches above him, shattering the ice into countless slivers, and stepped out into the snow. Taking a deep breath, he massaged the back of his neck and watched the air exhaled from his lungs take shape and hover in front of his face for a moment before being dispelled. He turned back to the pine tree to wake Siv and show her the new day when an arrow pierced the hard surface of the snow at his feet. Raef froze and scanned the trees for the archer, but all was still.

"Clever," he called out. "Lay your trap while we shelter from the storm. Most would not have the will to wait out the night in such weather. You show much fortitude, Bryndis of Narvik."

Behind him, the pine branches parted as Siv was drawn out by the sound of Raef's voice and he could hear others stirring from within their cocoons of ice.

"Stay where you are, Siv," Raef murmured. But he could not warn them all and soon his warriors were stepping out into the open air. "Bryndis." Raef's voice rang out through the trees, made sharper, it seemed, by the ice. "I am not your enemy."

"No." The woman's voice came from his left. "No, it would seem you are not." Bryndis of Narvik stepped forth from her hiding place. She was dressed in dark leather and a cloak that glittered with ice, her pale white hair bound back in intricate braids, her eyes made fierce by charcoal paint sweeping away from her bottom lids. As she revealed herself, the trees came alive on all sides of Raef's camp as warriors stepped forth. Raef let his gaze drift over them and saw that they were poorly clothed and poorly armed. They were farmers and fishermen dressed in leather, their hands used to holding rod and line or shears, not the tall spears they clutched to their chests. Warriors they might not be, but their faces were grim, their eyes determined, and Raef knew there was strength to be found in Narvik. "Skallagrim?"

"Yes."

Bryndis came close to Raef, head tilted up as her eyes searched his for a moment, and then she held out a hand encased in a leather glove. Without taking his eyes from hers, Raef clasped her forearm and the tension slipped from the air.

⟨ ⟨ ⟨

"How did you know it was me? It could have been Fengar with an arrow aimed at you." Bryndis had removed her gloves and stood with her hands over a fire. In the presence of such warmth, her cloak was melting and she brushed excess water from her shoulders.

"Fengar would not have had the will to endure the storm. But if he had, that arrow would have been aimed here," Raef said, tapping a hand to his heart.

Bryndis nodded and then looked over her shoulder to where Raef's men mingled with those of Narvik. "Is this all?"

"Vannheim has suffered much, lady. I made no demands on my people, only took those who wished to come. More might have been gathered, but that would have taken time I did not care to waste."

Another nod from Bryndis. If she was disappointed by Raef's numbers, she did not let on. "A hazard of having your people spread over such a vast amount of land. Others might beg the gods for such a dilemma." She stared hard at Raef and then broke into a smile that flitted quickly away from her features. "We do not stand alone. Not quite. I have sought help from many. Garhold does not answer. Sverren of Bergoss sent back a frozen piece of horse shit instead of my messenger. Axsellund is silent. Silfravall says little. Leska of Kollumheim promises nothing."

"Uhtred of Garhold is dead, lady. As is Torleif of Axsellund. Who rules in those lands, I cannot say, but we will have no help from them."

Bryndis took this news with a twist of her lips and a nod.

"Who, then, answered your plea?"

"Balmoran."

Raef frowned. "Last I saw Thorgrim Great-Belly, he was content to let his hall play host to a new king."

"Perhaps at first, though he managed to avoid committing warriors to battle, the cunning whoreson. But the Great-Belly is failing and I do not think the decision to ride to my aid was entirely his."

"What do you mean?"

"His son is lord in all but name." Bryndis shot Raef a look of annoyance. "They quarrel endlessly."

"And Fengar? Where is he?"

Bryndis turned solemn. "He is holed up a day's ride from here. His position is well-defended."

"His numbers?"

Bryndis shook her head. "Uncertain. Many." She bit her lip. "Enough to burn a great many of my people's homes."

"We saw evidence of his passing as we came south. I hope some survived."

"Most. They have fled to Narvik's fortress and sit and wonder if they will starve."

Raef nodded his sympathy. "Fengar slaughtered many good animals."

Bryndis's gaze hardened. "Fengar burned farms, yes, and killed those who might have opposed him, but you are wrong, Raef Skallagrim. My people butchered their own animals."

"Why?"

"Better that the enemy be unable to feast on what we have lost, no?"

"A harsh way to live."

"Narvik is small and has always fallen prey to wolves who would pluck up land the gods did not give them. The people here learned long ago that the world is harsh." Her voice and words defied her years and Raef nodded his respect.

"You have a warrior's spirit and a ruler's head, Bryndis."

"You flatter me. But tell me, do you speak as a king? Or a fellow warrior who knows what it is to rule?"

"What do you think?"

The smile threatened to return. "Perhaps I will reserve judgment." Bryndis's gaze narrowed and her face grew hard. "But I want to know, Skallagrim, I have made my intentions to you clear. When Fengar is dead, I will call another gathering. Will you hinder me?"

"No."

"Bluntly spoken."

"The truth is often blunt."

"Is it, then? The truth?" Bryndis did not wait for Raef to answer. "Come. The Great-Belly will wish to see you." She turned to go to her horse, a tall black creature waiting with little patience, but Raef called her back.

"Bryndis."

She looked over her shoulder, eyebrows raised.

"Has a man called Vakre come this way?"

Bryndis shook her head. "I know of no such man." She seemed about to speak, but the question remained behind her lips and she pulled herself into the saddle. "Have your men fall in, Skallagrim."

ᚱ ᚱ ᚱ

The hall of Narvik was nestled in the elbow of two valleys that joined on the shores of a deep lake. Bryndis led the approach from the northwest, but their progress down the valley was halted while the lake still shimmered in the distance. A party of riders cascaded out of the trees, enclosing the Vannheim and Narvik warriors with a well-timed maneuver, but Bryndis did not seem alarmed. Raef caught a grimace twist her face and heard the sigh escape from her lips. Her gaze flickered to Raef but she kept silent as one rider pushed ahead of the rest.

"So, the lady of Narvik returns unscathed." The speaker had the look of Thorgrim Great-Belly, but younger. His face, ruddy in the cold, was wide and already fleshy. His torso was rounded with muscle that would sag and turn to fat with time.

Bryndis smiled. "Do you have so little confidence in me?"

"I only wonder if such risks are necessary. Your safety is paramount."

The smile remained but Raef could see it was strained. "Your concern is kind, Eiger, but my safety is no more important than that of any warrior. Much must be risked in war." The fleshy man's gaze shifted to Raef, who had pulled his horse up alongside Bryndis. The lady of Narvik answered the unasked question. "The lord of Vannheim has joined our fight." Bryndis looked to Raef and nodded in the direction of the stranger. "Eiger of Balmoran, the Great-Belly's son."

Eiger's gaze returned to Bryndis without comment. "Your hall awaits, lady."

Bryndis flashed another smile at the Great-Belly's son, but the moment he turned his horse and called for his men to ride, Raef was sure he heard her mutter, "Yes, do not forget whose hall, fat man."

The hall was long and low, a solid, durable structure lacking embellishments and fine features. The walls that surrounded the village were tall and thick, but here and there the timbers were rotten away, their strength eaten at by time and wet weather, and Raef was not certain the gate would withstand even the most tepid of assaults. Inside, the village was overcrowded. Children dodged between men and horses, their grimy faces laughing at the shouts flung their way. Dogs backed away from the onslaught of hooves, tails tucked between their legs. Men and women watched the arrival of the warriors with calculating expressions, no doubt wondering how they might all expect to be fed. Raef took one look at the place and signaled for his warriors to halt. He angled his horse toward Skuli and Dvalarr, who had ridden through the gates at the rear.

"We will not burden the lady Bryndis. Set up our shelters beside the lake. As long as we are here, we will eat only our own provisions and what we can hunt or forage," Raef said.

The Crow assured him it would be done and Raef found Siv. Leaving their horses with the rest, they continued on to the hall. The doors, thick slabs of smooth, darkened wood manned by a pair of boys, swung open to admit them, and Raef stepped into the hall of Narvik.

A single fire blazed in the middle, surrounded on three sides by tables. Eiger had already seated himself at one and was calling for meat and ale. Bryndis picked her gloves from her fingers, her pale hair gleaming silver in the light of the fire as she spoke in quiet tones to a woman of middle years. Only after the serving woman had turned away and Eiger had taken his first eager swallow of ale did Bryndis acknowledge Raef.

"The Great-Belly?" Raef asked.

Bryndis opened her mouth to answer, but Eiger spoke first, ale dripping into his beard.

"My father is not well," Eiger said. He wiped an arm across his mouth, then drained his cup and called for more. "He keeps his healer close," Eiger went on. "If a poultice or broth will save him, he will find it."

"Is he dying?" Raef said.

"Are not we all dying?" Eiger seemed amused by his own question, then brushed it away. "The illness will claim him, I believe, though perhaps not until the spring thaw. If the gods favor him, he may see high summer."

Raef had no liking for the son of the Great-Belly, but he tried to offer the sort of words a man might like to hear. "The gods will welcome him into Valhalla and give him a place of honor."

"No, I think not." Eiger was not smiling now. "He is a weak man, unworthy of high honor. Too long has he lived off the fame of others, too long has he gotten fat on riches bought not won." The son seemed oblivious that those same riches were already weighing on him.

"Your father was a bold warrior in his youth," Raef said. "Can he not be forgiven for seeking comforts later in life?"

"Youth is not enough. A man must live all his years, be they many or few, with purpose."

"Perhaps your father holds to a purpose still. Have you asked him?"

Eiger's face darkened, but any answer he might have was forgotten at the appearance of a servant bearing a platter of withered apples and winter plums.

"How many times must I tell you," he said to the servant, who would not meet his eyes. "The lord of Balmoran requires meat." He waved an arm, sending ale splashing to the floor. The servant bowed and scurried off. Eiger took a swig of ale and nodded at Raef with a conspiratorial eye. "My father thinks the gods hold fruit dearest above all things. But you and I know they crave meat. Would Thor nibble on an apple? No, he sinks his teeth into dripping haunches of elk." Eiger laughed and did not seem to notice that Raef did not join in.

A new platter was brought, this one heavier than the last and piled high with cuts of venison and legs of pheasant. A plate of bread was also brought. Eiger did not hesitate and his fingers were soon smeared with the juice of a hunk of meat. A dribble ran down his chin and he did not bother to wipe it away. Raef watched but it was Bryndis who stepped out from the shadows, her face betraying nothing. She sat close to Eiger and refilled his cup, this time with sweet mead.

"How is it that you call yourself lord of Balmoran when your father yet draws breath?" Raef seated himself at the bench opposite Eiger and watched the other man through the shimmering heat above the flames. Siv remained standing at the edge of the hall, arms crossed, shoulders stiff, her dislike of Eiger obvious.

Eiger shrugged his meaty shoulders. "He has given much of that burden to me, it is true." Thorgrim's son cracked a smile and then shoved the pheasant leg between his teeth. "It is better this way. When my father dies, no man in Balmoran shall question me for they will already know me as lord."

"How peaceful," Raef said.

"Indeed. Tell me, Skallagrim, have you heard of Dae-gren Clefthand?"

Raef shook his head.

"The Clefthand makes his home in the south of my lands. He fishes in my lake and farms in my earth, and yet always has he pretended to be something other than a dog. Each summer, we hear rumblings of unrest in the south, of promises made by the Clefthand of uprising and bloodshed, and each summer my father sends a gift, gold more often than not, and the rumors die to nothing. When my father breathes his last breath, I shall look to the south and Dae-gren Clefthand will regret his own birth." Eiger's voice had risen and his cheeks, flushed with anger and ale, showed his fervor. When Raef did not react, he went on. "It is I who will lead Balmoran to greatness, not that insolent dog. Odin knows this."

Bryndis's gaze met Raef's from across the fire and though he caught a hint of aversion in her eyes, she smiled as she offered him meat and mead. Only when Bryndis herself began to eat did Raef do the same. A moment later, five hounds burst into the hall, each baying with eager voices, tails whipping back and forth. They skidded to a stop in front of Eiger and he laughed as he tossed them morsels of fatty meat and let one lick the grease from his fingers.

"Do you keep dogs, Skallagrim?"

"A few," Raef said. "I prefer to hunt in silence."

Eiger laughed again. "Hear that, girls? The lord of Vannheim is too good for the likes of you." He did not seem offended. "Me, I like to feel my blood rise when the hounds begin to bay."

When Bryndis had finished her mead, she stood and looked to Raef. "I will see if Thorgrim is well enough to join us."

Raef was quick to rise to his feet. "Let me assist you."

When they had left the smoke of the fire and Eiger's noisy chewing behind, Bryndis led him through the back of the hall and out a small door. There, in the narrow passage between buildings, Raef caught the lady of Narvik's sleeve.

"How many of your people will go hungry this night because of his great appetite?"

Bryndis flushed. "We are not so poor as that, not yet."

"His hounds are at liberty to roam your hall, he commands your servants as though they are his own, and you sit by and smile and pour his mead. Does Bryndis rule here? Or Eiger?"

Bryndis drew herself up and did not flinch from Raef's stare. "You insult me, Skallagrim."

"And there she is again, the woman I met in the ice this morning, a woman accustomed to authority, a woman who does not shrink in the presence of men. Where did she go, Bryndis?"

"What does it matter to you? I may do as I please in my home, Skallagrim."

"You are right. Perhaps it is not my place. I hardly know you. But I cannot understand why you would sit by and let Eiger hold sway. This is your battle, the fight you wanted, your land and home at stake. Not his."

Bryndis looked at Raef for a moment, the anger in her eyes fading. "I cannot fight Fengar alone. I am not beautiful. Men's eyes do not seek me out like bees honey. Eiger is happy. He has his hounds. His belly is full. I need Balmoran's shields, Raef, and so I will do what I must to keep him happy." Bryndis placed a hand on Raef's arm. "Remember, I told you that Narvik has often been at the mercy of greater powers, that its people have learned to survive in a harsh world. The same can be said of Narvik's ruler. I do what must be done." Bryndis turned and took a single step forward before spinning back to face Raef, her face hard with emotion. "And when all this is done, when Fengar is dead and a true king has been named, when I no longer have need of Eiger, I will show him my claws."

Raef did not doubt her intent, or the fire that burned in her eyes, but misgivings still plagued him. He swallowed them down and said only, "Take care that you do not dig too deep a hole, Bryndis."

She was already turning away and did not respond. Raef followed her to another building, this one an old stable converted into living quarters. The interior was lit only by candles, their flames flickering in the gust of air that followed close on Raef's heels as he stepped over the threshold. The air was smoky and smelled of lavender and dill, as though long-forgotten herbs had been left too long. A pair of servants kept to the edge of the candlelight, one stooped and bent so far that he could barely lift his head to see their arrival, the other a young woman who watched Raef and Bryndis with wide eyes. At the far end, a large chair sat before a huge, blackened hearth and a figure was ensconced deep within its hulking grasp, half-hidden under layer after layer of thick furs.

Had he not known Thorgrim Great-Belly was ailing, Raef might not have recognized him. Gone was the proud lord and the remnants of strength and youthful vitality that had clung to him when he had called the gathering. His was still a large man, encumbered with fat, but he sagged now, as he heaved himself out of the chair, the pelts cascading off of him, and his steps were slow and sluggish as his feet dragged across the floor. His cheeks were pale and his eyes sunken. He kept his head down, gaze intent on his feet as though he feared he might stumble on the smooth floor and fall to his knees. He managed no more than four steps away from the hearth before he was forced to stop and steady himself. The young female servant rushed to his side and Thorgrim leaned against her slender frame. Only then did he raise his eyes high enough to take in his guests.

"Do you know me, lord?" Raef asked.

The noise that came from the Great-Belly was both cough and

laugh. "Know you? You spilled blood in my hall once, Raef Skallagrim. I do not forget such things."

"Skallagrim is my guest," Bryndis said. "Whatever has passed between you has no place here."

Thorgrim brushed this away with a feeble wave of his hand. "Where is my son? Has he gotten himself killed yet?"

Bryndis answered in smooth tones. "Eiger has only just returned from scouting Fengar's position."

Thorgrim snorted. "More like he slept off a bellyful of mead in some stinking place and has come out in search of the next cask." The Great-Belly laughed at his own wit and coughed again, his body convulsing with the force of it. His grip on the young woman grew tighter, Raef could see, the pale skin over his knuckles stretching thin as the coughing fit subsided. The young woman bore the violent motion and the Great-Belly's weight without even a grimace.

When Thorgrim had regained his voice, he glared at Bryndis. "I am tired. Leave me. Skallagrim can stay."

Bryndis met Raef's eyes, but neither spoke a word as Bryndis passed from the smoky room, leaving Raef with the Great-Belly. The girl helped Thorgrim reclaim his seat by the hearth and she rearranged the heavy furs with care, including the fine white pelt that Raef and his father had given Thorgrim at the gathering. The Great-Belly motioned her away and sank back into the chair, a grimace of pain flashing across his face. Only when the servants had retreated in Bryndis's wake did Thorgrim venture to speak again.

"Are they gone, then?" He peered around Raef and then stood once more and walked to the hearth. His strides were firm and sure and his hands did not tremble. The watery eyes that had stared at Raef were now clear and bright.

"What is this?" Raef asked, wary at the sudden change in the lord of Balmoran.

The Great-Belly did not answer right away, instead he put a log on the fire and then seated himself on the bench by the hearth, his broad shoulders bent over his chest, his hands clasped together while his elbows rested on his knees. "My son will have told you I am dying, and this is the truth. Only I do not intend to go to Valhalla as soon as he would like." He caught Raef's gaze. "Oh, I stumble and I limp and I complain of pains and aches in my head and bowels. But I am not so weak as that. Not yet."

"Why such pretense?" Raef stepped closer to the fire, watching the older man carefully.

Thorgrim's eyes grew harsh. "The wolf and the bear have been enemies since the dawn of days. A wolf would never presume to attack a strong bear, hale and whole. But a dying one? Riddled with pain and prone to fever? So weak he can hardly grasp a horn of ale? A wolf might misjudge this bear. A wolf might act rashly."

Raef grasped the meaning, if not the entire story. "And yet a wolf hunts with a pack. A bear would not fall to the teeth of one, but the jaws of many?"

Thorgrim gave a nod and Raef knelt to tend to the fire. "True, my son has those who would follow him. But I am not yet friendless. He is uncertain of himself, his position, his power, though he pretends otherwise. For now it is enough that he thinks me disabled by my illness. This way I may watch and make my own plans."

"Perhaps the bear will recover?"

"No." Thorgrim gazed into the small flames that now ate at the log. "The bear will not. And Eiger knows this as well as I."

"How can either of you be so sure?"

"Because he has made sure of it. This is no natural illness, Skallagrim. My own son has had me poisoned. He thinks I do not know, of course, and I play the part he has given me. As I said, I have plans of my own."

"And those might be?"

"Retribution."

Silence fell over them even as the fire grew, sending light into the dark corners. At last Raef spoke again. "Why tell me?"

"Because I must make do with the man Odin has sent to me. You help me, I help you. A simple bargain, no?"

"I am here for Fengar, not to interfere in Balmoran's affairs. And what do you think you could offer me?"

Thorgrim scratched at his beard and continued as though Raef had said nothing. "You lend me your ears, tell me everything you hear in my son's presence, and in return I will see that he keeps his hands off the girl."

"Bryndis? She is capable of fending for herself." And yet Thorgrim's words were a confirmation of Raef's fears.

The Great-Belly's gaze narrowed. "The last time my son took interest in a woman, she did not see the light of day again. Her body was a mangled piece of flesh, disposed of with the kitchen refuse. Would you have the lady Bryndis suffer the same?"

Raef kept silent and Thorgrim got to his feet. He called for the serving girl and the moment his voice rolled off the timber walls, Raef watched as his shoulders slumped forward, his back bent in a painful stoop, his hand shook as it reached to steady him on the back of the chair, and, as he went to meet the girl, Raef heard his feet shuffle away, one agonizing step after the other.

TWENTY-THREE

"IT IS NOT much," Bryndis said, her gaze roving over the spare chamber that had been opened for Raef and Siv. The room was little-used and smelled of damp earth. "But it will keep you dry."

"The day is not yet old, Bryndis. Show me where Fengar is."

"My men are worn to the bone. There will be no more scouting today." Bryndis raised her voice as Raef began to protest. "Tomorrow." Raef accepted this with a nod, though it did not sit well with him. "I have little to offer you, but there is one thing my hall is rich in that few have. Steam. A hot spring runs under these hills and long ago a bathhouse was built to harness its warmth. Even in darkest winter the stones are warm to the touch and the waters hot. You are welcome to it."

Bryndis did not lie. The bathing room, stone from floor to ceiling, was filled with steam. A shallow pool covered much of it and a single servant, a young boy, collected their clothes as Raef and Siv slipped into the water. Raef submerged himself for a long moment, glad to feel the heat penetrating through his winter skin. Standing, the water came to the middle of Raef's chest and he floated on the surface until Siv offered to scrape his back. Raef agreed and seated himself on the edge of the pool, the steam rising and swirling, the stones warm beneath his skin, and closed his eyes as Siv went to work on his back, first rubbing oil and then scraping it away with a strigil. When she had finished, he did the same for her, and in time he felt the tension slip from his muscles.

Raef set the strigil down on the stones and wrapped his arms around Siv, resting his chin on her shoulder blade. The short hairs behind her ears curled on her damp skin. "We could do it. Here. This very night. I am sure Bryndis keeps a priest."

Siv leaned back against him. "Not here."

"Have you changed your mind?"

Siv smiled. "No." The smile vanished. "But not here. This place, I do not like it."

"Then we will wait." Battle with Fengar loomed and there was little chance of another opportunity presenting itself in the coming days. But Raef understood Siv's misgivings.

"Do you think Hauk has joined Fengar?"

It was an unexpected question but one Raef had turned over in his own mind many times. "Perhaps. His list of friends grows thin. And now that he has been exposed, there would be little point in pretending he does not follow Fengar." Raef paused and watched a trickle of water slide down Siv's neck. "Fengar will have need of him if they are to survive."

Siv was quiet for a long moment. "I think of Eira often. I wonder if she has found a measure of happiness, if, indeed, a Valkyrie knows what it means to be happy. She was never at peace. Perhaps this new life will fill the emptiness in her heart."

Raef had not spared the newly-made Valkyrie much thought. "It is Visna I wonder about. I imagine her releasing her sword, letting go of the last piece of Asgard she had claim to. And I wonder what has become of her."

"Cilla said she wished to see the Valkyries. Do you think she lives?"

Raef had not thought of the young girl from Kelgard in a long time. So young and yet so fierce and determined. He had no answer, and could only hold Siv closer.

In time Siv stirred and said she wanted to visit with the three shieldmaidens from Vannheim who had followed Raef south. They were young, she said, and uncertain, and she would ease their fears if she could. Raef smiled and watched Siv dress in the fresh clothes that had been brought from their packs. After she left, he enjoyed the heat and the steam for a moment longer, but as he rose from the pool, the door opened and the steam parted to reveal Eiger on the threshold.

Eiger was swathed in a black fur, but the coarse chest hair and pink skin visible below his neck told Raef he was naked beneath. He held a wooden cup in his hand and raised it to his lips, draining the contents before casting it to the stone floor where it rattled and rolled to a halt.

"I have found the steam is best at this hour, Skallagrim. No, no," Eiger said as Raef made to dress. "Stay. I would speak with you in private." Raef retreated back into the depths of the pool, trying to discern Eiger's mood. There was no impatience or demand in his face, only calm words and earnest eyes. "My father has ears every-where. Only the baths are safe."

The steam was thick, the light dim. Raef watched Eiger shrug out of his fur, a bear shedding its skin, and then sink his wide girth into the pool. He let out a groan of pleasure and lay back in the water, the rolls of fat and muscle on his chest and belly protruding like a rising whale.

"These waters have been known to heal," Eiger said, his voice floating off the stones. "The spring is ancient. Frigg herself is said to have bathed here when there was nothing but trees and open air encircling the waters. They say Freya is the great beauty among the gods, second to none. But it was Frigg, when the sun's light was still new and the grass fresh beneath her bare feet, who caught Odin's eye. She is the one we should sing of and cherish." Eiger swam closer to Raef so that they might see each other clearly through the steam. "Do you love the gods, Skallagrim? Have you known their presence, felt a strong hand at your back in battle when all is chaos and darkness? No," Eiger hurried on, "you make your home by the sea, perhaps you have felt their caress in the form of a swift breeze that fills your sails and sets your course for home." He looked at Raef with a hopeful expression, but Raef kept his features still even though his mind was filled with thoughts of ravens and his own dream-like meeting with Odin. Eiger went on. "Long have I felt the gods are my true family. The father, mother, brothers and sisters that are my blood are but a poor substitute, shadows of the family in Asgard that I yearn for. Much of my youth was spent hoping the gods might find reason to call me home. Gladly would I have given up any dreams of valor and renown for this." Eiger paused and took a deep breath, closing his eyes. To Raef, his fleshy face had grown younger, almost childlike, as he revealed his dreams. "Sometimes I think I can hear them. Can you feel their presence?"

"I regret that my ears are deaf to such a marvel," Raef said. But for him the marvel was not the presence of the gods, but Eiger himself. Some might think him mad, but there was no wildness, no raving. Only fierce obsession and utter sincerity. A far more dangerous combination.

"As I grew into a man, I began to understand that I should not be waiting for the Allfather to bring me home, to summon me to his shining hall. He is beset on all sides by terrible foes, each more deadly than the last and each striving to bring about his destruction and the annihilation of Asgard. He fights to stave off that dreadful fate, every breath holding back the tide, every breath a lifetime of woe and desperate survival. Who am I to ask the War-Maker to spare a moment for me?" If Eiger wanted Raef to answer, he did not wait long, but rushed onward, his gaze turned inward now. "I must find my own way to my father's hall. I must gain Asgard."

This statement lingered in the steam and Raef began to ask how he thought to accomplish this, but Eiger spoke again. "A perilous task, a dangerous journey, but one I have prepared for my whole life. I can see it before me, the bifrost leading me to the gates of diamond and gold, gates that reach up and mingle with the stars. And there, where the grass is ever green, the winds always gentle, the skies always bright, I shall at last make my home where I belong. For I have begun to understand the purpose of my life. The Allfather will have need of me when the twilight comes."

Raef asked the only question he could. "And my part in it all? Why do you tell me this?"

Eiger's fingers slid across the surface of the pool toward Raef, stopping just short of touching him. Eiger's brow lowered and his eyes narrowed in a pained expression, interrupted by a small, almost wistful smile.

"They told me he would come with stars in his hair and a storm in his eyes. They told me that together we would walk the path to Asgard and together we would bring victory to the gods in their hour of need."

"Who?"

"You, Skallagrim." The words were a caress, full of longing and promise.

"You are mistaken, Eiger. My fate does not walk with yours. My fate is mine alone."

"No, no, do you not see? You are meant to walk with the gods, not alone."

Raef shook his head, trying to find words that would dissuade Eiger. "But stars? A storm? There were no stars in the moment of our meeting. The skies were clear and filled with the sun."

Eiger smiled. "A storm of ice staked claim to the world this morning and it was as if the stars themselves had come to earth. What is ice if not the child of the stars? You were wreathed in that embrace."

Melting ice was no sign from the gods, Raef might have said. But he could see that nothing he said would defeat Eiger's ravenous belief. Eiger raised a hand from the pool, water dripping from his fingers like liquid gems, and reached out to Raef's face, stopping to hover over Raef's cheek, so close that Raef could feel the heat of Eiger's skin.

"The gods have given you a great gift, Raef, son of Einarr, and made you as one of their own. They never told me you would be formed like one of the gods descended from Asgard."

"They?" Eiger's arousal was obvious now. Raef chose to ignore it.

"Those who have vowed to guide me from the realm of men. Let me show them to you. Hear what they have to say. And then together we will take the first steps on our glorious path."

Raef searched for words. "You speak of a path that is not mine, Eiger, though surely any man would wish for it. You are mistaken. I am not the man you seek. My place is on the field of battle, where I will end this war."

"You are too humble, Skallagrim."

"Eiger. Hear me. I have come to Narvik for a single purpose, to see to Fengar's defeat and destruction. What you seek is beyond me."

Eiger's mouth tightened, the sincerity gone from his eyes, but he kept his voice pleasant. "I can only hope you will discover the mistake you have made, before you come to regret it."

It was not a threat, but Raef, as he climbed from the pool and pulled on his clean clothes under Eiger's watchful eye, was sure he had run afoul of whatever good will the Great-Belly's son possessed.

When Raef reached the room he and Siv would share, it was the Great-Belly who waited for him, half-hidden in shadow, a deep hood pulled down to hide his features.

"You have seen my son." Thorgrim plucked back the hood as Raef closed the door behind him and settled the iron latch into place. "Does he rage against Daegren Clefthand? Does he speak of the captains who will follow him?"

Raef studied Thorgrim's worn face, understanding then that the Great-Belly did not comprehend the depths of the workings of his son's mind.

"His mind is far from Daegren Clefthand tonight."

"What do you mean?" The Great-Belly's brow creased as his eyes narrowed.

"Your son is consumed with an obsession he has long harbored. I do not doubt that he intends to supplant you and claim Balmoran for himself, but this is not what drives him."

"Speak plainly, Skallagrim."

"He dreams of Asgard. He believes Odin is his true father and that he is meant to find a path to join the gods in their halls," Raef said.

Thorgrim stared at Raef in disbelief. "Preposterous. His mind is bent on mead and hunting and bloodshed. He has no thoughts for the gods, he does not even honor them." Scowling Thorgrim paced toward Raef. "I do not know what he has promised you in return for forging lies to tell me, but I see through your deceit, Skallagrim." The Great-Belly made to push past Raef and leave the room, but Raef would not let him go.

"What of your assurances, Thorgrim? What of your son's interest in the lady of Narvik? You promised you would draw his attention elsewhere," Raef said, his hand on Thorgrim's shoulder as he blocked the door.

"These lies you have fed me deserve nothing in return," Thorgrim snarled. "And the lady of Narvik is nothing to me." He shouldered into Raef and this time Raef let him go. The door swung behind him and Raef watched as Thorgrim Great-Belly assumed his crippled stoop, his pained gait, and vanished down the hall.

TWENTY-FOUR

"SO YOU SEE." Bryndis shielded her eyes from the blinding sun and she squinted into the distance. "He is well-defended."

Fengar had chosen his position wisely. Or perhaps it was Stefnir of Gornhald, if he still lived, for Raef knew Stefnir to be a veteran of many battles and more skilled in strategy than Fengar.

The ruins of the ancient fortress lay across a narrow valley and high above them, perched at the top of a cliff and surrounded on all sides by sheer rock. Bryndis had pointed out the sole access route, a narrow stair carved into the cliff. A perilous path, full of switchbacks and uneven footing. Any man who dared the climb would be easy prey for an archer above.

"Why not return to Solheim?" Siv asked.

Bryndis shrugged, her eyes still on the cliff. "News of the Hammerling's death came to us only with your arrival. If Fengar remains ignorant of it, he would keep clear of his home lands, as he has done all winter."

"The fortress is far more secure than your hall, lady," Raef said. "Why did the rulers of Narvik abandon it?"

Bryndis laughed. "To answer that I would need to tell you a long, bloody story involving so many twists and turns and broken oaths that even I have trouble remembering all of it. It is enough to know that someone was very clever and cunning, and someone else was very stubborn and proud. They were friends until they were no longer friends. Such is the way of things."

"And there is no other way? Not even from the high passes above?"

"A goat might manage it, Skallagrim, but not an army."

"Then we will starve them out. As I have said before, lady." Eiger had pulled his horse up alongside Bryndis and spoke now with brash certainty. He had been quiet on the ride east from Bryndis's hall that morning, though Raef had caught him staring more than once. Whether it was a malicious eye, or merely a watchful one, Raef was uncertain.

"And as I have said, we believe Fengar to be well-provisioned. He pillaged enough storehouses to make it so. There is no telling how long they might last. And through it all, our own warriors would sit and shiver, at the mercy of the winds and the snow, while Fengar waits behind stone walls." Bryndis sighed. "And yet, I do not know what else can be done."

They retreated to the large white tent that had been erected on the valley floor. Around them, the warriors of Narvik, Vannheim, and Balmoran were at work setting up shelters and starting fires. They were within sight of the cliff-top fortress, though well out of arrow-range, and no doubt more than a few pairs of eyes were taking note of their every movement. It had been Raef who had insisted on staking out ground so close to the fortress. He wanted Fengar to know what waited for him and Bryndis had been willing to agree. The array of small tents would be an intimidating display, made even more so by the fact that fully a third were being set up merely as decoys to create the image of a far larger force.

Inside the tent, Raef waited while Bryndis spoke to a grey-bearded warrior who seemed to trail her like a shadow, her father's brother, she had told Raef, and then went and spoke quietly in her ear.

"I would have you show me how a goat might access the fortress."

Bryndis studied him, her green eyes intense above the black charcoal paint that lined her lower lids. "If it could be done, Fengar would be dead already, his head on a spear outside my hall, and we would be choosing a new king."

"I do not question your courage or your resolve, Bryndis, I only wish to know what you know."

The lady of Narvik was silent for a moment. "It cannot be done." Her mouth curved into a smile. "But if it could, you would have to begin at the Dragon's Jaw."

"And where might I find the Dragon's Jaw?"

Bryndis pushed aside the tent flap and surveyed the far side of the valley. She pointed. "First you would climb to the top of that ridge, there. Follow it to the shadow of the mountain. From there, you must go underground."

"A tunnel?"

"Of sorts. It will lead you high above the ruins of the old fortress." Bryndis's brow furrowed as she looked at Raef. "In truth, I have only seen the entrance. No living man or woman has set foot inside. Not since my great-grandfather was a boy has the Jaw been climbed."

"Why so long?"

"Some say the Jaw is home to a dark alf, one who was cast out of Svartalfheim. Others say a great serpent dwells there, a child of Jörmungand who sleeps in the deep." Bryndis blinked and her voice grew sharper. "Perhaps it is no more than a stair carved in the stone, full of treacherous paths and bottomless crevasses."

"Whatever it is, I will climb it. Tonight."

But no sooner had Raef spoken than a shout came from across the camp. A man raced to Bryndis's tent, nearly tripping over his boots in his haste, arm outstretched behind him in the direction of the cliff face.

"Someone," he slid to a stop and was forced to catch his breath and begin again, "someone is making the descent. He bears a flag of peace."

Bryndis was on her horse in a moment, throwing herself over the tall black's back though he was unsaddled. With her fingers twined in the horse's mane, she took off across the snow, threading her way through the shelters, and Raef followed hard at her heels, his own horse eager to catch and race hers. The commotion caused many to follow them across the valley, warriors and shieldmaidens strung out behind them, watching with curious eyes.

Raef could see the peace flag now, borne aloft by a single man who was making the descent down the narrow path with deliberate steps. Bryndis's uncle was not far behind them, and he called out a warning that Bryndis ignored as she leaned over her horse's neck and urged him onward. By the time they had come within a spear's throw of the cliff, the man had reached the bottom. Bryndis did not slow, but raced so close that her horse's tail whipped against the man's shoulder as she passed. He did not flinch as she wheeled the horse and circled him.

Stefnir of Gornhald watched Bryndis pass in front of him, but his gaze did not follow her as she continued to trace circles in the snow around him.

"You will not harm me, Bryndis," Stefnir said.

With a snarl, Bryndis vaulted from her horse's back, landing just in front of him. She took a step forward, so close now that Stefnir would be able to see the deep brown ring on the edge of her irises. She came only to his chin, but she stared at him as though she were looking down at him, not the other way around.

"What do you want?"

"Fengar asks for your surrender."

Bryndis said nothing and Raef was pleased to see her remain calm.

"The king does not wish for further bloodshed. He seeks peace with Narvik."

"The king is no king of mine," Bryndis said. "But if it is peace he wants, perhaps he should not have laid waste to Narvik's farms. Perhaps he should have thought of peace instead of slaughtering innocent people."

"A regrettable outcome, lady," Stefnir said. "But surely you do not wish to see more of Narvik's people die? For that is what will happen if you resist."

"It is you who will die, Stefnir. You will waste away up there. What will you do when your stock of meat runs out? When the warriors grow gaunt and weak with hunger? Will you kill the ones closest to death and feast on the flesh of men? Is Fengar willing to go to such lengths?" Bryndis leaned closer. "I think not."

But Stefnir was unmoved. "I do not speak of the deaths of the warriors behind you, lady. I speak of the one and twenty men and women and children up there," Stefnir said, gesturing to the ruins above, "who live only as a token of Fengar's generosity." Bryndis froze and Raef felt his heart rise into his throat. Stefnir smiled. "They are well taken care of. For now. But one will die with every rising sun that sees you still here in this valley. Beginning tomorrow. Go home, Bryndis, and spare them."

"I do not believe you!" Bryndis's voice burst out of her, wild and full of fury. She was trembling but still she held her ground, as though sheer strength of will would make Stefnir's words a lie.

"A child will die with the sunrise, Bryndis. Think on that." Stefnir turned and began to retrace his steps.

"I will not yield," Bryndis called after him. "That is the only answer you will have from me."

"Do not be hasty. In his kindness, Fengar has given you time to make your choice. Do not throw away such a gift."

"A foul gift, full of poison." Bryndis spat but Stefnir did not look back a second time.

"Come, away." Bryndis's uncle dismounted and put a hand

on her arm. She did not at first respond, but after a moment she let him lead her away to where her horse waited. She spoke not a word as they returned to the camp and shut herself alone inside the white tent.

The sun had slipped below the horizon by the time Raef ventured to disturb Bryndis. Her uncle stood guard, his face creased with worry, but he let Raef and Siv pass, then followed them inside.

The interior was dark and Raef's eyes took a moment to adjust. Bryndis sat hunched on a small stool, her forearms resting on her knees, her head cradled in the crook of one elbow. An untouched cup of ale stood at her feet. Her uncle knelt at her side and pushed the hair from her face, then planted a kiss on the top of her head. With a sigh, Bryndis uncurled herself and looked up at Raef and Siv.

"I meant what I said to him," Bryndis said.

"I do not doubt you," Raef said.

"The guilt and the blame will rest with me alone, Skallagrim, you need not worry."

Bryndis's uncle put a hand on her shoulder. "Are you so eager to give them up? To let them die?"

The lady of Narvik burst to her feet, her eyes flashing with anger. "Eager, uncle? You know I am not that cruel. But if it comes to choosing between one and twenty lives that will bring me Fengar and countless lives lost should he live, unchecked, then I would make the same choice again and again."

"The time for such words may yet come." Raef waited until Bryndis released her uncle from her gaze before continuing. "But first we must know the truth."

"Yes. Odin's eye, if Fengar holds no hostages," Bryndis was shaking now, "if he lies to save his own skin, I will keep him from joining his fathers in Valhalla."

ᛉ ᛉ ᛉ

Raef had been forced to take Eiger with him. Better that than leave him alone with Bryndis, who had reluctantly agreed to remain. The fat man had grumbled about not being informed the moment Stefnir of Gornhald had flown his flag, and he had questioned Raef's decision to bring only Siv and Skuli on the climb, but beyond that he had kept his mouth shut, no doubt compelled into silence by the exertion required to labor his way up to the ridgeline Bryndis had shown Raef in the light of day.

In the dark, the distance seemed greater, but at last they reached the top of the ridge and worked their way along it until the mountain rose up in front of them, barring further progress. There Raef allowed Skuli to unveil the lantern they had carried with them, the light concealed by thick leather coverings. Aided by its feeble glow, they soon discovered a cleft in the rocks, just large enough for a man to squeeze through.

"Does it go anywhere?" Skuli's voice seemed unnaturally loud and Raef shot him a warning glance as Siv wriggled her way between the stones. She slid out of the lantern's light, then returned a moment later.

"Yes."

Raef turned to Eiger. "You will wait here."

Eiger scowled. "I am no common warrior for you to command."

"And yet your girth will not fit." Raef did not bother to keep his face neutral. "Indeed, you are far too well-muscled and strong." Siv placed a restraining hand on Raef's back where Eiger would not see it, but Raef grinned at Eiger's displeasure. And yet it was the truth. Eiger would not be able to pass into the Dragon's Jaw. "Keep the lantern covered until we return." Raef nodded for Skuli to hand it over, but Eiger would not take it and Skuli was forced to set it on the ground between them. Raef tossed the leather cover over it, encasing them in darkness once more, and then turned and plunged into the mountain.

He could hear Siv and Skuli behind him, the worn leather of their boots scuffing on stone as they went, their breathing filling the air around him. The way was narrow and they had no choice but to shuffle along at a sideways angle. Raef kept one hand on the wall that pressed in from the right, his palm gliding over rough rock, and the other out in front of him to discover any sudden obstacles. The blinding darkness seemed to steal away his senses but Raef was certain the path was rising at a steady, nearly imperceptible rate. He tried not to imagine the stone floor dropping away in front of him, tried not to think that his next step might send him plummeting into a yawning abyss.

The passage was straight and seemingly without end, but at last Raef came to a halt as he felt the space around him widen. Though he stretched his arms to their fullest, he could no longer touch both walls. Behind him, Skuli muttered something about the air in the mountain being cold enough to freeze his balls. Five long strides were enough to cross the distance between the walls, but in tracing that path Raef discovered something that chilled his blood more than the winter air. He reversed his steps to be certain, his fingers taking in the surface of the stones.

"A dead end?" Siv's voice, though hushed, resonated off the rock.

"Worse. The way divides." Reaching out into the darkness, Raef took Siv's hand and led her forward, showing her hands where the rocks fell away to reveal three new passages. Skuli cursed and asked if he should return for the lantern, but Raef knew it would not help. "Three passages. Three of us. This is no accident. We are meant to continue alone and hope that blind Hodr will carry us through the darkness."

Skuli let out a nervous laugh. "You mean the mountain knows we are here? That this is some trick played by one of the gods?" The young warrior laughed again, almost sure of himself now. "The paths cannot change."

"I have seen stranger things."

Skuli had no answer for that.

Raef sighed and balled his fist against the cold stones. When he spoke, he was glad to hear his voice remained even and calm. "Skuli, choose your path." He could hear the other man's breathing, short, shallow breaths that told of fear. "I told you to save your nerve, Skuli. Now you must find it."

After a moment, Skuli spoke. "The middle one."

Raef stepped through the blackness, fingers groping for Skuli's arm. He found it and grabbed the warrior's wrist. "Keep your wits. Recite a poem in your head to measure time. Count the hostages when you find them." Better to say when than if. Skuli's courage was fragile. "You must avoid being seen by Fengar's men at all costs."

"And if the way splits again?"

"Make a choice," Raef said. "And remember it so you can return." He released Skuli's arm but the warrior lingered. Raef reached up to his own neck and worked his numb fingers over the knotted cord that held his Thor's hammer in place. He had worn the hammer to war, it had seen him through Alfheim and Jötunheim, but he knew Skuli had lost his to a wager before leaving Vannheim. He gripped the familiar, smooth shape in his palm once more, then pressed it into Skuli's hand. "Take this." Raef wrapped Skuli's fingers around the hammer. "Thor will guide you. Now go."

"Yes, lord."

Raef, trying not to think about the absence of the hammer around his own neck, listened as the sound of Skuli's boots faded down the middle passage, then turned to Siv. He sought her out, twining his fingers with hers. He did not need light to know that her face would be tense, but her eyes full of determination. Her hand reached up and touched the hollow in his throat where the hammer usually rested. Raef brought her palm to his lips.

"Left or right?" he asked, his mouth moving against her skin.

She answered without hesitation. "Right."

"Then I will see you before the sun rises. Now, go." Raef released Siv and felt her retreat from him. He heard her turn, heard her take the first steps into her chosen passage, and then, before he could regret sending her into the darkness alone, Raef felt out the left-most passage and went to meet whatever waited for him there.

He counted his steps at first, to ease the burden of darkness and pass the time, but it was not long before the numbers turned to words, words spoken in Gudrik's voice. The story was the same, the one that had always come to him as a boy when alone in the forest. It had stolen upon him then, creeping unaware into his young mind until the tracks of deer and the song of birds were forgotten, and it came upon him now in such a manner, slipping into the corners of his heart and seeping through the marrow of his bones. It was an old friend, the story of the beginning of all things, of the creation of the nine realms, but it was Gudrik's voice as he had told the story all those nights ago that was the greatest comfort in the darkness. Raef might have wished to have the dead skald at his side, but it was enough to carry a spark of him.

By the time the giant Ymir was being carved up to form the mountains and valleys of Midgard, Raef's path began to climb and the ascent was so steep that Raef had to clamber forward on his hands and feet. In places, the tunnel had been worn smooth and round, as though rubbed away for countless years, and there Raef was forced to leap upwards, propelling himself onward with his toes as his fingers sought something to catch hold of. Before long, sweat dripped down his forehead and ran into his eyes, and the tips of his fingers grew numb as the skin wore away on each handhold. More than once, he felt a faint residue on the rocks, as though they had been dusted with honeycomb. When he raised his fingers to his lips, the taste was of rotten meat, and no matter how hard he tried to wash it free from his tongue with his saliva, it lingered, foul and resilient, and a sudden thirst came over Raef, incessant and as fierce as a storm in summer.

It was only then that Raef became aware that his breaths were coming short and fast, that the blackness before him swam with flashes of light, that he was no longer sure where the sky lay and where the earth waited below, ready to swallow him. The urge to run washed over him but his limbs were as weak as wilting wild-flowers and he could feel his fingers slipping from the narrow shelf of rock he clung to, could feel his heart pounding as the ocean does against cliffs. Fighting back the dizziness and the fear, Raef forced himself to swallow and he closed his eyes, as though he might chase away the darkness with the blackness inside his own lids.

The swaying in his head dissipated, but he could not catch his breath, could not calm his heart. A sound came to him then, a sound full of terror, and then he realized it was his own breathing, his own great, gulping breaths, and it seemed to him that he heard his own death.

His right arm gave way first, wrenching his left at the shoul-der, and he slipped back down the slope. When the left could hold no longer, he felt himself drop, sliding, tumbling back down the tunnel. With a cry of pain, he crashed against a jutting shard of rock and landed, draped over it, his heartbeat reverberating through the heart of the mountain. And in that moment, he became aware of the handle of his knife gouging into his side from where it lay twisted in his belt.

The sensation of this proved stronger than anything else. Gone was the weakness in his arms, gone was the pounding in his tem-ples, the lights that danced in his eyes, even the thirst. Trembling, Raef reached for the knife and let it whisper out of its scabbard. The hilt was cool against his skin and he could not shake the thought that it was vital he know how sharp the blade was.

The edge bit into his forearm and the first trickle of blood was hot against his skin. He could not see the crimson blood, and in his mind's eye it was the color of molten gold, thick and viscous as it spilled forth. He pushed the blade deeper, drawing it across the flesh. There was no pain, only a sense of cold, as though the mountain was stealing into the spaces vacated by his blood. Raef lifted the knife and held his arm out, marveling in the curious sensation of blood seeping through that narrowest of slices. It rushed down his arm and seemed to pool just behind the cut. It was not enough. He would have to go deeper.

The blade kissed his skin once more and then Raef heard the scream. Faint, muffled, consumed by the mountain, but filled with terror and pain. The sound of it sent a wave of nausea rolling up Raef's throat and his fingers fell slack. The knife fell away, skittering down the tunnel, and only then did Raef understand what he had done, that his lifeblood was dripping away and he had been the cause.

The knowledge that he had been a moment away from severing his veins, that he had wielded the knife without thought, awoke a fear that had slept in him since the labyrinth of Jötunheim had threatened to swallow him. For a moment he could do nothing but cling to the rock, the darkness crushing down on him, the fear gnawing at his heart, but then he realized the mountain had gone silent. The screaming had ceased and this was enough to stir him.

"Siv!" His shout echoed back at him and, though he knew it was fruitless, he called again, hoping against hope that he might hear an answer. There was only silence.

Reaching under his leather jerkin and woolen layer, Raef untucked the hem of his linen shirt and tore a wide strip away. Using his left hand and his teeth, he wrapped the self-inflicted wound and fashioned a knot. It throbbed under the pressure of the bandage, but Raef was glad of the pain, glad of the reminder of what the Dragon's Jaw had cost him.

Mustering the limbs that had betrayed him, Raef heaved himself off the cold, hard flesh of the mountain and began to climb once more. The way up seemed less steep, the walls of the tunnel less smooth, the handholds more frequent. Gone was the sticky residue and gone was the comfort of Gudrik's voice. Raef could hear only the memory of the scream.

When the tunnel leveled off into a flat chamber, Raef could smell fresh air and felt a slight draft on his cheeks. He knew he was close. The path turned left and narrowed again, so constricted that Raef had to turn sideways and even then the rocks pulled and scraped at him. His scabbard caught time and time again as he made agonizingly slow progress and more than once he caught his head on low-hanging rocks. Stooping, Raef was forced to creep forward, feeling his way forward with his hands and wondering if the his path would continue to shrink until he had nowhere to go, no way to turn around.

So intent was he on finding his way that at first Raef did not notice that something other than blackness was ahead of him, but when he did look up, he doubted at first the faint change in light and wondered if his eyes told the truth. But soon there was no doubt. There, ahead of him, was the night sky, full of stars, waiting for him.

Raef traversed the last section of tunnel on his hands and knees, the stones pressing in on all sides, but at last he broke free, stepping out onto the shoulder of a mountain bathed in starlight. It was a treacherous place, slick with ice and snow, and the steep drop-off to Raef's left promised a sudden fall and a broken body, but after the dark, blind confines of the mountain, Raef breathed in the night air with relish.

But he was not alone. A figure crouching at the edge of the drop-off stirred, standing tall and catching Raef's gaze. He reached for his axe, but his fingers only brushed the worn handle before he recognized Siv in the shadows.

"You are well?" Raef went to her, and though she nodded and appeared unhurt, her eyes, solemn and unblinking, told him the mountain had taken a toll on her, too. He raised a hand to her face and brushed away a strand of hair that had escaped her braids, but she caught his wrist with her hand, her gaze on his crude bandage stained with blood.

"What happened?"

Raef met her eyes. "The work of the mountain." And he told her of the sticky residue, the thirst, the dizziness, and his strange need to test the knife's blade. "I do not doubt that I would have cut again and again and watched my blood drip from my veins until I could watch no more if I had not heard the scream." Siv's gaze flickered back to the mountain behind Raef. "You heard it, too."

"Yes," Siv said. "I fear for Skuli's life."

"We will search for him. After we have what we came for."

Siv released Raef and walked to the edge. "There."

The ancient fortress was open to the sky, the roof long destroyed by wind and water and falling rocks. Among the remaining walls, broken as they were, two fires burned and men clustered to them, but far more men were left in the cold and the dark, shivering, for Fengar had only what wood he had carried with him. When he ran out, there would be no more warmth.

"Difficult to count them," Siv said, her voice no more than a murmur. She was right. The half walls and tumbled towers shielded much of the ruins from Raef's view, but it was clear that Fengar still commanded enough men to wage a war, however brief it might be. "They have fresh water." Raef nodded, for he had seen the spring-fed pool at the base of the cliffs that towered behind the fortress.

"And the hostages?"

Siv pointed, but kept her gaze on Raef, and as he looked in the direction she indicated, he understood her anxious expression.

A small group of people was clustered in the half-light just outside the circle of the fire nearest Raef and Siv's overlook. Their hands were bound and their feet tethered to each other so they might not escape. Men, women, children, just as Stefnir had promised. But it was the sight of one slight figure among them that caused Raef to suck in air.

"Serpent's balls," Raef muttered. "Cilla."

There was no mistaking the little girl from Kelgard. She held herself apart from the other hostages, crouching as far from them as the rope lashed around her ankle would allow. She had shaved the sides of her head, leaving only the hair on top to grow long and this was tied in three braids knotted together. Her arms were still thin and Raef did not think she had grown much since he had seen her in Solheim, but she had proved to be stronger than she looked during her brief training with Siv and Eira, and Raef had no doubt she nursed deadly anger in her heart.

"Eira said Cilla chose to stay in Solheim. How is it that she came to Narvik and fell into Fengar's path?"

Siv had no answer and Raef saw that she was watching the hostages with care, though her eyes seemed focused on something far away, something only she could see.

"I should never have left Cilla. She was under my care and I let her drift into a world she should never have had to face alone."

Siv roused herself. "You are not at fault. Would you have taken her into the dangers of Hullbern and Ver? And the burning lake?"

"No, that was no place for a child, however brave." Raef turned and looked at Siv. "I will not leave Cilla up here to starve or die under Fengar's knife."

"You know what Bryndis will choose. She is willing to see them all die."

Raef was quiet for a long moment, trying to fathom a means to thwart both Fengar and Bryndis. "There must be another way." And yet he could not see it. "Even if we bring warriors through the

Dragon's Jaw, even if we gather up here," Raef flung his arm above them, indicating the ledges and level places that made up the side of the mountain, "in numbers greater than Fengar's, there is no way down. We might kill some with arrows, but then the rest will hide and wait and the hostages will die."

"And the fortress will never be breached from below." Siv's voice was calm, but Raef sensed an underlying sorrow that she was not yet willing to release to him.

They stood in silence, each contemplating the ruins below, until Raef sighed and glanced at the stars and the moon above.

"It is time we went back. The night is no longer young," Raef said.

Siv nodded but her gaze lingered on the hostages until Raef had ducked back into the tunnel from which he had emerged. Then she frowned and followed, though she stopped and hesitated where the starlight still fell upon her.

"You came this way?" Siv asked.

"Yes."

"As did I."

"Something is at work here well beyond us." Raef was quiet, stalled on hands and knees in the passage. "I have seen its like before, though I had hoped never to know it again."

"The labyrinth of Jötunheim?"

"Yes." Raef crept forward and heard Siv enter the tunnel behind him. "In Vannheim, we are told that mighty Ymir's heart is buried in the deep waters of the fjord. I wonder if it lies here instead, and if that heart burns still with rage over what the Allfather did to him."

TWENTY-FIVE

THEY EMERGED AT the base of the Dragon's Jaw to the sound of weeping. The sobs were soft and weak, and at first Raef could not see their source. Eiger's bulk was hunched over, but his broad back did not shudder and when he stood and turned to face Raef and Siv as they emerged from the Jaw, his fleshy face, free of tears, was twisted with revulsion.

At Eiger's feet, Skuli shivered on his knees. Spittle hung from the young warrior's open mouth. His cheeks were streaked with tears and blood. And his eyes were nothing more than mangled, pulpy orbs, all crimson gore where once they had been pale blue.

"What happened?" Raef went to Skuli and dropped to his knees in front of the younger man, but his words were for Eiger, who had retreated into the glow of the lantern. Raef placed a hand on Skuli's shoulder, his own fingers trembling almost as much as Skuli's body, but the slight touch sent a shudder through Skuli and he jerked back and began to scream.

It was the scream Raef had heard in the mountain and now he was desperate to silence it for no doubt the whole valley could hear Skuli's terror. But his words, his pleas, went unnoticed and Raef, grimacing to himself, placed one hand over Skuli's mouth and then wrapped his arm around the warrior's neck and pressed Skuli against his chest, muffling the blood-curdling cries. Skuli fought him at first, fought for air, fought against Raef's restraining arms, but Raef held him there until the will to resist fled from Skuli's limbs, leaving him limp in Raef's arms, his breaths reduced to wretched, mewling gasps. Skuli's head hung back and the ruined eyes stared up at Raef.

"What happened?" Raef asked once more.

"He came out like that." Eiger's voice was flat and free of compassion, but there was something else picking away at the edges of his words, something like fear that might unravel any moment.

Siv nudged something with the toe of her boot and Raef saw it was a knife, long and lean in the moonlight, but the blade was stained with blood, as were Skuli's fingers, and Raef thought of his own knife, lost now to the Dragon's Jaw, and his own blood that lined the edge.

Raef stood and hoisted Skuli onto his shoulder, draping the young warrior as he would a deer downed in the hunt. To his relief, Skuli whimpered but made no other sound.

"What are you doing?" Eiger stared at Raef, the lantern highlighting his disbelief. "Better to end his misery."

Raef glared and gave no answer, but turned and headed back the way they had come.

Bryndis waited, wrapped in a woven robe dyed a deep blue and trimmed with white fox fur. A single candle lit the tent and a bowl of soup that no longer steamed was discarded on a stool. She was sitting when Raef pulled aside the tent flap, but he could guess that the ground had been well-worn by the tread of her impatient feet. The black ink that lined her eyes had been wiped away, leaving her looking vulnerable and young.

Bryndis began to speak as Raef entered, but she stopped short when she caught sight of Skuli hanging from Raef's shoulders.

"Is he?" She let the rest of her question linger unspoken on her lips.

"Alive," Raef said. With Siv's help, Raef unloaded Skuli and propped him on a pile of furs. The warrior was quiet now, his distress visible only in his tightly clenched fists. The blood on his face had turned to a crust but his ruined eyes still leaked fluid and Bryndis stared in dread and horror.

"Odin has abandoned us, lady." Eiger had followed Raef into the tent and now he loomed at Bryndis's shoulder, his bulk separating her from the candlelight.

"The Allfather had nothing to do with this." Raef snarled, advancing on Eiger, who held his ground.

"And you know the Allfather's mind, Skallagrim?"

Raef bit back the words he might have spoken and turned his attention to Bryndis.

"Stefnir spoke the truth."

Bryndis closed her eyes for a moment, though whether to blot out the sight of Skuli's disfigurement or the thought of the innocent life that would be ended in the light of the rising sun, Raef could not be sure. She went to the tent flap and called for aid for Skuli. When she turned and looked at Raef, her resolve was visible in every line of her face.

"You know where I stand."

"I do," Raef said, "and were they all of Narvik, I would defer to your right to decide. But there is a girl among them. She was in my care once. I do not intend to abandon her." A woman came with fresh water and a clean strip of linen. She set to work dabbing the cloth to Skuli's face.

"Would that we could save them all," Bryndis said, "but I do not see how it can be done, not without letting Fengar go free, and this I will not do."

"Send word that we will retreat, that the hostages must be released, that Fengar may leave Narvik unmolested. We can ambush him when he leaves the safety of the fortress."

"You would make me a liar?"

Raef tried to hide his frustration. "I do not think you can be honest and victorious, Bryndis. Not this time." The lady of Narvik looked unmoved. "Are you so fond of this harsh world you have known that you would see no other option? Are you so eager to show your resilience that you would send children to their deaths?"

Bryndis recoiled from Raef, the tendons in her neck straining against the skin, her eyes sharp with anger. "You think I do this for myself? I do this so that we might be free of Fengar, so that we might have a new king, one chosen by the voices of the warriors, not the voices of a few."

Raef shook his head and spread his hands. "There are other ways, lady."

"Perhaps I was wrong to call on Vannheim."

"Do not make me your enemy, Bryndis. We have enough of those."

"Do you threaten her?" Eiger placed one hand on Bryndis's shoulder and the other on his sword hilt.

Raef kept his gaze on Bryndis. "She knows I do not."

Before Bryndis could speak again, a new voice interrupted them, weak and trusting, as Skuli spoke his first coherent words.

"Lord? Are you there? Will you not help me?"

Raef held Bryndis's gaze for a moment longer, though what he might hope to convey to her, he could not say, then went to Skuli's side.

"Here, I am here." Raef took Skuli's hand between both of his. The other man's skin was cold and dry.

"I had to." Skuli's voice took on a measure of strength. "I had to do it." Skuli's fingers tightened around Raef's and he grew agitated, pushing himself off the furs with his other hand and reaching out as though he might latch onto Raef or whatever he could find.

"I know." Raef took Skuli's other hand and held them both,

hoping to calm him, to give him some peace. "I know." They were not empty words. Whatever had found Skuli in the Dragon's Jaw, whatever had brought him to mangle his own eyes, Raef had felt it, too, and it lay over him still. When Skuli grew calm again, Raef pulled him to his feet and led him to the tent flap. Raef pushed aside the heavy canvas and then looked over his shoulder at Bryndis. She met his gaze but neither of them spoke and Raef left her.

Raef had not heard Siv leave the tent, but she was gone and had not lingered nearby. But whatever troubled Siv would have to wait. The Vannheim shelters were quiet when Raef, supporting Skuli, approached, but a few men left on watch rose to meet him.

"Find ale, mead, whatever we have, and clean cloth," Raef said as he laid Skuli out beside a fire. Two warriors hurried off to do as he asked. A third stared at Skuli's face, his fingers finding the hammer amulet that hung at his neck. Only then did Raef remember that he had tied his around Skuli's neck. It was no longer there and the loss of it gnawed at Raef. Ignoring the gaping warrior, Raef pulled his remaining knife from his belt and ran his whetstone along the edge until it satisfied him. By then the two warriors had returned clutching several full skins. Raef opened one and took a swig, glad of the sweet mead as it lined his throat. Then he signaled for them to prop Skuli up so that he might swallow.

"You know what I must do, Skuli?"

"Yes, lord."

The sockets had to be cleaned. Raef was no healer, but he knew he could not leave the remains of Skuli's eyes to fester and rot.

"Then drink. And then drink some more."

Skuli emptied three skins of mead before he slumped against the knees of the men holding him up and let the skin fall from his hands. Raef held the point of the knife in the flames until it began to glow, then, steeling himself with a steadying breath, began to carve out the pulpy eyeballs. Skuli flinched under his touch but did not cry out and Raef hoped he could not feel the searing heat of the blade, could not feel his flesh being scraped from bone.

When he finished, Raef splashed mead across the empty, blackened eye sockets, then followed that with water to wash away the rivulets of blood that lingered on Skuli's cheeks. The bandage was ready and waiting and Raef wrapped it again and again around Skuli's head, sealing away the wound. When it was done, Raef leaned over and pressed his lips against Skuli's hair.

"You are in the gods' hands now." Raef got to his feet. "Do not leave him alone." The three warriors nodded as Raef rinsed his hands with more water and took another gulp of mead. He longed to rest but the night was not through with him yet.

It was not difficult to find Siv. She was perched on a fallen tree at the edge of the camp, and though the ruined fortress was cloaked in darkness and beyond their sight, Raef knew she saw it as clearly as if the sun were shining.

She acknowledged Raef with a small smile and he sat beside her for a long moment before speaking.

"I have never seen you like this." Raef took her hand. "Will you not tell me what troubles you?"

"My sister is up there."

They sat in silence. Raef brought her fingers to his lips and kissed the tip of each.

"You never told me her name."

"Bekkhild."

"And what are we going to do about Bekkhild?"

TWENTY-SIX

THEY HUNG THE hostage at dawn.

It was not a child, as Stefnir had promised, and Raef breathed a sigh of relief as he tilted his face up to the cliff top where the body dangled. Cilla lived. Raef wondered if Fengar's belly had roiled at the thought of slaughtering a child.

The dead man had been stripped of everything but his lank, dirty hair and his skinny corpse would be left for the crows. Raef had only to look at Bryndis's face to know that the lady of Narvik knew the man. But she remained resolute and her eyes harbored no trace of tears as she turned her horse away from the cliff and urged him back across the valley.

Siv gazed up at the dead man for a long moment, then she and Raef turned their horses and followed in Bryndis's wake. They had reached the outer shelters when a startled cry rang out and Raef saw a warrior staring back at the cliff, pointing and shouting words he could not make out.

The body was on fire. It burned without wood, without oil, but even from that distance, Raef could see the flames had consumed the corpse with ease. As voices around him murmured that perhaps Fengar meant it as a kindness, that he had chosen to spare the dead man from scavenging beaks and teeth, but Raef knew in his heart that the fire was not of Fengar's making.

"Vakre is here."

But Siv's eyes were on Bryndis, who had spared the flames only a glance, then continued on into her tent.

"I will speak with her," Siv said.

"Do you want me to come?"

"No." Siv ran a hand down Raef's forearm, then she, too, vanished inside the tent. Raef waited for a time, pacing, catching snatches of murmured words, but as the sun rose higher and higher in the sky and still they did not emerge, he resigned himself to a long wait and returned to the Vannheim shelters.

Skuli's bandage had been changed already that morning. The soiled one had been burned and a fresh cloth layered over his eyes, but already it was stained with blood and other fluids. He had spoken only a little, Raef was told, but neither had he appeared to sleep. Raef could only imagine what tormented Skuli's mind, could only imagine what ravaged in the self-inflicted darkness. He had been placed in a shelter and made comfortable with warm furs, and a steaming bowl of broth and a hunk of hard cheese had been set within easy reach, but Skuli reacted only a little to Raef's voice and said nothing in return.

"His mind is gone," Njall, another captain and Skuli's good friend, said to Raef as he stepped out of the shelter.

Raef shook his head. "No. His mind wavers. But it is not yet gone."

Njall looked uncertain but Lochauld, the young warrior from Axsellund, nodded his agreement. "The gods will give him back to us, but only if Skuli makes that choice."

Raef did not think the gods had much to do with the twisted blackness of Skuli's mind, but he kept his doubts to himself, for Njall seemed to find understanding in Lochauld's words.

"We have preparations to make," Raef said to the two warriors. The knowledge that Vakre lived and walked among Fengar's men had steeled his resolve to the promise he had given Siv in the grey hour before dawn. "More hostages will die if the lady Bryndis will not retreat from this valley. She does not seek my counsel and the far greater part of the warriors here are hers, so I cannot force a decision upon her. I mean to assault the fortress tonight." Raef looked up at the sky. Heavy clouds drifted on the western horizon. "With luck we will have cloud cover to shield us from the moon's light."

If Njall doubted Raef's plan, if he found it foolish and dangerous, he kept that to himself as they spoke of the preparations that had to be made, and Raef was sure he saw the lure of battle-fame in Njall's eyes. The chance of success was small, the chance of death great, but if they could succeed, their names would be carried on the tips of reverent tongues, even to the very gates of Asgard.

Leaving Njall to seek out Dvalarr the Crow carry out his orders, Raef was returning to Bryndis's tent when a commotion on the edge of the shelters drew his attention. Raef hesitated, for he longed to know what had transpired between Siv and Bryndis, but the shouting grew louder, rougher, and Raef had no choice but to address it.

The scene was grisly. A body lay on the ground, the skin sliced in countless places and marred with rope burns everywhere else. The man's face was beaten beyond recognition, and a symbol was carved into his chest. The Odin rune.

Two men, warriors of Narvik Raef recognized, knelt beside the body while three more stood above them, weapons bristling, curses and accusations flying from their tongues. They faced four men wielding axes and there was death in the eyes of each man.

The first attack came from one of the Narvik warriors as Raef stepped into their midst. He seized the man's cloak, halting his momentum, and yanked hard, putting the warrior off balance. He stumbled back among his comrades and turned, seething, on Raef.

"Enough!" Raef drew his sword and saw fear in the Narvik warrior's eyes. The men eyed each other uneasily but no one moved. "What has happened here?"

"These dogs hung Buruld from a tree," one of the Narvik warriors shouted. "Trussed him up like a pig and bled him."

Raef turned to the other four men. "What offense did he commit?" They were silent. "Answer me."

"They have only done the Allfather's will."

Raef spun to face Eiger, sword pointing at the other man's throat. The Great-Belly's son had approached silently and he stood before Raef without fear. His thin lips were turned up in a satisfied smile that spread across his fat cheeks.

"What have you done?" Raef tried to keep his anger contained, but it seeped into his voice.

Eiger spread his hands. "I have sought only to return us to the Allfather's good will."

"By murder?"

"Odin hung himself upon Yggdrasil for nine days and nine nights." Eiger gestured at the dead man on the ground. "These have only done so for the span of a morning. What is that compared to the Allfather's suffering?"

Raef flung his sword to the ground and lunged at Eiger. The fat man could not react in time and Raef, gripping Eiger's fur collar, hauled him to his knees. "These?" Raef, leaning so close to Eiger's face that he could see a tiny scar in the other man's eyebrow, fought the urge to draw his knife and slit open Eiger's belly so his guts might worm free. "There are others?" Eiger clenched his jaw shut. "Where are the rest?" Still Eiger would not speak and Raef threw him to the ground.

By then a crowd had gathered and Raef sought out Lochauld's face. "Start a search," Raef said as he picked up his sword. The young man hurried off, calling other Vannheim warriors to him as he went. Raef seized Eiger's thick hair and pulled, forcing him to scramble to his feet. "I am bringing you to meet the Crow, Eiger. We shall see how you like suffering then."

Leaving Eiger in Dvalarr's capable hands and well guarded by Vannheim warriors, Raef saddled his horse and joined the search for the rest of Eiger's victims.

The bodies were spread out through the forest that lined the northern edge of the camp. With each new discovery, the hatred in Raef's gut grew. They cut down eleven bodies, each as mutilated as the first, each bearing the Odin rune in blood upon his chest. Two were of Vannheim. The rest were men of Narvik. Raef knelt beside his men, one so young he had not yet fought his first battle, the other a farmer who had sought to win silver to bring back to his family.

Reflexively, Raef reached for the hammer that no longer hung from his neck. His fingers grasped air, but Raef hoped Thor would still hear the plea for retribution.

"Lord, come quickly." Lochauld burst into the clearing where the bodies had been stretched out in the snow. "This one is still alive."

Raef followed Lochauld through the trees until they reached a large, gnarly oak. There, a twelfth man was tied spread-eagle against the trunk, his right arm bent at an excruciating angle, the rope around his neck so tight that Raef could not see how he was still alive. Raef's men were working to cut him down and Raef stood underneath him as the ropes fell away, taking his weight bit by bit until the last restraints were severed and the warrior was freed.

He was alive, though just. His eyes were slits in his bruised, puffy face. The Odin rune leaked blood onto Raef's leather jerkin, but it was a surface wound, far less severe than the slashes that covered his flesh. His lips moved, though whether in prayer or in fear Raef could not know for nothing came out. Lochauld pressed a skin of mead to the man's lips, wetting his tongue, and Raef drew his axe and tucked its handle into the man's hand so that he might have a weapon and draw the eye of the Valkyries.

He slipped into death so quietly that Raef could not be sure when life left him, but still the Vannheim warriors stood in silence under the spreading arms of the oak, still Raef held the man's fingers in place around the axe, wondering if Odin was watching, if the Allfather could feel the depth of Raef's anger toward Eiger.

"His name was Fjorstark."

Raef had not heard Bryndis and her uncle approach, but it was Siv, standing just behind Bryndis, who Raef looked to and her gaze softened the rage that burned in his heart.

"Eiger must answer for this." Raef got to his feet and brushed past Bryndis, intent on finding the Great-Belly's son.

"We need Balmoran's shields."

Raef stopped but did not turn until he knew he had mastered his face. "Do we? We sit and wait and let Fengar kill defenseless farmers and children. Balmoran's shields make no difference."

Bryndis had applied fresh ink under her eyes. The bold black lines curved away from the outer corners and her pale irises were stark in comparison. "We need Balmoran's shields if we are to ambush Fengar away from this valley."

Raef looked to Siv, hardly daring to hope that Bryndis had changed her mind, but Siv's quiet nod told him everything he needed to know. And yet the thought of standing beside Eiger in the shield wall twisted Raef's gut.

"The Great-Belly commands the warriors of Balmoran, not this foul murderer," Raef said. "Thorgrim will agree." They were uncertain words, at best, for Raef did not know if the Balmoran warriors were loyal to the father or the son. But he meant to see Eiger undone for his crimes.

"The Great-Belly rests in my hall, Skallagrim, and does not like to travel."

Raef was tempted to reveal Thorgrim's secret, to tell Bryndis that the lord of Balmoran was not as weak as he pretended to be, but he held his tongue. And he was aware of the ears and eyes around them. This was not the place to discuss alliances, even among loyal men of Vannheim.

Raef took a deep breath. "Let the order be given to break up the camp. I will bring word to Fengar of our departure. We will determine Eiger's fate once the hostages are no longer threatened."

Bryndis nodded and swept from the clearing with her uncle at her side. Raef went to Siv and, smiling, took her face in his hands.

"What did you say to her?"

"The truth. I think Bryndis is capable of withstanding a great deal when it comes to her own person and to those she bears responsibility for. The world has molded her that way. She has grown hard and she takes refuge in her strength. But her heart is not so cold that she is deaf to a sister's pleas."

Raef kissed Siv's forehead as Lochauld and the other Vannheim warriors carried Fjorstark's body from the trees. "I am glad."

"Will Fengar honor his promise?"

"He has no reason not to. When he sees the valley empty, he will be glad to be rid of the burden of more mouths to feed. And he will be glad, I think, to be gone from this place. Narvik is not the quiet sanctuary he hoped it would be."

Siv nodded. "And Vakre?"

"Vakre must know what he is doing." It worried Raef that the son of Loki was so deep behind enemy lines. He would rather have Vakre at his side as they set a trap for Fengar, but Vakre had come to a decision about his uncle and Raef would not interfere.

Taking Siv's hand, they returned to the camp. Already shelters were being broken down, horses saddled and burdened, and fires dashed out with river water. Raef spoke with Njall, reversing the orders he had given the captain to prepare for a night assault on the fortress, then made certain Dvalarr had Eiger well in hand and gave strict orders that he was not to be released. The Crow would keep a heavy guard close to deter Balmoran warriors who might attempt to free Eiger. Then Raef saddled his horse and rode alone toward the cliff, the banner of Vannheim streaming behind him.

He was left waiting for some time. His horse, sensing Raef's mood, would not wait idly and Raef was content to let the grey mare pace the base of the cliff as he kept his gaze trained on the narrow footpath above him. At last a figure appeared, followed by three more, and the party of warriors began to make the descent. Fengar led the way, swathed in grey furs, his face newly gaunt, his eyes bloodshot. Stefnir was but a step behind him and Raef, as he watched them traverse the uneven path, wondered if the lord of Gornhald regretted turning Fengar into a king or harbored ambitions of taking his place. Raef had hoped for sight of Hauk of Ruderk, but if he had made it to Fengar, he did not show himself. Behind Stefnir walked Romarr, Vakre's uncle and the lord of Finnmark, and his faithful dog. The sight of Ulthor Ten-blade, sour-faced, mouth filled with rotten teeth, wove a knot in Raef's stomach, but he forced himself to look to Fengar as the four men followed the last switchback and then came to a standstill at the bottom of the cliff.

"Release the hostages, Fengar," Raef said. He kept his horse moving, turning in tight circles in front of the would-be king.

"Not until you are gone from this valley, Skallagrim." It was Stefnir who answered him, though Fengar had the will to maintain eye contact with Raef.

"How will I know you mean to honor your word?" Raef addressed Fengar, hoping to wring a promise from him, but still Stefnir spoke as the king's voice.

"Ten-blade will accompany you out of good faith," the lord of Gornhald said. "The hostages will be released when we are certain you have been true to your word. We will direct them north toward the lady of Narvik's hall. When they reach it, you will allow Ten-blade to return to us."

Raef accepted the terms, though he knew Ten-blade's part in it had nothing to do with good faith.

"One more thing, lord," Stefnir said. "We must have your assurance that you will not attempt to follow us."

"You have my word." It was not entirely a lie. As they spoke, Bryndis was already moving the warriors south, away from her hall, to cover the routes Fengar was most likely to take. They would not follow Fengar. They would be waiting for him.

"An oath, Skallagrim." They were Fengar's first words.

Raef grinned, showing his teeth. "Give me Hauk of Ruderk and I will swear whatever you wish."

Fengar scowled but it was enough to tell Raef that his father's murderer was alive.

"The lady Bryndis has no desire to dishonor her fathers. She will keep the terms." Raef waited, hoping his assurances about Bryndis would be enough. He did not wish to make an oath before the gods, an oath he would have to break.

But Fengar was not satisfied. "Swear upon your sword that you will not bring us harm."

Raef laughed. "Swear upon it? Or ride you down and cleave your head from your shoulders with it?" But Fengar had chosen his words poorly and Raef did not hesitate. Drawing his sword from its scabbard, he wrapped his gloved hands around the blade, gripping the cold steel. "I swear to Tyr, lord of battle, and to Odin Allfather, I will bring you no harm. Let Odin carve my heart from my chest and feed it to Fenrir if I lie." Without taking his gaze from Fengar's face, Raef raised the hilt of the sword to his lips and kissed it.

TWENTY-SEVEN

"YOU SWORE HIM an oath?"

Raef smiled at Bryndis's surprise. "Yes. But it changes nothing."

"You cannot mean that. An oath binds us from making the ambush."

They had retreated from the sightline of the cliff top ruins, working their way over the hills that lined the eastern edge of the valley. Raef had caught up to Bryndis before she reached the summit and she drew her horse to a halt in anger.

"It binds me and me alone. Had Hauk of Ruderk been there, no doubt he would have chosen better words, but Fengar spoke for himself and the rest were not clever enough to see the mistake. I cannot harm Fengar. I cannot harm any of them. But the oath spoke of no one else. You are uncompromised, lady."

Bryndis nodded her understanding. "And your warriors?"

"Free."

"Then we will proceed as planned. What will you do?"

"Fengar will not leave before nightfall, and even then he will send out riders to be certain of our departure. These must be avoided and kept alive at all costs," Raef said. Bryndis nodded, impatient. "While you stalk him and lay the trap, I will bring Eiger before his father."

Bryndis frowned. "The Balmoran warriors are restless."

"Then I will make a show of releasing him and let it be known that an urgent message has come from your hall. The Great-Belly has need of his son, you see." The frown did not vanish right away, but Raef could see the lady of Narvik was warming to his notion. "I will keep Eiger close and Ten-blade closer."

Raef had left Ulthor Ten-blade among his own warriors at the rear of the host. He was unbound and free to ride as he pleased, for he was no prisoner, but Raef had made it clear to Njall and the other captains that he was to be watched and men should hold their tongues in his presence.

"And when Ulthor Ten-blade understands the deception?"

"By then it will be too late," Raef said. "Now go. You must reach the ford before they do." Fengar's passage south would take him to a wide, lazy river in the farthest reaches of Narvik. If he hurried, Bryndis said he would reach it in a day's travel, more if he lingered. There was no other easy crossing within two days ride and she knew the place well, knew how it might be used to trap Fengar's larger force.

Bryndis nodded. "To victory, Skallagrim."

"Your victory, lady. But if you find Hauk of Ruderk, spare him. My axe means to make a home in his skull."

Bryndis spurred her horse over the crest of the hill, reclaiming her place in the column. Raef watched until she disappeared, then turned his horse and rejoined the Vannheim warriors at the rear.

When they had left the valley behind and it was time for Raef to turn north, Dvalarr pleaded once more with him.

"Let me go with you, lord."

"Bryndis will have need of every man, Dvalarr."

"I do not trust Ten-blade."

Raef laughed. "Then you are a wise man, Crow." He held up a hand as the big man began to protest once more. "I need you here, Dvalarr. Njall is clever and bold and the men like him well enough and will obey his commands, but you are the heart of Vannheim's shield wall." The Crow said nothing but Raef could see the argument had faded from him. Raef risked a glance toward Siv. "Keep her from harm, Crow."

"I will."

Raef clasped Dvalarr's forearm, then brought his horse forward to where Njall rode with Ulthor Ten-blade at his side. The young captain had done his work well, for Ten-blade stared at Raef with a vacant expression, then tried to squeeze a final few drops from the mead skin he crushed within the palm of one dirty hand. The scent of mead was heavy on Ten-blade's breath, the sweet brew chosen carefully from a reluctant warrior's stash because it would hide the taste of the ground root that was already at work taming Ulthor's mind and rendering him less aware of his surroundings. The effects would not last the length of Raef's journey to Narvik's hall, and Raef would not risk dosing Ulthor a second time, for the root powder was potent and had been known to kill men who used it too freely. Raef would not mourn Ten-blade, but he meant to keep his oath.

Raef exchanged a glance with Njall. "Skuli?" Raef asked.

"There," the young captain said, pointing to where the blind warrior rode at the edge of the column. Skuli sat tall in his saddle and his hands held the reins loosely. He was armed as a warrior should be and Raef caught sight of a pair of arm rings at the edge of his sleeve. Were it not for the thick bandage that covered his eyes, he would have been a warrior like any other, content, eager, riding for war. "He screams in his sleep, lord."

Raef had heard. "He will recover in Bryndis's hall." Njall seemed to take comfort in that. The coming battle was no place for a blind man; taking Skuli with him as he went north had been an easy choice for Raef.

Raef turned to Ten-blade, who sat his horse and stared ahead, content to let the beast follow the rest. "And now you come with me, you corpse-eating maggot." Raef seized the reins and extracted Ten-blade from the column, angling their horses back past the warriors until they reached Eiger. Unlike Ten-blade, Eiger was all sullen anger and he stared at Raef with storm-edged eyes. He rode with hands bound before him, his horse led by another of Vannheim's captains.

"The Allfather will strengthen Fengar's shields for this, Skalla-grim. He will splinter the whore's spears and fill the enemy hearts with battle-fury," Eiger said as Raef approached. Raef held his tongue as he worked at the knot that held Eiger's horse. "My death will only anger the Terrible One more."

"It is not your death you will face," Raef snapped. With a sharp yank, he pulled Eiger's horse forward, nearly unseating the fat man. There was no time to appease the warriors of Balmoran, who rode and marched ahead, no time to parade Eiger, unbound, before them as Raef had told Bryndis he would do. His men would spread the word that Eiger had gone north to answer a message from his dying father; Raef had to hope that alone would subdue any thoughts of treachery that simmered in the hearts of the Balmoran warriors.

They were a strange party that separated from the rest. Raef at the head, belligerent Eiger tied to him, drugged Ulthor follow-ing with careless, lazy eyes, and blind Skuli, his horse tied to Ult-hor's to keep him from losing his way. Alone, Raef would have raced through the hills, but he set an easy pace and kept to the high ground so he might see anyone ahead or behind, friend or foe.

"I offered you a place in the Allfather's hall, Skallagrim," Eiger said. They had passed beyond hearing distance of the host that moved south into the next valley.

Raef grimaced. "Offered? That is not what I heard. When you spoke of your scheme before, we were to be partners, you and I. Have I been reduced so much?"

Eiger was quiet for a moment and Raef did not need to turn in his saddle and face the other man to know that Eiger was uncertain if Raef spoke in jest. "Odin has need of me. You should not mock my purpose." The uncertainty in Eiger's voice was startling, but Raef was reminded of the strange, earnest vulnerability that had been about the Great-Belly's son when Eiger had found him in the hot spring fueled bathhouse of Bryndis's hall. It seemed strange that a man could contain two such different parts of himself, the cruel, savage man who committed atrocities, and the solemn, heartfelt man who dreamed of the gods. Raef could not like Eiger in either form, but he wondered which nature would hold true in the face of chaos and fear.

They rode in silence as the sun slide across the sky, the light always shifting as banks of clouds drifted by. Cruel gusts of wind battered the hills, whipping Raef's cloak forward under his arm and lashing the horse's tail against his legs, but Raef would not retreat to more sheltered ground. It would not do to be caught unaware in the thick pines below, not when his were the only hands capable of wielding a sword should they need to defend themselves. And yet a chase across the open slopes of the higher ground would not go in his favor. He would lose Skuli and Ten-blade first. The drugged man's horse, content to follow Raef's, would grow frightened and bolt, dragging blind Skuli along. Neither man was fit for a hard gallop. But the land around them was empty and Raef tried to keep his mind on his task.

Raef did not know what would become of Eiger, what the Great-Belly might say when told of his son's offenses. He rode north out of necessity, out of the need to keep himself from the fighting and preserve an oath. Better this than watch the ambush from afar, his axe silent on his belt while the steel song filled the air, knowing he could do nothing.

"Lord." Skuli had not spoken, but now he called to Raef, his voice urgent. "Look south and tell me what you see."

Raef slid from his horse and scrambled up a slab of rock so he might have a better look. He lifted one hand to shield his gaze from the sun, which hung heavy in the western sky amid a sea of pink and purple clouds. To the south, the clouds were grey and blue, their edges lined with the sunset.

"I see much, Skuli," Raef called. "What troubles you?"

"Do you not smell it?"

The words were not yet out of Skuli's mouth when Raef saw it. There, camouflaged against the swath of blue and grey, was a smear of smoke. And then the wind brought Raef the scent of fire, ash, and burning things.

"You see, Skallagrim, already the tides turn against the whore of Narvik." Eiger's voice, sly and satisfied, slunk into Raef's ears and Raef had to swallow down the urge to seize him and choke the breath from his fleshy neck. Raef watched the smoke, distant and dark, his heart thudding in his chest once, twice, and then he vaulted down from his perch, drew a knife, and approached Eiger, who, eyes wide with fear, tried to use his bound hands to urge his horse away. Raef grasped Eiger's wrist and sawed at the rope until it fell away. He kept the rope linking their two horses intact and went to stand at Skuli's side.

Raef placed a hand on Skuli's arm and the eyeless man tilted his face as though he would look at Raef.

"I need you to do something for me, Skuli."

"Yes, lord."

"You must stay here with Ten-blade. He will regain his mind and his strength and his will before the moon is high. I will secure him, but you must be his keeper. Can you do that?"

"Yes." And Raef believed him. There was more life and less terror in Skuli's voice than Raef had heard since the return from the Dragon's Jaw.

Ten-blade was loose and limp and pliable in Raef's arms as he took him from his horse. Descending a short distance from the summit of the ridge they had been following, Raef chose a white pine of wide and sturdy trunk and lashed Ulthor to it. Then he led Skuli there, showing the blind man's hands where the tree lay, where the horses were tethered, where the spare blankets were tucked, where the skins of water hung, and where the hard cheese and dried meat were nestled in the packs. It would be enough to last them several days, though Raef did not want to think they would need it.

"Ten-blade is clever and cruel, Skuli, and when he recovers he will be as furious as Jörmungand when Thor caught the great serpent on his fishing hook. Do not untie him, you hear? Let him piss himself."

"Yes, lord."

Raef hesitated, searching the bandaged face before him. "Someone will come for you." Raef tried not to let his uncertainty be heard in his voice. If things went badly, no one would know where Raef had left a blind man to guard a savage warrior.

Skuli nodded. "Go, lord. I will wait."

Raef backed away, desperate to ride south and yet reluctant to leave Skuli so vulnerable, then he turned and raced back to the summit and mounted his horse.

"Why not slit his throat and be done?" Eiger asked as Raef set a quick pace to retrace their steps. "You go to fight Fengar. Why leave one of his warriors alive?"

"Someone has a greater claim to Ulthor Ten-blade's life than I."

ᚦ ᚦ ᚦ

The sky was one hundred shades of blue and black by the time Raef drew his horse up at the edge of the ice-dotted river, but the blazing pines on the far bank lit the night.

There was little to see. Smoke, thick and dark, poured out of the pines and drifted across the river, obscuring Raef's view. He could hear only the rushing wind of the fire. There was no sign of battle, of Fengar, of Bryndis's host of warriors.

"I am not going over there." Eiger had halted his horse as far from Raef as the rope tethering them together would allow.

"You are." Raef no longer had anger to spare for the Great-Belly's son. He urged his horse into the water and Eiger's followed.

The river was deeper than he had expected and soon Raef found himself in icy water to his waist. The horse's legs churned beneath him as the beast was forced to swim, head raised high to fight off the water, nostrils wide in fear, and Raef felt the current dragging him, threatening to sweep him away. By the time the horse found its footing in shallower water, Raef was drenched and shaking with the cold. The far bank was steeper and the horse struggled up the slope, hooves sticking in the slick mud and snow. Raef dismounted in a tumble and dragged Eiger, who flailed in the river, his foot caught in a stirrup, up onto land.

On his knees, Raef caught his breath and stared into the blazing forest, the heat welcome against his skin and soaked clothing. Further down the bank, a man stumbled from the trees, his cloak a ribbon of flame behind him. His fingers worked uselessly at the clasp on his shoulder as the fire consumed more and more of the cloth, and, just strides from the water that would save him, he tripped over a protruding root and sprawled on the ground. The flaming cloak settled over him. Raef raced to the warrior and caught hold of one of his arms, hauling him the remaining distance to the river. The flames extinguished with a hiss and a rush of steam and together Raef and the warrior scrambled to shore.

The man was unburnt and unknown to Raef and for a moment they stared at each other, each wary of the other.

"What has happened here?" Raef asked, wiping river water from his eyes. The cold was deep in his bones and he had to work to produce the words.

The warrior stared back into the smoking forest and shook his head, remembering. "There was no warning."

Raef made to grab the man's shoulder, hoping to shake some words from him, but he restrained himself. "Where is Fengar? Or the lady Bryndis?"

"Walls of flame. Stinging sparks. A sea of smoke. So sudden." The warrior looked back at Raef and took him by the shoulders. "Without warning," he said, again. "It hounded us, no matter where we fled." Removing his hands from Raef, the man fumbled for the hammer that hung from his neck and after his fingers latched onto it, his lips moved silently, words for Thor's ears.

Raef turned from the man and searched the fire for further signs of life. It was clear the blaze had spread and traveled. Raef looked to the northwest, where the land swept upward, where Fengar's path from the ancient fortress would have taken him. The trees there were scorched and blackened, their branches still smoking. Raef did not doubt that most of Fengar's men had been caught in the thick of the fire, lungs gasping for air, skin blistered and bleeding. The forest had gained an army of corpses.

As he watched the smoke billow from the treetops, a roar filled Raef's ears and a rush of wind sucked past him, so strong that it lifted Raef's heels from the ground and he stumbled forward to keep his feet. The wind surged into the trees and then rose to the stars and, as though the cold, wild air had caught up the flames in its embrace, the fire was gone, disappearing into the dark expanse of sky, leaving only the sweet scent of smoke, a shower of sparks to drift to the ground, and silence that poured into Raef's senses.

Raef felt for the hammer that no longer hung from his neck. He had been certain that Vakre had caused the fire, that the son of Loki, in desperation, had set the blaze to keep his uncle from escaping. But though Vakre could birth flames from his fingers, he could not send them to the sky to be swallowed by darkness, he could not command the winds. No, this was something else at work.

Raef returned to his horse, where Eiger waited. The big man avoided Raef's gaze, but he could not hide the trembling of his jaw as he fought to control his fear. Searching in his small pack, Raef pulled out a clean cloth meant for bandaging wounds and went to the river. Kneeling, he soaked the cloth in the icy water, wrung it out, then tied it around his mouth and nose. Raef turned to Eiger.

"Well? Do you wish to choke on the smoke in there?"

Eiger grimaced and tore a strip from the hem of his shirt, then followed Raef's example and tied it, dripping, around his face.

"Will you not give me a weapon?" Eiger asked, his voice muffled by the wet wool. His dark gaze scanned over Raef's assortment of weapons and there was greed in his eyes.

"Are you afraid of corpses?"

Eiger's eyes narrowed and Raef was sure that if the moon were brighter he would see a flush of embarrassment on the fleshy cheeks that bulged above the wet cloth. "You do not know what we will find in there."

"I know that I do not trust you, and that is enough."

Without another word, Raef cocked his head toward the smoking forest and waited until Eiger was three steps ahead of him before following. With a final look back at the warrior who lingered on the riverbank, staring at Raef, he plunged into the smoke. Only then did he draw his axe from his belt, taking care to do so silently for he did not wish Eiger to know that he, too, felt the edge of fear.

The wet cloth provided welcome relief from the smoke, but as they pushed deeper into the ruined forest, Raef's eyes began to sting. He drove Eiger onward whenever the other man hesitated and directed him to turn now and then, though there was little to guide them. When they came across the first body, the river was out of sight, lost in the ash. The warrior's skin was blistered, his fingers black and charred. After that, the corpses were everywhere. Some were less damaged, recognizable, even, had Raef known their faces, and at length he came to see that a few clung to life. These stared up at him, only their shifting eyes giving indication that they had not yet gone to Valhalla. Raef saw pain in those eyes.

It came as a surprise when they found one young warrior, a woman, nearly untouched by the flames. She was limping through the trees, the point of her sword dragging behind her, her face a mask of ash that hid pale skin. The leather boot on her left foot had melted away, and the wool underneath, leaving her foot bare and bloody. When Raef came up behind her and took her hand, for she seemed not to hear his approach, the shieldmaiden looked at him in confusion and tried to twist out of his grasp.

"Steady," Raef murmured, tucking the axe back in his belt. He let go and raised his hands to show her he meant no harm. He turned to Eiger. "Take her back to the river. See that she drinks water."

Raef could see Eiger's relief in his eyes, but he hesitated. "How do you know I will not flee?"

"Because you need me. Remember, I had stars in my hair and a storm in my eyes," Raef said, throwing Eiger's own words back at him. He was rewarded with a look of loathing, but Raef could see Eiger still clung to his dream. "You will not gain the gates of Asgard without me."

Eiger grabbed the shieldmaiden and propelled her before him in the direction of the river.

"You will not touch her," Raef said, wondering how far his control over the man extended. He watched them go, and then continued on into the forest.

Raef, following the swath of burnt trees up into the hills, found twelve more warriors who were more living than dead. After scanning their faces to be sure Fengar, Hauk, and Romarr of Finnmark were not hiding behind smears of ash, Raef gave each a sip of water from his skin and directed them down to the sanctuary of the river.

The night seemed endlessly long and more than once Raef searched the eastern sky for signs of the sun. He came across a small pond, the clear water now soiled with ash and burned branches that had come to rest there. Removing the wrap around his face, Raef drenched it once more and tied it again, but a ripple across the pond's surface stilled his movements.

Still crouching, Raef waited for the ripple to subside, but no sooner had the pond gone still than it was disturbed once more and this time the surface of the dark water writhed and boiled and Raef watched in astonishment as a small figure, her shoulders breaking the surface, rose from the depths until she stood before Raef, the water lapping at her slender waist.

"Cilla?" Raef asked, rising to his full height to stare at her.

The girl had always been small, but now, soaked and dripping, she was reduced to so little that Raef could hardly be sure she was not a creature from the stories of his childhood.

Raef's astonishment doubled when Cilla splashed her way out of the pond and threw her skinny arms around him, her face buried in his chest. Raef put one hand on her head and was wrapping the other arm around her when she pulled away and stepped back, allowing herself only that small moment of comfort. Cilla wiped at the water dripping from her chin, looking up at Raef though she kept her head lowered. The air in the forest was still warm from the fire, but the pond was cold and Raef could see Cilla was fighting the urge to shiver.

"Cilla," Raef said again. He pulled the cloth down from his face and unhooked his cloak. He had left his heavy fur cloak in Bryndis's hall, content to rely on a thinner, lighter woven one for travel, but it would seem a warm embrace to Cilla's slight frame. Raef went down on one knee and held out the cloak. Cilla hesitated, then stepped into it and let Raef do the clasp at her collarbone. Raef put a hand on Cilla's arm, then reached around her neck and drew her limp, dripping hair over her shoulder with his other hand. With gentle fingers, Raef wrung the water out of her hair, and only then did he look her in the eye, catching her gaze just before it flitted away. The tangled mix of hope and mistrust he saw there wrenched at his heart.

"You are the bravest eleven year old I will ever know."

"I am twelve now," Cilla said. "I think."

Raef smiled and straightened the cloak on her shoulders. It was far too big and threatened to slip off. "Let me be brave for you now, Cilla. For both of us."

Cilla looked at him and he could see her struggle against giving in, could see her resist the vulnerability he was offering her, but after a moment she nodded and her eyes flooded with relief. Raef stood and offered his hand.

"Come, you must help me search."

"What are we looking for?" Cilla put her palm against his and Raef wrapped his fingers around her small hand. She had new calluses.

"Life."

TWENTY-EIGHT

THEY FOUND FENGAR in a ravine. The would-be king was drenched in snowmelt and the rocky sides of the ravine were dark with running water. Soon the cold air of winter would have dominion once more, but the heat of the fire had created a myriad of tiny, surging waterfalls and Fengar had found refuge from the gorging flames deep in the earth.

It was Cilla who spotted him, but Fengar, sitting with his head in his hands as water dripped onto the back of his exposed neck, did not stir when Raef called down to him.

"You will have a hard time climbing out when all this water turns to ice," Raef said.

Fengar raised his head. "Perhaps it is better if I stay down here."

It would be easy to agree with him, to walk away and let Fengar slide quietly into death. The three kings spawned by the gathering would all be gone.

"Have you ever watched a man starve to death?" Raef let his question hang in the air before continuing. "I have not. But I have heard that it is a cruel way to go." Raef waited another moment. "First your belly will beg for food until it no longer knows it is hungry. Then you will wither to nothingness, but not without pain. Your limbs will weaken and the slightest touch, a leaf floating on a gentle breeze, will have you screaming in agony. And you will linger. Starvation is not swift, Fengar."

It was a long time before Fengar answered. Raef stifled a yawn and rubbed his tired eyes. Cilla watched.

"The gods have forsaken me, Skallagrim. Perhaps this is the death I deserve. I am tired of this life. Up there," Fengar craned his neck, twisting to take in the sliver of lightening sky above him, "up there is only shame and hatred for me."

"I know not if the gods have forsaken you, Fengar, but I know you are not deserving of such a death. I would not wish it even on my most hated enemy." As Raef spoke the words, he knew they were true. He had deprived Jarl Thrainson, the man whose spear had ripped the life from his father, of a seat in Valhalla, he had made the blood eagle on Isolf's back, and he would bring death to Hauk of Ruderk even at the breaking of the world, but even Hauk would die a warrior's death.

"What do you gain from seeing me live?" Fengar asked. He used the slick rocks to pull himself to his feet.

"Nothing."

"Is it true you were named king?"

"Yes."

"Then you most of all should want me dead."

"I will not be king."

Fengar frowned.

"Bryndis will call a gathering. And the voices of the warriors will be heard. As they should have been," Raef said.

"I underestimated her," Fengar said, his voice low and weary. "We all did. Stefnir most of all. And I trusted him. As I always did." Fengar hung his head. "She will not rest until I am dead. If you share her vision for a gathering, Skallagrim, you will kill me and be done."

Raef took a deep breath and looked to the sky, pink and grey and gold beyond the reach of the burned, blackened trees.

"The fire burned hot and fast. Few escaped. Many of the bodies are charred and blistered beyond recognition." Raef paused. "That ring on your finger. It is fine silver."

Fengar looked up at Raef, reaching for the band of silver on his right hand as his eyebrows knit together. "What are you saying?"

Raef shrugged. "Only that it is valuable. Tell me, what is etched around the band?"

Fengar's frown deepened. "The ring bears the name of my ancestor, Bryngolf Brightshield."

"Beloved of the gods was Bryngolf."

"Yes." Fengar's voice was laced with suspicion.

"And famous, still, as the ancestor of Solheim."

"Yes."

"No one would doubt the authenticity of that ring."

Fengar held Raef's gaze and Raef knew the other man at last understood.

"Take your life and go, Fengar. Leave the ring and I will see that your death is known. But you cannot go home. You must no longer be Fengar of Solheim. Buy sheep, find a woman, learn how to make cheese."

"You would let me go?" There was wonder in Fengar's voice.

"Do you not wish to live? To be free of the yoke Stefnir of Gornhald and Hauk of Ruderk burdened you with?"

"To live in such a manner would bring shame to my ancestors."

"The time for such thoughts is long past, Fengar. You shamed them the moment you stood above the rest in the Great-Belly's hall, the moment you let a few lords name you king without the consent of the warriors."

Fengar dropped his gaze, but when he raised it again, Raef saw a measure of acceptance in his face and then the lord of Solheim began to climb from the depths of the ravine.

When he reached the top, taking Raef's arm to haul himself over the edge, Fengar stripped the fat silver ring from his finger, stroked the band once with his thumb, then placed it with care in Raef's palm.

"Bryndis was waiting to the south," Raef said. "Where she went when the fire started I could not say."

"Then I will go west first," Fengar began, but Raef shook his head to silence him.

"Do not tell me where you mean to go. I do not wish to know."

Fengar nodded and then, without another word, he pulled up his hood and turned his back on Raef, who watched him weave through the flame-licked tree trunks until Fengar was out of sight.

"Why did you let him go?" Cilla had watched in silence and her gaze rested on the ring that rested still in Raef's open palm. He closed his fingers over it and dropped his hand to his side before answering.

"Fengar was ambitious and it pleased him to be named king, but his ambitions were a gentle spring rain compared to the torrential flood that drives some men. Fengar's fault lay in his lack of will and his inability to rely upon himself, and for that he deserves some of the blame for this war that has ravaged so much of the world. But far greater blame rests on the shoulders of two men, for the war was of their making and Fengar was never more than a tool, wielded as it pleased them."

Cilla frowned and Raef could see that his answer did not satisfy her.

"Would you have wanted me to kill him?"

Cilla shrugged. "He wanted to die. You could have let him."

"Yes, I could have. But I have done him no great favor. The winter has been long and cold and the wilderness is ever hungry to claim the lives of those who cannot face it. He is alone and I doubt he carries more than a scrap of dried meat, if that. Food will be difficult for him to come by."

"You said you did not want him to starve."

"And that is true. But if that is his fate, better that he face it head on than wait for it to find him while he cowers in the dark and grieves for what he has lost," Raef said. Cilla nodded, though Raef was not certain she understood.

It was not hard to find a corpse that could pass as Fengar. What was left of the hair was the right shade of brown, the height and weight of the dead man were accurate, and the singed beard needed only a rough trim under Raef's knife before it was short enough. The man's face was badly burned, making it impossible to determine his eye color or even the shape of his nose. Raef pushed Fengar's ring onto the dead man's finger, working it over a thick knuckle, and wondered if Bryngolf Brightshield was laughing in Valhalla.

Raef shouldered the corpse and set off in the direction of the river. When he and Cilla emerged from the burned forest, the sun was glowing in the east, but the cold morning light was not all that had arrived on the opposite bank of the river.

Bryndis was there, dressed for battle, a naked sword in her grip, and surrounded by grim-faced warriors. She had fresh charcoal around her eyes and new ink that traced the outside of her ears and down the length of her jaw. From across the river, she was all bright blade and fierce eyes.

Eiger was waiting with the warriors Raef had found. He had not gone to join the lady of Narvik, Raef noted.

But it was Siv who caught Raef's eye as he set the corpse in a muddy patch of snow. She was apart from the rest of Bryndis's company, and though her face brightened at sight of Raef, he could see that concern for her sister weighed heavy on her.

Bryndis's gaze fell to the body at Raef's feet, the unasked question blazing from those eyes lined with midnight.

"The last king, lady," Raef called out.

Bryndis called for a horse and soon splashed across the river. She dismounted and prodded at the body with the toe of her boot.

"You are certain?"

Raef knelt down and grabbed the dead man's wrist, holding up the hand that bore Bryngolf Brightshield's ring.

Bryndis came close and bent over the finger and the fine silver. She kept her hands away from the burned flesh and Raef could see her nostrils flare slightly as she caught the scent of death.

"The heirloom of the lords of Solheim, lady."

Bryndis straightened and nodded. Her gaze fell to Cilla. "The hostages?"

"I have found one." Raef placed an arm across Cilla's shoulders.

Bryndis nodded again and now looked to the trees behind Raef, who sensed she would rather not look at the devastation. "What caused it?"

Raef dared not answer and he let the question linger and then vanish between them.

"We will search for the rest," Bryndis said. She called out across the river, shouting directions to her uncle, who led across a large group of warriors, perhaps forty in number. They spread out and entered the trees in a thin line, each man close enough to stay in sight and hearing distance of the man on either side of him. To Raef's surprise, Siv had hesitated on the far bank. Raef mounted his horse and urged it into the water once more. The icy water gripped at him and he grit his teeth against the cold, though this time he entered the river where Bryndis had exited and was glad to find the crossing easier, the current less fierce, the sandy bottom within reach of his horse's hooves. Siv did not take her eyes from the still-smoking trees as he dismounted at her side.

"Was it Vakre?" Her voice was tight and lined with pain.

"I do not know." Raef took a deep breath and found he had nothing else to say.

"If he has killed her," Siv paused, her voice shaking, "if Vakre's fury has killed my sister, he will answer for it." A tear slipped out of the corner of her eye and Siv brushed it away with a hurried swipe of her hand. Raef caught that hand and took it between his, and at last Siv turned her head and looked at him. A ragged gasp burst from her and she thumped Raef's chest with a balled fist. "I love him as a brother." The tears came freely now and she did not fight them. Raef pulled her close to him, longing to chase away her pain, but he knew his arms could not release her heart from its grief.

"She may yet be alive," Raef murmured. Siv nodded against him, then pulled back and wiped at her reddened eyes. Raef leaned forward and kissed her forehead. "Tell me how I might know her, and I will go search until she is found."

"No," Siv said, shaking her head. "I will go."

They crossed the river together, then Raef splashed water on his face, refilled the skin at his belt, and took a few bites of hard cheese. His stomach pleaded for more and an ache spreading from behind his ears up to his temples told him he needed to rest and breathe air that wasn't filled with smoke, but he would not leave Siv alone.

Cilla would not be left, either. She followed them without a word and Raef did not have the will to argue with her. Siv asked the girl where she had been when the fire started, and if the other hostages had been with her. Cilla said they were grouped together, though no longer bound like the links of a chain, but when the fire sprung up behind them and bore down on their backs, they had fled, separating. She had seen none, alive or dead, since.

Raef struck off in a more northern direction than the one he had taken on his first foray into the trees. The route would take them directly toward the fire's point of origin, though much of their path traced the curving edge of the burned swath of land and they walked a line between blackened trees with crumbling bark and untouched birches, stark white, solemn sentinels standing watch over their burned kin. They walked in silence and the forest was quiet around them, the birds and rabbits and squirrels chased away by the smoke. The stillness began to wear on Raef's nerves and the sound of his own footsteps grew irritating to his ears in the absence of bird song and the chatter of territorial squirrels.

Their path dipped here and there, but always climbed higher than before, and soon they found themselves high above the devastation. The air was fresher and Raef stopped to breath it in for a moment, closing his eyes as a shaft of sunlight glanced across his cheek. Cilla wandered ahead as Siv paused to adjust the quiver of arrows that hung from her belt.

"Fengar is not dead," Raef said.

"You let him go."

"Yes." Raef breathed in, letting the cold air sink to the bottom of his lungs. "For all his faults, the war was not of his making. The blame for that rests with Hauk of Ruderk, Stefnir of Gornhald, and Torrulf Palesword."

"And Einarr of Vannheim." The voice seemed to claw at Raef's ears and he spun, reaching for his axe and scanning for the owner of the voice among the trees as Siv nocked an arrow on the string of her bow with one swift motion.

Hauk Orleson, lord of Ruderk, stood twenty paces away, half in shadow, half in sunlight. He held a knife, the blade bright in the sun, and its edge rested against Cilla's neck. His left arm was wrapped across her collarbone but the flesh of his forearm had been seared, the hair burnt away, and a bloody gash, half cauterized, ran from his elbow to his wrist. Whatever he had worn to fend off the cold had been discarded when it caught fire, but Hauk seemed impervious to the winter air. He stared at Raef, unblinking, his eyes blazing with desperation, and yet his face was strangely calm, his hold on Cilla strong but easy.

"Let her go." Raef ran his thumb across the worn shaft of his axe, felt the weight of it in his palm, and wondered if he could bury it in Hauk's forehead before the knife cut deep enough to guarantee Cilla's death.

"Have you heard me, Skallagrim?"

"I hear a liar's tongue, nothing more." Raef kept his voice steady but he was sure Siv, standing off his shoulder and ahead of him, could hear his thundering heart. He did not break his gaze from Hauk's but the world around him was sharp and vivid. He could see the sweat-darkened hair at the base of Siv's neck. He could see the grime beneath Cilla's fingernails. He could see the pulse thrumming at Hauk's temple.

"Would you like to know your father's darkest secret?"

"My father would never have manipulated Fengar as you have, he would never have relished this war."

"Oh, it is not of this war that I speak, or Fengar, or even of the promises your father broke in the days before the gathering in the Great-Belly's hall. This is a far deeper secret, one he harbored since before you were born."

Raef felt himself shake his head. "I will not hear you."

"You will. Because you do not wish to watch her die." Hauk tightened his grip on Cilla. The girl's eyes flared but she did not cry out, did not even flinch. Siv released some of the tension on her bowstring and lowered it so that the arrow was no longer aimed at Hauk's head. When Raef made no move to protest, Hauk urged Cilla forward until they halved the distance to Raef, but he was careful to keep the greater part of his body angled behind a tree. "Do you know how your uncle died, Skallagrim?"

The question was so unexpected that for a moment Raef let go of his anger. "My uncle?"

"Your father's brother. Older brother. His name was Dainn, was it not?"

"It was."

"Yes. It was. And do you know how Dainn died?"

"He drowned," Raef said.

"A truthful answer, but not the entire truth."

"I grow weary of this game, Orleson."

"Then you better discover your patience, Skallagrim." Hauk shifted his weight, his face twisting in a grimace of pain as he moved. "The deep waters of the Vannheim fjord filled your uncle's lungs, this you know. But you do not know that your father watched him die and did nothing to save him." Raef wanted to close his eyes, to stopper his ears against the vile words Hauk spoke, but he could not look away. "I was there, Raef. I saw it all. I saw them quarrel, I saw the oar raised in your father's fist. I saw him swing, saw your uncle's neck snap back so far and so fast I was sure it had broken. I saw Dainn fall overboard, but he was alive yet, and he struggled. He fought the pull of the deep, fought to keep his head above water, but the blow to his head had sapped all strength from his limbs. I saw him sink and I saw his last breath bubble to the surface."

Raef wanted to rip Hauk's tongue from his throat but his own limbs were as worthless as Dainn's must have been.

"I do not believe you." The small, shattered voice was his own.

"Your father begged me to keep his secret. He vowed he would pay for my silence, whatever I might demand. I could have asked for gold, silver, a horde of treasure to put the mighty Fafnir's to shame, a sword from that bladesmith of yours, a ship, even, and Einarr would have seen it done. But I asked for none of this. I told him one day I would need something from him, and we would consider the debt paid. That day came last spring when the snow first grew soft and the ice began to wither. The king was old. He was dying, you see. Did your father not tell you?" Hauk's voice remained level, betraying little, but his eyes grew bright and Raef knew he was laughing at Raef's ignorance. "Do you know how many men have called themselves king since first our ancestors knelt to one man?" Hauk waited for Raef to answer and then continued as though he had spoken. "I learned their names as a boy, and I learned the stories of their lives and deaths. Think, Skallagrim, of the destruction they have wrought, all to be king. Battle after battle, year after year, ravaging our families and our lands. Think of the blood spilled in their names, think of the drain upon the future of Midgard." Something earnest had crept into Hauk's voice and his gaze grew unfocused, but his grip on Cilla never wavered.

"You speak as though we have always been at war," Siv said. "It has not all been steel song and bloodshed since Kyrrbjorn Wolfbane hunted down his rivals and our ancestors knelt."

Hauk brushed Siv's words aside but Raef spoke before he could. "Why do you talk of Kyrrbjorn Wolfbane and all the men and women who have sought power? Speak plainly."

"We need peace, Skallagrim. We need a peace that will last so that our sons and daughters and their children can live without the shadow of war."

"You started a war, Hauk," Raef said, his voice ripping forth, low and angry. "How dare you speak of peace."

"Could I have done what needed to be done without spilling blood, I would have. But we are crude beings, we warriors, and we consume violence as the gods do mead."

"What did you hope to accomplish?"

Something shifted in Hauk's face. The hard lines of his cheeks softened and his eyes lost their sharpness as he spoke of his ambition. "Deliverance. No more gatherings. No more kings."

"Impossible."

"Do not be so quick to make that assumption, Skallagrim."

And Raef knew the pull of Hauk's words, knew there was a

grain of truth in what he said. Raef remembered Sverren of Bergoss, who had refused to ally with Raef, whose messenger had said Bergoss would stand with no king. He remembered his own pride in Vannheim's resistance of Kyrrbjorn Wolfbane so many generations before. He thought of little-known lords who made their homes in the farthest reaches of the wild, lords who paid no mind to the greater world outside their hidden valleys and high vales, whose people had never seen a fortress made of stone and lived and died without leaving the small village that birthed them, and he wondered if they would not rather be free of any king.

"There will always be men who seek to rise above the rest, who believe others should kneel," Raef said. "And there will always be men like you, men who try to write the fates of others, who would hide behind an honest face and a hope."

"Then you think there is hope?" Hauk's eyes were lined with scorn, but his voice, eager and hurried, betrayed desperation.

"I think you have betrayed all the codes of gods and men. But what does this have to do with my father?" Raef dreaded the question and the answer he might receive, but he asked it without hesitation.

"And so we come to it at last. For twenty-eight years I waited, holding onto the debt your father owed me. In the spring, when the king was ailing, I met your father in secret on the border between Vannheim and Bergoss and I demanded what I was owed."

"Twenty-eight years is a long time, Hauk," Siv said. "Long enough that the lord of Vannheim might no longer fear retribution for his brother's death. Who would punish him? He was well-loved by his people."

"It seems, lady, that Einarr of Vannheim did not rest so easily as you believe. Or at least he was willing to honor the promise he had made to me as a young man." Hauk looked from Siv to Raef. "He agreed to support me and the path toward our liberation."

That his father would have harbored such a secret, that he would have thrown himself behind Hauk's scheme, seemed like madness to Raef.

"Then why kill him? More likely he spurned you and you had to silence him for fear of discovery."

"By the time we gathered in Balmoran, your father had weakened. The wisdom that had shown him the virtue of my plan had abandoned him. He clung to the illusion of the gathering and would not be reasoned with."

"And for that you had him butchered like a beast of the forest." There was anger in Raef's voice, and fury burned in his belly, but for all Raef tried, he could not summon the sight of his father's corpse, could not see Einarr stretched out in the tall grass, eyes staring, sword in hand, wound gaping. Instead he saw a fjord, dark and beautiful, but deadly, and he saw a face much like his father's slip beneath the surface, saw his uncle thrashing, striving to live, and succumbing instead to death. He could not bring himself to speak, nor move, and at last Siv broke the silence.

"What do you want, Hauk?" Siv's eyes had been full of concern as she looked at Raef, but now she fixed the lord of Ruderk with a cold gaze and raised her bow once more, aiming at a point between his eyes.

"My work is unfinished. Peace can be attained. But there can be no gathering. Join me," Hauk said, shifting his gaze from Siv to Raef. Raef felt that stare like a knife in his chest. His breath caught in his throat, though his heart pounded between his ribs. "Join me, Skallagrim, as your father should have. We can return Midgard to the greatness we knew before we kneeled. Fengar may be dead, but I am not without friends. There are those who have kept their spears unbloodied, who have watched the three kings break each other. We can release all the lands from the burden of kings."

"I will never join you." The words were nothing more than a

whisper. Raef tried again, forcing air from his lungs though he still felt caught in the grip of the fjord his uncle had drowned in. "I will never join you." Raef kept his eyes locked with Hauk's, but a slip of a shadow moving between trees behind Hauk's shoulder caught Raef's attention. He did not need to look to know who approached. He knew only one man with such wolf-like movements. "You must be desperate, indeed, Orleson," Raef said, intent on keeping the lord of Ruderk focused on him, "if you think I will ever hear what you have to say, if you think I will ever join hands with my father's murderer."

"You could rise above all your ancestors, Skallagrim, you could be the greatest of them all," Hauk said. "Or you could cling to the same faults that plagued your father and be no different than a man who killed his brother."

Raef blinked, then, for the image of his drowning uncle that shadowed his vision vanished, replaced by a pair of lungs, quivering, red and bloody in the cold winter air, framed by the splintered shards of Isolf's white ribs, the gaping ruin of his cousin's back and spine searing into Raef's open eyes.

But then Vakre was there, emerging from the shadows, his knife caressing Hauk's throat, and the son of Loki was commanding Cilla's release. Hauk's grip on Cilla was slipping, his eyes widening, his muscles stiffening against the cold steel on his skin, and then a quick hammered strike to Hauk's temple with the hilt of the knife sent the lord of Ruderk crumpling to the ground.

Raef turned away, a long breath shuddering out from deep within his lungs. He put one hand against the smooth, soft trunk of a pale birch and only then did he see the tremors in his fingers and feel the weakness in his legs. He did not dare let go, though he wished to be far from that place, wished to run as though his strides could carry him away from the horror Hauk had unleashed in his mind.

Raef closed his eyes, summoning shreds of memory, his father showing him how to steer a long, lean ship, the first deer felled by Raef's arrow under Einarr's watchful eye, the jarring blows of Einarr's sword against Raef's shield as father taught son to keep it raised high, no matter how heavy, no matter how weary the arm grew. Raef could hear the blows as the sword battered again and again against the wood, he could smell the leather his father wore and the sweat that warmed the skin beneath, he could feel the burning in his shield arm and the calluses on his left hand, his sword hand, slick with his own sweat. The memory grew and grew until Raef no longer knew he was in the wilds of Narvik, until he no longer remembered Hauk, Vakre, or Siv, but then it changed and Einarr's eyes were no longer his own. Raef saw his father's face shift, saw his own anger and fury burning back at him from those blue depths, saw what it was like to look into the face of the Skallagrim in Vannheim and see death there.

Pain brought Raef out of the depths of his mind. Blinking, he saw a droplet of blood welling on his palm, saw that he no longer held the smooth bark of the birch, that he had stepped into the thorny embrace of a blackthorn bush. He plucked the thorn from his palm, let the dark blood gather and pool, then knelt and placed his hand atop the snow. He waited until the snow had cooled his palm, then rose, leaving behind a stain.

"Raef?"

Raef looked over his shoulder. Vakre had left Hauk where he fell but he had not shed the hunter's stance.

"Do you want me to kill him?"

"I must," Raef heard himself say. The words seemed to rouse him further and he could feel the sunlight on his face once more. He looked to Siv. "But not now."

Vakre nodded and sheathed his knife. "The fire," he said, "it spread far too fast, as though carried on the wings of eagles. I only meant to separate my uncle from the rest but no sooner had I set the spark than the forest was blazing."

Behind Vakre, Siv closed her eyes and Raef could see her eyelashes darken with tears. Vakre, seeing Raef's gaze shift, turned and went to Siv.

"What have I done?"

Siv blinked back the salty tears that threatened to spill over. Her cheeks were pale. "Nothing. I grieve only for the hostages who did not escape." Siv reached for Cilla and took the girl's hand, together they knelt beside Hauk of Ruderk and Siv withdrew a pair of leather thongs from a pouch at her belt. With nimble fingers, she began to fashion knots that would bind the prone man's wrists.

Vakre looked at Raef, his anguish plain. "What have I done?" he asked again.

But Raef would not betray Siv's truth, whatever had caused her to hold her tongue, so he told Vakre of the strange wind that had vanquished the fire so suddenly. "The spark may have been yours, but I think the fire answered to another."

"My father?"

"It seems that way. But I do not pretend to understand the will of the gods or the workings of the nine realms."

Vakre looked to Hauk. "And him?"

"Will you take him to the river? Bryndis's army awaits on the eastern shore. The men of Vannheim must be there, though I have not seen them. Find Dvalarr." Raef glanced at Hauk. Ordering Einarr's death had been the work of much preparation; the savaging of Einarr's reputation was the work of only a moment but it had proved no less thorough or painful to Raef. "Keep Hauk for me. I will return when I can."

Vakre nodded, though Raef could see he had not set aside his guilt and the son of Loki glanced at Siv once more before returning his attention to Raef. "I heard what was said. Do you believe his claims?"

Raef did not trust himself to answer. He put a hand on Vakre's arm. "Go. Please."

Raef watched as Vakre, Hauk draped over his shoulder, took to the descent. Cilla, still wrapped in Raef's cloak, trailed after. She clutched the hem up to her chest to keep from tripping on it as she picked her way down among the trees and Raef looked away only once they were out of sight. Siv had come to stand beside him, and he saw now that her eyes were dry.

"You did not tell him?"

"It is yours to tell."

"What will you do?" Her voice was raw, but she did not accuse, and Raef knew what she did not say.

Though the thought of choosing Siv over Vakre opened a pit in his stomach that seemed deep enough to swallow him, he would, if it came to that. "I will be guided by you," he said. Raef took her in his arms and kissed her. "I am yours," he murmured.

TWENTY-NINE

EKKHILD'S HAIR WAS longer than Siv's, but the sisters shared the same bright, rich blonde color, suffused with so many undercurrents of red and gold. She wore it loose, the long strands falling to her waist.

She had gone on hands and knees, Raef could see, in search of air that was not thick with smoke. The skirt of her dress was damp and muddy where it had dragged across the melting snow and her hands were black with dirt and ash. In the end, she had curled up at the base of a pine tree, one arm crooked around the slender trunk, the other held across her face, the drape of her sleeve shielding both nose and mouth.

The fire had not touched her, save for singeing the hem of her cloak, and her face was a refuge of peace amid the scorched earth and trees. Raef wondered what color irises lurked beneath her lids, what her voice sounded like, and how she might have smiled to see her sister again.

Siv lingered five paces from the body after catching sight of it and Raef waited, keeping his distance, until she crossed the empty space with deliberate steps and knelt beside Bekkhild's body. She reached out and pushed a lock of hair away from her sister's face, then put a hand to the pale, cool cheek.

"I often wondered if I would know her face or if the passing of so many years would make her a stranger to me." Siv's voice was quiet but strong. "I should not have doubted." Siv raised her head and looked at Raef. "She was close." They were not far from the edge of the fire's path. Raef could see trees untouched by the black fingers of the flames, could smell the clean breeze. Only six spear lengths lay between Bekkhild and air that might have saved her life. "Do you think she knew?"

Raef shook his head, though he wished he might have a different truth for Siv, but she nodded, accepting it.

"I am glad, at least, to know her fate."

The sun had set, leaving only bands of clouds washed in hues of orange and purple. To the east, the sky was already deep blue and the first stars were unveiled. Raef carried Bekkhild away from the place of death and stood by while Siv washed her sister in a quiet, shallow pool south of the ford. The dirt rinsed from Bekkhild's hands, Siv combed through her sister's long tresses of golden hair with her fingers and was beginning to braid it when Vakre approached and sat beside her.

"Your hands are cold," Vakre said. "Let me."

Siv hesitated, then let Vakre take Bekkhild's hair from her. The son of Loki worked with precision and care, crafting a neat braid. Without a word, Siv handed Vakre a length of twine and Vakre secured the braid. Only when he had tied the knot did Vakre raise his gaze and look at Siv.

"Now, tell me, Siv, who is she? What have I done to you?" Vakre's voice was so soft that Raef could hardly make it out, and at first Siv did not answer, but then she began to speak and Raef moved away, content to give them privacy. He crossed the river once more and found the Vannheim warriors where they had gathered on the riverbank.

Hauk of Ruderk was awake and among them, bound to Dvalarr's saddle. He watched Raef approach with eyes that did not leave Raef's face, but his own face was blank, his emotions carefully hidden away. The lord of Ruderk was a short man and surrounded by warriors all taller and broader than he, but to Raef he seemed a giant among them. Raef forced himself to look away and sought out Njall and Dvalarr the Crow. The young captain was full of questions, Raef could see, but Njall held his tongue when the Crow cuffed him on the back of the neck.

"Send Horik and Berrgund north," Raef said, addressing Njall and naming two of his warriors. "Skuli awaits." He went on to describe how the pair of warriors would find the blind man and his captive on the ridge where Raef had left them. He reiterated that under no circumstances should Ulthor Ten-blade be loosed from his bonds. Njall listened and raced off to issue Raef's command, leaving Raef alone with the Crow.

For a moment Raef stood still, lost in thought. Across the water, barely visible in the deepening darkness, Vakre had drawn his sword. The son of Loki was offering the hilt to Siv and though Raef could not hear what Vakre was saying, he understood well enough.

"What are your orders, lord?" The Crow's voice cut in but Raef could not look away from the bright blade in Vakre's hand. "Lord?"

At last Raef tore his gaze away and forced himself to focus on Dvalarr's weathered face, but it seemed that his heart had lifted from his body, that it lay now on the cold steel between Vakre and Siv, and for a moment Raef could not summon any words.

"The prisoner, lord, who is he?" Dvalarr persisted, ignorant of Raef's struggle.

Mention of Hauk brought Raef back to himself and he could feel his heart beating inside his ribs once more. "He is the lord of Ruderk," Raef said, "and he is responsible for my father's death."

The sudden rage that flooded Dvalarr's face was an old friend to Raef, for it was the same rage that had burned in him for so long.

"When will he die and how will it be done?" The Crow did not ask to kill Hauk himself, but Raef could see that he yearned to do so.

"He will die tomorrow," Raef said, the decision coming to him without thought. But he had no other answer for the Crow. He had waited so long for the moment he would bring justice to his father, but he had given little thought to the manner of death he would choose. And now, as he turned away from Dvalarr, his belly knotting as he saw that Siv and Vakre had vanished, he could not see Hauk's death before him, but he could taste the salty water of the fjord, could feel its cold embrace, could see his uncle's corpse sinking, forever beyond the sight of the stars and the sun and far, so far, from Valhalla.

There was no telling where Vakre and Siv had gone. With one eye on the western bank, Raef gave orders for suitable ground to be searched out so the Vannheim warriors might make camp, raise shelters, and build fires. He did not consult with Bryndis, did not even send for word of Eiger, whom Raef had last seen on the eastern bank when the sun was still high. He was weary and desperate for food and he wanted only to know what had passed between Siv and Vakre.

The Vannheim war band moved south, out of sight of the fires lit by Bryndis's host, and set up camp on a rise above the river's edge. The men were quiet, for, though they had moved downriver, they had not escaped the lingering smell of smoke and the memory of the fire that had blazed in the sky the night before hung over them. Raef knew he should sit among them, should speak with them, encourage them to laugh and sing, but he had only the strength to sit at the edge of the camp and stare into the dark. Cilla was near, he knew, lurking close to the spot Raef had claimed for himself, but, though she had deposited the borrowed cloak on Raef's pack when he had stepped away to relieve his bladder, she did not emerge.

Sleep came with devastating swiftness, overwhelming his exhausted spirit and body with ease. He fought it for a moment, straining to keep his eyelids from closing, desperate to stand watch until Siv and Vakre returned, but he succumbed, head tilted down to his chest, blanket settled loosely over his legs, his torso cradled in the split trunk of a two-pronged birch.

The dreams came later, dragging Raef from oblivion. He saw his father standing in the prow of a small fishing boat, saw the boat rock as his uncle was thrown over the side, saw Dainn suck water into his lungs, but most of all he saw his father watching Dainn slip beneath the surface. Again and again the scene played. Sometimes his father watched with horror, but sometimes that face that Raef knew so well was still and grim and there was satisfaction in Einarr's eyes as he became the heir to the seat in the Vestrhall.

The struggle changed, though, and in time the faces of his uncle and father were replaced with faces Raef could not name, though he was sure they were familiar to him. They were brothers, too, he knew somehow, and he watched, as a wolf watches, from a distance as the brothers fought. Weapons were discarded as the men exchanged vicious, bloody blows, and Raef knew this was a long-simmering feud that would end only in death. When one of the brothers had pinned the other down, kneeling on his throat and chest, he brandished a sputtering, sparking torch and it was then, as the flickering flames were held to the restrained brother's hair, that Raef knew these men and their story. He watched, unable to intervene, unable to look away as the brothers Kell-thor and Ulflaug, long-dead ancestors of Vannheim immortalized in the carved wood of the chair in the Vestrhall, broke every bond of blood and brotherhood between them. Kell-thor heaved Ulflaug off his chest, his muscle-bound arms straining, his hair blazing, and in the scramble that followed, it was Ulflaug who was caught by a wild blow to his jaw. He sprawled in the dirt and Kell-thor sprang upon him, his fingers scrabbling for the knife he had abandoned moments before. Raef saw the knife descend. He heard Ulflaug scream.

But the scream was Isolf and Raef was removing his cousin's lungs with his blood-slick hands. Isolf was bent at a grotesque, ghastly angle, bones piercing his skin all over his convulsing body. And he would not stop screaming. Desperate to silence him, Raef wanted to end his cousin's suffering but he could not find the knife that would allow him to slit Isolf's throat and bring him peace. Instead, he began to stuff the lungs back into the cavity of Isolf's chest, only they would not fit and he lost his grip and the red, pulsing organs slipped from his hands, and still Isolf screamed.

Silence.

Raef took a breath and saw that he was alone in darkness. All was still and quiet and he knew this was all that would exist after the nine worlds came to ruin, after the great wolf Fenrir swallowed Odin Allfather and Black Surt's fires burned out.

A flash of lightning split the darkness above Raef's head and out of that sudden, painful brightness swooped a bird of black and white, its feathers gleaming in Thor's white fire. A swift. He knew the bird. He had seen it before. And as Raef was drawn from his dreams, woken by a hand on his shoulder, he could hear the words spoken by a young boy, words of hope that defied everything the Norns had carved into Yggdrasil's bark.

"The swift knows the way," Raef said, waking, opening his eyes, finding Vakre hunched over him. His relief at seeing the son of Loki was shadowed by the words the boy Anuleif had spoken and for a moment he could not shake them away.

Vakre frowned. "What did you say?"

Raef shook his head, dispelling the last dreamthreads. "I dreamed of," he paused, for the dreams had shown him much, "of Anuleif." He told Vakre of the last part of his dream, of the lightning and the bird, just as they had appeared on the bald top of

Old Troll, the hill in the northern part of Vannheim where Ailmaer Wind-footed had searched for golden apples and found only an empty cave. "I did not remember it then, but Anuleif said the swift knows the way. That bird I saw, spawned by the lightning strike, it was a swift."

He could see that Vakre did not understand, and he did not blame him, for Raef himself hardly knew what he was saying and he was only beginning to grasp at the stray threads in his mind. He did not know what would unravel when he pulled. Raef shook his head again and cast aside the blanket. He stood and blew warm air on his hands.

"You offered Siv your sword," Raef said. His toes tingled as the blood rushed back into them.

"Her sister's death lies with me. I had to."

"And yet here you are."

"She has forgiven me." It was clear from Vakre's tone and face that he had not forgiven himself.

"I am glad."

Vakre was quiet for a moment. "I wanted to believe the Far-Traveled. "

"Believe him? What did he say?"

"He said he did not know what the future held for me, that when he looked at me he saw my blood burning with Loki's fire, saw things he could not understand. But he said I could find peace in my father's gift. I asked him how, for I wanted his words to be true, but he had no answer for me. But I see it now. Every day, my father's claim over me grows stronger. I can bring only destruction. Death." Vakre took a deep breath. Raef waited. "I told you once before to let me go, to leave me to my fate."

"And I told you I would not turn my back on you. Never, Vakre."

"And I will not ask you to. I ask only for your sword hand to do what must be done."

Raef felt himself shaking his head. "No, no. This I will not do."

"I am resolved, Raef." Vakre's voice was sure and steady, but gentle. "I have caused too much pain and misery. I have become a tool to be wielded by my father. I will not be the source of more suffering."

"No." It was all Raef could muster.

"If you will not do it for those I have harmed, then do it for me." Vakre's voice had a new sharpness to it and he made a visible effort to calm himself. "End my suffering, Raef. There is no one I would rather have do this, and there is no other hand I trust. I will not ask another, Raef, I cannot."

Raef closed his eyes. He had been dreading this, he knew, from the very moment Bekkhild was found dead, though it had been nothing more than a nebulous fear burrowed deep within him.

"What of your uncle?" Raef threw the question to the wind, trying to find some means to forestall Vakre.

Vakre sighed. "He is not among the dead. But," he went on as Raef started to speak, "I will not hold my hatred of him above the well-being of countless lives. If he is gone and out of reach, so be it."

"You do not know what lies ahead, Vakre."

"Yet I see clearly what lies behind."

Raef forced himself to hold Vakre's gaze. "Today I bring death to Hauk of Ruderk and avenge my father. When it is done, then," Raef paused, the words sticking in his throat, "then I will do what you ask."

Relief stole across Vakre's face, and with it came a rush of heat emanating from the son of Loki's skin, so warm that Raef drew back.

"Where is Siv now?"

"She said she would give her sister to the river. She wanted you to join her."

Raef nodded, but he hesitated before turning away from Vakre, as though he might yet undo what he had promised if only he remained, but he could not see how to loosen Vakre's resolve.

Raef separated a drowsy horse from the rest and walked it north along the river's edge until he came to the shallow ford. Siv waited across the river, her cloak pulled tight about her, the moonlight caressing the shadows on her face. Patting the horse's neck, Raef mounted, murmured encouragement, and urged the horse into the water. Tossing its head, the horse stepped nimbly through the black and silver eddies. Siv smiled as he dismounted and Raef was glad to see true warmth in her face.

Together they lifted Bekkhild's body and walked along the river until they reached a spot where they could easily wade into the water. Raef walked backward out toward the middle, feeling the current tug at his calves.

"This will do," Raef said. "It is not deep, but the water is strong here. It will take her south."

Siv nodded.

"Do these waters flow past the valley that was your home in Wayhold?"

"Perhaps."

"We could have burned her."

"No, she would prefer it this way. She always liked the sea." Siv lowered her sister's head, setting it gently into the water. Raef did the same with the feet. They released Bekkhild at the same time.

For a moment, the body lingered at their feet, then the current caught her up and she was swept away. They watched until she was lost to the darkness and the bend of the river, then waded to shore.

"Are you cold?" Raef asked.

Siv took her eyes from the river for the first time. "Is the eagle proud? Is the sun bright?" Siv teased. Raef laughed and spread wide the folds of his cloak, tucking her in against his chest when she stepped close.

"But are you well?" He hardly dared ask the question, for he could not bear the thought of Siv without the joy that gave her light.

She was still against him for a moment, and quiet, but then she nodded. "Yes." Silence. Raef waited, sensing there was more. "I hardly remember a time when I was not searching for my sister. I was guided for many years by the vow I made and I do not regret it. But now it is ended." She looked up at Raef and smiled, but when she saw the stillness in his face, she frowned. "Do you think me coldhearted for letting go?"

Raef shook his head. "Cold is the last thing you are, Siv." He kissed her forehead and then, taking her face in his hands, her lips. "I stare only because I marvel at your strength of spirit and the love you have for the world."

"Sometimes I think your ancestors were trees and rivers and mountains. Sturdy oaks and towering spines of rock with roots that go deep."

Raef laughed. "Why do you say that?"

Siv remained serious. "Because your love for the world is far greater than mine. It is in your blood. Your heart beats in time with the earth." She placed a hand on his chest, then looked at him. She started to speak, then thought better of it, smiling instead.

"What is it?" Raef asked.

"A thought only."

"Tell me."

Siv held Raef's gaze. "Long have I thought that is the reason you will not see Valhalla or fight alongside the Einherjar at Ragnarök. Because you will be here. Your last breaths will be the heard by the trees. Your final heartbeat will be felt by the earth. And when the end comes, you will be its witness."

Her words should have troubled Raef, but instead he felt no fear for his unknown fate, no fear of the words the Allfather had chilled his blood with. He knew only a great swelling of peace under the light of the moon and in the embrace of the woman who was the sun and the stars in the sky of his heart.

THIRTY

THE SKY WAS spitting sleet and snow when Raef awoke curled alongside Siv. He raised his head out from under the thick wool blanket and felt the tiny shards of rain strike his face. For a moment, he could hear only the quiet, steady voice of the river, but then the sounds of men stirring and the smell of morning fires came to him and all that had happened in the past day came rushing back.

Raef ducked back under the blanket as Siv stirred next to him, as though he might be able to close his eyes and lose himself in sleep and memories once more.

"You are solemn, Raef," Siv said. "And troubled."

"At last Hauk of Ruderk will answer for his crime," Raef said. "Today my father will know that I have not failed him."

"But this does not please you."

Raef sighed. "I do not know what is in my heart. Strange, that I should have lusted after this death for so long, and now, when at last I shall avenge my father, I can find no joy in what will happen today." He looked at Siv. "I can think only of my uncle."

"Then you believe the story Hauk wove about Dainn's death?"

"I do not wish to," Raef said, irritated with his own uncertainty, "but seldom did my father speak of his brother. When he did, there was sadness there, I could see, but also reluctance and something I am not ready to name, something with an edge, like a blade shrouded in darkness." Raef felt for the Thor's hammer that no longer hung around his neck, his fingers plucking at nothing.

"Could you forgive your father if it were true?" Siv prodded with a gentle voice.

Raef was quiet for a long moment and when at last he did speak, his words were no answer to Siv's question. "It troubles me that I cannot answer that. He was a good father. Stern when he needed to be. Affectionate when he wanted to be. Fair, always, even when it caused me pain. He had my respect as well as my love. And yet when I begin to soften, when I want to forgive him for that moment of rage and wrath that killed my uncle, a moment I am sure he regretted, I see my own hands slick with the blood of my cousin."

"Isolf was a traitor to your shared blood," Siv said.

"But he was my blood." Raef swept away the blanket and emerged once more into the grey, wet morning, no closer to understanding his mind. Standing, he stamped his feet to encourage the flow of blood as Lochauld approached bearing two bowls of steaming broth. These he set down on a flat rock as Raef gave thanks and retrieved strips of dried venison from his pack.

"Our supplies are running low, lord." Lochauld said.

Raef nodded. "We will see home soon, Lochauld. Once this day is finished, we will set our sights to the sea." Lochauld turned to go and Raef called after him. "Tell Njall to organize a hunt and seek out Bryndis or her uncle to discover if there is a lake nearby where we might fish through the ice. We will feast tonight and have plenty for the journey home."

"Yes, lord."

"And tell Dvalarr to be sure the prisoner is fed. I will not have it said that I did not grant him the comfort of a full belly."

"Yes, lord."

Raef strapped on his sword belt and fastened his knives and axe securely on the worn leather, then cradled one of the bowls of broth and handed it to Siv before taking the second for himself. The sleet pricked his face, harder now, and already the broth had lost much of its heat. Raef slurped it down and then bit off a piece of venison and began to worry it between his teeth.

"Cilla," he called. "I know you are there. Come eat."

It was a moment before the girl stepped out from behind the tree she had sheltered under during the night, but she took the meat Raef offered her with eager hands and chewed quickly, eyes wide, her jaw working hard.

"Have you been training, Cilla?" Siv asked.

The girl nodded, her cheeks too full to speak. But her eyes turned flinty and when she swallowed she spoke with vehemence. "They took my bow. And my knife."

Siv smiled. "I will make you another."

"Can I have a shield, too?"

"If you like."

"What will we do now?" The question was directed at Raef before she tore off another piece of meat.

"What do you mean? The war is done." This did not satisfy the girl, Raef could see, but he was not willing to speak of the final battle that he waited for with every breath. "It is time I went home, Cilla."

Cilla wrinkled her nose. "That is all?"

"No," Raef said, finding a smile despite his mood. "No, then I shall find someone to conduct the ceremony that binds me to Siv and her to me. But," he went on, knowing Cilla craved something she could not name, "the lady Bryndis means to call a gathering so that the warriors might choose a king, as should have been done before the snow."

The young girl's eyes gleamed. "Will you go? Who will you

name?" It was clear the girl had not heard of Raef's own naming, and he was glad of that.

"If anyone asks my opinion, I will tell them to consider Eirik of Kolhaugen." The choice came to Raef without thought, but it pleased him. The new lord of Kolhaugen would make a good king, if the final battle did not begin before he could be chosen. "But I will not go, Cilla."

She snorted, showing her disapproval of that decision, then returned her attention to the last of the venison, her teeth flashing with all the fervor of a dog.

"And what will you do, Cilla?" Raef asked.

"Are you going to tell me to go back to my brother and sister?" Cilla was trying not to show her disappointment at the thought of being sent north to the foster home her siblings had found in Finngale.

"No."

She beamed. "I would like to stay for the gathering."

"You must ask the lady of Narvik."

Cilla nodded, then rose from the stone she had been seated on and skipped off into the trees, no doubt intent on searching out Bryndis immediately. When she had gone only a few steps, she paused and Raef could see her straighten her shoulders and hold her head high. When she began again, her gait was steady and without the restlessness of a child.

"Perhaps I should send her north to Finngale," Raef said, more to himself than anything. "But I cannot make her want to see her family again. When the rooster crows and sends the Einherjar into battle, she may come to that understanding on her own."

"She is too fierce to run to them in fear."

"Yes, but that does not mean she should not, when the time comes."

"Would you run, Raef?" Siv's question seemed to squeeze Raef's heart and it beat faster in his chest as he imagined the fires and the flood coming for him.

"What man would not?" And yet the words tasted strange in his mouth. Siv watched him bend and pick up the two wooden bowls as though she knew what was in his mind. Raef took her hand with his free one. "Of one thing I am certain, Siv. I fear that we will never be joined in the sight of the gods."

Siv pushed her palm out to face him, fingers spread. Raef's hand rested against hers, reflecting it. "I am yours and you are mine. What need have we for the gods in this?"

Raef smiled, his heart lighter than it had been since waking. "None. But I should like the Allfather to know that I have found a woman superior to the goddesses in Asgard." Siv laughed and the sound warmed him. But no sooner had he turned away than the darkness of the day seemed to settle on his shoulders once more, and he did not think even the sun, if it found the strength to break through the clouds, would chase the cold or the melancholy in his mind away.

ᚾ ᚾ ᚾ

It was past midday when the warriors gathered to see the lord of Ruderk die. Raef had chosen a spot deep in the pines, finding level ground where the trees grew further apart, letting in what light there was. The sleet had changed to snow, coating the exposed ground in fresh whiteness, and then back again so that it pricked at the necks of those who did not draw up their hoods.

Many were the faces who had come to see Raef enact his vengeance. All the warriors of Vannheim were there. They were quiet, their jaws tight, their brows creased as they anticipated the death that would bring long awaited retribution to all of Vannheim. Some had been with Raef and his father in Balmoran and these, above the rest, had reason to wish for Hauk's death, for their own honor was at stake as long as he lived and their lord, slaughtered under their watch, went unavenged.

Eiger, Raef saw, watched with open interest. The Great-Belly's son did not hide himself in the trees, but stood at the forefront of the watchers, nearly as close to Raef as Dvalarr the Crow. Cilla watched at Siv's side, her young face carefully blank but Raef was sure he could see an undercurrent of impatience.

Behind the first ring, Raef saw Bryndis and her uncle and many warriors of Narvik and Balmoran. They knew only that Hauk would fall to Raef's sword and that it was right. Little talk of Einarr's death had spread to them, leaving the reasons for Raef's actions unclear. It did not bother most; they were long accustomed to blood feuds.

Raef searched the crowd for Vakre, but if the son of Loki was present he did not show himself, and his absence lowered Raef's spirits even further. He closed his eyes, trying to shut out the murmuring voices around him, and ducked his head against the sleet. His mind ran far away until he was immersed in a different forest, this one green with summer and rich with life. He knew the place and in his mind he climbed the hill above him until the forest fell away and there was nothing but sky, blue and vivid, and the rays of the sun, warm and bright.

With a deep breath, Raef opened his eyes, exhaling white vapor as he raised his head. He nodded to Dvalarr.

"Bring the prisoner, Crow."

Dvalarr left the ring of watchers, and the moments of his absence seemed to press down on Raef, stifling him with the weight of what was to come. When he tried to remind himself what this was for, instead of his father's voice, he heard Isolf's screams. Raef tried to push away the weakness that threatened him, but it persisted, making his heart pound though he hardly seemed to draw breath. By the time Dvalarr returned with Njall and Hauk of Ruderk between them, Raef's palms were hot and he could feel sweat beading on his back.

Vakre appeared, trailing just behind Hauk. If he had stayed to watch the prisoner and make certain there was no chance of escape, Raef did not know, but seeing Vakre's face calmed his racing heart for a moment. He would not let himself think of what would come after, of what he had promised Vakre he would do. If he let that in, it would destroy him. He had only his strength left to him, and even that seemed uncertain.

He watched as Vakre took a place next to Siv and did not wish to look away, but then Hauk was being forced to kneel at his feet and Raef had no choice but to turn to his prisoner.

The lord of Ruderk's wrists were bound behind his back, but he kept his balance as Njall and the Crow shoved him in front of Raef, coming to his knees with as much dignity as a man could hope for. Raef nodded at the two warriors and they backed away.

The hatred Raef had for Hauk simmered under his skin and Raef drew strength from it. But even then the knowledge that avenging his father was right was not enough and as he looked into Hauk's eyes he saw his uncle drowning, saw Isolf's agony.

"We can still rid the world of kings, Skallagrim." Hauk spoke quietly but the words bit into Raef. "You and I can draw swords together and out of this dark hour we will shape a new world."

Raef was shaking now, for with every word Hauk spoke he felt one of Isolf's ribs crack in his hands once more. Summoning every last shred of control, Raef willed his body to obey him.

"There will be no new world, Hauk," Raef said. He could not keep his voice steady and he was glad no one was close enough to hear his ragged reply. "Just as there will be no world soon enough." He saw Hauk frown but his own turmoil was so great that it barely registered. "Ragnarök is coming. Soon Heimdall will summon the Einherjar to the last battle. Odin will know the sharpness of Fenrir's teeth and mighty Thor will take his nine steps and fall with the serpent's poison in his blood. And all will be darkness, for the wolves will devour the sun and the moon and the stars will fall. But the world does not end in that darkness. No, first the flames will bring a terrible light, Hauk, for Black Surt is coming and nothing will escape his blazing sword. Yggdrasil will burn. And then Jörmungand, the great serpent, will lash the seas and send the salt waters flooding over land. The fires will go out and then, yes, then, there will be a darkness eternal."

Somewhere amidst that tumble of words, Raef had drawn his sword and he held it now against Hauk's neck. His hands no longer trembled.

"When you see my father in Valhalla, tell him who sent you, and then tell him I am sorry I will not join him," Raef said. He stared at Hauk for a moment, wondering if the other man comprehended what he was saying. Hauk was very still and seemed without fear. Behind those dark eyes, Raef was sure Hauk's mind was at work, for this was a man always thinking, always planning, even as death touched him.

But then Hauk's eyes shifted away from Raef, focusing instead on something over Raef's shoulder. His face betrayed something at last, though whether it was fear or triumph, Raef could not have said. He did not turn, did not have to, and he kept his blade pressed against Hauk's neck.

"Did you know she would come?"

Hauk shook his head.

"Why, though? What brings her back to save you?"

"You would have to ask her that."

Raef turned at last and the chaos that heaved within him vanished. This was the steel song, then, nothing more.

Eira had changed since last Raef beheld her. She was taller, her skin more pale than ever. The blood that had stained her throat when she had swept Hauk away from the walls of the Vestrhall was washed clean, leaving no trace of the wound Siv's arrow had given her. Her eyes promised depths and knowledge Raef could not grasp and yet there was still the same wildness about her, as though she could not shake the part of her that had watched her mother kill her younger siblings, as though she were still fighting for survival, even now, when she had been made a Valkyrie. She remembered Raef, he could see, unlike the last time when her confusion had likely spared his life.

Around them, the ring of watchers had gone silent with fear. Though only Siv, Vakre, and Hauk knew what Eira was, the others could sense it, and many reached for weapons. More reached for hammers that hung from their necks.

"Is this how it is to be, then?" Raef asked.

When she spoke at last, her voice was as he remembered Visna's to be when all nine Valkyries had descended on the burning lake.

"There is only this, Skallagrim. And then you will be finished." Her voice was the grinding of rocks, the rush of a waterfall taking flight, and the scream of an eagle. Among the pines, few could withstand its pain and the fear it spread. Warriors, tall and proud, dropped to their knees. Others stared in horror. Cilla's face showed only fascination.

"Why, Eira? Why come for him?" Raef asked. Siv and Vakre had started forward, but Raef motioned for them to stay clear.

"You would question me? You are but a man, far beneath me. I am of Asgard now and my name is Roskva."

"If I am but a man," Raef said, feeling a strange laughter bubbling up from deep in his chest, "then so, too, is he." Raef pointed at Hauk, who had come to his feet. "And yet you are like a dog on a chain. You cannot leave him to his fate because you, a Valkyrie, are still bound by an oath you made when you were merely mortal. How that must burn your proud heart." He snarled the last and

Eira answered by drawing her sword. Raef did laugh, then, though he hardly knew it. The blade was still dark, with none of the sunlight it had flashed with when Visna wielded it before her exile from Asgard. It was sharp and deadly in a Valkyrie's hands, but it was still just a sword.

She came for him, the dark blade arcing with such swiftness that Raef was forced to throw himself clear, but he came up on nimble feet and his sword shivered against hers as they met at last. The clash reverberated through every bone in Raef's body, and he was sure the earth beneath his feet and the tall pines standing watch shuddered with the force of it. Her strength pushed him down and nearly sent him to one knee, but Raef, baring his teeth at her, stood tall once more and drew his axe with his right hand. Eira saw it coming and she drew back, avoiding his swing. Raef pressed on, lashing out with both hands, but Eira deflected and dodged with breathtaking skill until she was no longer on the defensive and it was Raef who had to work to keep his footing. Soon every movement was one of desperation. He knew he could not win. The edges of his vision darkened, leaving only Eira's blade of death and the feel of his own weapons in his hands. He moved on instinct, but it would not be enough in the end and his mind, empty of all else, reached out for the fate he knew would come soon, the fate that would not send him to Valhalla.

He brought the axe up late, catching only enough of Eira's sword to keep it from taking his arm, but her blade bit into the flesh of his right shoulder and then it was gone. The axe fell from Raef's hand and he saw her sword come again, this time meant for his right side. She would carve into his torso, drag the sword up into his ribs. The leather would not stop her. He would fall and he would feel the blade as it ripped out of him, taking flesh and bone with it.

But the blow never came. Eira's swing slowed, the sword hovering, waiting, hungry for Raef's blood, and Raef had time to bring his sword across his body and knock her blade away. She did not resist. She did nothing but twist her torso, an awkward movement that reminded Raef of a deer caught in a trap. And then she opened her mouth as though to scream, but there was no sound.

Only then, in that strange moment that should have seen Raef's heart beat slow and then cease, did Raef see Cilla.

The girl's arm was soaked in blood, but not her own, and she still held the knife that was buried in Eira's back at the base of her spine. The Valkyrie twisted again, wild gaze roving in search of what had done her such harm, but then Cilla withdrew the knife and Eira collapsed, her legs useless.

The shadow that came for her was cold and darker than midnight and the air ripped from Raef's lungs as it swept over him, but then it was gone and there was no trace of Eira but for the blood in the snow and the dark sword that had dropped from her hand.

Raef sucked in a breath and fell to his knees, drained by something other than Eira's speed and fury or the wound in his shoulder, but as his head cleared, he saw that Cilla was unmoved, untouched by the darkness that had come for Eira. The girl reached down and, with a gentle hand, set the small knife in the snow, then walked to where the dark sword lay, the blade streaked with Raef's blood, and bent over it. Raef watched as her small fingers touched the hilt, then curled around it. When she lifted it, a sunrise spread through the dark, cold metal until it was blazing with all the brilliance of day, a ray of sunlight in her hand.

Cilla met Raef's gaze, and already he could see her eyes were changing, deepening, growing, filling with strength and power, but there was nothing of Eira's rage.

Without a word, Cilla stepped close to where Raef knelt in the snow and picked up the axe that had fallen from his hand when Eira wounded him. She contemplated the sharp edge, the smooth handle, as though it were important that she know its shape, weight, and balance. She held out the handle and Raef put out his hand, palm up. She settled it there against the spatter of his own blood and did not let go until Raef had clasped it tight in his grasp. Then she turned and looked to the sky, expectant.

The horse came from above, pale and luminous like the moon, just as Raef remembered when the nine Valkyries descended on the burning lake. It landed at Cilla's side, towering over her, and bumped its nose against her chest. She put a hand on the smooth, broad space between its eyes and then the horse kneeled, bending its front legs until its back was within reach. Cilla, still holding the radiant sword, wrapped the fingers of her free hand in the horse's silky mane and pulled herself up until she could settle herself on its back. When the creature straightened to its full height, Cilla's legs dangled and she seemed so small, so insignificant, and yet Raef could not doubt that she belonged.

If the horse ran or flew, Raef could not say, but it was gone in an instant, leaving no trace of Cilla or the sword of sunlight. Only the small, blood-drenched knife in the snow gave testament to what had happened and those who had watched it all amid the trees began to speak in frightened whispers.

In a daze, Raef glanced down at his axe and then walked to where Hauk of Ruderk stood. Their eyes met and then Hauk sank to his knees. For a moment Raef thought he might beg for his life, but Eira's sudden presence and unexpected death and Cilla's ascension had brought a great stillness amongst the pines and Hauk, it seemed, had no words. Raef planted his sword in the snow and switched the axe to his left hand, but as he drew back and aimed for the side of Hauk's neck, a rustle of wings drew his gaze to the sky.

The swift was true to its name, passing over Raef's head with the speed of an arrow loosed from a bow, and yet the world seemed to slow and Raef saw the flashing white belly and the darting black wings clearly. He followed its flight, craning his neck to catch sight of it as it disappeared over his shoulder and into the trees.

Raef looked once more at Hauk, who seemed not to have noticed the swift pass over. He glanced at Siv and Vakre, then back to the man whose blood he had vowed to spill.

"Forgive me, father," Raef said, his words a whisper. He turned his back on Hauk, pulled his sword from the snow, and walked away, sheathing his weapons as he went.

Warriors moved aside to let him pass, their faces riddled with fear and uncertainty, unable to comprehend what they had witnessed. Raef had eyes only for the path ahead of him, though he knew not where it would take him.

He had left the ring of warriors behind when the land began to rise beneath his feet and he climbed, scrabbling his way over rough, steep ground, ignoring the throbbing in his shoulder where Eira had made him. When he came to the top, the hills were spread out around him and there was no sign of the swift. There was only wind and sky and clouds.

Raef closed his eyes, felt the wind on his face, felt the earth beneath his feet, then opened his eyes and kicked away the snow with one boot until he had exposed the bare, frozen ground. He placed his hand on the dirt and the brown grass, trying to make sense of all he had done, of what had led him there.

"The swift knows the way."

The words had never been far from his thoughts since his dreams the night before, and he spoke them now, first quietly, tasting them, then with more certainty, more resolve.

A gust of wind crested on Raef's small summit and then the air seemed to sigh, and in that moment the sky grew dark with wings.

Countless birds took to the air as one, rising from every tree, every valley and hill Raef could see. The roar of their flapping wings and the sound of their voices was deafening and the horizon grew dark in every direction as they blotted out the grey swaths of clouds, rising higher and higher. Raef could see tiny sparrows and soaring hawks, glossy black crows and even a white, sharp-eyed owl, but together, heaving across the sky as one pulsing beast, the great flock turned west. On and on they came, flying over Raef in droves, and then at last there was silence and the sky emptied, leaving Raef alone on his hill.

It took only a moment for Raef to make his decision, and even then he knew his choice had always lain in his heart, slumbering, waiting. He left the barren hill and hurried back down the slope, weaving through the trees, nearly tumbling over in his haste as he took the shortest path back to the riverside camp.

The warriors of Vannheim called out to him when he came within sight of their shelters, but he paid them no heed, hurrying on until he came to the boulders he had slept between. His pack was as he had left it, damp now after the sleet of the morning. Raef stuffed the last of his belongings in it, rose, and turned, swaying slightly at the rush of blood from his head. He looked down at the wound Eira had given him, studying the damage for the first time.

"Let me bind that for you." Siv had come. Vakre and Dvalarr stood behind her.

Raef nodded. Siv spread open the slashed cloth with her fingers and poured river water across the wound, washing away the sticky blood. Then she took a strip of clean linen from her pack and wrapped it around Raef's arm, pulling tight as she cinched the knot.

When she finished, Raef, calmer now though no less determined, went to Dvalarr.

"Lead them home, Crow," Raef said, gesturing to the camp of Vannheim warriors. He might have said more, he should have said more, but the solemn nod the Crow gave him stopped the words in his throat. Raef held out his hand and the two men clasped forearms.

And then he was alone with Siv and Vakre.

"Come," Raef said. He led them to where they had tied their horses and began to saddle his, the tall, fleet-footed grey mare. "Fate has come for me. I do not know what lies ahead. I only know that I am as certain that I must do this as I am certain of the love I bear both of you. Perhaps I am wrong to ask this, but I would regret it if I did not. Will you follow me, one last time?"

Siv reached out and took Raef's hand, stopping him as he strapped his pack behind the saddle. It was answer enough.

Vakre was quiet, his face marred by dark circles under his eyes, and Raef saw a weariness there that was deeper than a lack of sleep. It worried him to see Vakre that way and for a moment Raef thought the son of Loki would refuse, would draw his sword and demand Raef fulfill the promise given. The smile that curved Vakre's mouth was small and sad and full of lost things.

"You know my answer."

Raef nodded at Vakre and kissed Siv's forehead. "We must go, at once."

They did not go alone. After crossing the river and heading into the charred trees on the western side, Raef caught sight of a small party pursuing them. Bryndis led them, her white fox fur cloak pure and bright amid the blackened remains of the forest.

"Skallagrim!" The lady of Narvik shouted after him, but Raef did not slow until he saw she would not give up the chase. They slowed and circled as Bryndis caught up. Eiger was there, his face flushed with the exertion.

"What are you running from?" Bryndis lined her voice with a touch of disdain, as though she might shame Raef, but he could see that her heart was not in it, that what she had seen and heard among the tall pines had upset her. Only Raef had seen the great flock of birds, but the rest could not have missed the terrible cacophony.

"I run from nothing," Raef said.

Eiger had regained his breath, but he looked from Raef to Siv to

Vakre as though he suspected them of some conspiracy. "That is no answer, Skallagrim."

Raef bit back his anger, but Bryndis spoke again. "What of the gathering? Your voice will sway many."

"Call your gathering, Bryndis. There is no place for me there." Raef turned his horse's head and made to continue, but he could see the lady of Narvik did not understand. "I will ask the gods to grant the warriors wisdom."

The words were a mistake, he knew, and he wished he could call them back to curl under his tongue once more, but it was too late and Eiger's eyes narrowed.

"Betrayer!" The Great-Belly's son brought his horse next to Raef's leaving him no choice but to draw his sword to keep Eiger's fury at bay. "You would leave me behind, I who first gave you the dream of Asgard, who wanted only to take the path together that we might kneel before the Allfather as one. False heart, I name you, full of black greed."

"Be careful of your words, Eiger. You know not what you say."

Eiger spat and drew his own sword, bringing it level with Raef's blade. "You deny that you have found the bridge to Asgard? That you meant to steal away and gain the glorious gates alone?"

"That dream is yours, Eiger. I do not aspire to such lofty heights." Raef kept his voice low and calm, though he was desperate to get away.

Bryndis was frowning at the exchange. "What is this you speak of, Eiger?"

But Eiger was too unsettled and he rounded on her, unleashing all the anger he felt toward Raef. "You are not fit to hear of it, sword-whore! You are filth, less than a dog." He swiped at her, his movement hampered by his protruding belly and his horse's neck, but Bryndis's stallion reared up, lashing out with his hooves at the sudden threat. The lady of Narvik clung to the saddle at first, but as her mount's hooves struck the other horse, she was jarred loose and fell in a heap. Her warriors leaped to the ground and one darted in and pulled her away from the stallion's feet, but then the stallion screamed, his neck nicked by Eiger's blade, and the Great-Belly's son was dismounting, his sword reaching for Bryndis.

Eiger came up short, dropping his sword as he howled in pain at the same moment that Raef seized him by the hair. Eiger clutched at his hand and fell to his knees, his palm seared and bloody, the flesh blistered and torn. The hilt of his sword hissed where it lay in the snow, steam rising as it cooled. Raef's gaze flickered to Vakre and saw grim satisfaction there.

Bryndis was on her feet, recovering faster than her warriors, and she gazed down at Eiger, whose cheeks were wet with tears, contempt blazing from her coal-lined eyes. Raef kept his grip on Eiger's hair and brought the tip of his sword to rest next to Eiger's spine.

"Too long have I indulged you, Eiger, son of Thorgrim." Bryndis's voice was sharp with wrath long-contained. "And now at last you show me the true shade of your spirit. I was warned, and I should have heeded those warnings long ago and cast you from me as a dog scratches away a flea. You think a woman beneath you? You think me weak because I have breasts and nothing dangling between my legs?" Bryndis leaned over Eiger, her face twisted in a dreadful smile. "There I have the advantage, you see, because no one can do this to me."

The lady of Narvik thrust out one arm, striking out with all the vicious quickness of a snake, and clamped onto Eiger's groin. The fat man shrieked but he was helpless, caught between Bryndis's grip and Raef's sword and in the throes of agony.

When she released him, Eiger fell back and Raef let him go as he sprawled onto the snow, the place between his legs damp with blood and fluid. The scream died on his lips, reduced to whimpers as Eiger shuddered through the lingering pain. Bryndis stepped back, her satisfaction turned to disgust, but before she could speak again, a loud, spiteful laugh filtered through the trees.

Raef spun to see Thorgrim Great-Belly emerge from among the charred trees. The lord of Balmoran, thought to be an invalid in Bryndis's hall, had abandoned his hunched back, his shuffling gate. He stood tall and proud, his hand resting easily on the hilt of his sword. The only hint of his illness lay in his eyes, edged with pain. Six warriors stood at his back, their faces grim as they witnessed Eiger's humiliation. Raef recognized them as the captains of Balmoran and knew then that Eiger had overestimated their loyalty. And he knew, too, that Eiger, even through the depths of his pain, was beginning to understand this.

"You are a disgrace to our ancestors." Thorgrim bent over Eiger, the pleasure he felt at witnessing his son's distress plain for all to see. When Eiger tried to worm away from his father's gaze, Thorgrim grabbed his jaw and held fast, forcing his son to look at him. "Yes, son, I am strong, still, despite the slow poison you have loosed upon my blood and bones. And now you will answer for it." The Great-Belly released Eiger from his withering stare and straightened, then signaled for two of his warriors to step forward and seize Eiger. They hauled him to his feet, ignoring his moans and incoherent curses, and dragged him toward the river. The Great-Belly marched after them without so much as a glance at Raef or Bryndis.

Bryndis watched until they reached the shore, then turned back to Raef, Siv, and Vakre. The blood lust had vanished from her eyes.

"Are you unhurt, lady?" Raef asked.

Bryndis snorted. "It would take more than his vile words to wound me." She paused, her gaze roving over Raef's shoulder where Siv and Vakre stood. "You are lucky in your friends, Skallagrim."

"Yes."

Bryndis nodded, as though she had come to a decision. "I do not understand why you are leaving, Raef, nor do I understand your haste or Eiger's strange accusation, and I can only begin to guess at what I saw across the river." She paused. "But go with my good will and the good will of Narvik. You do not need it, of course, and having it means little to you, I think. I was never going to change your mind, was I?"

"No. But you do not regard yourself highly enough, Bryndis. Your good will means a great deal and I am glad to carry it with me where I am going."

He saw the question on her lips and saw her bury it with a smile. "Long may there be friendship between Vannheim and Narvik."

"It will endure until the last battle, lady, when all bonds are torn asunder." Raef reached for his horse and remounted. He urged the mare onward, looking only once over his shoulder at the lady of Narvik, solemn and proud in her fox furs, but alone.

THIRTY-ONE

"IT IS AS if I was watching Hoyvik work at his forge, but only now do I see the sword take shape beneath his hammer."

The night was bitter under a sea of stars and Raef coaxed the fire to burn bright and warm them. They had ridden at a steady pace into the darkness, stopping at Bryndis's hall to supplement their provisions and pay silver for grain for the horses, but still Raef had not explained what he had woven in his mind in the daylight hours. Siv and Vakre waited, the firelight flickering in their eyes.

Raef met Vakre's gaze. "Do you remember when we were taken by Fengar below the eagle's nest? And Anuleif risked his life to find me, to speak to me? He said he was the ancestor, that there could be life after the fires burn and the seas rise." Vakre nodded. "That night, I dreamed of lightning. First I knew fear, but then, as each bolt struck closer and closer to my feet, blinding me, I felt hope kindle in my heart and I knew not to be afraid." Raef poked at the fire once more with a bare branch, sending up a shower of sparks. "The dream was lost when I woke. Until last night when I dreamed it again. And I know now that the lightning was not the work of Thor, but of the very earth we stand upon, of the waters that flow around us and the air that we breathe." Raef looked to the sky, as though he might see something among the stars. "The swift knows the way." If the bird was darting in the night sky, he could not see it. "I do not know what that means, but those are the words Anuleif spoke that night. I saw the swift today, in the moment that I meant to take Hauk of Ruderk's life. But that was not the first time. The Old Troll, Siv." Siv was nodding, understanding widening her eyes. "The lightning fell at my feet, just as I had dreamed, and the swift was born in it."

Raef paused and the silence stretched between them. Vakre passed around the single skin of mead they had been given by Bryndis's steward. Raef let a trickle of the sweet liquid pass his lips, then swallowed and spoke again.

"I believe the first rooster, the crimson one, has crowed," Raef said, hardly daring to speak the words. He did not name Fjalar, the red rooster whose voice would signal the approach of the final battle. "The birds heard him and fled in terror. The giants will be stirring, gathering."

"Can we know this?" Siv asked.

"By the time we know, it will be too late," Raef said, his voice harsher than he intended. He rose and paced away from the fire.

"Too late for what?"

Raef flung his arms out, frustration taking hold. "I do not know!" His shout was quickly swallowed by the darkness.

"I think you do." Vakre spoke quietly.

Raef shook his head. "I am certain of nothing."

"But you believe the boy."

Raef hesitated, wondering if Siv and Vakre would reject his words. "I believe I must try." He took a deep breath. "I was never meant to fight in Ragnarök. At last I think I understand why."

"You want to save the nine realms from the long-told fate?" Siv's face was mired in wonder and doubt.

"Not all nine." Raef looked up at the stars once more. He closed his eyes and breathed in deeply, seeing a world made green with spring. "Just one."

Siv got to her feet. "How can you succeed when Odin himself cannot turn back this tide?"

Raef shrugged and wanted to laugh at his helplessness. "I hope the swift will show me. I will not give up this world, Siv, not without a fight."

To his surprise, Siv smiled. "Did I not tell you your ancestors were the mountains and rivers of old?"

"Then you do not think it is madness?"

Siv came close and took one of Raef's hands between hers. "If it is madness," she said, "I will share it with you." Raef leaned forward and rested his forehead on hers. "Back to the Old Troll, then?"

"It is the only place I have to begin."

"Do you think the golden apple tree is there? The one Ailmaer sought?"

"I think Ailmaer chased a legend. But something lies beneath that hill."

Raef returned to the fire and settled down on a fallen log. Siv sat next to him and began to braid a small portion of hair at the base of his neck.

Vakre stretched out beside the flames and settled his hands behind his head. "Why did you let Hauk live?" he asked.

Raef was quiet for a long moment, trying to find words to express what he had felt in his heart the moment the swift flew overhead while Hauk was under his axe. "This is the wolf-age, the sword-age. Hauk said it. We are warriors and we consume violence as the gods do mead. We revel in it, and in this time before the darkness, we will get drunk on it. You know the stories as well as I. Brother will turn on brother. We will descend into depths we cannot emerge from. I had a choice, but it was no choice at all. Take my revenge and become death just as my father was for his brother, just as Ulflaug and Kell-thor were for each other, just as I was for Isolf. Or choose," Raef paused, struggling to make himself understood, "choose something I cannot yet name but that speaks to me. And though it shames me to say it, this voice is stronger than my father's pleas for justice."

"You think if you had taken Hauk's life, you would not be able to follow the swift, wherever it leads?" Vakre's voice was soft.

"No," Raef said. "I think I would not have wanted to. I think I would have craved the end, longed for it." Siv tucked her hand into his.

"And now?" Vakre's voice slipped out of the darkness.

"Now, I will defy the Norns and everything they have carved in Yggdrasil's bark."

Silence across the fire.

"All for a bird." Raef could hear the grin in Vakre's voice and it lifted his heart.

"All for a bird."

ᛝ ᛝ ᛝ

The first wolf came before the dawn. The horses grew nervous from the threat they could not see but whose scent came to them. Raef stirred at the sound of their snorts and stamped hooves, but he could see nothing in the grey half-light. Clouds had come in the night, slinking through the valleys, and had settled into the low places to await the sun, reducing Raef's world to mist and the half-seen shapes of trees. Rising, Raef went to the horses, calming them with quiet words and gentle hands. He listened, straining to catch wind of what had made them anxious, but he heard nothing.

The chill had set into his bones as he slept and Raef longed to rekindle the fire, but warmth was a comfort they had to forgo, as was lingering over a meal. They would eat in the saddle. Raef leaned down over Siv's sleeping form and was about to wake her when he caught sight of the four-legged shape stealing into the edge of his vision. Raef froze, his hand hovering over Siv's shoulder. His sword was within reach and the wolf, a grey and white child of winter, was not close. The yellow eyes rested on Raef, steady, unafraid, and for a long moment man and wolf stared at each other. Then at last the wolf turned and trotted away into the shroud of the morning.

Raef exhaled the breath he had been holding and shook Siv on the shoulder. She woke slowly, her eyes searching Raef's face as her senses were restored to her from the clutches of sleep.

"Come," Raef said. "We must move on."

They were mounted and headed north in a matter of moments, and Raef said nothing of the wolf as they ate in the saddle, sharing the dried plums, cold meat, and day-old bread from Bryndis's hall. As the sun rose and light began to filter through the thick cloud cover, once or twice he caught a glimpse of something loping through the trees, first to their left, and then, not long after, to the right. Whether the lean, grey shape was the same wolf or whether there was more than one, Raef could not say with certainty.

By midday, the sun had burned away the clouds, leaving them exposed to the cold winds, but it was the sound of a wolf's howl, unnatural under the blue sky and bright sun, that made Raef shiver. He exchanged a look with Siv and Vakre and together they increased their pace, taking advantage of an open stretch of land. The wolf went unanswered, but Raef found no comfort in that. They set a watch that night, each taking a turn before the small fire, but the pack did not show itself under the watchfulness of the moon.

↑ ↑ ↑

"The land is quiet," Vakre said, as they rode within sight of a small village the next morning. By Raef's judgment, they were well within the lands of Silfravall, but they had crossed paths with no one and the village seemed deserted. Raef broke off from Siv and Vakre and brought his horse closer to the thatched roofs. He could see a well and a set of hides strung out to dry, but there was not even a boy fetching water or a hen pecking for food in the snow.

He was about to turn his horse away when movement caught his eye. A door creaked open and at first Raef thought the wind had done it, but then he saw a face in the crack. The face jerked out of sight, but then Raef heard a brief scuffle and anxious whispers. He waited, not wanting to make sudden movements in case an unseen foe had an arrow trained on him. He glanced to his left and saw that Siv and Vakre had angled around the tiny village and come to a stop on the northern edge.

The whispers grew louder and then at last a boy came bursting out of the door, stumbling forward as though he had been shoved. He caught his balance and faced Raef, defiance in his eyes, an axe in hand. But the boldness went no further and the boy could not find the courage to speak and challenge Raef.

"Where is your father, boy?" Raef called.

"Gone." The boy swallowed. He was tall, but young. "Gone with the rest to hunt the wolves."

"How long have they been gone?"

"This is the third day."

It was too long and Raef could see the boy knew it.

"Tell your brother to come out of hiding."

"I am alone." The boy's face flushed at the lie. Raef could see his knuckles were white from gripping the axe with all his strength.

"I am not going to hurt you."

Still the boy did nothing. He was biting his lip against his fear.

"What of your mother? The other families?"

"Sick." His gaze shifted from Raef to the small house closest to his own. "Maybe dead."

"What ails them?"

The boy hesitated. "Fever."

"When did it begin?"

"After the birds flew off."

Raef's heart constricted in his chest. "And the wolves came then, too?"

The boy nodded.

"What is your name?"

"Eddri, son of Ragnarr." There was pride in the boy's voice.

"I knew a man named Ragnarr, once." Raef thought of Ragnarr Silenthand, the half god, the son of Heimdall. He had killed Ragnarr at the burning lake. "If your father is half the man he was, you are fortunate."

Raef's words seemed to please Eddri and the edge of his fear grew dull. Raef dismounted and walked closer.

"Do you have grain?" Raef drew an arm ring over his wrist and held it up so the boy could see it glint in the sun. "This is good silver and my horse is hungry." Bryndis's steward had given them enough grain for the horses for three days. They would need more to reach the Old Troll.

"We have grain."

Raef smiled, trying to distill the last of the boy's trepidation. "Perhaps your brother will help you carry it."

After a moment, a grin split Eddri's face. From the shadows of the doorway, another boy appeared. This one was small, his face streaked with dirt, and he glared at his older brother for giving him away.

"What is your name?"

The small boy turned his glare to Raef but his lips remained sealed

"He is called Tjorvi. He does not speak. Not to strangers, at least," Eddri said. "He fell on his head as a baby," he added.

"Well, perhaps he is not strong enough to carry the grain, then," Raef said, trying not to laugh. It felt good to smile.

The younger boy flared up, his dark eyes growing fierce, and darted off around the corner of the house. When he reappeared a moment later, he was dragging two sacks of grain behind him and trying desperately to make it look easy. Raef drew his axe and set the arm ring on the ground as Eddri fetched two more bags. Taking careful aim, Raef chopped off four slender circles of silver. It was far more than the grain was worth and Eddri stared, speechless, as Raef dropped the payment into his palm.

"Thank you, sons of Ragnarr. Have you tried yellowhorn for your mother's fever?"

Eddri shook his head.

"Look for it near water, dig up the roots, and boil them until you can no longer stand the smell." Raef wanted to say more, wanted to give them something other than silver that would be of no use to them, wanted to shelter them from the storm that was coming to Midgard, but he could do nothing but signal for Vakre and Siv. Together, they strapped the grain to their packs, then, with a final wave to the watching brothers, rode off.

"The fever came with the flight of the birds," Raef told Siv and Vakre once the houses were out of sight. "And the wolves followed that night. Their father left to hunt the beasts with the other men. They have not returned." Raef glanced at Siv. "I fear this is what we will find everywhere. Already Midgard is in the grip of death and ruin."

Shadows the wolves had been, sensed yet never seen, but as the light failed and the sky darkened, those shadows grew bold, weaving their way between the trees to either side of Raef, Siv, and Vakre, staying just clear of the well-traveled path worn through the snow. Raef counted twelve. A large pack. They looked strong, as though they had prospered during the long days of winter. As they stalked the three riders with more aggression, Raef resisted the urge to increase his horse's pace, though she strained under his hold on the reins, her instincts telling her to run. He did not need to tell Siv and Vakre that they would not be stopping for the night, but they could not risk overtiring the animals.

Siv unslung her bow from where it rested on her back and, balancing the long, slender yew across her lap, guided the horse with one hand and reached with the other into the pouch at her belt where she kept her strings. Gritting her teeth in concentration, Siv attached the string at one end of the bow, then released her hold on the reins. Raef watched, ready to intervene if her horse bolted, but Siv was quick, bending the yew bow under one knee with precision and speed and fastening the string in place. She knocked an arrow on the string, drew, aimed, and loosed. It was an awkward shot, made difficult by the length of the bow. It was a weapon made for hunting on foot, not for firing from horseback. The arrow flew long, sailing over the shoulders of the nearest wolf.

Undeterred, Siv chose another arrow, but her horse, eyes rolling with fear at the smell of the predators, lurched to the right, driving into the hindquarters of Vakre's horse. Siv grabbed the reins in time but the impact caused Vakre's horse to stumble and Siv's horse reeled, half-rearing. The bow, catching on a tree branch, was ripped from her hands.

The commotion and the scent of fear set the wolves off and the twilight came alive with the sound of snarls and hungry whines. Raef circled his horse, intent on retrieving Siv's bow from the snare, but found his path blocked by four wolves, feet planted, hackles raised, teeth bared in silent growls. Raef's horse reared up, screaming, front hooves flailing in terror. Raef felt her lose her balance, felt her begin to topple backward and threw himself from the saddle.

He landed hard, so hard his shoulder went numb, but he staggered to his feet, sword already loose, the naked steel eager to drink wolf blood. The horse had come to her feet, too, her fear now laced with pain. The smear of blood trickling down her left hind leg registered in Raef's mind, but he had no time to assess the damage. The wolves were ready to spring.

But the attack never came.

The wolf closest to Raef, a tall black thing with yellow eyes, whimpered and flattened its ears back, then dropped to its stomach. The others imitated it and Raef spun in search of the source of their sudden fear. One by one the wolves began to slink away, bellies brushing the snow, but as the last one vanished from Raef's sight, an animal scream blazed out of the twilight. Raef heard bones breaking and flesh ripping and then all was quiet and he knew one of the wolves had not escaped.

"Raef, get in the saddle." Vakre's words were quiet and full of dread. Siv was there, tugging her bow free, and Vakre was reaching for Raef's horse, who still snorted and tossed her head after her encounter with the wolves. Raef did not hesitate, his own fear hammering in his chest, and put his foot in one stirrup. Grimacing against the painful tingling in his shoulder, Raef pulled himself into the saddle and as three they raced away. He did not dare hope they had gone unnoticed by whatever had hunted the wolves.

THIRTY-TWO

IT STALKED THEM through the night.

Raef was sure of it, though he never caught sight of anything. Instinct told him the creature was just out of sight and keeping pace with ease. The horses knew it, too. Whether the wolf-killer toyed with them or was judging them, Raef could not say. He could only hope the light of day might bring a measure of safety.

They halted when the horses were at the brink of exhaustion. Dawn was not far off and the trees had given way to open land and a pair of narrow lakes between high hills. Vakre spotted an abandoned summer farm and they took refuge there, leading the horses within the three walls that remained to one small building and removing the heavy saddles. Their backs steamed in the air and they were too tired to eat the grain that Raef offered.

The other building they took for themselves and Siv began to work on a fire. Raef did not want to stop for long, but he knew the value of rest, knew he could not arrive, wherever he was going, drained and without wit or strength. As smoke wafted through the one-room house, Raef stepped outside to empty his bladder, his gaze on the horizon. There was no sign of pursuit, but to Raef the air that should have been clear and bright and cold seemed tainted with a vile scent, so faint he could not be certain, but the feeling persisted and Raef was uneasy as he returned to the warmth and closed the door.

"We should watch the horses," Raef said. "Something is coming. We cannot lose them." He rummaged in his pack for some morsels of food, careful to take only what he needed to sustain him. It would not do to exhaust their supplies. With dried meat and a scrap of hard cheese in hand, Raef went to the door once more, but Vakre stopped him.

"I will do it."

Raef began to protest, but Vakre was already out the door.

Raef found him hunched under the rotten remains of the roof of the second building. Two horses slept; one munched on the grain Raef had left.

"Are you angry?"

Vakre's shoulders rose as he inhaled and he untucked his arms from where they had wrapped around his torso.

"I am," Vakre paused, "tired." It was not sleep that Vakre spoke of.

"I have not forgotten my promise."

Vakre acknowledged this by meeting Raef's gaze. His face softened. "I know." Vakre rubbed a hand down the side of his face. "I am well enough, Raef. Sleep. While you can."

Raef hesitated, but he was suddenly weary and did not resist. He left Vakre with the horses, wondering if the heat he could feel radiating from the son of Loki was a warmth Vakre welcomed or dreaded. Siv was asleep already, curled before the fire, her face burnished by the low orange hues. She stirred but did not wake as Raef kissed her cheek. It was only a moment before he followed her into slumber.

When Raef awoke, the small fire had burned only a little and by the light streaming under the door he knew he had not slept for long. But it was the smell that consumed him as he pushed aside the blanket, choking on the thick, foul odor, like the smell of spoiled meat and a battlefield under the heat of the sun. Fighting back a gag, eyes watering, Raef woke Siv and reached for his weapons. He stumbled from the house, retching, but the high meadow was quiet and empty. Raef ran to the broken-down building and saw that the horses were safe and well. They showed no fear and the foul smell seemed to fade and shrink until Raef was left wondering if he had imagined it.

Siv came up behind him and the troubled look on her face told him she had caught the scent as well. There was no sign of Vakre or a struggle.

"He would not want us to worry," Siv said, voicing Raef's uneasy thoughts. Vakre would not have wandered off without a purpose and Raef was sure whatever foul creature brought the odor was responsible for Vakre's absence.

They waited. The sun climbed higher in the sky. They saddled the horses and prepared to ride but still Vakre did not appear across the meadow or on the snowfield that stretched up into the higher places behind the summer farm.

When he could wait no longer, when the shadow of the countless birds rising to the sky darkened his mind, when he began to wonder if he would hear Heimdall blow the Gjallerhorn to call the forces of Asgard to the last battle, Raef swung into the saddle.

He did not look back at the summer farm as he and Siv followed the narrowing meadow to where it vanished between two hills, but the gap in the hills was still far away when Raef heard Siv's sharp inhale at his side. He followed her gaze to the snowfield and saw a figure running, fleeing. Vakre.

For a moment, Vakre was alone and his silent, distant flight seemed like something from a dream. But then fear clutched at Raef's gut as the hunter emerged, sweeping up over a hidden rise in the white-washed terrain on dark wings that skimmed the snow.

The creature was massive, its wings stretching wide, its long serpent neck thrust forward as it narrowed the gap between itself and its prey. Vakre ran on without looking back, but then, perhaps catching sight of Raef and Siv and seeing they were on their way to safety, Vakre stopped running. He turned to face the winged death.

Raef buried his heels into his horse and she charged forward, reaching full gallop in a few strides. As he drew closer, the sheer size of the creature became more apparent as it settled in front of Vakre, landing in the snow with all the lightness of a sparrow. Its wings remained spread, each longer than the tallest giants Raef had seen in Jötunheim, and from the tip of its lashing tail to the end of its snorting nostrils it exceeded the length of his father's hall.

The arrow whistled past Raef, unleashed from Siv's bow where she rode behind him. It struck the creature's throat, lodging there, and the creature swung its neck around, a fierce rumble charging up its throat as it registered the new threat. Dashing forward in the moment of its distraction, Vakre slashed his sword at the base of its neck, drawing blood that sprayed across the son of Loki's face, but the beast took little notice of either wound and instead launched into the sky with effortless power and a single stroke of the immense wings.

Eyes of starless midnight narrowed on Siv, and the beast, hovering on high like an eagle, tucked its wings and dove. The silence was overwhelming and then Raef heard his own shouts, hoarse and desperate, but the beast was not to be distracted and there was nothing he could do, his sword, his axe, all useless as the creature descended from the sky.

The jaws opened as the beast closed in on Siv's terrified horse, whose legs churned in fear, and Raef saw at last the pair of great, curved teeth protruding from the upper jaw, as long as a spear and bearing a promise of death and gore. The jaw snapped shut and did not miss, closing around the horse's head. If the horse screamed in the moment of its death, the sound was caught in the creature's throat.

Siv still clung to the saddle as the creature flung the headless horse through the air and opened its maw in a scream of triumph that reverberated through Raef's limbs. Siv and the horse's corpse landed in a heap in the snow, the impact throwing the shieldmaiden clear of the saddle. She lay still.

Raef had no chance to go to her, for the creature rounded on him now, but this time he and Vakre faced the attack together. Raef felt the heat of Vakre's anger wash over him in a wave less than a heartbeat before the flames roared to life, consuming Vakre, billowing outward with ferocious hunger. The creature answered with a bellow of rage, rearing up and beating its wings at the flames. The air churned, tossed about by the strength of the creature's wings, and the flames bent toward Raef. Throwing himself to the snow, he felt a heat so unbearable, so searing, it forced a scream from his throat. And then his cloak was on fire, his hair was smoking, his very skin seemed to smolder. Raef rolled through the snow and at last the flames went out and he was able to look up.

Vakre, tucked into the heart of his cloak of fire, had risen from the snow, drawing the creature with him, and for a moment they hung high in the air, suspended in silence, and then they moved as one, Vakre's blaze bursting forth even as the creature twisted and lashed out with one wing, striking the flames, and Raef watched as Vakre fell.

The fire around Vakre went out, but not before taking root in the creature's wing, and in that moment of bewilderment, the arrow found its mark.

The shaft drove into the creature's eye until only the tip of the fletching could be seen and Raef whirled to see Siv, on her knees, bow in hand as the creature's scream ate into his ears, his heart, his bones.

The beast plummeted to earth and struck the ground with a roar of fury and pain, but Raef was already moving to finish it before it regained its feet. The flaming wing beat against the ground but the fire only seemed to spread as Raef vaulted onto the creature's belly and drove his sword down into the thick muscles of its chest. Again and again he plunged the blade and ripped it forth but still it howled at him, still it fought on, twisting so violently that Raef was thrown from his perch. Scrambling to his feet, Raef raised his sword over his head and brought it down onto the creature's neck. The steel bit deep, severing bone and tendons, and the creature flopped in agony, the head dangling loose.

When it lay still, Raef found he was on his knees, his heart thudding still in his chest, his shaking hands clinging to his sword. The will to breathe had left him and he had to work to force air into his lungs, his whole body tense, ridged, but at last he could breathe and he was able to rise.

Siv was still kneeling in the snow when Raef got to her side, her face pale and still, but she grasped Raef's hand as he laid his palm on her cheek. "I am fine," she whispered, her gaze shifting to where Vakre lay, the air around him still shimmering with heat. "Go to him." She got to her feet, clutching Raef's arm for support, and he could see she was hurt. She would not put weight on her left ankle, but she steeled her face. "Go," she said again.

Vakre was alive. He stared up at the sky, his eyes empty, his breathing shallow, but he flinched when Raef put a hand on his chest and a storm washed through his irises as he inhaled sharply.

"Be still," Raef said, examining Vakre for injuries. There was nothing, not a bruise or a scrape. "Does it hurt to breathe?" Raef asked, sure Vakre was bleeding internally. The strength behind the creature's wing would have leveled a house.

Vakre was quiet for a moment, as though assessing his body, then pushed himself into a sitting position. "I am unhurt."

"It should have killed you."

"Yes." Vakre hesitated, his brow creasing. "The blow was painful. But there was something else. Memories, I think. Pieces of thoughts so primal I cannot begin to comprehend them. Tastes and sounds and smells." Vakre looked at Raef, his eyes shining with wonder. "It was full of malice and hatred long-fermented in a black heart. It knew only savagery. But I think you know what it was."

Raef turned and looked over his shoulder to where the creature lay in the snow. One wing still smoldered but the flames had not continued to spread, as though the cooling blood in the creature's veins prevented the fire from growing.

"An elder kin," Raef said quietly. He rose and walked to the tip of the unburnt wing. The skin was stretched thin between slender bones, dark in color but suffused with something Raef could only describe as drops of dawn on the surface of a fjord still black with night. Vakre followed him, one arm supporting Siv as they came to stand at Raef's side. "An ancient dragon, born in the first light of the sun, old when the gods were young." Raef wished he could ask Finnoul for the secret name of such a creature.

"The last dragons vanished from the nine realms even as the first men drew breath. Odin and his brothers hunted them to extinction," Siv said. "How is it that this one has come to be here now?"

"The borders between the realms are withering," Raef said. He could not remove his gaze from the elder kin. "Imagine what ancient, forgotten horrors might call Niflheim home." The realm of the dead belonged to the goddess Hel, and Raef did not doubt that she ruled over more than those who did not earn a place in Valhalla.

"Was it merely chance that brought it to our path? Or was it set upon us?" Siv spoke the question that had been forming in Raef's chest.

Neither Raef nor Vakre answered at first, but then the son of Loki spoke, turning away from the elder kin. His gaze fixed on the snowfield above them and the path he had taken in flight from the dragon.

"I left the horses because I knew something was out there," Vakre began. "It was waiting, watching, calculating our strengths. A dragon dragged from the depths of Niflheim has never before seen or hunted man. Wolves, it knew. Wolves were not a threat. But it did not expect to find us in the woods, I think. We walk on two legs. If the Allfather hunted these creatures in a similar form, perhaps it feared us."

"Then why attack when it did?"

Vakre frowned. "Perhaps when I got close enough to where it was hiding, it knew I did not smell of Asgard. The fear turned to hunger."

"Or you did smell of Asgard," Raef said. "And the dragon sought revenge." A whisper of wind on Raef's neck reminded him that time was against them. He looked to the sky and the path of the sun. "We cannot linger. We have lost too much time."

With only two horses between them, Siv straddled Raef's horse behind the saddle, one hand resting on his hip. She kept her bow strung, the arrows within easy reach, and all three of them waited for another winged shadow to fall across the sun. But their passage north was untroubled and when they came to rest under the cover of darkness, they had reached Vannheim lands.

Raef knew the place, knew the river and the waterfall that, in spring, would roar. In the depths of winter, the cascade would be half frozen, but still Raef could hear the telltale fall of water just out of sight to the west. They crossed, leading the horses through ankle-deep, unhurried currents, and took shelter on the northern side.

"With luck we can buy another horse tomorrow," Raef said, dismounting and taking Siv's hand. She slid down from the horse, her feet unsteady under her and her knees buckled. Raef caught her, thinking she was sore from riding without a saddle, but then he saw her eyes in the moonlight and knew her suffering had a different cause. When she did not protest when Raef scooped her up in his arms to carry her to even ground, his stomach clenched in fear.

Siv grimaced and bit back a cry of pain as Raef stretched her out on a patch of earth free of snow. Her right hand flew to her side, to the bottom of her rib cage, but she yanked her fingers away at the first touch and this time her cry was sharp.

As Vakre placed a blanket under Siv's head, Raef undid the buckle of her belt and began to peel back the layers of leather, wool, and linen while trying to disturb her as little as possible. A sudden flare of light from Vakre's hand made it bright enough to see a deep purple bruise spread under Siv's skin when Raef pulled up the edge of her linen tunic. It stretched from her hipbone up to her lowest rib, sustained, no doubt, when her horse was flung from the dragon's mouth.

"You should have said something," Raef said, meeting Siv's eyes.

"Would you?" She stared at him, unblinking, and Raef regretted his words. Vakre offered her a skin of ale, but she shook her head and closed her eyes as she leaned back to rest her head on the blanket.

Keeping his touch as light as possible, Raef placed his fingers on the discolored flesh, trying to determine the extent of the injury, but his probing revealed nothing. He sat back on his heels.

"At the least, you have cracked the bottom of your rib cage," he said.

"And the worst?" Siv murmured, her eyes still closed.

Raef was sure she already knew the answer, but he said it anyway. "Ruptured organs. Blood flowing into places it should not be."

"Then I would be dead already," Siv said.

"Can we be sure of that?"

Siv opened her eyes and met Raef's gaze but said nothing.

Vakre rested the back of his hand on Siv's forehead. "No fever. Yet."

That was a good sign. Raef rose and paced away from where Siv lay. "Tomorrow we will turn west. There is a village a day's ride from here. We can seek a healer."

"No, Raef," Siv said, her voice quiet but firm. "You must go north. To turn west now will place two fjords and a stretch of hills and valleys between you and the Old Troll. It will take time you cannot spare. You must take the shortest path, and that means staying on the eastern end of Vannheim's fjords."

"You need care," Raef said, suddenly angry.

"And what good will that care be when Hati and Skoll swallow the moon and the sun?" Siv remained calm. "Do not choose me over all of Midgard, Raef. If we do not save the world, it will not matter if I go to the last battle with broken ribs or with all my strength."

"I do not know how to save the world," Raef shouted. "I am helpless against this fate. It is madness. What can one man do in the face of the end of all things?" His eyes burned with tears of frustration and Raef turned his back on Siv and Vakre and strode into the pines that lined the river.

His steps took him to the waterfall and he let himself take refuge in its thrumming rhythm, in the blurred rush of water where the fall was strongest, in the steady, delicate trickle where streams of water found their own paths down the glistening rocks and icicles. After a time, he stretched out a hand and let the water play across his fingers. For a flashing moment, no more than a heartbeat, Raef felt the tumbling water in his veins, felt the strength of the river even while winter kept it chained, felt what it might be like to exist only as a drop of water, constantly moving, following the curves of the world on a path etched out by every other drop of water, destined to roll into the sea and drown. A bleak, yet beautiful life.

Raef drew back his hand and studied the droplets that ran down his fingers to pool in his palm. The fate of those droplets had changed the moment he came to the falls, the moment he thrust his hand into their existence. He tipped his head back and poured the water onto his tongue, thinking of Finnoul and her relentless belief that Raef had come to Alfheim for a purpose. His arrival had been an accident, an unforeseen consequence of Eira's decision to keep him alive, and yet he had taken a place in Finnoul's rebellion, had disrupted the flow of Alfheim's future just as he now disrupted the waterfall.

"What was it all for?" Raef murmured as he watched the moon-light play across the water. "Fate," he said, looking up at the stars, "I do not fear you. I do not fear what lies ahead. I defy you." The last words were whispered but never had Raef felt such conviction burning in his heart.

When he returned to the riverside camp, Siv was asleep. Her face was free of pain and for that Raef was glad. Vakre was hunched by the river's edge, filling skins with the clear water. Raef squatted next to him.

"Take care of her," Raef said. "Perhaps rest is all she needs. I will return with the second dawn."

"Where are you going?"

"In search of an answer." Raef rose, settled a hand on Vakre's shoulder, then walked away.

The horse was tired, but she pricked her ears when Raef approached and waited patiently while he cinched the saddle and drew the reins over her head. Raef stroked a hand down her nose.

"Are you ready, friend?"

As if in response, the horse bobbed her head and snorted into Raef's gloved hand. He pulled himself up into the saddle and turned her away from the river.

THIRTY-THREE

RAEF CAME INTO the valley from the east, just as Fengar had done before him when the lord of Solheim had sought refuge from the war in the furthest reaches of Vannheim. Riding through the night had brought Raef to the eastern entrance to the valley in the late morning and he stopped to water the horse and give his own body a period of rest. The climb would come next, but he granted himself a long, sun-drenched moment at the edge of the river that split the valley in half. To the north, across the water, rose the slope to the eagle's nest, the hidden fortress of Vannheim. But that was not the steep climb ahead of him. Raef looked over his shoulder to the southern summits, to a ridge where he had flown, once, the ridge where he had watched the smoke-colored kin breathe her last.

He was not sure what drew him to return to that place. And even then, with his destination in sight, he could not escape the feeling that he was wasting precious time. That he should have continued on to the Old Troll without further delay. But the decision was made and could not be unmade, and so, after steeling himself for the climb, Raef pushed his doubts into the deepest recesses of his mind and, leaving the horse tied to a tree, he began his ascent.

The way was easy at first, a gentle trek through tall pines. The snow cover on the sheltered ground was thin and Raef's strides ate up the ground. Soon the way grew steep, the trees more scattered, the ground slick beneath Raef's boots. When he crossed the tree line, he cast a quick glance over his shoulder toward the eagle's nest. The deep bowl was in full sun, the steep walls bright with the light's reflection. Taking two deep breaths, Raef pressed onward, attacking the bare, ravine-carved slope above at a run that soon made his thighs burn and his lungs cry out for respite.

Only when shadows flitted across his vision and a stumble nearly sent him sprawling did Raef realize he was dizzy and weak with hunger, not having eaten since the previous day. He collapsed in the snow and dug out his skin of water, but his shaking hands caused him to spill more than he swallowed. Raef set the water skin aside, closed his eyes, and forced himself to slow his breathing, to command his thundering heart.

When he had regained his lungs, Raef pulled out the small ration of food he had taken from his pack. The crumbly cheese broke apart as he opened its cloth wrapper, but Raef brought the cloth to his mouth and ate like a dog, his tongue snatching up every stray piece. The strips of dried venison took more time, more patience, and Raef resolved to continue his climb at a slower pace while he tore at the meat and chewed.

The sun beating down on his back as he climbed on soon had him soaked in sweat but Raef knew that if he stopped for any length of time again, the winter air would need only a moment to chill him. He could not risk that.

He could see his destination in his mind, a narrow crest of stone, a shoulder between the heads of two peaks. Enough room for one man and a loyal dragon-kin to wait for death. The ground would drop away on either side. A perilous place but one that held claim over a piece of his heart.

When at last he reached the top of the ridge, Raef was drained and he dropped to his hands and knees on a slab of granite, the tip of his nose brushing the stone as he sank down. To his relief the air had gone still. There were no cruel winds whipping over the ridge.

"Perhaps there is a goddess yet in Asgard who still watches over the world of men," Raef murmured to the cold stone. At last he gathered the strength to raise his head, to see what was left of the smoke-colored kin.

The snow had come to cover her, he remembered, but snow never lingered in exposed places for long and any trace of the storm that had descended on the peaks after her death was long swept away. Her body remained, the grey skin still stretched over the bones, the sunset eyes still masked by eyelids. The cold had kept the teeth of decay at bay. But tears flooded Raef's eyes at the sight of her so shrunken, so bereft of life and strength.

Raef knelt at her side and stretched out one hand until it came to rest on her nose. The cold he found there startled him, though he had known it would be that way. Yet he could think only of the first time they had met, when she had been set to watch him while he awaited his audience with the Guardians, of how she had stretched out her nose, both curious and tentative, to smell his outstretched palm. Her warm breath had tickled his fingers.

"Why?" Raef whispered. "What brought you here? What brought me to Alfheim when I should have died on the seas?" He ran his fingers down her neck to her chest, remembering how he had felt her heart go still. "Would that you could help me now. That you could tell me what it is I must do. If I can do anything at all. This fate is as old as the void at the beginning of all things and I am but one drop of water waiting to drown in the sea. And still, I will try, though I expect nothing for myself in return. Because I do not know any other way to live." Words sprang to Raef's mind unbidden, the Allfather's words, as he spoke to Raef about foolishly hanging himself upon Yggdrasil, all because he knew no other course.

Those words seemed to Raef a seed in his mind, but he felt blind to whatever might grow from it. Raef sighed and sat close to the crook of the kin's neck, his knees tucked up to his chest. "I killed one of your ancient cousin," he told her. An involuntary shiver coursed down his spine and Raef knew he could not linger. As he stood, his boot brushed against the kin's outstretched foot, the impact jarring loose one of the talons from the sunken joint. Raef picked it up and stroked a finger along its curved length until he reached the tip. It was as long as his hand and deadly sharp. "Perhaps I have come in vain, for I will return to Vakre and Siv no wiser. But you have granted me a final gift and so I do not count it a wasted journey." Raef tucked the talon into his empty food pouch and leaned down to touch the kin one last time. "Farewell, friend."

The descent passed quickly as Raef tracked the sun through the western sky. There could be no rest, no fitful sleep, not if he meant to return by dawn as he had promised, and so Raef, after filling his water skin once more, mounted the mare and turned her back the way they had come, first east, through the valley, and then south to the river where Vakre and Siv waited.

He beat the sun, returning to the small camp near the water-fall when night still held sway. The horses greeted each other as Raef approached, waking Vakre. The son of Loki held the mare's bridle while Raef, stiff and weary, dismounted.

"How is she?" Raef asked, looking at Siv who slept beside the dying embers of a fire.

"No worse." Vakre's gaze searched Raef's face. "Did you find what you sought?"

"I am no closer to understanding how I might change fate, if that is what you mean. But Odin sacrificed himself for something even he did not understand." Raef met Vakre's gaze. "Are we not made in the Allfather's image? Do we not share the follies of his heart, the strength of his anger, even his hunger for knowledge? We are weak of body and spirit when compared to the gods, but my course is laid before me and I know no other."

Raef let Siv sleep, even drifted into a half-sleep himself, until the sky lightened. They shared the last of their bread, dry and stale, and half the cheese they had remaining. Vakre heated water over the fire and they drank to warm themselves from the inside. Siv gave no complaint when Raef helped her onto the horse, though her lips tightened and her face grew pale. She smiled, though, when Raef showed her the smoke-colored kin's talon.

"I would have liked to know her," Siv said, returning the talon to Raef. She held to his waist more tightly than she had before, but she gave no sign of weakening as they rode north to curl around the double forked end of the fjord.

They made good time in the daylight, their route made easy by a wide valley. Prevailing winds had swept the snow into hulking drifts as tall as farmhouses, leaving swaths of frozen ground clear. The empty land around them was uninhabited, a bleak part of Vannheim home to little but rocks and stunted trees. The good soil for farming lay to the west and north at lower elevations, and the waters of the fjord were a great distance away. Looming to the east, the highest peaks in Vannheim and the vast glacier stretched over those slopes were the only landmarks, the only means to gauge distance and location. The summits were shrouded in cloud, as they nearly always were, Raef knew, but their sharp shoulders, their bald faces, their jagged silhouettes, were known to him, as were their smaller brothers and sisters clustered at their feet.

Raef pointed toward the northeast, at a finger of glacial ice that delved lower into the foothills than any other. It dipped in and out if sight as they crossed the rough terrain.

"When we are level with the Serpent's Tongue," he said, "the fjord will no longer obstruct our passage west. We will find gentler terrain and, with the gods' help, a farm with meat and bread to spare."

They rode on, Raef with one eye on the Serpent's Tongue, watching it draw closer, but his mind was on Siv, who had grown quiet and seemed to lean more heavily on him. He slowed his horse to a walk, hoping to give her a respite from the constant jarring of their faster, ground-eating gait. It would come again all too soon.

But he was too late. Siv, her eyelids fluttering as she slipped into unconsciousness, began to slide from her perch behind Raef. Twisting, Raef caught her around the waist and halted the fall, but one look at her face told him the fever had come. With Vakre's help, Raef settled Siv on his lap, her head cradled on his collarbone, his arms encircling her as he held the reins, her fevered brow warming his neck, his cloak pulled around them both. They rode on, for there was no place to turn back to, and they would find nothing but darkness if they lingered.

They turned west when they drew even with the Serpent's Tongue, but Raef, consumed by the fever that burned in Siv, felt no relief at their progress into the lower lands away from the mountain plateau. The closest farms were still out of reach and Raef's sleepless night was wearing on him, but they pressed on until the light began to fade, lengthening the shadows across the glen they rode through. They chose a grove of oaks, tall and proud, to shelter them and Vakre lifted Siv from Raef's lap, then began to build a fire. He kindled the spark with his hands and they wrapped Siv in all three blankets they carried, laying her as close to the flames as they dared. Neither Vakre nor Raef spoke until the sun dropped out of the world, leaving them among the blues and purples of twilight and the first stars. The moon, a fat crescent, hovered among the black branches of the oaks above them.

"You should go on," Vakre said. He sat apart from the fire, though whether he was simply warmed by his own heat or he wanted to distance himself from the flames he had come to loathe, Raef was not sure.

The words were an echo of those in Raef's mind but he did not respond.

"Take what food we have. I can hunt with Siv's bow. There is fresh water here. If she does not worsen, I will take her to the closest farm. Then, if it is not too late, I will follow you."

"I will not leave her."

Vakre was quiet for a moment. "Would you choose her over all of Midgard?"

"Do not ask me to make that choice, Vakre," Raef said, his voice sharp though it was Vakre's words that had cut. "There is no certainty of success. I do not know what I am looking for. I do not know if the Old Troll will show me anything."

"Will you wait here, then, by her side? Wait for Black Surt's fires? If the red rooster has crowed, Heimdall will soon sound the Gjallerhorn. Staying with Siv will not save her."

"And leaving will?" Raef shook his head. The truth in Vakre's words hounded him. "Do you know what I fear most?"

Vakre met Raef's gaze, unblinking. "What?"

"I fear achieving the impossible, only to discover that I alone have eluded Ragnarök, that I am left to walk Midgard in isolation, that I will save this world that I love and take no joy in it because to live in this world alone would be the worst fate imaginable. And I fear that is the unknown future the Allfather spoke of." Raef stood and turned away from the too-hot fire.

"I cannot save Midgard, Raef," Vakre said, his voice filled with a sad certainty. "I know it in my bones, in the very air I breathe. And Siv," Vakre hesitated, his gaze shifting to Siv's face. Her forehead was damp with sweat as she dreamed a fever-dream. "It was your fate Odin One-Eye could not comprehend, Raef, your runes

384 | <small>T L Greylock</small>

he touched and could not read. I do not know what lies ahead. I do not know if this is folly and madness. But I know you."

Raef closed his eyes, as if shutting away the world could delay the moment he would have to say goodbye to Siv, for Vakre spoke as Raef's own heart did.

"She will forgive you."

Raef turned back to Vakre. "We never found a priest. And now it is too late." He glanced to the stars, bright in the velvet sky. "Perhaps it will all be too late," he murmured before returning his gaze to the light of the fire and Vakre's waiting eyes, then went to his mare and lifted the saddle onto her back.

"The world is full of hope, Raef, though we are often too blind to see it. Remember that."

"Let it fill the hearts of others," Raef said. "I claim none for myself." He could not look at Siv as he drew the reins over the horse's head.

He was in the saddle when the wolf song shattered the night and the earth began to tremble. The mare reared up and Raef slipped backward, tumbling from the saddle as the shuddering ground lurched up to meet him. So violent was the shaking that Raef could not stand, though he tried to crawl to Siv's side.

"Raef."

Vakre's voice was calm, his eyes on the sky, his face full of dreadful anticipation and Raef, ceasing to fight against the heaving ground, followed Vakre's gaze.

The moon was gone.

The wolves went silent, their song of triumph echoing into the gulf of darkness in the sky.

"Hati has come."

THIRTY-FOUR

RAEF WAITED. WAITED for the gaping hole in the sky to descend and swallow him. Waited for the wolves to strike. Waited for the stars to fall. Waited for the end of all things.

But there was only silence. The earth grew still, the vibrations diminishing into nothing, leaving Raef pressed against the ground, waiting, his fingers reaching for Siv's hand. The fever held tight; Siv did not stir.

"Skoll will not be far behind his brother," Vakre said.

"We ride together." Raef stood and went to quiet the horses. He dared not look at the hole in the sky where the moon should have been lest he lose his resolve; instead he fixed his attention on saddling Vakre's horse and tried to ignore the fear storming through his heart. "No one should be alone."

To Raef's relief, Vakre did not argue and they were soon mounted once more, Siv on Raef's lap. They rode hard, as though if they went fast enough and far enough they might discover the moon in a different part of the sky, but there was no escaping this, Raef knew.

As the dark hours passed and the ground flew under them, Raef did not look to the sky, did not look over his shoulder, though he longed to see the first glimmer of dawn behind the eastern hills. In his mind he saw the sky grow bright with the sunrise, saw the first lining of gold spread over the horizon, saw the waves of pink and purple, faint and timid at first, then bold and brilliant as the light danced with the clouds. Raef clung to the hope of sunlight as a dying warrior does his sword, but he did not pray, did not ask Odin to bring the sun once more. Odin had his own battle.

The relief Raef felt when the sky grew light behind them was profound. So strong was the light, so sharp, it seemed to him a show of defiance that lifted his spirits.

"If this it to be our last sky, at least it is clear," Raef said to Siv, hoping she might hear him through the veil of the fever.

The day grew warm, softening the top of the snow they rode through. Snow fell from tree branches in wet clumps and sweat beaded on Raef's spine under his warm layers.

"A breath of spring," Vakre said. They stopped to let the horses drink from a narrow stream. With one arm still wrapped around Siv, Raef rummaged in his pack until he found the last strips of dried meat. He handed Vakre two pieces, kept two for himself, and returned the rest. "It will grow cold before the end."

"Do you think the Einherjar are gathering on the field of Folkvangr? Or do they squabble still over mead and old quarrels?"

Vakre managed a small smile as he urged his horse onward. "I think they will fight among themselves until Fenrir comes for the Allfather."

"I wonder if my father and his brother will stand side by side."

Vakre had no answer.

"And Cilla. I wonder what Cilla will do."

"Her duty. She is of Asgard now," Vakre said.

"Yes." Raef was quiet for a moment, his mind skittering here and there. There was so much to consider, so much that might be said. And so little time. "I kept Ulthor Ten-blade alive for you."

Vakre frowned. "For me?"

"You had more right to send him to Valhalla than I did."

Vakre's eyes narrowed and Raef saw the feral look he had come to know so well, the look he had first seen on Vakre's face. "You should have killed him."

"Raef." Siv's murmuring voice was so quiet that Raef was not sure she had spoken until her eyes opened, green and golden in the newly risen sun. Raef kissed her forehead. The fever still burned hot.

"How do you feel?"

Siv did not answer, but the look in her eyes was answer enough.

"Sleep." Raef kissed her again. "Sleep and get well. Do not leave me here alone." Siv closed her eyes but Raef could see that sleep did not claim her.

She grew worse even as the day grew bright and Raef shed his cloak to savor the light. Her rest was fitful, punctured by spasms of pain, but when Raef asked her if she wanted to stop, she refused. He did not tell her of Hati's victory over the moon.

But when the twilight came and the moon did not appear in the sky, her gaze, though clouded with pain and fever, roamed the stars above Raef's head and he could see understanding come to her.

"I am not blind, you know," Siv managed. The grin Raef might have expected did not appear. He smiled for them both, even as his chest constricted and her hand found his on the reins and held tight. "How far?"

"Too far."

⚡⚡⚡

Two days moving northwest through the hinterlands of Vannheim, desolate and deserted. Two nights of darkness that chilled Raef more than the cold and two sunrises that brought him a measure of strength. When the sun was high on the second day, they passed two farms sharing one valley, abandoned, the sheep left to huddle in the barn, a cow desperate to be milked. The animals would not survive much longer. It was not starvation that would take them, for there was fodder enough in the barn. But wolf tracks rimmed the open fields and Raef knew the pack would come again, bolder this time, and sure of an easy meal.

They took what food they could find. Fresh cheese. Dried apples. A sack of nuts. Grain for the horses. Vakre discovered dried flowers preserved with care, including one that might chase away Siv's fever. Raef released the cow from distress and searched for evidence of what had driven the families away from their homes, finding nothing.

A third farm passed late on the second day seemed just as empty but when Raef pushed open the door, he startled a young woman, upsetting the cream she was churning to butter. She jumped away from Raef as it spread on the packed dirt floor, her back pressed against the wall, her eyes darting around the small house in search of escape. An old dog in the corner struggled to get to its feet, its movements slow and limited. It made a brave attempt at ferocity, though there was no fight in its eyes.

Raef held up his hands and came no further. "Forgive me. I do not come to hurt you. I thought there was no one home."

The young woman swallowed. The dog watched Raef. "Then you came to steal."

"No." Raef took a small step through the doorway. "Do you know me?"

"Once I might have thought you the lord of Vannheim. I saw him once, a few summers ago, before he was lord. We took maple syrup to the Vestrhall to sell that year. But he is dead in the south."

"I live. The war is over and I am returning to the Vestrhall," Raef said, summoning the lie quickly.

"Then what do you want?" The young woman shushed the old dog, who grumbled still at Raef's presence, but she remained wary of Raef.

"Your closest neighbors have left their homes," Raef said, choosing his words carefully. "I was looking for answers and thought this one, too, was abandoned."

"It will be soon enough." She gestured to the dog. "We are the only ones left. We will have to leave soon. Go to my sister's, if she will have me." Dropping her eyes from Raef, she grimaced at the cream she had spilled and got to her knees with a cloth to soak up what she could.

Raef stepped forward and bent to retrieve the bowl, righting it. "The only ones?" He remained at eye level with the woman.

"My husband's brother went out three days ago. He likes to set snares for rabbits and we were eager for fresher meat. He came back at dusk, raving, saying the trees had chased him, saying there were shadows where none should be, saying a squirrel had spoken to him and sung a song of death." The young woman shook her head, but her dismissal was tinged with fear. "We put him to bed and hoped the morning would make it right, but he slipped away in the darkness and did not come back." She stopped and Raef could see unwanted tears brimming on her lower lid. "Though I begged him not to go, Karvol went looking for him the next day," she continued, fighting to keep her voice level. "I have not seen either of them since."

"And your neighbors?" Raef asked. The other farms were set in separate valleys, but the families would still have known each other well. "Did something similar happen there?"

The young woman shrugged. "We had not visited in some time. Karvol and Ferrun did not always get on well.

Raef nodded and found the young woman was looking at him expectantly. He did not know what to say.

"I am sorry for your trouble."

"What should I do?"

As lord, he should have an answer. As lord, he should protect her. Raef could not protect her from Ragnarök. Whatever the truth of what her husband's brother had seen and heard, Raef did not doubt that something had disturbed the valley and brought both brothers to their deaths.

"Tell me your name."

"Brama."

"Is your sister far away, Brama?"

Brama nodded, her long brown hair falling across her face. She brushed it aside.

"I do not think it is safe to travel any great distances," Raef said, forming his answer as he spoke. "How much food do you have?"

Brama considered for a moment. "With just me, plenty." She shivered a little and Raef wondered when the hearth had gone cold and if grief had kept her from rekindling it.

"Then stay here, where it is safe." The lie tasted foul on Raef's tongue, but he had nothing else to offer her. "Come, show me your stores while my friend starts a fire to keep you warm." Guiding her with his arm, Raef led Brama out of the house. As she blinked back the sudden light, Raef whispered for Vakre to carry wood inside and light a fire. Vakre nodded his understanding and brought Siv inside, and Raef kept Brama occupied, nodding as she showed him the small storehouse and the cured meat hanging above the winter vegetables, nuts, cheese, and dried fruit, until he judged enough time had passed for a man without Vakre's talent to start a fire. Even so, the flames were tall and the house already filled with warmth when Raef and Brama returned, though if she noticed she said nothing.

"Will you stay?" Though Brama mourned her husband, it was clear their presence was welcome. "Perhaps I can help your friend," she said, motioning to Siv, who sat, listless, in a chair.

"Thank you, but we must go on," Raef said. Brama nodded and Raef hesitated after lifting Siv into his arms. "I will ask Frigg to keep your husband safe." It was a wasted promise. Karvol was dead, he was sure, and Frigg would not notice such a small plea amidst the turmoil in Asgard, not when her own husband was preparing to face the great wolf, Fenrir. But it seemed to give Brama some comfort, even though Raef was sure she, too, knew her husband was not coming back. He wondered if she had noticed the absence of the moon. They exchanged farewells, and then Raef was mounted once more, ready to push onward.

"If we ride through the night, we will reach the coast and the Old Troll by midday tomorrow," Raef said to Vakre, who was taking a turn with Siv on his lap. "We will stop when the moon," Raef paused, realizing his error, "when the last of the light has gone, and rest the horses and ourselves for the final stretch of the journey."

They rested at a merging of two streams as the sky grew deep and dark and the long reach of the sun's rays slipped at last over the western hills, black and stark on the glowing horizon. As the horses drank, Raef crushed the dried flowers Vakre had found and added the powder to Siv's skin of water. She was awake and alert enough to swallow when Raef lifted it to her lips.

"Elder flowers," Raef said. Siv gave a weak nod and took a sip from her skin. It was a stronger remedy than the yellowhorn he had suggested to the boys Eddri and Tjorvi, but harder to come by in winter. "You must eat. The flowers will unsettle your stomach." Siv had swallowed no more than a few mouthfuls of cheese and meat in the past three days. She nodded again but her gaze drifted from Raef to the early stars above them. "You need your strength, Siv," Raef said, drawing her attention once more. "And I need you to be strong."

She accepted the meat he handed her. "The stars are bright," she murmured, and Raef looked and saw it was true, as though they burned hotter to compensate for the loss of the moon.

They rode onward through the black world and Raef waited and waited for the sun to come and release the shadows. The hours passed, measured by the light of the stars and by the hills they wove through and still the darkness persisted. A knot of primal terror grew and twisted in Raef's stomach and neither he nor Vakre said a word, refusing to give life to the dread swirling within.

The hour of the sun had long come and gone without a change in the sky when Raef could deny it no longer. He looked to Vakre and saw his thoughts mirrored there. The endless night was upon them.

THIRTY-FIVE

"STRANGE, THAT THE moon should go out with a shudder and a howl, and the sun in silence," Vakre said. The darkness seemed to press on Raef, crushing him, and Vakre's voice sounded muted to his ears.

Without thinking, Raef drew back on his reins and his horse came to a halt. Vakre circled around, watching Raef.

"What will there be left to save, without a sun?"

It was a question that had not come to him until that moment of loss, but now it consumed him.

"Without light and warmth, the world will wither and die, even if there is a way to spare it from Ragnarök. I have failed. I am too late."

Vakre stretched one hand out, palm to the stars, and a flicker of light bloomed there. Siv stirred in Raef's arms. The elder flowers had helped her sleep. It was too early to tell if it would calm the fever.

"What is it? What has happened?" Siv asked, struggling to sit up straighter.

Raef found he could not answer, his tongue dry in his mouth, his throat tight.

"The morning has not come," Vakre said. The tiny flames still danced on his skin. The son of Loki looked away from his fire and glanced at Siv, then fixed his gaze on Raef. "It will not come." He let the fire spread until it reached his elbow. "Perhaps there is another way."

"What do you mean?" Raef asked.

Vakre was quiet for a long moment. He dismounted, his arm still burning, then with a flick of his wrist, the fire went out, leaving them in sudden darkness. Raef lowered Siv to the ground, then swung himself out of the saddle to look Vakre in the eyes.

"When my father took me to the mountains of the far north, when he made me open the heart of the mountain and release Freyja's army, he told me something of my future." Vakre was utterly still as he spoke. "I had forgotten because I would not trust a word from Loki's mouth, and it seemed not to matter, for it is a future that all can claim. He said I would know pain and suffering. I asked him what man or woman does not and he laughed in reply." Raef felt a wave of heat surge from Vakre's skin. "But I think perhaps he told the truth, though he could not have foreseen this moment, for I can think of no greater pain and suffering than to burn forever."

Raef's heart dropped to his stomach and he forgot to draw breath as he comprehended Vakre's words.

"Could you?" Siv asked. Her voice was stronger than Raef had heard in days, but he was supporting nearly all her weight. "Burn forever, I mean?"

"Only one way to know the answer to that."

"But you said it does not hurt."

Vakre nodded. "Not here," he said, touching the skin of his palm. "But here," he brought his fingers to his head, then lowered them to rest over his heart, "and here most of all." His gaze shifted to Raef. "That is why I asked you to end it all."

"Then you cannot," Raef said, finding his voice. "It is too much to bear, Vakre." Whether he spoke of Vakre's suffering or his own sorrow at the prospect of saying a final farewell, Raef did not know.

"What other choice is there? You will reach the Old Troll soon, but a sun must rise, or there is no hope."

Raef blinked. "The rising sun," he said softly, remembering. "Something Anuleif said, though I do not think he understood. He left because he said he could not remain in the land of the rising sun. I thought he misspoke." Raef stared at Vakre. "He knew. He knew without understanding, without even knowing what you are."

A silence spread between them and Raef's grief raged against the hope Vakre had kindled.

"What will you do?" Raef asked at length.

Vakre looked to the line of hills to the north. "I think I must find higher ground."

⟨ ⟨ ⟨

Raef did not watch as Vakre and Siv shared a goodbye. He heard Siv whisper something, heard Vakre's easy, warm response, a laugh even, as the tightness in his own chest threatened to steal all breath away. When he turned back to face them, Siv was smiling and Vakre looked content.

They left Siv with the horses, her bow strung and resting across her lap should she need to defend herself, a knife and her sword in reach. There was no question that she had to stay. In her weakened state, Raef and Vakre would have had to take turns carrying her on the climb, slowing their progress. Raef leaned over her and kissed her, glad to see some strength in her face even though her skin was still feverish, and then he and Vakre set off.

Vakre led the way and with every step Raef could feel the son of Loki growing warmer, the heat radiating off his back until Raef had to fall back in search of cooler air. He did not think Vakre was conscious of the change.

The first crow was nothing more than a rush of wings across the stars, though Raef heard it settle on a branch somewhere above them, heard the gentle croak in its throat. It was the first bird he had seen or heard since the day in Narvik when the birds had risen to the sky in a swarm of wings and flown west. Its sudden presence made Raef uneasy, though he could not have said why. If it watched them, if they passed right under it, Raef did not know, and soon they were approaching the edge of the trees and heading into the high reaches of the hills. He breathed more easily once they passed out from the tree cover and came under the open embrace of the night sky.

They paused on a shoulder of rock. Above them the summits were still far away. Even in the dark Raef could see the air around Vakre shimmer with heat. Vakre's gaze, though it rested on Raef, seemed very far away.

"I will go on alone. You must reach the coast."

Raef nodded, not trusting his voice. For a moment, they looked at each other, then Vakre extended his hand. Raef, his heart pounding, reached out and grasped Vakre's forearm. In that touch, Vakre's heat vanished and Raef wrapped his other arm around Vakre's shoulders, pulling him close in a fierce embrace. Neither said anything, though Raef's mind ran with words, words that were not enough, and he held his silence, lest speaking break him.

As they released each other, the warmth rushed back into Vakre with sudden force and Raef had to yank back his hand as Vakre's palm grew too hot to touch. He stepped out of reach of the heat but his eyes remained locked with Vakre's.

At last the son of Loki took a deep breath, exhaled, and then turned to face the hills above. He had gone only three steps when he stopped and faced Raef once more. Only then did Raef see the fear in him, see how it had caught him up in its cold grasp, see how it threatened to tear him apart.

"I am afraid." The words came out hoarse and shaken. Vakre tried to laugh, but it was a mangled, broken thing that lifted neither of their hearts. "I am afraid of what it will feel like to burn forever. I am afraid of what I will remember." He stared, unblinking, at Raef, as though he dared not look away. "And what I will forget."

Vakre was shaking, his control weakening, and Raef felt his very blood tremble. "I should have honored the promise you asked of me. I should have ended your suffering in that moment, spared you from an eternity of torment."

With visible effort, Vakre steeled himself. "No, no. If you had done as I asked, the world would be a dark place."

"I would live in darkness if it meant peace for you," Raef said, a sudden vehemence rushing through him.

"I told you once that you cannot save us all, Raef," Vakre said, his voice gentle. "My fear will pass." Vakre looked to the sky. "It will be lonely." He dropped his gaze to Raef once more. "Perhaps I will make friends with the stars."

There were no more words, it seemed to Raef, nothing but grief. Vakre held his gaze for a long moment. When he turned his back for a second time, he did not look back.

Raef watched him go, unwilling to leave until Vakre had climbed too high, too far into the darkness for Raef to follow him with his eyes.

He was yet in sight when the wings passed over Raef, the sudden stir of air in the still night raising the hair on the back of Raef's neck. Raef glanced to the sky just as the flock of crows turned, twisting as one in the air, and dove at him. He ducked the first pass but the birds doubled back and rushed him again. This time their wings beat against his face and arms as he tried to shield himself, and on the third pass their talons and beaks found his skin, raking his forearms. So relentless was their assault that Raef could not draw his sword for fear of exposing his eyes to their sharp beaks. With one arm covering his face, he tried to beat them back, flailing blindly against the storm of wings. If he struck one, another replaced it, and Raef dropped to his knees, his arms and neck stinging where he bled. As he hit the ground, the flurry of wings grew silent and Raef drew his sword from its scabbard as he opened his eyes.

The crows stood on the ground around him, their black eyes staring, their feathers glossy in the starlight. They made no move, no sound, and Raef, sensing a breath of something behind him, spun.

The figure was difficult to make out. It was robed in a darkness that moved as though alive and Raef was reminded of the sea foam that the giantess Barra had worn when at last he saw her in the feeble light of Jötunheim. But this was no sea foam; it was midnight bereft of stars.

The face, regal and cold, was unknown to Raef, though the piercing eyes he found there seemed somehow familiar. It was a man, or something like a man, tall and handsome, flawless.

"Where is my son?" The voice began as a terrible thunder, beating on Raef, and ended like rain falling on green hills. A beautiful voice, but deadly. Loki.

The god laughed at Raef's silence and the crows croaked along with him, their voices chilling Raef's blood. Any of Vakre's heat that had lingered on him was gone. "Hold your tongue if you like. It matters not. I will find him." But Loki lingered and Raef began to see the uncertainty in the god's eyes. Loki took a step toward Raef, who willed himself to hold his ground, head high, gaze unrelenting. "I see the workings of your mind, human. You are scheming at something." There was frustration in Loki's voice now, and anger. "I will peel you to the core to discover it, exposing your every hope and joy, your deepest fears and scars."

"I spilled your blood once, Loki, I can do it again." Raef's snarl ripped across the air between them and set the crows cawing.

The god laughed again, a mirthful sea at storm, delighting in his own superiority. "In that weakened form, yes, yes, you drew a drop of blood. Try again, boy, and see what I am made of." Loki seemed to grow before Raef's eyes and against his will he took half a step back as the god filled his vision. "Or better yet, I will show you the true form of Loki, the form I was born in, the form that will bring destruction to the nine realms, the form that the eyes of humans cannot endure." The darkness that cloaked Loki began to hum and flicker, but then the god grew still, as though he was reconsidering, and the midnight he wore was still and quiet, too.

"Where is my son?" he asked again, and Raef again sensed Loki's doubt.

"He will be greater than you soon."

To Raef's surprise, Loki did not shake this off, did not laugh at Raef's bold words. His pale eyes narrowed. "The gods cannot be saved from their fate."

"I know."

"Then what is it that you want?" Loki shouted.

Before Raef could reply, the crows took flight, their frantic wing beats taking them up, up the slopes above Raef and Loki, up to the high places where Vakre had disappeared. Without thinking, Raef began to run, certain the crows knew where to find Vakre and desperate to defend him, to keep the sun alive long enough to be born.

He was slammed to the ground by an unseen force before he had gone five steps and though he struggled to rise, a great weight kept him pressed to the snow. Raef cried out in pain.

"The crows are agents of fate, Skallagrim. You cannot stop them." From the edge of Raef's vision he could see that Loki was gazing into the darkness. "And I think they have found my son."

"But you can stop them." The words came out in a crush of air as Raef fought to stand.

Loki moved without Raef seeing, suddenly crouched next to

Raef, their faces almost touching, Loki's hand clutching Raef's cloak. "Why should I?"

The pressure on Raef's body vanished and he sucked in a breath before answering. "Because he goes to destroy himself." The truth came rushing out and Raef could not hide the pride he felt. "Because he goes to take the sun's place in the sky."

Loki did not move, did not draw back, but was quiet for a moment. "So, this is what you intend." Raef held the god's gaze. "It is in vain. There is no dawn for these realms." Silence.

And then Raef was lifted from the ground, the earth shifted beneath him, the sky spun, and when he could see again, he found he was high above the place where Loki had come upon him. The crows swarmed overhead, dark wings blotting out the stars. Loki held tight to Raef, still, his eyes not leaving Raef's face, and then the crows went silent and began to fall from the sky. One by one they dropped as though turned to stone and they did not rise again. Only when the last crow hit the snow, its heart gone cold and quiet, did Loki release Raef.

"There," the god said, stepping back. "I have spared him from the crows."

"Why?"

Loki looked up to the crest of a hill above them. A fire burst into life there, distant and small, but Raef's heart erupted with joy. When he looked at Loki again, the coldness there turned his blood to ice. "Because now you have your hope. And when it is crushed at last in the defeat of Odin, in your defeat, my victory will be all the more complete."

Raef did not quail before Loki's words. "I have looked into the eye of the Allfather. I do not fear you." Raef stepped close to the god and looked up into that pale, handsome face. "Heimdall is waiting for you."

The flinch was almost imperceptible, but Raef was sure he saw it in the muscles around Loki's eyes, in the tightening of his mouth. It seemed Loki, for all his eagerness to destroy the Allfather and the nine realms, was not so impatient to face his fated battle with the other god, the battle that would kill them both.

"The shieldmaiden is badly wounded, Skallagrim. Do you think you can save her?"

Raef's heart skipped.

A smile played across Loki's face. "Let me look after her for you."

And then the god was gone and Raef was left to scream at nothing but the sky.

ᚱ ᚱ ᚱ

How he came down from those hills, Raef could not have said. He ran, sliding when his feet got too far ahead or behind, but when he reached the place where Siv should have been, he found only the horses.

There was no sign of a struggle. If Siv had seen Loki coming for her, she had not had a chance to fire, for her quiver was not missing a single arrow. The knife and sword had not been disturbed and the bow lay alongside them, placed with care.

Raef dropped to his knees and stretched out a hand to touch the smooth, curved bow. Once he might have hurled his anguish at the sky, shouting at the gods, cursing Odin and Loki both, but he did not have the will now.

He collected the weapons and strapped them to his pack, then mounted his horse, leaving the other behind rather than slow himself by tying the horses together. Casting a glance to the hills, he saw only darkness and no sign of Vakre, no fire in the sky.

"Alone, then," he said. "Let it come."

With a shout Raef urged the mare onward, west now, to the sea and the hole in the earth that might give him an answer.

THIRTY-SIX

THE COAST WAS white with foam. Waves, released by
Jörmungand in the deep, crashed against the shore, spewing salt spray high into the air. The Old Troll stood tall,
stone eyes facing the sea, waiting for the flood that would come to
swallow the land.

Raef's mare, breathing hard, reached the top of the lone hill and
came to a halt, legs trembling with exhaustion from the hard race
through darkness to the sea. Raef swung out of the saddle, then patted her neck and thanked her for her swift legs and strong heart.
With steady fingers, he loosened her saddle and freed her from its
weight, then removed the bridle as well. Steam rose from her back
and she snorted at him, blowing hot air on his neck. Leaving his
pack alongside the saddle, he stroked her nose once more, then
turned to the sea that he had dreamed of so often, that had called
him westward in search of unknown lands. The sea road was as lost
to him as Vakre and Siv. Closing his eyes, Raef turned away from
that distant dream and faced the hole the lightning strike had made
in the top of the troll's skull.

Without a means to lower himself, Raef was forced to brace
his back against one side of the tunnel, his legs against the other,
and slide in halting, grating bursts down through the earth. Then

the small cavern opened up beneath him and Raef fell, striking the stone floor hard, the impact jarring through his bones. Wincing, Raef righted himself and strained his eyes for a sign of something, anything, but darkness reigned uncontested by the stars.

But he could hear. The sound was faint, but Raef knew at once what it was. Water. Tiny ripples lapping against stone. There had been no water in the cavern when he last visited, when he saw the strange, glimmering image of Yggdrasil fade from the walls and ceiling. Lowering himself to his hands and knees, Raef felt his way across the cold stone floor until he felt water at his fingertips.

Raef dipped his hand into the icy water and lifted it to his lips, testing it. Clean. Better than the best mountain streams Raef had drunk from in the high places of Vannheim. This gave him courage, though had the water tasted vile he still would have unfastened his cloak, set it to the side, and stepped into the pool.

The water dragged him down. There was no bottom. It filled his ears and nose, it tumbled him around, and just when Raef ran out of air in his lungs, the current vanished, leaving him suspended in water that threatened to freeze his blood.

But there was light above him and Raef kicked to the surface, breaking through at last, sucking in air.

He was in a lake. The surface of the water was smooth and flat around him, the ripples made by his limbs dying away almost instantly. Above him were stars, but they hung low in the sky, illuminating the lake in bright light. In one direction the lake extended unimpeded, stretching away into a flat horizon, but it seemed to Raef that there was an edge, and that the water there must form a waterfall large enough to swallow all of Midgard. There was a shore, though, and it was close to Raef. And it was green, impossibly flat, just as the lake was, but vibrant and rich even in that strange starlight. Raef swam to it and only when he climbed onto the grass did he see the tree.

It stood away from Raef and the lake, but he found he could not guess the distance. The trunk was wide and straight, the limbs curling and twisting into the stars. And three roots burrowed into the green earth at its base.

"Yggdrasil."

The name came to his lips as though placed there by some force other than his own mind, and he could taste it. It was soil and summer fruit and lean venison and silver fish and root vegetables. Sunshine and mead. All the bounty of the earth.

Raef began to walk across the endless green meadow but he had not gone far when he sensed something following him. He stopped and turned and saw the lake was lapping after him. It did not frighten him, for there was no malice in the water, and by the time he reached the tree, the water had closed the distance, too, coming to rest by the roots. Perhaps there had been no distance at all. He peered once more into the lake and in that moment he saw Odin's lost eye, the pair to the one he had looked into when the Allfather had come to him in the labyrinth of Jötunheim.

The eye covered the entire lake and yet was also a tiny thing hovering just below the surface, so close that Raef could have reached in and plucked it up.

"Then this is Mimir's well," Raef murmured. Odin had sacrificed his eye to the well in return for ancient knowledge. The borders between the realms must have weakened a great deal for Mimir's well to reach to the Old Troll.

The bark of the great ash tree was covered in carved runes, some orderly and neat, others scrawled in haste or maybe pain and falling at angles down the trunk. But as Raef paced around the trunk, he saw that one part was rotten, the bark oozing with decay and slime, though he could see it had been smeared with wet clay from the lake in an effort to stave off the rot. There were scars in the trunk, too, and Raef was certain he was seeing the marks left by the ropes Odin had used to bind himself to Yggdrasil for nine days and nights. A squirrel chattered at him from a low branch as he passed underneath. Raef wondered what message he was passing between Nidhogg, the serpent in Yggdrasil's roots, and the eagle perched in the ash tree's highest branches.

He had passed around the tree at least three times, he was sure, before he found those who had scooped the clay from the lake and spread it across Yggdrasil's wounds.

The Norns were sitting between two of the roots. One was dressed in white, her hair almost as pale. The second wore black and her raven-colored tresses fell across her face. The third was ready for battle in gleaming armor made of fire and moonlight. She had red hair and it was her eyes that found Raef first.

"You should not be here." The red-haired Norn's voice was no more than a whisper.

"Did your runes tell you that?"

"The stars are falling, child of Midgard." It was the Norn dressed in white who spoke next. Raef looked up and saw that it was true, almost as if her words had begun it. The orbs streaked across the sky, plummeting into the lake or beyond the edge of the green plain.

"The battle has begun. Fenrir has come for Odin. Jörmungand has slithered from the seas to face Thor. Even now Black Surt sets a fire to the walls of Valhalla." This from the dark-haired Norn.

"The long-told fate has come." The red-haired Norn rose from her seat on the root and Raef saw the serpent Nidhogg was curled around her waist.

"And you think you can undo what was made when Yggdrasil was no more than a seed." The white-blonde Norn spoke again.

"You are Urda." Raef was not sure how he knew this but she did not correct him. "I have met your son." He turned to face the dark one. "And you are Verdandi." She gave a slight nod, though he thought it was against her will. "Then you are Skuld." Raef said to the third as he reached out and ran a hand up Yggdrasil's ancient trunk, his fingers sliding among the runes. He heard one of them hiss at his boldness. "I have not come to save Odin. The Allfather knows his fate. But I do not know mine. And so I have learned to hope."

"It matters not." The Norns spoke as one and then they were gone and in their place was a three-headed creature. Its body was that of a massive wolf, but the wings of an eagle had sprouted from its back and the heads were all different. A dragon bristled in the middle but the other two creatures were too ancient for Raef to name.

The beast came for him but Raef was ready, eluding the three heads as they sought to snatch him up. Diving first out of the reach of one, he slashed into the tendons of the second just as the dragon's teeth snapped over his head. Whirling, Raef threw his axe, catching the dragon in the throat. The creature wailed as Raef lunged forward, his sword stabbing into the wolf heart. Writhing, wings beating the earth, the creature dropped to the ground, but it was Siv who fell, who curled up in agony, hands trying to stem the flow of blood from the gaping hole in her chest. She called out to him, her pain taking life in the air Raef tried to breathe.

He knelt by her side, fear and horror reaching into his heart with cold fingers. But there, just at the edge of his vision, the blue of Odin's eye flashed from the depths of the well and his mind steadied. "You are not Siv. You are here to break me. Know this: I was already broken in the labyrinth of Jötunheim. My mind is my own and belongs to no other. You cannot take it from me." Without thinking, Raef drew the dragon-kin talon from where it rested in his belt. It was warm to his touch and seemed to pulse with the last heartbeats Raef had felt in the smoke-colored kin's chest. The thing that was not Siv cried out, begging him to help her, pleading, but Raef, as the stars fell around him, buried the talon in her chest.

When he drew it out again, hot with blood, the form of Siv vanished, leaving behind only a spreading stain to darken the green grass at the edge of Mimir's well.

Only then did Raef feel how his heart raced, how his breaths came shallow and short, how his limbs were weak and unsteady. He sank to the edge of the lake and rinsed the blood from the talon, and as the water touched his skin, as his hand was swallowed up by Odin's eye, he was able to catch his breath.

"You are watching me still, Allfather," Raef said.

Rising, Raef turned and took in the great expanse of Yggdrasil, larger, it seemed, than ever. Before it had been merely a tree, ancient and carved with runes, but nothing more than bark and limbs and leaves. Now he could see eight realms cradled in Yggdrasil's strong arms and one, a dark, cold place, nestled between the roots. This was Niflheim. The green plain was gone, leaving only stars above and below Raef. They were fewer now, the expanses of dark sky between them larger and threatening.

He knew each realm. Muspellheim burned, its fires raging as it sensed the end coming. And there was Alfheim, empty and silent. Raef was certain that realm had long since succumbed to fate. Asgard, golden and bright, was highest of all, but a shadow lurked over it. Fenrir's breath, Raef knew.

And then there was Midgard. Raef's heart ached to see it, smaller than the rest, green and vulnerable. It seemed about to be extinguished.

Raef began to climb. The runes became handholds, the wet clay hardened beneath his boots, giving him traction against the smooth ash and the rot. He vaulted into the branches as swift and sure-footed as Ratatoskr the squirrel, and then he was crawling along the length of a branch, Midgard trembling at the far end, ready to go dark and plummet into the nothingness that awaited below

Yggdrasil's branches. Mimir's well was shrinking and Odin's eye was spinning.

Raef was halfway to Midgard when he stopped. He had nothing with him but the dragon-kin's talon and this he began to saw into the ash wood. Back and forth again and again, each cut making the world tree bleed.

When the branch hung by nothing but a thread of Yggdrasil's fiber, Raef stood and stepped across the wound he had gouged, landing lightly on Midgard's branch, and in that moment the world tree broke free.

It was not the branch that fell, though Raef felt his heart plunge from his chest. Instead it was the great ash that dropped away, taking the other eight realms with it. It spiraled into the waiting void and the last of Mimir's waters drained away after it. Raef watched the ash tree until he could see it no longer and he was left suspended on Midgard's branch, the world he loved still beating alongside him. Beside him floated Odin's lost eye. Raef plucked it from the air and, stretching as tall as he could, placed it high above Midgard.

"It is done. And you will always be watching Midgard."

A star, the final lingering shard of light, fell without warning, striking Raef in the heart. He dropped from the branch and was swallowed by darkness.

THIRTY-SEVEN

I T WAS ODIN'S eye he saw when he woke, though it was not the eye from the well. It was set in a sad, worn face. But the Allfather was smiling.

"I am dreaming."

Odin shook his head. "No."

"You are fighting Fenrir. You cannot be here." Raef looked around. He could see nothing.

"The wolf is swallowing me. I let him take me the moment I felt Midgard break free. Soon, my son Vidar will avenge me, ripping the great wolf's jaw apart. Thor has fallen already, though he lingers through the pain of Jörmungand's poison even as the serpent draws its last breath."

"Then how are you here?"

"Because this is where I need to be." Odin smiled again, his face suffused with a light of its own, his burden stripped from him at last. He seemed young again. "I never dared hope. And yet hope came to me unbidden. What could be done against the long-told fate? Nothing, and yet here we are. Here you are, at least, Raef Skallagrim, the living heart of Midgard. I never spoke of it to anyone, never let my dream of Midgard's survival live in my heart for fear of its discovery." Odin lifted a hand to his missing eye. "It lived here instead, out of reach of Loki and all the rest who sought destruction. I could not even tell you, though I longed to share my hope of what you might achieve through strength of will. Even when I began to understand that perhaps the reason I could not read your fate was because it was your fate to survive, to contradict everything these nine realms have ever known, I had to keep my silence." Odin studied Raef for a moment. "Your friend spoke the truth. Yours is a great heart, Raef Skallagrim, and it alone has done what nothing else could."

Raef closed his eyes as the Allfather spoke of Vakre. He could not fight against that grief. When he opened his eyes again, Odin was watching him. "Why Midgard? Why not Asgard?"

"Because it is man, not the gods or the giants or the alfar, I cherish most, and Midgard was the world most dear to me, the world I made after my own heart. Men and women are beautiful in their weaknesses, Raef, beautiful in their faults and their failings. And because of this, because their lives are fleeting, they are worth saving."

The Allfather stood, though only then did Raef realize he had been sitting. His own body seemed to be stretched flat on a table made of air.

"And now you have done it. Take your world, Raef, and set it free. Make it grow. Live."

"Do I survive alone?" Rushed, desperate, those words were.

Odin's sad smile returned, and with it Raef could see his pain, pain at having lost a fragment of himself. "I can no longer see Midgard, Raef. Not the bright rivers or the wind-swept peaks or the warmth in the earth that waits for spring. It is for you to discover what remains."

Raef blinked and Odin was gone, leaving behind a great emptiness, a gulf that Raef felt in his gut. The gods were no more. The nine realms were no more. There was only one realm.

But Raef was not alone. A gentle breath blew across his face, followed by a horse's velvety black nose. The horse bumped his cheek and Raef inhaled, suddenly feeling as though he had not taken a breath in a very long time. He came to his feet, suspended still where the green plain had been, where Yggdrasil had grown from a seedling at the edges of Mimir's well. The horse was waiting and Raef knew its name.

"Sleipnir."

Eight legs the father of horses had, a tail made of wind, and a star in each eye. Tears pricked the corners of Raef's eyes.

"You are all that remains of Asgard. Did Odin send you for me?"

The tall black horse pressed his head against Raef's chest. Raef twined his fingers into Sleipnir's silky mane and pulled himself onto the bare back. Exulting in his own strength and speed, the horse reared up, calling to the lost stars, hooves sending sparks into the darkness.

Raef clung on to Sleipnir's neck and murmured, "One last ride, then, before you follow him."

Odin's mighty steed whickered in response and then they were racing through the dark and everything was a blur and Raef felt his heartbeat slow and then stop.

THIRTY-EIGHT

WHEN RAEF BEGAN to understand that he was alive, it was the cold that stirred him, that opened his eyes.

He lay atop a slab of stone. The world was dark around him. A single star tinged with blue fire glimmered above him and Raef knew he looked upon the eye of Odin, the one he had placed in the sky. But there was no light to see by, nothing to show Raef what he had salvaged from the grip of fate.

He stood on his cold stone and realized that the world he had saved was a bleak and empty one, that whatever life lingered there would soon perish in the dark. It was as he had feared.

How much time passed, Raef could not have said, and it did not matter, for there was only time and nothing else. The cold seeped into him and his eyelids grew heavy.

It was through this lash-strewn vision that Raef saw light. He blinked, sure it was imagined, but as he strained his eyes in the dark, the faint glow he had doubted began to grow, to spread rich fingers of golden light across the land, illuminating harsh mountain slopes and a shining river and cool forests, green forests free from the burden of winter.

When at last the light took shape, bursting over the horizon, the sight of the flaming disk brought Raef to his knees and he wept.

THIRTY-NINE

THE STARS HAD come back to live in the sky.

Not as many as before, and the brightest paled when compared to the memory of their lost brothers and sisters, but the night sky was no longer a place of darkness and doubt, of fear.

A moon had been birthed, too, following the sun that was Vakre across the sky, though where it had come from Raef could not be sure. The pale face seemed familiar, friendly, even.

But it was the daylight that brought him joy. He watched every sunrise in the days that followed the severing of Midgard, waiting for Vakre's light to break across the world once more, reveling in the warmth and brilliance. It was in those moments of first light that he felt Vakre was near, that he might have looked over his shoulder and seen the son of Loki as he once was.

He mourned, too, in those days. Siv had never been found. Raef had waited at the place of her abduction, had searched for her, but when the new spring passed into summer and still there was no trace of her, he looked to the eastern forests less and more to the western seas. He hoped Loki had been kind to her, had brought her a swift peace.

A king had been named. Bryndis had called her gathering, as

she had promised, and though Raef had sent warriors and shield-maidens of Vannheim to speak their voices as they wished, he had lingered in the west and waited for word to reach him. When a rider came bearing the name of Eirik of Kolhaugen on her lips, Raef thought of Finndar Urdson, the Far-Traveled, the last man to bring news of a king to Vannheim, and wondered where the son of Urda had met his lonely end.

The Vestrhall and the village were alive with the voices of children. The market was flourishing with fish and pelts and food. The soil was richer than it had ever been, the farmers said, and the fishermen spoke of fish in the fjords in numbers greater than ever before. Few spoke of the dark days before the new sun had come, though rumors reached Vannheim of a changed land, of mountains where none had been, of rivers altering course, of fjords snaking new arms through the wilderness and coastlines changing form. They talked of the gods still, though always with something left unsaid, as if they understood that world, the one under Odin's watchful eye, was gone, even if they did not quite understand their new one or how it had survived. It was a time of contentment.

But not for Raef. He smiled to see his people laugh in the light after the long winter. He found joy in the forests beneath the canopy of green leaves with a bow in hand and an axe at his back. He swam in the fjord and waited for the sun to warm him every day. But he was restless.

The ship was finished on the longest day of summer. Raef had worked much of the wood himself, had designed it to be fast and strong, and now, as the ship builders drifted away from the fjord at twilight, drawn to the scent of meat roasting in the hall, their work done, Raef was left alone on the deck.

The crew was chosen, the supplies gathered, the weapons sharpened. They would set sail at first light, striking out across the sea road in search of the unknown, and Raef would hoist the sail using a set of beloved, well-used seal skin ropes that had belonged to the brothers Rufnir and Asbjork, who had dreamed of taking the sea road with Raef and were now a memory of Valhalla.

The sea dream had come back to Raef not long after he had returned to the Vestrhall, fueled by his grief, embedding into his heart with such strength that he could not ignore it. The preparations had given him a means to lose himself in work, to forget, for a moment, the wound he hid at his core, the toll extracted in Yggdrasil's dying moments.

Raef leaped to the sheer strake at the bow, wrapping his arm around the smooth prow that leaned out over the water. Above him, the smoke-colored kin's face, rendered in wood, stared out, ever vigilant, at the western horizon. Raef could already taste the sea spray on his face, could feel the ship riding the waves, could see the wind filling the black sail.

At Raef's back, a summer storm lingered in the eastern sky, moving north, so distant the thunder could barely be heard though the bolts of lightning that split the sky and reflected down the length of the fjord promised savagery. The western sky promised nothing, and yet, somehow, everything, and Raef knew Vakre would follow wherever the wind took him.

The sound of boots on the deck of the ship drew Raef's ears but not his eyes.

"Is there room for one more?"

Raef, his heart racing, dared not look, lest his eyes shatter the voice he had heard.

"Look at me."

And then she was there, her hair of red and gold burnished in the light of the setting sun, her eyes, green and warm, searching his face, her hands reaching for him.

"Siv."

She smelled of sunlight as Raef took her in his arms.

"How?"

"Even Loki has regrets."

There was more to be said, more questions to answer, but that could wait.

Raef did not let go of her as she turned to face the sunset and the sea. He rested his chin on her shoulder and breathed in time with her beating heart.

"What are you looking for out there?"

Raef was quiet for a moment.

"I was looking for something to make me forget."

"And now?"

"Now? Now I search for whatever it is I will find. I know no other way."

Siv ran a hand down the dragon-kin's wooden neck. "What is she called?"

The name came to Raef unbidden, for he had not yet let himself speak it aloud, and grief constricted his chest. "She is *Sun-Sister*." He could feel Siv smile, could feel his heart smile with her.

"I have never sailed on the sea," she said.

Raef, his arms wrapped around her still, entwined his fingers with hers. "Then take my hand."

LIST OF CHARACTERS

Raef Skallagrim, lord of Vannheim, dispossessed
Vakre Flamecloak, half god, son of Loki
Siv, presumed deceased
Eira, a metamorphosis gone wrong

Tulkis Greyshield, fancies a fancy chair
Isolf Valbrand, Raef's cousin, usurped a fancy chair
Aelinvor, daughter of Uhtred, lord of Garhold

Visna, proud, like all Valkyries
Rufnir Bjarneson, Raef's childhood friend
Anuleif, He Who Burned, an odd little fellow
Dvalarr the Crow, warrior of Vannheim
Skuli, a captain of Vannheim, eager
Njall, a captain of Vannheim

Torleif, lord of Axsellund, a new, untested ally
Eyvind, warrior of Axsellund

Fengar, lord of Solheim, the unlawful king
Griva, knows best

Alvar of Kolhaugen, jealous
Romarr, lord of Finnmark, Vakre's uncle
Ulthor Ten-blade, a bad egg
Valdemar, the broken man
Tora, deceased
Inge, very much alive

Finndar Urdson, the Far-Traveled, half god, son of Urda
Ailmaer Wind-footed, in search of golden apples
Brandulf Hammerling, lord of Finngale, Raef's former ally
Eirik of Kolhaugen, a good egg
Hauk of Ruderk, crafty, big schemes and big dreams
Bryndis, lady of Narvik, fierce
Thorgrim Great-Belly, lord of Balmoran, may or may not be dying
Eiger, the Great-Belly's son, bursting with filial love
Cilla, brave, likes sharp things

Dainn, Raef's uncle, awfully troublesome, as dead men go
Bekkhild, Siv's sister, missing

ACKNOWLEDGMENTS

Thanks to Alisha at Damonza, who stuck with me on this third and final cover until we got it right.

Big shout out to my comrades from the SPFBO, who have populated my little writing world quite nicely. Don't get emotional on me, but, uh, you're all winners in my book. I hope we will continue to ~~grow~~ pillage the world together. Thanks, especially, to Travis, who loaned me his eyeballs when I needed them.

Most of all, I want to thank my readers, who met Raef a few hundred-thousand words ago and took every step of the journey with him.

ABOUT THE AUTHOR

T L Greylock is the author of *The Song of the Ash Tree* trilogy, consisting of *The Blood-Tainted Winter*, *The Hills of Home*, and *Already Comes Darkness*.

She can only wink her left eye, jumped out of an airplane at 13,000 feet while strapped to a Navy SEAL, had a dog named Agamemnon and a cat named Odysseus, and has been swimming with stingrays in the Caribbean.

P.S. One of the above statements is false. Can you guess which?

www.tlgreylock.com

 @TLGreylock

 @tl_greylock